Producer & International Distributor
eBookPro Publishing
www.ebook-pro.com

WORDS APART
Lilac Sigan
Copyright © 2023 Lilac Sigan

Originally published in Israel by *Yedioth Books* 2017

Editor in Chief: Dov Eichevald
Editor of original prose: Navit Barel
Editor: Michal Heruti
Secondary editor: Yael Madar

Translation into English: Yael Nussbaum
Translation editing: Juliana Starkman

Page 9: Screen shot of opening a new Gmail account.

Page 323 Paraphrased paragraph from Erich Fromm's *The Art of Loving* (Harper & Brothers).

The reality program *Masterpiece* that is mentioned along the book was aired on the public broadcasting channel in Italy for one season in 2013.

All rights reserved; No parts of this book may be reproduced or transmitted in any form or by any means, electronic or mechanical, including photocopying, recording, taping, or by any information retrieval system, without the permission, in writing, of the author.

ISBN 9798872211631

Words Apart

LILAC SIGAN

Dedicated to my daughters
In hope that they have inherited their father's emotional fortitude
and not mine

I'm a pupa
Not a moth, nor a worm
I'm a pupa
Non-existent, eyes veiled
I'm a pupa
Never died, never breathed
I'm a pupa
One day my life will be real

Part One

Name

| Sheera | And Michael |

Choose your username

softspoons @gmail.com

Create a password

••••••••••

Confirm your password

••••••••••

Location

Israel (ישראל)

Next step

To: <softspoons@gmail.com>
From: <softspoons@gmail.com>
January 2, 2016 at 11:25 p.m.
Subject: The story of how we met

Earlier, curled up with Tom in his bed, waiting for him to fall asleep, I tried to figure out how to reconstruct it all. How should I begin telling this odd story? I considered opening with a portrait of my life before we met, when I was just another out-of-breath single mom running the daily race for survival in the television industry, and everything was still relatively normal. But I immediately vetoed my own idea – too boring! Better to kick off with something more dramatic, right? I began searching my memory for things that happened to us over the past few months, and an awkward little laugh escaped my lips. How does that expression go, about reality surpassing all imagination? I suddenly realized it was true. There are certain incidents you have no way of predicting your response to before they happen. You know how you'd *like* to react, but at the moment of truth, your reaction is entirely different. Maybe reality does outdo all imagination, especially when it forces you to discover something about yourself that you'd never have guessed on your own.

Tom was breathing softly into my neck, slowly melting into sleep, while I ruminated where the hell to begin. The first time I saw you? That look? No, it didn't really begin with that look, it started the night before. It all began that one night two months ago, with a random dream that still remains unexplained.

I closed my eyes and tried to restore some clarity to the hazy details. I was riding through the desert on a motorbike covered in so much dust I couldn't make out its color. I wore a jacket and a huge helmet in spite of the oppressive heat, and the dirt path was endless, surrounded by a bleak yellowish expanse. It was the type of obscenely serene landscape that always makes me anxious, but I wasn't tense at all. Even the loud clatter that broke out of the engine didn't bother me. As if the woman riding the motorbike wasn't really me.

In the middle of the desert I saw a red light. There wasn't a soul to be seen, but I obeyed the law and stopped, suddenly noticing a tiny figure on the horizon, making its way towards me. I quickly checked myself out in the side mirror, as if fearing some physical change in my appearance. I was relieved to find my familiar brown eyes peeking back and the chestnut hair that emerged from under the helmet. The figure came closer and closer, white shirt, beige chinos, short dark hair. At some point I realized it was a man. I squinted and tried to make out his face, but just before he was close enough, the dream ended. Morning came.

I awoke with an inexplicable urge to write it all down. I keep a little pad next to my bed. Sometimes at night, before I fall asleep, an idea suddenly sprouts and I jot it down before it slips away, and that's what I did with the dream. An unfamiliar sensation hovered over me and accompanied me all day. I don't know how conscious I was of it, I thought it was just a random good mood. Could that be what you meant when you said that sometimes I don't register the details in real time, as things are actually happening to me?

A few hours later, on my way home from work, I stood in line for bread at a bakery on Pinkas St., watching the clock impatiently. I had exactly 14 minutes until school let out, which meant that if I didn't hurry, Tom would wait outside alone – that in itself being completely inconceivable – when I suddenly saw you. You were real, flesh and blood, just standing there. It was as if life had hit the brakes, a split-second freeze frame where something unexpected occurs and you can't decide if it's really happening. Your image from just before dawn came back to me like a wave crashing against the shore and then pulling back into the sea. I was so certain it was you - the guy from the dream - but I had no way of explaining it. You stood about six feet away, white shirt, beige chinos, thin white earphone wires snaked around your neck, Aviator glasses perched on your head. You seemed preoccupied as your eyes were looking around the store, and when you saw me, a tiny muscle in your chin jerked and something in your expression seemed to collapse. Like someone who felt a sudden jab of pain or had just witnessed an accident.

Ma'am, anything else or just the French sourdough? The cashier startled me. Uh, no, that's all, I mumbled, my nervous fingers tugging the wallet out of my bag, fumbling for a ten shekel coin and then another five. I handed them to her and peeked in your direction. You were slouching, hands in your pockets. An inexplicable feeling of alarm flooded me just as you turned sharply, throwing another half glance at me, and as your shoulder crossed mine in a barely palpable touch, you left the store empty-handed, turned right, and disappeared.

I grabbed the bagged bread and hurried outside. I stood by the store, my eyes scanning the bustling street in search of you, wondering if it was your back I had just seen breezing away. For a second I wanted to run after you, put a hand on your shoulder and ask, wait a minute, who are you? But that was only how I wanted to react. In reality I just stood there, hesitating, until I remembered that Tom was waiting and rushed to the car, telling myself it was just my imagination.

You kept invading my quality time with Tom throughout that entire afternoon. I was hoping we'd clean up his room together, but he only wanted to watch TV and fidget with his PlayStation and I wasn't in the mood to argue. Your image continued to hound me. Tom stayed unusually close to me, hugging me a lot and stroking my hair, but when I pulled him close I wasn't sure which one of us was protecting whom. You barged into my thoughts from the most unexpected corners, ignoring the fact that I can leave work early only two afternoons a week to spend time with him - even if all we ever do is homework, while I text the whole world as it continues its mad dash out there without me.

The next morning, after dropping Tom off at school, I headed to a big meeting with Gaya, the producer of our flagship program, "Big Fear". Our fifth season premiere was coming up in November, which left only a month to tie up loose ends before the launch. I stepped into the elevator with Erik, who was armed with his trademark cowboy boots that grant him a full extra inch. The very thought of having to watch his face bursting with self-important expressions over the next hour was irritating – a sneak preview to my usual reaction whenever he cuts in obnoxiously while I present my part, though he knows nothing about PR. I was starting to boil over before any of it even happened.

Erik pushed the twelfth-floor button, and just before the steel doors kissed closed, a mysterious hand pushed through, making them part again. I didn't know what to think as you entered the elevator casually, as if you were an innocent passenger. Again the white shirt, the delicate earphone wires around your neck, hiding a tiny smile that twisted slightly to the left. I almost blurted out: You again? But I said nothing, although it was clear that this was more than just a mere coincidence. Our eyes locked with a silent click, like the elevator doors just did. Erik was busy with his phone when you pushed the button for thirteen and stood right in front of me. Something familiar glimmered through your cologne, and I tried to smile but couldn't because your tiny smile had vanished, and the mischief in your eyes was replaced by something so hungry I was almost swallowed whole. I quickly looked away as Erik lowered his phone, surveying us both suspiciously. When he went back to tapping at his phone, you winked and put your hands in your pockets. The steel doors opened on the twelfth floor and Erik rudely stepped out first, the soles of his boots echoing through the hall. You managed to whisper - It's not what you think, Sheera, I'm not following you - and at the sight of my startled face you winked again, with a hint of a smile that disappeared behind the closing doors. I paused for a moment, stunned. Not following me? Then how do you know my name? And how did you know I'd be here? But Erik had already entered through the glass doors and I had to catch up with him, balancing carefully on my thin heels, trying not to slip on the marble floor.

A slight anxiety twitched inside me all day. Before falling asleep I read the scribbled note from the little pad beside my bed. Not that I believe in that kind of thing, but I thought it might provide a clue. Who knows. The only clue came after I fell asleep, when you reappeared in the exact same dream. Desert, dirt road, motorbike, red light, and you walking towards me, at first distant and blurry but clearer with every step. Only this time you didn't disappear at the last minute. You approached me with that burdened look from the bakery, allowing me a glimpse of your face while you said - some things can't be explained rationally.

The next morning I woke up troubled, shifting from fear to attraction, from curiosity to apprehension. I grabbed the little pad and shoved it into a drawer. I kept feeling the anxiety tap dancing in my bowels, as if the very stability of my life was being threatened. Funny, because up until that moment I hadn't even considered it stable. I'd grown so accustomed to seeing the bumps and squeaks and problems and daily battles, but now I had the sudden realization that my chaos had become a routine, and that's what it was, my life. Stable.

When I took Tom to school, my eyes searched for you behind the green dumpsters. As I stopped at the light I cast a suspicious look to the side, but all I saw was a blonde smoking in a Fiat Punto on my right, and on my left just a panting green bus loaded with passengers, none of them you. The morning programs chirped incessantly from the radio, and only when Tom asked me to explain something they were saying on the news did I realize that I my thoughts had drifted, and I hadn't really heard anything.

Mom, why aren't you listening to me? He turned his honey-colored eyes up at me as we stood by the gate. I'm sorry, sweetie, I apologized and tried to embrace him, but he slipped away when he noticed some friends and quickly started towards them, his huge backpack concealing his head, back and tush, making him look like a backpack with feet. Just to be on the safe side, before I left, I asked the guard to keep an eye out for my mother when school let out to make sure Tom didn't leave alone.

I was afraid of you. But everything was normal at the office, and nobody sprang out from behind any corner, or surprised me on my way home. Normally I would at least mention it to Rona, but something stopped me.

What's with the silent treatment, sister, everything ok? She texted me in the evening, after we hadn't spoken all day.

Crazy day, I responded a few minutes later. I wasn't in the mood for her inquiries or the sarcastic code names she liked pinning on everyone – The Poet, The Short Guy, The Smartass, The Philosopher – perhaps if I told her, your code name would be "The Intruder", but for some reason I didn't feel like joking about it with her.

At night, I was somewhat afraid to go to bed. After Tom fell asleep I closed all the shutters and checked the front door several times. I remember it was pretty late when I called Oren and that he was surprised – we'd only known each other for a few weeks, and it was the first time I called for no reason, just to chat from bed. I didn't tell him about you, obviously, and the conversation was so dull that at a certain point I wondered why I'd called, since his voice did nothing to calm me. What was I afraid of, you ask? I was afraid you'd start harassing me - which is the exact opposite of what actually happened. But what did I know back then. I really didn't know a thing. I was a curled up fetus, unaware of the contractions or of the fact that the warm womb would soon spit it out.

I kept expecting you to appear every day, and after a week went by, I stopped at the bakery again. Walking in, my eyes searched the little store for you as if of their own accord. There was something so empty there, so vacant, as if they were in the middle of spring cleaning.

After that, life kept travelling along the same road: alarm clock, coffee, school, work, work, work, and then at night - collapsing into bed with Tom. Everything was fine, except for a faint bitter aftertaste, a hint of disappointment maybe, and I couldn't pinpoint its source. The days piled up into weeks but you didn't reappear, my fear subsided and then drowned beneath the waves of routine, and was replaced by a vague emptiness. I thought it was just that familiar feeling of senselessness that raises its head every once in a while and whispers – so where are you headed? What's the point in all this?

A whole month went by before I realized my feeling was connected to you. But it's late, I'm too tired already. Tomorrow I'll try to write up a replay of that evening when everything changed. To reconstruct the exact moment when I understood that I wasn't really afraid you'd pop out of somewhere, uninvited, but the exact opposite. I was afraid you would never return.

To: <softspoons@gmail.com>
From: <softspoons@gmail.com>
January 3, 2016 at 10:20 p.m.
Subject: The story of how we met – continued

So where were we? On that evening you suddenly reappeared after I'd spent about a month trying to forget you existed. The babysitter was in the living room with Tom when I stepped out of the shower and into the bedroom. Oren was picking me up for dinner, and I scanned the closet trying to decide whether to wear something nice or something comfortable, since we'd already known each other for six weeks and I wasn't sure if we still need to try to impress each other. I suddenly caught my naked image, still glistening with tiny drops that managed to escape the towel, gazing back at me from the mirror. Somehow set off by that glimpse, the jaws of a beast opened wide - a beast of lust that had been sleeping inside me. I shivered as I tried to remember the last time I'd had really good sex. The kind that makes everything tremble, the bewitching kind, that's predatory yet fragile. The beast roared for a moment but immediately curled back into its slumber, and I stood there at the closet, staring. Yes, I wanted to keep seeing Oren. Maybe because Rona introduced me to him, maybe because when she described him she said – forget the details, he's got a neon "husband" sign flashing on his forehead – and we both laughed but we weren't really joking. She immediately decided to name him "The Husband" and I too was sure he was my ticket to that last train everybody wants to board for some reason, the train to a normal family and a father figure for Tom. But suddenly I realized that this was the price I'd pay. The beast would remain in hibernation, and I would never feel that way again.

Oren was a few minutes early and was already texting from downstairs, but I lingered for a moment, carefully opened the drawer in my night stand, fished out the little notepad and read that forgotten dream again. The memory of your image flashed before my eyes, and I automatically scolded myself – stop it, you're not a kid anymore, enough with the daydreams. I knew it was time to make up my mind. I couldn't toy with fantasies forever, and I would probably never find someone better than Oren.

When I went downstairs, Oren came out of the car and opened the door for me like the perfect gentleman. We drove to the pier, to a restaurant that my boss Moni mentioned casually at some meeting, being an expert on food, and generally – an expert on everything. The radio hummed on low volume while we exchanged polite nothings, but my mind was on the premiere of "Big Fear" that aired that night. Believe it or not, I've never watched it, Oren said and changed the subject, and the whole way to the restaurant I tried not to peek at my phone too often, though I was dying to see what people were tweeting about it.

It's strange to reconstruct the details from that evening, to have them resurface. It hasn't been that long, but since I met you it's as if I've erased him. Sometimes I think that the decision to leave Oren was not even mine. It was made after a secret vote that evening, in some grey matter boardroom hidden away in my skull, and I, slow on the uptake, only realized it much later. I was sitting across from Oren over fancy plates, surrounded by soft music, dim lights, the occasional fragment of conversation floating over from another table, and suddenly, in the middle of the roasted eggplant, I saw you. You were following the hostess with catlike steps, tall and present, streaks of silver shining in your hair. Why did it seem you'd left home in a hurry? Maybe because of the careless way you were dressed. Jeans, a grey t-shirt and bright orange sneakers. You fired one quick glance in my direction, and all at once I turned pale and flushed and sweated and shivered from the cold. What's *he* doing here? I almost choked on my food, a huge lump formed in my throat and refused to slide down, and I slowly placed my fork on the plate, feeling like I'd never be able to eat again.

You sat at the next table, just behind Oren's back and right in my face, flashed your half-smile at me, and then theatrically put on a baffled expression, pointed at Oren and mouthed – who is that? I stifled a smile and looked away. When the waiter approached, you refused the menu and just pointed at Oren, looking right at me and saying you wanted what he was having. So they poured you some wine, served you curried shrimp, and whenever Oren looked down at his plate, we touched each other with our eyes. I couldn't understand a thing although I understood everything perfectly, and my heart was pounding so hard I was sure everyone around us could hear it.

Do you want to order something else? Oren asked when he saw I'd stopped eating. No, it's all right, I mumbled, truth is I'm not that hungry. I poured myself another glass of wine, and behind Oren's back you raised yours, then waited for me to drink before taking a sip. My cheeks were burning, everything felt one size too tight and I fidgeted restlessly in my seat. Even when I wasn't looking I could feel your eyes interrogating me. I wanted to go to the bathroom but was afraid you'd take it as an invitation and follow me there. I'm a little embarrassed to write this, but something in me wanted it so badly, a dirty little hookup in the tiny stall, you pushing me inside without saying a word, kicking the door shut behind you and pinning me to the wall. But I guess life's a bit more complicated than porn, and besides, I really was scared. I didn't even know what your name was back then.

Nobody has ever become as superfluous as Oren did while sitting there facing me. We slowly got up to leave, the air felt so thick and pasty I could barely walk through it. I didn't know how you'd found me again. I couldn't think of any reasonable excuse to approach you with Oren watching us, yet couldn't believe I was on my way out without knowing who you were. I felt your eyes piercing my back like darts on a board. When we stepped out onto the street I nearly bumped into a big grey Yamaha motorbike that was standing near the door. For a moment I could've sworn it was the bike from the dream, minus the dust, innocently parked on the sidewalk.

When Oren dropped me off I gave him a quick peck on the cheek, and left the car saying I have to get up early before he could even respond. I rushed upstairs and paid the babysitter, you look great, she said over her shoulder just before leaving. I was pumped with so much vitality I didn't know what to do with myself. I wanted to dance, run, rescue a few stray cats, give a speech in the Knesset, throw a huge party and invite everyone I knew. The end-of-the-day fatigue had completely evaporated. I told Oren I had to go to sleep early, but not only did I lie, I had no idea how I'd be able to fall asleep. I couldn't settle down.

I crowded into Tom's bed and stroked his silky dark hair. He's been refusing to cut it for over a year now, and I've also kind of fallen for this new look of his. He moved around a little, fluttered an eye open for a moment and shut it, smiling at me through his dream. I held him and clung to the warmth he created under the blanket in his sleep, but the harsh buzz of the intercom startled me. Don't go, Mom, it's no one important, Tom mumbled, but I pulled away anyway and whispered I'd be right back. When I went to the door and asked - who is it? - my voice sounded pretty impatient. Hey, it's Oren, he said, his insecurity creeping at me through the little round holes on the speaker, as if ground into metallic worms of air. When I opened the door he stood on the straw doormat, trying to smile. For a minute I really felt sorry for him. Suddenly he seemed a bit lost, too thin and gentle, too fair.

You want something to drink? I asked without waiting for an answer, and went into the kitchen to pour us both some vodka on ice.

He just stood there, we clinked glasses, we sipped, I smiled.

So what's up with you? He asked with a man-in-charge voice, and I said – Nothing, everything's fine, why?

He put the glass down, then took off his glasses, paused for a moment before taking my face in his hands, and just before he kissed me, said – I didn't understand why you ran off like that. Funny how you can always smell something in kisses. The good ones have such a heady aroma they instantly make you forget everything, but this kiss had only the faded scent of a consolation prize.

I slept with him later, after carefully shutting Tom's door. His little mumble was echoing in my head – Mom, it's no one important. Still, I forced myself to sleep with Oren that night. It was a bit like swallowing medicine, if you shut your eyes and avoid breathing through your nose you hardly feel anything. I figured it would take less energy to fake sex than to actually end it in a long patient conversation.

I still get upset when I think about it. Why did I sleep with him that night? I didn't want to, Michael, I swear I didn't, not even a little. Maybe I just wanted to prove to myself that everything's fine, that despite the surprising encounter at the restaurant I still hadn't jumped off that last train, that nothing had really changed.

I was so close to a normal relationship, the kind I'd always wanted, but a week after that meeting at the restaurant, I chose you so naturally. It's completely absurd. I'm not sure I know the real significance of that choice other than the fact that from then on everything became complicated. You once told me that only a person's actual choices reveal who they really are. That people lie to themselves about the real reasons behind their choices so they can feel better about themselves, appear more heroic. Denial makes it easier, like licking your wounds, it's soothing. But if you don't insist on seeing the truth you learn nothing, and those wounds never heal.

So why did I choose you? I told myself I wanted to know what the deal with you was, and that it was unfair to continue dating Oren at the same time. But maybe that's not the real reason. After all, I'm not even sure I was honest with myself about wanting that "normal relationship". In theory, the idea always appealed to me, but look what I did in reality - had a child who would never have a father, and even when I had the chance to fix that, I easily passed it up. Oren was a really good guy, sometimes I still feel bad for him. But life with him would've tasted like sand. Faking sex every once in while is okay, but counterfeiting your whole life, even at home? I guess even I have my limits.

Maybe the real reason I chose you was that invisible key you gave me, though it happened long before you actually did offer it to me. Is it possible that even back then something dormant in me already wanted to find out the truth? Funny, because back then it never even occurred to me that I don't know it.

    11:23 p.m.   Hello? Hey, are you even reading all this?
    11:23 p.m.   Of course. You and your strange questions.
    11:24 p.m.   Okay, just making sure.

To: <softspoons@gmail.com>
From: <softspoons@gmail.com>
January 4, 2016 at 10:10 p.m.
Subject: The never-ending story of how we met

I woke up at six thirty the next morning, all frenzied and haunted by the foggy tails of a thousand dreams. I hurried through the morning routine and walked into the office at nine a.m. sharp, tired but alert, a little more edgy than usual due to our encounter the night before and also due to the meeting I had scheduled with Moni for later on. Another where's-my-career-heading discussion, or to put it more accurately, my illusion of a career. In the past years it's become a pattern - every few months I break down, complain, suck up to the boss, and in a charming yet assertive tone tell him I've had enough and want a different position at the station, while he pretends to listen but eventually dodges my plea and convinces me to stay exactly where I am.

I turned on the computer, sat down, and the first email that caught my eye was from Gidi, head of the promo department.

Hey sister, could you help me out here and show some enthusiasm on Facebook? Share the clip of the dudes who made it through the auditions last night, it'll only take you a second.

I surrendered with a little smile. I'd already poured my heart and soul into the promotion of "Big Fear", so why wouldn't I sell out my personal Facebook page for the benefit of the station? Instead of attending to the tons of emails that were still pouring in, I logged onto my Facebook page and uploaded the promo clip featuring the nut-jobs who survived the bungee challenge and the leech bath, and captioned it with the dramatic question from the show: "Few are blessed with the courage to battle the darkest human dreads.... so what's your Big Fear?" I wanted to get back to my emails but noticed two new friend requests. I didn't have much time to waste but curiosity compelled me to take a peek anyway. I recognized the profile picture of the receptionist at Gaya Productions and accepted her as a friend, but then I froze. My eyes fell on the most recent friend request, fresh from only thirty five minutes ago, from someone called Michael Eden.

That photo is still on your profile by the way. It's the one where you're standing on the beach while the orange sun is about to set, simple white t-shirt, hands hidden in the pockets of dark running shorts, smiling, hair a little stray. A wave of momentary happiness washed through me. You're back. You exist. You have a name and even a profile pic. It wasn't my imagination, it was real.

But a zillion questions sprang up and cut the surprise party short. How did you find me? Did you follow Oren's car when we left the restaurant, or what?

"It's not what you think, I'm not following you," the words you said in the elevator came back to me as I clicked on your photo, which linked to a locked page. You knew I wouldn't be able to help myself and that if I wanted more details I would have to accept you as a friend. Not following me, yeah right, I muttered as I clicked 'confirm' and let my eyes drink up the meager information – Michael Eden, forty four years old, lifeguard.

Lifeguard? No way, he doesn't look like a lifeguard, I thought. I searched for other photos, but that was the only one. I zoomed it to the maximum size on my computer monitor. Your enlarged face on my screen made me feel like you were right there in my office, and a light shiver went through my body as I examined you carefully. Handsome features, but not too handsome. Full lips, a bit pale in color. Short stubble, looks like someone forgot to shave this morning, maybe the night before as well. It appeared to be kind of soft, the stubble, except for the tiny groove between your upper lip and your nose – where it was coarse and dense. I tried to capture the exact color of your eyes, what was the right word – amber? I glanced at the door to check that no one was coming from the hall, then lingered on the rounded shoulders underneath the white shirt, stared at the baggy shorts, tried to imagine what your feet looked like when they weren't laced into the orange sneakers. Who had taken this photo? A friend? A girlfriend? Maybe a child? Or... a wife? I tried to check out your friends, but the list was blocked. I was so busy looking for what you had to be hiding that I didn't notice the little chat window that had popped up at the bottom of the screen. It took me a few minutes to realize you were there, online, waiting, trying to talk to me.

Why are you so stressed? It read.

My heart stopped. I hesitated for a second, then smiled and typed – I'm stressed because I'm in the middle of work and all of a sudden some lifeguard I don't know starts chatting with me.

They say stress is caused by the belief you're not going to get what you want, you wrote.

Really? Is that what they say at the beach?

You ignored this and just wrote – so what do you want to get today?

I asked myself whether this question had a pornographic tone to it, or if it was just my imagination.

I'm not sure you really want to know, I typed, and the truth was I didn't like the way things were going. I was expecting the dialog to be a bit more sophisticated.

But you persisted – I do. Tell me. What've you got to lose?

Okay, that's it, he's obviously looking for cybersex, I said to myself, and when I read my previous answer I was afraid you might interpret it as a hint that I was into it too.

You'd be surprised, but most of all I'd like to hear that the season premiere of "Big Fear" scored over thirty percent last night, I wrote.

Is that all? You asked. I still couldn't tell if you were trying to drag me into some kind of sexting session. I had to make it totally clear that I was not in any way the type to go for that sort of thing.

No, I started pouring out, I also want the charming VP Content, who always takes credit for everything, to admit that the campaign I sweated over was what got us those ratings. And later when I meet my CEO, I want him to finally agree to move me to a better position in the station. And *that* is all, since you're so interested.

You didn't respond for about thirty seconds, and I began to think I'd been too aggressive. At first I told myself off - is that how you come on to guys, stupid? Then I just mumbled - fine, whatever, just another prick, who needs him.

But after all that you suddenly answered with only one word.

Done.

I raised my eyebrows at your strange proclamation, and while I was still wondering how to respond, you wrote – talk tomorrow - and disappeared.

I shut down Facebook, ignoring the disappointment seeping through me along with the thought that somehow I always attract the wrong men, and tackled the emails that awaited me. The account exec at our advertising firm wanted another meeting. What a tedious woman, a professional time-waster. First give us a decent quote and then we'll meet as much as you want, I wrote back, with an annoying little thought pecking away at the back of my head – can't he just come on to me like a normal person? The next mail was a file of media clippings headed by a scathing review in Rona's paper: "Big Fear" misses no opportunity to scout ego-filled and brain-drained contestants, encourage adolescents to injure themselves in reckless stunts, and flatten human bravery into pornography.

I became more furious with every word. I forwarded the email to Rona and wrote – if there's one thing I can't stand, it's washed-up journalists who think they'll gain some self-worth by belittling someone with real talent. Like it was her fault.

What do you care, as long as they spell the show's name right, she wrote.

What does that mean, "done"? That he's not really into me? I tried to ignore the mousy little thoughts gnawing away in my head and moved on to the next email. But then the cell phone buzzed, making the whole desk vibrate, and the usual pain stabbed through my stomach, the stab that goes along with daily rating stats we get from the research department. I took a deep breath as I touched the screen, and a surge of bliss infused my little heart. Thirty eight! I screamed at whoever happened to be out there, the echoes of my cheers resonating back from the other rooms. I was so relieved. The night before, when I texted Avi from Sales, he'd managed to contaminate me with his fear. He thought that the viewers' enthusiasm would decline in this coming season, and the ratings for the premiere would plummet below twenty five percent, like they did with "The Human League", a flop from hell which of course Erik tried to pin on me when he said it was all because I "hadn't sold it well enough". But with "Big Fear" there's no room for mistakes – it's our oxygen tank - the station's very existence depends on the success of the show. I immediately texted Avi – how was our ad share last night?

Through the ceiling, he wrote. You're the best, I wrote back, I knew you'd line them up again this season. I leaned back in my chair to enjoy that blessed relief that floods my joints on mornings that begin like this.

When I heard Erik's cheery voice coming from down the hall my joy instantly evaporated. Here comes the loser to pat himself on the back, I muttered, and went back to my emails, praying he wouldn't come into my office. But his voice came closer, and there he was, his head poking in, followed by his stumpy body with his chest inflated ridiculously, and he just stood there like a peacock in his pointy steel-tipped boots as if waiting for me to bow or something, so I was forced to look up and struggle for a smile.

So, he said, thirty eight fucking percent, huh? I always knew you can do it when you put in that extra mile.

I searched his face for a glimmer of sarcasm, waiting for some sharp follow-up, but it didn't come. Erik just turned away and went out into the hallway to continue his victory lap.

What's up with him? I bet he's finally getting laid, I told myself and considered texting Avi to find out if he knew anything, but I didn't have time. In less than thirty minutes the hyperactive social media brigade would scurry in to discuss network distribution (which meant nobody would let anyone finish a sentence), and right after that I'd have to make the press rounds to get some feedback about last night's premiere. At noon I was supposed to have a kvetch session with Rafi Hadar, our biggest talent and the host of "Big Fear", who was planning to leave his wife and was confiding in me to consult on the "best way to communicate it". And at one p.m. I was supposed to see Moni. It's a little embarrassing, but at that point I still didn't realize what was going on. The constant pressure at work had turned life into a marathon, or maybe just an endless string of short sprints that chase one after the other. The race requires complete focus on running, and at some point you stop thinking about the reasons that made you start running in the first place. So when something unexpected gets in your way, your first instinct is to hurdle it. You can't stop if you're programmed to always proceed.

I continued going through my emails but then the phone rang, and Ruthie's name was blinking on the display. She probably wants to push back the meeting because Moni doesn't feel like hearing me whine, I thought as I took the call. Sheera, she sang coquettishly in her didactic tone, is there a chance you can push up the meeting with Moni and come right now? We had a cancellation and it would be perfect if I could squeeze you in.

Oh yes, sure, I said, surprised, give me three seconds. I snatched my phone, leapt out of my chair and began to march quickly over to see the big boss.

I've really grown to love Moni, but whenever I get summoned to his office I get slightly anxious. He trusts me and recognizes my total loyalty, but still. I'm always afraid he might want to reassign the troops, who knows, that's what it's like in this whimsical industry, it's erratic. Whenever he sends for me I wonder if I'm about to get fired, though I've been proven wrong hundreds of times.

We ruled last night, I said as I breezed past Ruthie, and she smiled back as satisfied as a grammar teacher who had just put a comma in the right place. I stepped into Moni's office. He was sitting on the orange leather couch, a fresh glass of diet cola fizzing on the coffee table in front of him, and he asked with his reserved smile, well, what do you think?

Funny, how every time I walk into his office and see his expression, my fears immediately dissipate.

I'm very pleased, I said, you?

Pleased, are you kidding? He said with a tight smile, the monster is always hungry and we have to feed it again tonight, so now we have to figure out how to keep those ratings up throughout the entire season.

I smiled at him knowing this was the perfect timing for my one-on-one talk. Notice how you spend less and less time enjoying the good numbers? I asked, sitting across from him. He glanced at his cell phone that flashed silently on the table, and then looked right into my eyes with a look that felt a bit too paternal, and my heart froze again. Listen, he leant over at me and said quietly, I've been thinking about your ambition to move to content, and I totally understand your motives and everything, but there's no opening at the moment, you know how it is, and besides, you're a PR wiz and I need you there.

I'll be polite and let him finish, I thought, but right after that I'm going to make it clear that I want to move ahead in life, and if not here, it will have to happen elsewhere. Or maybe I shouldn't make threats, I suddenly hesitated, where would I go if I left? I needed to have a backup plan before firing blanks. But then Moni started talking again.

I have an idea about the new show we want to import with Gaya, he said.

"Masterpiece"? I asked, wondering why he was suddenly changing the subject.

Yeah. Do you think you'd like to take it on? He asked casually, as if he offered me stuff like this every day.

What do you mean? I asked, confused. I didn't know what he meant by "take it on".

It means you'll have to work very hard, he said. We start in about a month, and you can oversee the entire adaptation process to Hebrew, along with your regular job. Take on one big production, I'll make sure Erik plays along, we'll see how the first season works out, and then decide how to take it from there. Agreed?

My tongue froze. I didn't know what to say, so I just mumbled something like - sure, wow, sounds great.

Okay, Moni said and grabbed his manically flashing phone and started typing a response to someone. So I'll talk to Erik and then ask Ruthie to set up a preliminary meeting, and in any case I'll see you in a couple of hours to check out tomorrow's promo clips, okay? Great, I mumbled again, as if it were the last surviving word in my repertoire. Moni was already deep into his phone, his brow wrinkled, which meant this was overtime and it would be best if I got up and said goodbye. I walked down the hall, completely baffled. My heart was bouncing around with excitement, but also with fear. What's come over him? And Erik, too. How exactly had this shift in attitude occurred? "Masterpiece", the new program we were planning to import with Gaya Productions, was not just another show. Moni was counting on it as a stepping stone for a binding partnership with Gaya, the production house that had bought the exclusive rights to the program from an Italian production company, and in exchange would become our in-house producer. So how come he just offered it to me?

I thought of the chat we had earlier, all the coincidences, that word that you'd written, "Done". How were you connected to everything that happened over the last hour? Who did you talk to? Do you know Moni? Are you friends? I suddenly remembered that Moni was the one who recommended the restaurant I went to with Oren. Is that how you found me last night?

But the faster my frenzied thoughts raced around perspiring in an attempt to put together a conspiracy theory about you – the less sense they made. Eventually I came to and stopped myself, because how could you have anything to do with this? You certainly don't know Erik or you would've said hello when we ran into you in the elevator last month. And how could you possibly affect the ratings? And if that's not enough, Moni obviously didn't make his decision on impulse this morning, so even if you had all the connections and all the right moves, technically you wouldn't have had the time to do anything. And why would you do anything? You don't even know me.

I sat at the computer again and texted Rona – I still can't believe it, but Moni just told me he's letting me run a show on my own.

No shitttttt, she wrote back, and who else will you have to sleep with for it except for him?

Unclear yet, I'll keep you posted, I wrote back. I added a smile emoji, though I no longer felt any happiness, just a few anxious worms squirming in my stomach.

Rona's sarcastic reaction echoed my feeling that something was off, illogical. I opened Facebook and clicked on my new friend's page, Michael Eden. Lifeguard my ass, I thought. Is this some kind of a stupid joke? What are you hiding? Who are you and what do you really do for a living?

Suddenly, at the top of your page, a new status line appeared, freshly written only seconds ago. I'm copy-pasting it here exactly as it originally appeared.

> *The world is full of hacks, but people who suspect everyone and spend life believing nothing good can ever happen to them, don't need the hacks. They cheat themselves just fine on their own.*

I felt my face turn pale and quickly reread my texts to Rona. An icy paw gripped my gut, and I had the inexplicable feeling that somehow you'd read them. What exactly did you mean back then in the elevator, when you whispered that you weren't following me?

Is it possible that this whole morning was just some crazy coincidence? Maybe, I thought, but I would still try to somehow find out whether Moni knows you. I'd milk it out of him casually during some random conversation. What were you even doing in that elevator at Gaya's office building? I'll have to grill the receptionist there as well. My feet twitched nervously under the table as I wanted to Google you, but suddenly my computer monitor flickered with a green flash and shut down. I jumped back gasping, and just stared at the black screen. Could that be you?

I tried to turn my computer back on, my heart was out of control as I fruitlessly jabbed at the keys. Should I call security? What's the deal with this guy? Suddenly, from within the cloud of fear that was already suffocating me, out of the corner of my eye I noticed that the computer was unplugged. My jittery legs had probably pulled the cord from the socket. I reached out to push it back in with quivering fingers, and it flickered on again.

God, what is wrong with me, I rolled my eyes when it came back on. Always blowing things out of proportion. Still, I knew very well that the world was full of hidden agendas. So what was yours, and why all the mystery?

You need to understand, Michael, ever since we met you keep lecturing about developing my sensitivity and reading the signs and clearing my view. But in the world in which I live, the only signs you need to read are the signs of deceit. Moni taught me long ago that when you've been sitting in a meeting for over thirty minutes and you still can't tell which of the participants is being screwed, then it's probably you.

10:48 p.m.	So tell me, how did a poetic soul such as yours get stuck with such a pragmatic personality?
10:48 p.m.	Is that all you have to say? Seriously, why ask me to rehash all this if you barely respond to anything? I don't understand what you think is supposed to happen here.
10:49 p.m.	Wait, it won't happen so fast. You said you'd give it a chance, didn't you?
10:49 p.m.	Yes, but I expected you to be more responsive. To give me some feedback, explain. Tell me something I don't know. For instance, how you planned everything the first time we met.
10:49 p.m.	Do you really think I planned it? Couldn't you see how startled I was?
10:51 p.m.	Yeah, but... you really didn't know? I was sure you knew everything up front.
10:52 p.m.	I didn't know squat. I mean, I knew we'd meet at some point, but not where or when. I didn't even know you were a woman. And when I first saw you at that store... I lost it. You were so tall, and that look in your eyes. I never pictured you like that. I recognized the station's logo on your cell phone, but I had to leave. I went around the corner to some playground, sat on the bench, it took me fifteen minutes just to catch my breath. Later I found your picture on the station's website and realized you were VP Communications for the number one station in Israel. Before that

	I didn't even know your name. That was the first time I started to inquire about you.
10:53 p.m.	So wait, how did it all happen? You want to tell me that our first meeting was really a coincidence? Now I really don't get it.
10:54 p.m.	Neither do I.
10:54 p.m.	And there I was thinking that as "The Guide" you're supposed to understand everything.
12:14 a.m.	Hey… if you're still up, I just wanted to ask how it went today.
12:14 a.m.	You're improving.
12:14 a.m.	What do you mean by improving..? How long does it take to master this shit?
12:15 a.m.	Will you relax? I already told you - you can't do this without patience. And don't get caught up in the technique. Technique is not your problem.
12:15 a.m.	So what is?
12:16 a.m.	Telling the truth. You're the most charming liar I know.
12:16 a.m.	What?? What are you talking about? I always tell the truth. Besides, what does the truth have to do with anything?
12:16 a.m.	Telling the truth is not as simple as it seems.
12:16 a.m.	Could you try to get off your high horse and explain what you mean?
12:17 a.m.	You need to know the truth behind your motives in order to be precise. Even when you write here. No one but us knows this email account exists. It's just you and me, like a journal. Or a diary. So don't be afraid, pour it all out, as truthful and genuine as you can.

12:17 a.m.	Okay, Guide. I thought that's exactly what I was doing, but never mind.
12:17 a.m.	Cut it out with the "Guide", OK?
12:18 a.m.	Okay, sorry... why are you so sensitive, I was just kidding.
12:18 a.m.	Your apology is humbly accepted. Go on, keep reconstructing everything, alright? Can't wait to read you.

To: <softspoons@gmail.com>
From: <softspoons@gmail.com>
January 5, 2016 at 9:32 p.m.
Subject: And now – the story of how we finally met

So what happened on that first night when we finally had a proper date? According to your theory about this weird journal, maybe now that I'm reconstructing the details I'll finally understand.

It was a unique evening, no doubt, although I didn't like the fact that you were shrouded in so much mystery. I thought you were doing it on purpose, and believe it or not, there were even moments I thought you'd drugged me. Funny, because as a little girl I was pretty keen on mysteries. I was captivated by the clues discovered by Nancy Drew, drawn to stories that slowly unfolded like a gypsy's accordion. But nowadays – who's got patience? If someone insists on being mysterious I immediately assume they're either a tedious bore or trying to hide something.

The day after the beginning of our beautiful Facebook friendship, you popped up in a chat window again. Congratulations on the show, you wrote, and I nearly choked. Don't panic, I'm on your side, you continued, the producer is also on your side, and if you play your cards right, Erik will be too. I don't know if you meant to calm me, because you only made me feel worse.

If there's anything we're all terrified of, it's industrial espionage. If our competitors found out about the new program or our plans for this future partnership with Gaya, I'd be totally screwed. I wanted to ask how you knew all this but didn't want to confirm it was true, so I decided to ignore it and sent back only a smile emoji.

Later on, during our morning meeting, I casually asked Moni – hey, do you know a guy called Michael Eden?

He stared back at me blankly and said – no, who is he? A lawyer?

No, I said, a lifeguard. (Why did I say that? I thought there might be a shred of truth in it though I'd already Googled you and realized it was just a bad joke).

A lifeguard? He looked at me, puzzled. No, I don't know any lifeguards, why did you think I would?

No, no... I stuttered, I meant he's some kind of hi-tech entrepreneur.

Never heard of him, he said, and gave me a funny look.

Forget it, doesn't matter, I mumbled and changed the subject. I tried sniffing around some more, asking other people, but eventually I gave up. Nobody knew who you were. I had to make do with the little I'd found on Google: a few news items from eight years ago about an exit you made when you were a partner in a start-up firm that was sold to a large global company for an impressive amount. I Googled the start-up – it was called "Tell-me-lies" and was based on a single product designed for HR managers: a tiny, almost invisible camera that installs on the back of a computer monitor, and tracks the interviewees' eye movements without their knowledge while they're interviewing, in order to rate their credibility. I still didn't know what you were doing these days, but it was pretty obvious you weren't really a lifeguard.

The next day you wrote me – did you know that the Italians are already selling your show to Spain's biggest broadcaster? You attached a link to an article that had aired on an Italian website less than an hour before. You managed to scare me. The more countries a format is sold to, the higher its price, and we didn't think there'd be much demand for "Masterpiece". It's a writing competition in an attempt to find "The Next Bestselling Author", so the entire program is built on writing assignments. Competitors experience things like spending an entire day with a blind person or with a couple on their wedding day, and then they have thirty minutes to write a story about it. When the time is up each contestant reads what he's written, the judges decide who stays and who goes, and the winner gets a contract with a big publishing house. It had potential, but we didn't think broadcasters would be standing in line because after all, who wants to be an author these days?

But that wasn't the only thing that freaked me out. You simply knew too much. What were your sources? We're extremely strict about confidentiality. It's so easy for other channels to copy an idea, make a few minor changes and air it as quickly as they can. It's not uncommon to do this sort of thing just to ruin your competitor's new show. So I had doubts about writing you back. I couldn't really figure out what you wanted from me, so I just sent you another innocuous emoji that gave nothing away.

There was still time until January, when we agreed to begin work on the new format, but during the morning roundup I asked if anyone'd heard about the sale to the Spanish channel, and Erik froze for a moment and then immediately texted Gaya. A few minutes later he looked at his phone and said – Gaya says no worries, the price was closed in advance and can't be changed. I was a bit surprised that he hadn't blown me off but actually addressed what I had to say, and for a moment I could've sworn that even his tone towards me had softened, something in his face. Only towards the end of the meeting, when I said we should start thinking about famous authors that could work well as judges, his smug expression reappeared as he told me not to get ahead of myself.

The next day you wrote – don't let Erik get to you, it's not personal, there's no way he'll start recruiting judges before Moni seals the deal with Gaya. I panicked. It all sounded very reasonable, but how the hell were you getting all the details? Were you bugging our meetings, do we have a mole? I decided to finally be direct and asked – hey, are you in the industry?

You know I'm not, you replied, didn't you Google me?

I couldn't decide whether it was a shot in the dark or you really had some way of knowing what went on inside my computer.

Two minutes later you wrote – I'm just a hi-tech geek. I used to be a partner in a small firm, and now I invest in start-ups.

In the media field? I asked.

No, you replied, in security.

So what's your connection to the television industry?

My only connection to TV is through the socket in my living room, you wrote. And when I didn't reply you added – and you, of course. I smiled, but didn't reply. I just didn't trust you.

Later on when I was talking to Moni, I mentioned that I understood that he didn't want to move on with the production before finalizing the contract with Gaya. He looked at me for a moment, then nodded and said – exactly. I had no idea how you knew it but I also knew how much Moni liked those moments between us when he thought I understood him without his having to explain.

We aired the second episode of "Big Fear" that evening, and I was still stressing despite the first episode's numbers. The auditions would last five weeks, during which we'd have to keep our numbers high because new viewers rarely come on board in later stages of the season. The next morning, your chat window popped up to ask whether I'd received last night's ratings yet, and I replied - for someone who has nothing to do with the TV industry you seem pretty obsessive about it.

It's not me who's obsessive, it's you, you replied. And it's you I'm interested in, not television, don't you get it?

If you're so interested in me, how come you never ask me anything else about my life?

I thought work was your life.

I couldn't decide whether this was a snipe or a clever dodge, so I didn't respond.

The next day you didn't write anything but when I checked your Facebook page I saw that you'd shared a link to a song. When I clicked on it, Elvis Costello's voice gushed out and flooded my office. *Sheeeee... may be the face I can't forget... a trace of pleasure or regret...* I jumped back and quickly shut it off, afraid someone would hear. Are you trying to tell me something? And if you are, why do it in such a twisted way?

The truth is that more than anything, I was waiting for you to ask me out. You had really piqued my curiosity, and I wanted to talk face to face, grill you about your sources. You'd helped me and didn't strike me as dishonest, but I still figured that if you were in the tiny camera business you might have some unsavory way of stalking me. And I couldn't understand why you hadn't asked for my number. If you were really interested, why didn't you want to call? What's the deal with you, anyway?

After a few days of this bizarre correspondence, I woke up one morning to the epiphany that this could actually work differently. Why the hell was I letting you set the tone? The more I thought about it, the angrier I became. When I got to the office, I turned on the computer, logged onto Facebook, checked to see you were online and wrote in your chat window: What's your stand on meeting outside this chat window?

A minute later you replied: Do you want to have dinner with me tonight?

I wanted to retort – Well, was that so hard? But instead, I took a deep breath and just wrote – Yes.

Something didn't add up. You've invaded my life but I was the one who had to initiate our first "meeting", I thought as I dabbed on some perfume in front of the mirror that evening. I hoped that all this mystery crap was just some sort of misunderstanding, the awkwardness of beginnings.

My parents came at seven thirty to fulfill their destiny as babysitters, and as I was leaving I kissed Tom, who asked: When are you coming back?

Not too late, I promised. And what about Harry Potter? He asked, raising his honey-colored eyes to me, and awash with guilt, I immediately suggested he read a few pages with my mother, promising we'd continue together the next day. He gave me that look of his, the one he knows no lifeboat can rescue me from, and when I hugged him he pulled out the maneuver that usually goes with that look - so can I skip the shower today, pleeease? My father raised his eyes from the paper and said – When I was your age, we would bathe once a week, whether we needed it or not, and then laughed at his own joke. When I saw Tom smiling at him admiringly, I glared at him and said – okay, Dad, a few other things have changed since you were a kid, and in this house we shower every day. Still, demonstrating that even as a grownup you keep kissing your parents, I kissed my father goodbye for Tom's benefit before leaving.

You were waiting for me outside the restaurant. You leaned against the dirty wall, ignoring the urban bustle of Ben-Yehuda Street, thin white earphone wires dangling from your ears, their ends hidden in the right pocket of your chinos. You were immersed in the music and didn't notice me as I slowly got out of the cab, walked up to you, almost stumbling, not entirely sure how I was supposed to say hello. You were a bit startled as you finally discovered me standing right next to you, but quickly recovered. Your eyes smiled at me as you pushed yourself lithely away from the wall. You placed your hand on my nape, drew me closer and kissed me on one cheek only, lingering there one millisecond longer than was called for by etiquette. Our attention was suddenly drawn by the deafening screech of a bus braking nearby, and your mischievous eyes pierced me for a moment and then bashfully fled sideways. I tried to remember the last time anyone in my life had had a look like that in his eyes, but couldn't.

We sat down with our menus, my heart beating so fast I had no idea how I'd be able to eat. You shredded a napkin with your fingers as you looked at me and asked – so how's Erik?

I smiled. Actually, a little better lately.

My mom always told me never to trust people who go through winter wearing the same boots they wore all summer, you winked. You know he's just intimidated by you, right?

By me? Why would I intimidate him? And how would you even know, do you guys know each other?

I don't know him, but I sniffed around a little, you gave a lopsided smile, and you're not the only one who can't stand him.

I wanted to ask who your sources were, but you suddenly asked if I was hungry.

Not really, I confessed.

Neither am I, you said, what do you say we get out of here?

It was the shortest low-cal no-carb dinner in history. We got up, accompanied by the waitress's annoyed stare, and stepped out into the noisy street. Do you like watermelon gum? You asked. Of course, I said, and you stopped and put your hands on my shoulders as if planting me in the sidewalk and said, then wait a second. You crossed the street to a convenience store and came back with two chilled cans of Diet Coke and watermelon gum that cracked sweetly in my mouth.

We started walking towards the beach. The light wind laughed in our faces, and it felt like the most natural thing in the world – walking by your side and getting carried away into the conversation as if picking up exactly where we'd left off last time, only the last time we'd met like this was actually never. A tall guy with a huge shock of Kramer-like hair walked by, and when we exchanged a smile you said you used to like sitcoms, but never really found a substitute that could measure up to Seinfeld, and I admitted that I no longer enjoyed anything on TV either. You? You opened your eyes wide at me and gave me a little nudge with your shoulder. I was sure you spent your days with your nose stuck in the screen and your nights spooning with the remote control.

I watch a lot, I just don't enjoy it anymore, I confessed, and if we're already on the subject, the last good movie I saw was somewhere back in the nineties. You paused for a moment and then said that in your opinion they just don't make monumental movies anymore, just like they no longer write monumental books. I asked what you meant, and you said that it'd been at least fifteen years since anyone made a movie that resonated in history like The Godfather or The Deer Hunter, and that authors are also not nearly as influential as they used to be. That something had happened to the world, eventually it really had become flat, because even when a movie is good, it doesn't remain engraved on your skin, it just stays there for a few minutes and then fades until completely forgotten. Sorry, I said, I totally disagree, but you insisted – really? Then give me an example of a movie or a book that did. I was silent for a moment, trying to think, because surely there'd been a movie or a book that changed the world since the turn of the millennium. I thought of "Masterpiece", my new show, and I wanted to say that you were actually claiming that there were no masterpieces anymore, and it was impossible to agree that the films and books that had once changed the world were gone, but I couldn't come up with any examples. I sneaked a glance in your direction as you glanced at me at the exact same time, and we both smiled, and something in the air between us was so pleasant that I agreed to postpone all my questions until later and for the time being continue to be ignorant about who you were, where you lived, where you'd parked, or why you thought that Erik was an asshole.

I had the feeling that the street was my home and the sea a private pool in my backyard. You held out another piece of gum, I declined, you insisted, come on, take it, at least I'll be able to say I took you out for watermelon on the beach. So we chewed and marched along to the urban soundtrack of cars, horns, bits of words said by people we passed, and the whisper of the night waves that grew closer, caressing the sand.

When we reached the boardwalk, you just stood in front of a bench for no apparent reason. I stood beside you and we watched the dark sea, and then, completely in sync, we sat down next to each other. You suddenly looked at me all serious and said – do you ever have the feeling that real life is going in another direction? I smiled awkwardly and said I didn't entirely understand what you meant.

Do you ever feel that life is a train, but you're not travelling on it, just running alongside of the track?

My pulse quickened, because I knew exactly what you meant, I just wasn't sure whether you were confessing something about your own life, or you'd somehow understood something about mine. I think everyone feels that way sometimes, I conceded diplomatically, and you watched the pedestrians for a few moments and said – yeah, it's just that some people feel that way all the time. I didn't really know what to say, and then you asked when I had to be home, and if Tom was alone.

How do you know about Tom? My stomach clenched. That's it, gone was the perfect moment where I didn't need any more information. My unanswered questions resurfaced and now I wanted to know everything.

I don't want to alarm you, but I know a few things about you, you said, and once again you made my heart race. I decided to just ask you, to simply be direct.

Listen, are you into some kind of industrial espionage? I asked, and you smiled and said, no, that's not really my field.

So where do you know all this stuff from, Facebook? I asked, half serious and half-kidding.

No, please don't panic, but I've known that we were supposed to meet for a while now.

You turned to me and crossed your legs like some kind of Buddha. I did the same and we sat facing each other, our knees almost touching.

Known that we're supposed to meet? What does that mean?

It means that I know some things, you said.

Look, I have to admit I keep getting the feeling you're following me, I persisted, and that it has something to do with that startup company you sold.

I swear it's not what you think, you said, and then smiled at the cliché that you'd already used when we met in the elevator. Your smile was so boyish that for a moment it melted away my suspicion like warm lava. My head refused, but somehow my body believed you. So what is it, you communicate with spirits? I asked cynically.

Only with the spirits of beautiful women, you said.

Okay, let's get serious for a moment, I said, I really want you to explain.

You paused for a minute and then said quietly, I promise to tell you everything, I'm just a little scared to do it right now.

Scared? I asked, wondering again if you were teasing me. You smiled a tired but naughty half-smile, like a street kid burdened with too much responsibility.

Will you agree not to talk about it anymore tonight, if I promise to tell you everything the next time we meet?

I didn't really like your suggestion, but I said okay, like some idiot. Something in your eyes was so cute I somehow gave in.

A small gust of wind surprised us, and you reached out and removed a stray strand of hair from my forehead, and when you smiled your teeth suddenly seemed exceptionally white. Two rows of perfect pearls. Something about you was so familiar, maybe that's why I seemed to take that whole conversation pretty lightly, instead of allowing it to set off about eight hundred warning bells and at least one mayday siren. But to be totally honest, a constant fear gnawed inside me, because it wasn't just me on the line. What about Tom? I couldn't believe how quickly I'd let myself drift, it's been years since I'd let down my defenses like that.

We sat there wordlessly for a few minutes, submitting to the gentle breezes, smelling the sea. We watched an elderly couple as they slowly walked by, arm in arm, slightly hunched. The sidewalk was scattered with prostitutes' calling cards, and we both smiled as the elderly couple carelessly stepped on them with their orthopedic shoes. On a nearby bench was a silver haired woman who didn't stop staring at us. She wore a long colorful dress, her lips a dark, purplish brown. Some invisible teenagers were laughing wildly somewhere in the distance, and every once in a while we were kissed by the mist that was coming off the surf. Something in our silence was so pleasant, but I kept trying to figure out why you were reluctant to tell me how you knew so many things, and the fear thickened in my gut. It wasn't that cold but I shivered, and reached for a thin cardigan that was neatly folded in my purse.

I have a headache, you said out of nowhere, closing your eyes. You placed a hand on the back of your neck, suddenly seeming a bit pale. I offered you my soda can, but you just put it on the sidewalk without touching it. You took the earphones out of your pocket, putting one bud into your ear and the other into mine, and then naturally took my hands in yours. You closed your eyes again, and for a minute I saw the pain in your face. I was silent, and without thinking too much I shut my eyes like you did, and we just sat there on the bench by the boardwalk in the middle of life, holding hands with our eyes shut, cross-legged and blind. The warmth of your hands felt like an electric blanket, and then that Coldplay song started playing, "Yellow". *Look at the stars, see how they shine for you, in everything you do...* It was beautiful despite the fact I'd heard it a hundred times before, and I didn't want to open my eyes and ruin the illusion that the band was right there playing for us on the sidewalk. The images running through my head were also too beautiful to just stop without a reason. I imagined us standing on the black waves as if they were some dynamic marble floor, you were holding me close, your warm face buried in my hair and your breath tickling my neck as if we were in the middle of a slow song at junior prom.

When the song was over I slowly opened my eyes. You were sitting across from me, your eyes wide open and webbed with thin red lines, watching me with a quiet ocean gaze, and everything around us was dark and empty. Where did all the people go? An icy wave encrusted my bones, and I quickly released my hands from yours. My fingers were numb, as if hardened in our entanglement and refusing to regain their flexibility. For a moment I wasn't sure if this was really happening or I was dreaming about you again. My voice sounded hoarse when I asked you what time it was. About one thirty, you said, do you have to get home?

One thirty?! I was sure I misheard. Yeah, the babysitter, I said, confused, because I didn't even remember that it wasn't the babysitter I had to release but worse, my parents, and I couldn't figure out how four hours had disappeared into thin air during one Coldplay song.

We walked slowly towards the road, and with each step I was sure the sidewalk was going to crack open and collapse under my weight like Styrofoam. Something felt so off-beat and strange, and I didn't know what it was. Like a really strong hangover, but without the headache and dry mouth. Everything around me looked like fake scenery, as if someone would soon yell "cut!" and turn on the lights, and the crew would come out of the dark and start to break down the set. You hailed a stray cab, and when I realized you weren't joining me in the back seat I asked how you planned on getting home, and you said it was okay, you felt like walking back to the restaurant, and you'd left your motorbike there. But what about your headache? I asked.

It's gone, you said and smiled, and then just before you shut the door you caught my gaze and casually added – It's been so long since I danced with someone.

The ride home was swift, the lights were all green while soft songs oozed out of the radio, and for some reason I felt so safe and secure just staring at the back of the driver's neck. What happened to me tonight? Had I fallen asleep sitting up? Did we really dance or did I imagine it? I recalled that strange dream I had before we met, and wondered if it was possible that I'd dreamt not only of you but of your motorbike as well. I couldn't understand anything.

But the strangest thing of all was that I felt no pressure. Nothing seemed suspicious, or fucked up, or frightening, or something I had to forget ever happened. I left the house to get to know you better, I came back with more questions than answers, and still something about the evening infused me with a rare and inexplicable sense of serenity. I floated, watching everything from outside, as if you had drugged me. The taxi screeched outside my house, and I scolded myself, you idiot, he put something in your soda, you drank it, come on, how naïve are you? Yet something refused to be angry, refused to be scared. As if I was watching a film about someone else.

I paid the driver, went into the dark building and switched on the light in the stairwell. When I walked in, my father glared at me grimly and asked, is everything all right? Sure, I said, sorry I'm late. He grumbled something while my mother smiled at me mercifully. I quietly embraced her, and for a moment she was so small and frail in my arms. The minute they left I squeezed into Tom's bed, clothes and all. He mumbled something from within a dream and twitched a little, and I wrapped one arm and one leg around him and fainted into a deep and heavy slumber. The next morning I was awoken by insistent little shakes of my shoulder, still shrouded in unfamiliar sensations, Tom's eyes anxiously staring at me, and his little mouth saying, Mom, you slept here by mistake. I smiled and gently pulled him into a hug, and for a moment I wondered whether today would be the right time to tell Oren - it's not you it's me, because it was clear I wouldn't be able to keep pretending.

I think I'm starting to understand what happened to me that evening, just now as I've finished writing everything down. Because what happened is really quite inconceivable for the limited human perception, especially mine. You could say it's the exact opposite of what I recited for Oren – it's not me, it's you. Despite the tangled up thoughts, the suspicion, the doubts, there was something about you I couldn't pass up, although I didn't know what it was. I could have disqualified you on so many grounds, I could've decided you were a con artist or a fraud or a psychopath, demand explanations and threaten to leave if you didn't provide them. But what I didn't understand about that evening is how in spite of all the warning signs, I simply chose to set the suspicions aside. The way our dialogue flowed, and then the warmth that flowed between our hands – it was more than just another date. Maybe it wasn't a drug that dissolves in your cocktail, but there was something addictive about it. I felt as if you'd seduced me with something I hadn't known existed. Despite my disdain for mystery, when I looked in the bathroom mirror, there was something different about my face. It was still me, but in a slightly altered version. So eventually, regardless of the person I'd gotten accustomed to be, and despite my unanswered questions and inability to understand, I agreed to be naïve and to semi-believe.

9:56 p.m.		You know there's no such thing as semi-believing.
9:56 p.m.		Oh, really? "Semi-belief" is the only explanation for why I'm still playing along with you.
9:56 p.m.		Come on, Sheera, you either believe or you don't. You know what you really chose? To keep all your options open.
9:57 p.m.		What, you mean Oren? Because what I told him was absolutely final as far as I'm concerned.
9:57 p.m.		No, not Oren, who cares about your boring exes. I mean what we're doing here. You want to believe, but you also want to keep suspecting.
9:58 p.m.		I don't see what you're getting at.

9:58 p.m.	I'm trying to show you how you think. You think like someone who's afraid to go all the way. You said you want to go through this process with me, but only half-heartedly. Half of My Heart. You know that song?
9:58 p.m.	Me?? I agreed to your crazy rules, I'm cooperating like the ultimate submissive collaborator while you just sit there, telling me nothing and barely responding, and you're complaining?
9:58 p.m.	The eternally deprived. I think I'll start a charity for you. What am I not telling you that you so badly want to know?
9:58 p.m.	Just tell me anything. Doesn't matter what. Even something technical like how you drink your coffee, what you studied at college, what you did in the army.
9:58 p.m.	You were so calm a minute ago, what did I say that set you off? You surge like a wave out of nowhere, transform like those creatures in Song of the Sea. All right, I get it. I'll write you something tomorrow. Good night.
9:59 p.m.	Good night? No practice today?
9:59 p.m.	If you want to practice on me, I'm always willing.
9:59 p.m.	Okay, give me a few minutes to get ready.

To: <softspoons@gmail.com>
From: <softspoons@gmail.com>
January 6, 2016 at 7:05 p.m.
Subject: Here's what I did in the army

The day we were stationed at the unit, fresh out of the oven, we waited for our first briefing. We were eight newbies. Officers with shiny new ranks in a conference room that stank of Lysol. I had butterflies in my stomach. The walls were bare except for a huge faded regional map in a cheap wooden frame. Everyone straightened as the base commander walked in with his polished boots. He tried to motivate us, but wasn't too good at it. "From now on, you decide who's assigned to the IDF's most classified units, and that's a great responsibility, are we clear?"

We all watched him, silent as fish, only a chorus of internal voices thinking the exact same thing – what's he talking about? We're not here for the responsibility, we're here for the perks. A prestigious unit so nobody could call us paper pushers, but smack in the center of Tel Aviv. Perfect combo. The officer next to me quickly scribbled something in a notebook. I barely remembered him from officers training. When the commander turned his head he passed the notebook to me so I could read it.

Are you good at math?

I didn't understand what he wanted. I nodded like an imbecile. He took the notebook and scribbled something else, passing it back to me.

A quick estimate – how much cash could we leave the army with if we charge each soldier 1000 for assigning him to the unit of his choice?

I looked at him, a fair skinned nerdy Field Security Officer with flushed cheeks, and when I realized he was joking I uttered a hoarse little laugh. The commander turned and gave me the look of death. I mumbled an apology. That's how I got to know Yanky. That's my first memory of him, and of course it has something to do with money.

After a few weeks at the base, I really did get to know him. His thoughts, his jokes, the kind of ass he liked on a woman, his dreams. Yanky wanted to get rich. He'd come up with a new idea every day, flapping his hands, explaining enthusiastically. He had a real talent for numbers, a pro at quick multiplication, percentages, roots, powers. The type who sees everything through the profit-line. Didn't let a day go by without making us both millionaires. In dollars, yes? Back then they were still worth something.

We sat in the same office for three years. You have to admit that's more quality time than a married couple.

Our office was relatively big, with an old wooden bookshelf that gave off a musty smell, a green steel cabinet on either side, and the cherry on top – a window with a broken handle that couldn't be opened. Sometimes we were so busy we barely raised our heads to look through it, but on slower days we'd put our feet up on the desk, drink stale black coffee and pretend it was whiskey. Real men, right? Yanky had sharp senses even back then. Not just about business or girls. He could sense one of my headaches coming on before I even would. He'd suddenly hand me two pills, wordlessly putting them in my palm, and only then would I realize the pain was already covering half my brain and I hadn't noticed. That's how he won me over. He cared. He knew how to be a friend.

We slipped into a boring routine. Eight to five, bland mashed potatoes and chicken a-la-grease for lunch, and a parade of uniforms passing before us all day. The only thing that managed to excite us was girls, and maybe one or two Sade songs. *"Diamond life, lover* boy..." Yanky was obsessive. I've never met anyone with such drive. He was the leader and I brought up the rear, living off his fumes. We'd stand at the commissary, leaning on some lame plywood counter as if it were a hip club in New York, constantly checking out the racks on the women soldiers. He'd elbow me in the ribs or step on my foot when a pretty one came in or leaned forward. When I was with him, I could come on to anyone without even stuttering. He taught me how to conquer a woman. You don't need looks - you need character, determination. He was my exact opposite. No inhibitions. The type who throws himself at the world and says – catch me.

We had codes. Out of nowhere he'd ask me – so what's your take on this issue? When the full question was - is she wearing a thong or isn't she - about some girl that just bent over. Or someone would walk in and he'd ask – smooth? Which meant he wanted me to bet on whether she was totally smooth down there or maybe she left a little landing strip. We'd often hit on two girls, he'd choose one and leave me the other. Thanks to him I had plenty of sex during my service, but plenty by my standards, not his. He really got around when it was still legitimate to behave that way, let me tell you. Got me all riled up, competitive, like a test I had to pass again and again. It took me some time to realize that I wanted to be like him, although I didn't, not really. I'd score and then get all depressed about it. For the first time in my life I felt like a man, but I was touchy like a woman. I didn't say anything, but a few years later, after we'd already founded our start-up, I stopped joining him on his screwing sprees. I still wanted sex all the time, and Yanky was still going on about nipple sizes, pear shaped asses, lips. Every random girl would undergo a screening to check if she was a potential lay. So we continued to joke about it, but then he'd go out and I'd go home alone and jerk off in the shower.

But you asked what I did in the army, right?

I did soldiers. A lot of them. They moved in front of my face and I shifted them around like Scrabble pieces. We'd imitate them after every interview. Yanky was a master of expressions. His best - that shocked, hollow look they all had when coming fresh out of boot camp. Lips slightly parted, jaw agape, shoulders slumped. He'd put on that face in a second, and I'd laugh my ass off, nearly crying. Later we started classifying them by types. The tight-asses, the horrified and petrified, the jokers, the buddies, the over-eager ones who repeated everything twice. But don't get me wrong, I didn't play with their fate, I took my job very seriously. We were supposed to screen the soldiers according to their credibility. There were long written tests, and they teach you what questions to ask, which body motions to look for, expressions, reactions, cross-examinations.

At first I was a little stunned when I realized everyone was lying. Just little fibs sometimes, but still, when someone lies to you without batting an eye it's upsetting. One morning the commander called me in and said I rejected too many soldiers, that I was exaggerating. I was so insulted, got all defensive – it's not my fault they send me all the liars. Yanky told me I had high expectations. That we should let the little lies slide. Well, he was right. I've always been over-sensitive about lies. But once I accepted the fact that humans are creatures who lie, I realized that credibility should be rated according to other criteria. That I shouldn't be checking if someone was lying or not - I should be inquiring what they lied about and why.

I was so proud of myself, like a bonehead who just discovered electricity. Suddenly my job became interesting. Finding out if someone was lying is boring, but finding out what stands behind the lie is a whole other story. I still used the questionnaires from the training, but developed my own system. I started tracking the data in matrices, and realized there were three groups.

The first group was The Obvious Cheats. The ones who are there to take you for a ride and it's written all over their faces. They were the easiest to reject, not very challenging. But many people lie because they don't want you to think they're losers. Insecure, you know? I'd put them in the second group. I called them The Wannabees, and had some sympathy for them, but I'd get rid of them too.

Those who needed some more looking into – I'd put them in the third group. I called them "The Sinceres". They'd look you in the eye and really try to be honest, but the problem was that they only thought they were telling the truth because they were lying to themselves as well. You know what I mean, right? People who are straight as an arrow, they'd easily pass a lie detector, because they don't lie consciously. They really believe in the story they've made up about themselves. You know the type?

Meanwhile, more and more soldiers came through, and I got pretty good at it, became this sorting machine. Sometimes we'd get audited by psychologists, especially when we were screening for senior positions. I was the only one who never missed. Yanky couldn't understand how I picked up on them so quickly. He'd gaze at me with dollar-sign-eyes and say I had a badass intuition for people. At a certain point I'd picked up on so many nuances I didn't even need to listen. I could sit there wearing headphones all day, seriously, listen to Sade's clean voice washing through my ears, *a license to love, insurance to hold, his eyes are like angels but his heart is cold*, and just by looking in their eyes, see exactly when they were lying and why.

Most people think that if someone looks you straight in the eye, that means he's not lying, right? But actually The Obvious Cheats make sure to constantly look you in the eye, they try to create an impression of sincerity. They don't look away for a second. They reveal themselves in their obvious attempt to be too credible.

The "Wannabees" are hesitant, they're afraid you'll figure them out for who they really are, so they shift their eyes too much in all directions. And The Sinceres look you in the eye most of the time, but occasionally look away when stopping to think or trying to remember something. It's amazing how everyone works exactly the same way. I bet I do the same as well, only I can't really see myself when I'm lying.

But here's the most interesting part. Sometimes I'd reject a Sincere one too, the ones who were too delusional. You know how I'd tell? They were the most persistent. They would stubbornly stick to their answer, incapable of hearing anything that contradicted it. If they were asked to reconsider an answer they'd automatically wave it off, saying they were entirely sure. No need to rethink. They'd defend their story with everything they had, and you could see it in their pupils. If someone's really thinking something over, their pupils contract and expand. But people who only pretend to be thinking - their pupils freeze; there are things they're simply unable to confront. If God forbid they'd discover they were wrong, their whole world would collapse. You know what I mean?

That's what I did in the army, Sheera, I found people who were unwilling to see things from a different angle, and I realized that the more persistent you were, the less you were willing to think. My commander was happy. I told him about the groups and the eye movements and he made me his protégé. He asked me to put together a presentation about my technique, and I started to teach trainees. Became an expert on the truth. Yanky began calling me "Polly" – short for polygraph. He still calls me that sometimes. Then we turned the system into an algorithm, a camera, a startup, and Yanky fulfilled his childhood dream. I made my share too. I still live off it, and sometimes I invest in new startups.

So now you know something else about me, not all that interesting if you ask me, but you're not really asking me, are you?

One last thing. Regarding your question about telling the truth. You asked why it was so hard. That's why I told you this whole saga. Believe me, as someone who's made a career of it, people who are totally honest also lie. Sometimes unconsciously, sometimes on purpose. Take Yanky for instance – my eternal best friend, knows me better than anyone, but even he doesn't know the whole truth about me. Everyone lies, Sheera. For all kinds of reasons. As do I, as do you.

7:27 p.m.	What did I lie about?
7:28 p.m.	Don't get me wrong, your sincerity is spellbinding. And contagious - I've never written anything like this. You're honest, but it doesn't mean you don't lie. Try thinking of something you know you lied about.
7:28 p.m.	Oh come on, don't play treasure hunt with me. If you think I lied about something, just tell me.
7:28 p.m.	Relax, Sheera, you're so impatient. It's not easy to dissemble lies you're so used to telling yourself. I mean when you wrote me you had a child who would never have a father. But you know who Tom's father is.
7:28 p.m.	Did I write that? I didn't even notice. And you know what? It doesn't count. I've become so used to saying Tom was a sperm-donor baby that I don't even notice it anymore.
7:28 p.m.	Sometimes we repeat a lie so many times we forget it's not the truth.
7:29 p.m.	Oh please, that's such a petty example. You really think I don't remember that's not the truth? Give me a break. I made myself get used to that lie but for a very good reason – for Tom's sake, and there's no other lie I cling to like that.
7:30 p.m.	Sorry, I didn't mean to upset you.
7:30 p.m.	Yeah, okay. I have to go. Good night.

To: <softspoons@gmail.com>
From: <softspoons@gmail.com>
January 7, 2016 at 9:48 p.m.
Subject: The story of how you hung me out to dry until we met again

I remember the morning after our boardwalk date very clearly. Tom was a little worried after finding me in his bed, still in my clothes from the night before. When I dropped him off at school he suddenly asked, Mommy, where were you last night?

At a work thing, I said, and something clenched inside, as if protesting the lie. I told him I was working on a new program. Pleeease tell me what it's about, he begged eagerly. He's thrilled when he knows what's going to be on TV before anyone else does. I said I'd tell him that night if he promised to keep it a secret. He smiled and quickly glanced out the window, then gave me a hug after making sure none of his friends were around.

After I dropped him off, Rona called. What's new? She asked, and instead of giving her the complete play by play of the night before, I found myself stalling. How exactly was I supposed to tell her?

Listen, Sheer, I'm clinically dead, it's been six months since my last cover story, she immediately started shooting out a volley of words, and I was relieved to realize she called to talk about herself, not about me. I went to the Predator in Chief to complain, but before I could get a word in he was already biting my head off, told me I'm not angry enough, not daring enough, not even strong enough on Facebook. He's such a bloodsucking vampire, die, asshole die, no matter what I pitch he snorts in my face, and you know they're making cutbacks, so I really need a kickass story, ASAP. Any ideas?

Don't worry, we'll come up with something sexy and boost your ratings, I said, enthused, especially about the temporary pass on having to tell her about you, and we scheduled coffee to figure out how to save her butt.

I was still afloat in the strange sensation of the night before, it felt as if someone had remodeled the regular landscape around me. Everything seemed more colorful, and there was something clean about the air, as if someone had taken a huge bucket during the night and washed all the buildings and the sky and the street.

When I got to the office the security guard in the lobby stared at me and I smiled back, confused. I wasn't even wearing anything special, just black jeans and a white t-shirt. In the elevator I ran into Julia the secretary, who was planted in huge platform shoes, and whipped out her gleaming smile at me as she said – hey, did you do something with your hair?

No, I mumbled, awkwardly running my fingers through my hair. Then at our morning roundup Avi sat down next to me, winked and said – what's with the glow, sister, is there anything you wanna tell me? I smiled and said nothing, but noticed that Erik was also measuring me with his eyes in a strange way.

Later when I was at my computer, you emerged from our chat window.

It was good to see you yesterday, you wrote.

I smiled to myself and decided to take a risk. I'm glad you're so polite after you hypnotized me last night and used me, you pathetic manipulator.

Pathetic? You replied. I'm anything but pathetic when it comes to manipulating.

I realized there was no escape from asking you directly: Okay, and now that we've had our fun, would you please explain what you did to me last night?

And you answered casually - What I did to you or what you did to me?

When I didn't respond, you continued – Don't be alarmed. We connected, so your channels opened up a little.

I thought you were still joking. What channels, I wrote, are you with the cable company? Planning to set me up with the premium package? Or is "we connected" your way of telling me you brutally raped me after drugging me and I just can't remember anything? And before you could even respond I added - And if so – how was I?

Relax, you wrote, I think you've been watching too much TV. All I did was wake something dormant for you, and in return you made my headache go away. Now we're even.

I couldn't understand anything, and it was starting to get irritating. You didn't strike me as one of those hippie spiritualists, but just to make sure I asked - Did you study Reiki or something? Transcendental meditation?

But you remained enigmatic. We agreed that I'd tell you everything next time we meet, you wrote. In the meantime, just try to pay attention. Look for small changes, and we'll see each other next week, OK?

I rolled my eyes and sighed. How come every time I like someone it all has to be so difficult? I wanted to write – Gee, thanks for finding me a slot in your schedule. But Julia's blonde mane suddenly appeared at the door, and she stared right at me with her big baby blues and asked: Botox? I looked at her, baffled, and asked, What? A hint of a smile escaped her lips as she gave me the look she usually reserved for talents like Rafi Hadar, until I caught on and giggled. I swear I didn't do anything, I said as she frowned disappointedly and clunked her heavy platforms down the hall. When I looked back at my screen, you weren't online anymore.

People are always comparing their situation to others, I told Rona when we met that night after work, maybe you should go for a story about relationships.

Are you nuts? Her eyes widened, what do you think I am? A reporter for Glamour magazine?

Everyone's into that kind of stuff, I insisted, and you want ratings, right?

It's too shallow, she argued, and I went on to convince her that there was a way to write intelligently about every subject, even scientifically, and maybe she could get a research firm to conduct the Grand Relationship Survey, Love Israeli Style 2016, which would bring forth fresh new findings.

Like what? She kept looking at me reluctantly, and I spread both my palms out and said – everything! How long it takes to know for sure that it's the real thing, how long it takes to realize that it isn't, top reasons why people get a divorce, how often they have sex, and who you should marry – "the one" that meets most of the requirements on your checklist or "the one" who steals your heart.

You think that would hold a feature? The contempt in her eyes softened a little, and I nodded confidently and suggested she add stories about couples in various stages of their relationships and experts who would analyze it all. She said she'll sleep on it, though something in her eyes was wondering why I'd thought of the subject in the first place, me of all people, the most single person in the world.

But while I was starting to take interest in in-depth studies of relationships, you went back to being interested solely in my work. The next day you popped up in our chat window and started interrogating me about the show.

How's it going with Erik? Did you meet with the producer already? You really gave me a jolt. I'm not supposed to discuss things like that with anyone outside the station. Plus - I couldn't understand why you didn't want to meet up again before next week.

Was I only imagining that something special had happened the other night? Or were you stalling because you didn't really want to tell me everything next time we meet? Maybe you really are using me. I couldn't understand what it was that you wanted.

Everything's fine. You? I answered laconically.

You didn't reply, and I thought our chat was over. But an hour later you were suddenly back.

About the delay with your show, you should know that Erik has personal motives. It's not just another show for him. The connection with Gaya is really important to him, but it's not only that. He wants a piece of the new partnership – a cut of the profits.

How do you know all this? I asked. You were scaring me with your stealthy sources. You had a few too many for someone who had nothing to do with the industry. You wrote that I shouldn't concern myself with it, advised me to just wait and let Erik resolve his issues, because once that was taken care of, things would flow. But everything irritated me. Erik's greed. Your meddling. There was something nice about having someone help me move forward, but still – I was wary of your motives.

The next day Erik stormed into Moni's office while we were in the middle of a work meeting.

Moni was eating his lunch, and placed his chopsticks down on the table. Erik sat down and without thinking twice, reached his stubby fingers out to Moni's plate and helped himself to a maki, dipped it in some spicy mayonnaise and crammed it into his mouth. I made a huge effort not to stare at the pinkish blob that stuck to his chin as he said, while chewing – That's it, I've talked to Gaya and we're starting to scout judges for "Masterpiece". My heart skipped a beat. Where was this turn of events coming from?

Maybe we should set up a three-way meeting, I suggested, and Erik said it wasn't necessary, Gaya was just starting to feel out the agents and she could do it on her own. I was infuriated that he'd started running everything behind my back, although it was so obvious that he would do just that. Play mister nice guy and tell Moni that he's fine with my running the show, but freeze me out and not let me do my job. I wanted to strangle him but I sat there with a frozen look on my face, nodding when Moni asked to set up a meeting in two weeks' time, and just said "sure" without revealing anything.

Later I went online and wrote you that Erik and Gaya had suddenly agreed to start looking for well-known authors to judge the show.

Great, you wrote.

What's so great? And how exactly does that comply with what you said about his sneaky maneuvering?

Complies perfectly, you replied. He got what he wanted, the agreement is almost finalized and now things will start flowing and everyone's happy. You wanted to move forward, didn't you?

I didn't respond. Sure, I got what I wanted, but everything pissed me off. Your interference. The anonymous sources. Erik's domineering takeover. Conceding and allowing him to take the lead. And yes, the fact that a few days had gone by and we still hadn't set up a date. I fluctuated between anger at your remoteness and anger about the way you'd invaded my life, infiltrating my smallest capillaries.

My nerves were still raw when Rona called to rave about her Predator in Chief that had surprised her by green-lighting the relationship survey, and it only became worse when I got home and had to deal with Tom's hyperactivity.

Mom, who was that person who came over last week in the middle of the night when I was asleep? He suddenly remembered while flitting around the house like a drop of mercury, and when I said that it was someone from work, he asked if I was trying to find him a dad. I froze for a second before asking – where did you get that idea? He stopped right in front of me, panting, pushed a strand of hair out of his eyes and said that's what grandpa had told him. I'm not trying to find anything, I said quickly, but his restlessness did not abate, and it took me an hour to wrangle him into the shower. When I finally lay in bed with him after texting a death threat to my father, I knew that if I wanted him to calm down I would also have to decompress. I took a deep breath and tried to halt my mind from the endless mushrooming of distressed, unanswered questions about you. Tom and I made a few pages' progress in Harry Potter, which he insists on reading though he's really too young, and I slowly stroked his hair until his reading became heavy and slow. I watched his eyes as they were closing in perfect sync with the movement of my fingers on his hair, and just before he fell asleep, he muttered – I love when you comb the thoughts out of my head.

And I love that boy's way with words.

The temporary tranquility didn't last very long. I had another eye-rolling moment the next day when I realized you had no intention of asking me out, and all I found was another song on your Facebook wall. When I clicked on the song, Barry Saharof began singing: *"it's like dancing with a demon – I'm falling further down – sparks of revelation – fly by time after time..."* I stopped the song decisively. I had no desire to encourage more indirect messages. If you want to tell me something, just say it.

A minute later you popped up on chat, asking if I had felt anything out of the ordinary since our date. For a second I panicked – I'm no expert on Facebook – could you have a way of knowing if I'd listened to your song?

Nothing, I replied.

Nothing?

Nothing at all.

A little more edgy than usual? You persisted.

No, I lied. I was determined not to cooperate until we met.

I waited for you to initiate something for a whole week, so the only thing I felt was my threadbare patience fraying, a little more every day. Why does everything have to be so twisted? I muttered one day in the car on the way to work. The air no longer clean, the city unwashed, and me hating my life and violently honking at anyone who dawdled more than a millisecond after the light turned green. Why does Erik always get what he wants? Why do other women manage to find normal men? I'm forty years old – is this ever going to change or am I always going to end up with all the freaks?

When I parked the car, I saw an incoming message from you. Any chance someone as beautiful as you would agree to see me tonight?

I was relieved. Finally you caught the drift, and we'd progressed from chats to texting, so maybe there was still some hope. I was upset that you'd dragged me on for an entire week, but you promised to answer all of my questions on our next date, so I extracted some more patience from my emergency stash. We agreed that you'd pick me up at nine, and for a moment I thought everything was about to work out, because obviously I had no way of knowing what you were planning on saying.

10:18 p.m.		Have you any idea how scared I was of the moment I'd have to tell you, Sheera?
10:18 p.m.		Really? And *I* was scared because you were reluctant to tell me… I couldn't figure out what your reason was.
10:18p.m.		You always want to know everything in advance. Why do you hate surprises so much?
10:19 p.m.		Because, Michael, for me a surprise is when something goes smoothly, without any problems!
10:19 p.m.		Yeah, but when something happens the way you expected it to, you have to agree it's not a surprise.
10:19 p.m.		I don't know how to respond when you suddenly pull out these Tibetan monk proverbs. Besides,

	you don't seem like such a big fan of surprises either. Aren't you bored by all this reconstructing? You were there, you know what happened.
10:19 p.m.	I like reading you.
10:20 p.m.	But is it really necessary to document everything?
10:20 p.m.	Don't you feel that it's helping you to sort things out?
10:20 p.m.	A little. But I still don't understand what I'm supposed to discover.
10:20 p.m.	You have to do something about that impatience of yours. Everything will come in its own time, it's part of the process.
10:21 p.m.	Okay, okay. BTW, how's your head tonight?
10:21 p.m.	Fine.
10:21 p.m.	So should I come?
10:21 p.m.	I'm always happy to see you.
10:22 p.m.	Okay. I'll be ready in a few minutes. Wait for me?

To: <softspoons@gmail.com>
From: <softspoons@gmail.com>
January 10, 2016 at 10:02 p.m.
Subject: The story of our second date

I drove to my parents' house after work today. My father was dozing off in front of the TV as usual, his chin slowly dropping as if magnetically drawn to his chest, and when I shut the door behind me he woke with a tiny jolt. What's up, Dad? I asked, trying not to reveal I'd seen him sleeping. No news, he said in a thick voice and then coughed obtrusively, cleared his throat and went silent again.

My mother was helping Tom with his homework as she dried dishes with a faded kitchen towel, occasionally leaning over the table, squinting to check for spelling mistakes. As we were about to leave she quickly dried her hands and said, Sheerie, I went through some old junk today and look what I found. She pulled a black and white photo out of the drawer and placed it on the table, and the three of us huddled around it. It was my kindergarten class photo, taken by a skilled photographer who managed to capture a moment of pure childhood happiness, thirty or so little gnomes arranged in rows and spilling over with merry peals of laughter. It felt as if a handful of invisible confetti from that ancient moment tickled our faces, making it impossible not to smile. Tom started laughing and said, come on, Mom, is that really you? You're the only one who's not laughing. I stroked his head and asked, how crazy is it to see your mom as a little girl even smaller than you?

My mother held out the photo between her forefinger and thumb and said, here, take it. I hesitated for a moment before reaching for it. I didn't really want it, but I didn't want to offend her, so I carefully placed it in a safe place within the mess of my bag.

After Tom fell asleep I took it out, planning to bury it in some drawer, but I suddenly noticed how right Tom had been. The girl in the photo is looking straight at the camera, slightly embarrassed, hiding a glimmer of a smile. All the children are crammed into each other, mixed up in a tangle and surrendering to the mutual laughter, but my chair is just slightly remote from the others. I'm the only one who isn't laughing, somewhere in a world of my own.

On the other end of the row was Benny, the disabled boy I went to play with when my mother complained that I had no friends. I remembered how happy his mother had been when I came in, hovering above us, offering me chocolate and other sweets, and how I couldn't understand why she called me an angel. When I looked at the photo I suddenly realized that though Benny and I didn't look alike, inside we felt the same. His mother may have thought differently, but we both knew what it was like to be weird, and what it was like to have no friends.

You're probably wondering why I'm telling you all this. I have to admit that this re-tracing does bring back some details I missed along the way, things that just passed me by when they happened in real time. You asked me something about that on our second date, remember? So maybe I'll answer you now, because back then I was too busy with other things and I didn't really feel like telling you about it.

Okay. So a week and a day after our boardwalk date I left work early, took Tom to McDonald's, we scattered the fries on our trays, slathered thick puddles of ketchup around them, and when I dropped him off to spend the night at my parents', he asked suspiciously, Mom, where are you going? And my mother quietly cocked her ear to listen to what I was going to say.

I have this important work thing, I lied again, and to compensate for the lie I hugged him as fiercely as I could. He hugged me back somewhat reserved, as if sensing my bluff. So is that why you didn't steal any of my fries today, because there'll be lots of yummy food there? He asked, and I nodded, a slight tremor going through me as I realized how nothing escapes this child.

You wanted truth and honesty, Michael, so here it goes: I wanted to conquer you that night. I decided that either the evening would end in bed and the beginning of a normal relationship – or that I wasn't going to take it any further. I couldn't understand why you were so reluctant, warm yet distant. It immediately made me think there was something wrong with me. I thought maybe I wasn't feminine enough for you, maybe all I needed to do was fix myself up a little, wear something nice.

I managed to get to the hair salon just before they closed. I showered, dappled on some perfume, and put on a simple but extremely sexy dress I'd bought for a friend's wedding once. Rona was with me when I tried it on, and her verdict was – perfect, that's a dress that says "I didn't really make an effort, I'm just naturally attractive and uncontrollably desirable". Eventually I wasn't brave enough to wear it to that wedding, and regretted listening to Rona, who knows nothing about dresses, and only wears jeans and button-downs herself. But on our second date I thought Rona may have been right after all – as if this was the dress I was supposed to win you over with from the very start. Standing at the mirror I hesitated over the generous cleavage and went to the fridge to pour myself half a glass of wine. It was the kind of dress that requires some alcohol to feel comfortable in. I painted my lips red, the wine melted the edges off my fervency, and at nine p.m. sharp the intercom buzzed.

You stood outside by the hedge. I walked towards you with sheer concentration, as if I was about to execute the most important mission of my life. When our eyes met, for a second I wasn't sure whether I'd overdone it or if something in the dress was doing the job just fine. I could almost hear you swallowing hard when you walked slowly towards me, and when you finally approached you reached one arm out and curled it timidly around my waist. A tiny quiver passed through me when you looked right into my eyes, your lips so damn close. But then you suddenly pulled away, and again I couldn't understand why.

You show up like that and then blame me for trying to hypnotize you? You winked, and then walked over to a cab that was standing there waiting, and opened the rear door. What happened to the motorbike? I asked.

I didn't want to drive because I have the feeling we're going to drink a little tonight, you said as we entered the back seat.

Our bartender was obnoxious, served our tequila with sharp movements and a grim face. Three shots and a beer later, with a plate of cold fries between us on the bar, I no longer cared about the bartender. The awkwardness had completely dissolved into the alcohol and swirled into a delicate yet stimulating cocktail. At a certain point you turned your body towards me and sat on the side of the stool, and I did the same. Our knees kept accidentally touching, we laughed a lot, I can't really remember what about, just the sensation the words left me with. At some point you looked at my hand, hesitated for a moment, and softly placed your long fingers on top of mine. I didn't understand why you were being so cautious. Dave Matthews' voice wafted around the velvety dimness of the bar, and you asked me what I was like as a little girl. Maybe I should have told you something along the lines of what I told you now about that old photo, but I wanted to listen to your story, not tell you mine.

So I smiled and said – You think I remember?

You persisted, but I hate being asked about my childhood, why would I want to remember anything about it? I was a little girl who couldn't wait to grow up already.

I was just a normal kid, I said, I don't know, there's really nothing special to tell.

I hate thinking about the past too, you said, but you remind me of a girl I went to grade school with. She had your smile, and something in your eyes that I can't really explain.

And did she like you back? I asked.

You smiled before saying – I guess she didn't really get me.

It's very encouraging to hear that even as a child you were inscrutable, I chuckled, and wondered if you'd noticed that my laugh came out a bit flustered.

She sat next to me in class, you said, and she smelled like honey drops. She taught me how to play Rummy, and I was in love with her so I kept letting her win.

Did you try to kiss her? I asked, and you smiled and pulled your hand away, raising your beer for another sip.

Only in my imagination, you said, and something in your eyes drew me in. All of a sudden an image of you as a little boy flashed in my head, lying alone in bed, all agitated underneath the blanket, unable to sleep. I didn't know where that thought was even coming from, but I wanted to kiss you so badly.

So have we come to that point in the evening where you keep your promise and finally tell me how you "know all sorts of things"? I finally asked what had been on the tip of my tongue the entire evening. You kept staring at me with that gripping gaze of yours, smiled, and then suddenly said - I can hear thoughts.

I rolled my eyes, half smiling. Great, I said, so can you hear me thinking that I don't find it funny and I'd like a serious answer?

You burst into laughter. It was an abrupt, slightly wild laugh, and the scowling bartender approached and asked if we wanted another round. Do you want anything? You asked, and I shook my head. I wanted him to stop interrupting and leave us alone. I just wanted you to tell me already.

You lowered your head for a moment and rubbed your eyes, as if weighing how to put together what you wanted to say. You leant sideways with your elbow on the bar, raised a tired look at me and said, listen, I really hate doing this kind of stuff, but in your case I guess there's no choice. I looked at you questioningly, waiting for you to explain. You moved closer and whispered in my ear - see the girl approaching the bartender? That's his shift manager. He thinks she's beautiful. They used to have a thing, but earlier she told him it's over and broke his heart. Or maybe just his ego. And on top of that, she said she'd let him know if he'll have to pull the late shift tonight, but he's pissed and he's going to say no.

I wanted to say something, but you motioned for me to stay quiet and listen, then turned to face the bar and we both sat there, watching the bartender and the tall girl as if they were the leads in a movie. The girl leant towards him and I couldn't hear what she said, but suddenly, without any warning, the bartender burst out and hurled at her – forget it, Sharona, that makes three times this week, no way!

I was dumbfounded. You slowly turned to look at me and your eyes were flushed with such heavy emotion – maybe fear. You held out your hand and touched my cheek, as if to apologize. A warm little current flowed thinly under my skin and accompanied your hand as it slowly descended to rest on the side of my neck. Just don't ask me to do it again another hundred times now, okay? You said.

Why not? I asked quietly. You were silent for a moment, then took your hand off and said, I thought you'd understand why it's not fun to be asked to expose your deformity over and over again like a traveling circus freak.

I looked at you and didn't know what to say. Deformity? Aren't you overreacting a little? I mean, if this was true – why would you want to hide such a thing? I wanted to hate you for lying, and at the same time sympathize and believe you. I tried to think of when you could've overheard a conversation between the bartender and the shift manager, maybe when we came in, but a thick discomfort filled my chest and I decided to keep my mouth shut from a sudden revelation that sometimes it's best to stay quiet. I held myself back from asking you what my father had always asked me when I was little – why do you have to be so odd about everything?

We were both silent for a few long moments, the awkwardness only getting heavier, the thoughts hurdling through my head like bumper cars. You scared me. I quickly replayed all the things you'd miraculously known about me since we met, and admitted to myself that your surrealistic confession accounted for quite a few of them. At some point you signaled the bartender for the check. I was dying to cross-examine you but suddenly felt really uncomfortable. The sour-faced bartender placed the check at your side and after you paid you tried to smile at me, but you seemed sad, maybe hurt.

My head was still swimming when we stepped outside. We walked to the edge of the sidewalk to catch a cab, and I wasn't sure, but it seemed like you were keeping a certain distance from me.

When we sat in the back seat of the taxi, I didn't know what to do. For a second I just wanted to take your hand and lace your fingers in mine, but I didn't. We sat there silently, our faces frozen. The streetlights kept beating in through the windows, punctuating the darkness. Now and again the two-way radio crackled indecipherable syllables by some invisible hoarse dispatcher, and meanwhile I was conducting an animated argument with myself. Something about you just didn't add up. You were cute and smart and funny – but then you'd suddenly say things that normal people just... don't say. For some reason I believed you weren't lying, maybe it was the look in your eyes. I tried to think of other possible explanations for what you said at the bar. For a moment I thought you were just plain crazy. But crazy people can't be crazy only in regard to one thing, and totally normal about all the rest, right?

You sat there, slumped. I mustered up some courage, put a hand on the back of your neck and asked - Why are you so sad? You turned your head and looked at me but said nothing. I kept looking you straight in the eye, and then you said – Crazy? This is my life, Sheera, I can only wish I was crazy.

An icy river flooded my veins. Did you really just hear what I was thinking? I waited for you to keep talking, but you were silent until the taxi stopped. When you came out onto the street with me I realized that you were planning to come up despite what had happened. We walked towards the entrance, our steps drumming the same beat on the sidewalk, right-left-right-left, and the faint chirping of the sickly city crickets was drowned in the clamor of the cars. Fear began rising in my throat, unsettling me. I wasn't so sure I wanted it anymore. Forget it, not tonight, Fear said, the moment is gone.

Don't worry, you suddenly said, I'm just walking you to the door, I'm not coming upstairs.

I startled again, and perversely, although it was what I wanted, I was also offended.

We stood there at the door and I decided to think about something completely unpredictable, something there was no way you could know. In my imagination I set up a row of bouncing can-can dancers kicking up their legs to the beat of some crazy music I hoped would block out any other thought you might hear. You looked at me and started to laugh, but quickly became serious again as you realized I wasn't laughing along. I wanted to step into the building, but you reached a long arm over my head and stopped the door. Wait a minute, you said. I turned right into your intense stare, from a distance of an inch away.

I want you to understand, you said, I'm not a magician or some kind of illusionist, I was just born with extremely exposed senses, more than most people's. And it's not always a picnic, I assure you.

I didn't know what to say. What do you say to someone who thinks it's no picnic to hear other people's thoughts?

So, what, you hear everyone's thoughts all of the time? I finally asked.

You smiled, and a boyish tone snuck into your voice as you said – no, not everyone's, and not all the time, God forbid. But with your thoughts it's different... I really like hearing you.

And suddenly, Michael, a huge wave of desire washed over me. The fear completely subsided and all I could think about was how much I wanted you. There was a wild rustle crackling ecstatically in the space between us, and you wrapped my face in your palms as if it was a fragile package. You leaned over and gently touched my cheek with your lips, but didn't kiss me, just lingered there for a moment, and your scent made me dizzy. I sent a trembling hand to the back of your neck, my fingers ran through your hair, and in one moment a pulse of confidence surged inside of me, and I pinned you to the wall and crushed my body into yours.

You suddenly stiffened, drawing back. I guess you didn't see it coming. You didn't push me away, but you didn't really cooperate either. I was dismayed by your rejection, but was incapable of letting you go. Assuming you'd soon surrender, I buried my face in your neck and breathed you in. I could feel the stiffness in your pants, pulsing against my stomach, and my hand reached down to touch you. You stopped me. Again.

Do you want to come up? I heard myself asking in a slightly cracked voice. But instead of giving me the answer I wanted to hear, you held my hand, laced your fingers in mine, shot that aching look of yours at me and said, listen Sheera, chill for a second, okay? We can't... this can't happen now. All I want is to surrender to this and then die or something, but there's something I have to tell you and there's no easy way to say it.

What, there's something else? I asked. I didn't know what to expect anymore.

Yes, you said, there's something really important.

Shit, I thought, what are you going to tell me next? That you're gay? That you have HIV? That you're married? On the run from the law? Okay, I said in the most disinterested tone I could muster, so tell me.

Don't you feel different? you asked.

What do you mean different, I smiled sarcastically, different from how I was when this evening started? Different from the other women in your life?

Different from others, you said, everywhere. At work too.

I didn't know whether you were trying to flatter me or pass some covert criticism, so I didn't want to disappoint you by saying that I wasn't different, pretty standard, really. I'm just always alone, that's all. Never completely connected to anything. Not to my parents, not to Rona since she married and started a family, not even to my job. I'm addicted to my work not for the substance but in order to make a living, to survive, to maintain my source of strength in the world. Actually the only thing to which I'm completely connected is my son, because he came out of me. But even with him it's the same, since he was born from my inability to fully connect to a man.

Only tonight, looking at that kindergarten photo, did it hit me. I was an outsider back then too, plagued by alienation, feeling unwanted. I'd always thought it was part of being an only child, sometimes I see it in Tom as well. Everyone sees nothing but indulgence in an only child, but those who felt it on their own skin can immediately identify the perpetual loneliness of someone who walks alone, someone who never had siblings.

When I was little, I had no problem lying to make people like me, just to make friends. And when we stood there outside my building I was willing to do the same. Willing to believe you could hear thoughts, to tell you I'm different – say practically anything if it would get you to shut up and come upstairs, though I already knew my mission had failed.

Okay, I said, let's say I'm different, but what are you getting at? I was confused and exhausted, and the remnants of my desire began dissolving into a murky puddle of disillusion.

You took a tiny step back and breathed deeply. You placed your right hand on your stomach, as if trying to balance yourself, and your left hand on my shoulder. You were very dramatic as you said: You're not who you think you are.

I'm not what? I wasn't sure I'd heard you correctly.

You're not who you think you are, you repeated. There are some pretty important details you don't know about Sheera Leitner.

10:32 p.m.	Do you have any idea how much willpower I needed to say no? That dress. And your scent in my nostrils. I had to tear myself away from you.
10:32 p.m.	Really?
10:32 p.m.	I swear.
10:33 p.m.	I can never tell with you. You don't give anything away. Too bad I can't hear thoughts, huh?

To: <softspoons@gmail.com>
From: <softspoons@gmail.com>
January 11, 2016 at 10:16 p.m.
Subject: The story of our second date - continued

When Tom was still a toddler I could persuade him to do anything, even things he really didn't want to do, if I promised him a surprise. It was a magic word, the ultimate weapon, and to this day it's maintained some of its power. We called it "a surprise" but we both had a pretty good idea of what we were talking about. So contrary to what you said, maybe I don't hate all surprises, but only those that stray from this childish definition. And as for our second date – it transformed rather quickly from "surprising" to "crazy", or at least to something way outside the boundaries of anything I knew. It wasn't supposed to happen this way. Nothing you said made any sense. This story was supposed to be about a surprising encounter, but a normal one. An extraordinary yet ordinary story, about two people who had somehow found each other within the chaos of the world.

You don't know who you are, you told me as we stood there by the door. You have certain abilities too, it's just that you're not even aware of them.

Abilities I'm not aware of? I repeated your words like a dummy.

Yeah, abilities. Capabilities. Powers, you said.

Powers? What are you talking about? And why does it seem that every time I want to set our relationship on some sort of normal track of progress, like kissing in the doorway for instance, you whip out some sentence I have no idea how to deal with? I wanted to say – Listen, sweetie, I really want to believe you, but give me a break, would you? How far are you planning to go with this line?

So I just smiled. Is that supposed to be funny? I asked cautiously.

I don't think so, you answered without a trace of a smile.

The first thing that popped into my mind was that I shouldn't have said anything to Rona. At first I hadn't told her because I wanted to wait for something more concrete than a Facebook friendship and a few random meetings, but when I saw her for coffee that day to brainstorm some questions for her big relationship survey, I couldn't hold it in anymore and it just came out. I told her I'd met someone, that he was a little strange, that I still didn't know what to make of him, but that he seemed interesting.

Strange? She asked suspiciously, running her fingers through her ultra-short, velvet-length fair hair, which had just undergone its monthly trim. I still need to get over you dumping The Husband I found you. What's strange about him?

I don't exactly know, he's not just another guy, I tried to explain, but how could I explain when I myself didn't understand? I regretted it instantly and changed the subject, but your name had already been burned into the database in her brain, and when we stood there that evening I knew that at some point she'd ask - so what's going on with The Strange Guy? And God only knows what I'd say. There are two options, and the easier one is to lie. Otherwise I'd have to hear myself saying - Oh, him? Well, on our first date he opened my channels, and on the second he told me he could hear people's thoughts and that I don't know who I am because I have powers I'm unaware of. Do you have any idea what kind of hell she'll put me through for my bad taste in men?

I looked at you dumbfounded, didn't know what to say. I was scared that despite everything, I had got myself mixed up with a nutcase.

I couldn't find one good reason for not pulling myself together, ditching you and forgetting you ever existed. For not thinking up an excuse along the lines of - listen, it's late, and I gotta get upstairs and feed my goldfish, so we'll be in touch, okay?

Let's just let it go for now, you said. We've had too much to drink and I realize this is a bit much to digest at the end of a romantic evening.

The end? The end of a romantic evening? Meaning... you're leaving? These questions ran through my mind but I didn't breathe a word. I just gazed at you, with the thoughts going wild in my head, flapping like fish trapped in a net. You reached over and touched my face. There was something so serene and pleasant about your touch. I closed my eyes, and you probably felt that I was willing to just forget everything you'd said so we could pick up right where we'd left off. But you didn't let me.

Sheera, listen to me, concentrate, you spoke quickly and tried to appear serious. You have abilities you're unaware of. You live a life that belongs to someone you'd like to be, but not to who you really are. Instead of using your most potent power, you live alongside it, it's like you drive on two parallel roads that never meet. You need to find it and learn how to use it. You know what I mean?

Not really, I stuttered.

You took a deep breath. I don't need to keep convincing you that my info about you didn't come from conventional sources like Google, right? You forced a smile, and for a moment I wondered if it was just my imagination or you were a little spooked.

Still, that part I found relatively easy to believe. Yeah, okay, you have a sixth sense or something. People like that exist, we even aired a documentary about it once. But the fact that you thought I had these "powers" that I was never aware of? That was a bit too much for me. What were you planning to do next, convince me to climb up on the roof, hold out my arms and try to fly? Do I get any accessories, like a cape or at least a bracelet or something?

You let out a sudden laugh, then stopped yourself. I'm sorry, you said, I'm dead serious, it's just that you're hysterically funny.

Did you just hear what I thought again? The air was cold and I was trembling. I knew this was completely irrational, and I was sure you were lying, but couldn't understand why. My head was jammed with a million questions, all jostling to be first in line, crowding at the exit, but I couldn't phrase anything coherent out of them.

So, are you trying to tell me that I can know all sorts of things like you do? I finally asked.

No, you said, I have my abilities and you have yours. We're different. We're similar only in our sensitivity. We're both hypersensitive. We can feel things most people are incapable of feeling, that's how we identified each other and connected this way. But our connection will be very unstable until you find your power. You're not aware. You need to develop your senses, try things, use them. I realize this sounds psychotic but I have to convince you.

But I can't feel anything, so how am I supposed to develop it? I asked. I felt like a clueless high school student.

Listen, I can't focus when you're standing in front of me like that, you said, I think it's best if I go home now. You absentmindedly placed a hand on your stomach again, and suddenly seemed so tired.

Can you just tell me what sort of powers? Give me some direction, so I get some sense of what you mean, I tried.

No pressure, you said, it's best if you find them on your own. Try connecting with yourself, with your roots, be aware of what's happening around you, of your influence. Try doing things you've never done before. Dare a little. If you still don't understand, ask me and I'll try to explain. I can be your guide if you want me to.

My guide? I wanted to grab you by the shoulders and violently shake you. Can you hear what you're saying? What's wrong with you?

But I didn't say anything, and you'd already turned to leave, then suddenly turned back to me and clutched my waist and planted a huge kiss on my lips, whispered "good night", turned absentmindedly and left.

That kiss really shut me up, I'll give you that. I could still taste you as I watched your cute little butt disappearing into the dark night, and I just couldn't believe that's how the evening was ending. You left me there like an orphan, with an invisible pile of hidden "powers" I now had to find on my own. Seriously? Do you really expect me to believe this bullshit? If I have special senses or abilities or powers, how could I have lived forty years without knowing about them?

I wanted to cast you aside, Michael, forget we ever met and kick your ass a mile away. But I couldn't. Not because I believed anything you said, I believed nothing, not one single word. So what was it? Maybe you aroused my curiosity. Maybe I had to figure out what you were really about. I didn't really know why, but I couldn't just discard you.

I went upstairs confused, bitter, angry, exhausted.

I had no idea what to do. There was a pretty good chance you were shitting me. I thought you were attracted to me, that you felt what I did, but maybe I was just spinning myself an illusion. I panicked for a moment thinking it was someone from the station, some sort of hidden camera gag and you weren't even real – as I'd suspected from the very beginning.

I went inside and turned on the light. Just to make sure, I glanced at the ceiling and the walls to check for tiny cameras. I blinked and smoothed my hair, breathing in the remains of your memory. You were almost there with me, for a moment I'd already visualized our bodies entangled in a burning hot jumble, passionately feeling our way to the bedroom, flinging shoes and belts in every direction. I stopped for a minute and quietly admitted to myself that I find you kind of attractive.

I filled the kettle and pulled out the instant coffee. As I waited for the water to boil, I considered just going to bed and then calling you tomorrow and telling you I'd dared a little and tried all sorts of new things and nothing had happened. But then I remembered your face in the taxi, and knew I couldn't lie to you like that, even if you were lying to me. So I took the coffee spoon and held it to my face, briefly looked left and right to make sure no neighbor was watching from the window, then I glared at the spoon with my most intimidating look, and tried to bend it with my mind. Go on, bend, you stupid bitch, I thought to myself. Would you fucking bend already? But the proud spoon wouldn't budge. It remained as erect and stable as all spoons, as if making it clear that its only role in my life was to stir the coffee, and my only role in its life was to make it clear I was no Uri Geller.

I sipped at my coffee and looked around. Connect with myself, with my roots, that's what he said, right? Jesus Christ. If my father ever found out I'm involved with someone who talks like that. How is a person supposed to "connect", for God's sake? Stick my finger into the socket? What a load of bull. I hate all this new age shit.

I noticed a few stray coffee grains on the counter. I picked up the dishrag and was about to mop them into the sink, but then stopped. Wait a minute, a grain of coffee would be easier to move than a spoon, right? I'd never been a master of physics, but that seemed logical. So I bent over the counter, focused on one of the little brown crumbs, and concentrated. Fly, fly into the sink, you little twerp, I said in my thoughts. Go on! Move your ass already! I lost my temper after two minutes of sterile attempts. Finally I furiously mopped away the crumbs and went to the shower. While lathering I tried to make Moni text me and ask what I thought about the Sports Channel's new late night program. When I got out, wrapped in my towel, I peeked at my phone but there was no message.

I felt like such a fool. Gullible. Stupid. My mood sank like a sack full of ashes, landing at the pit of my stomach with a thud and raising a cloud of filthy dust. I'm pathetic. You'd caught me by my worst weakness. Your special senses must've picked up on how badly I wanted it to work out between us, that no matter what you said, I'd believe it. Why did I let myself get dragged along like that? How low would I go and would I do anything for a relationship with someone who didn't want to have sex with me until "I found my power"?

I started to get myself all worked up about how you were humiliating me. What's your problem? If you want me, just come, and if you don't – so don't. Why did you feel the need to sell me these ludicrous stories?

I sat at my laptop, agitated, and saw that you'd started a chat. No preambles. Just one little sentence that made me believe that maybe you could really hear thoughts.

Not everything in life is as fast as instant coffee... relax, patience, just be a little bit aware.

I smiled. Your words were like a tiny ray of sun that illuminated the corner of my living room. I couldn't understand how, but I realized you were still there, that you'd left but didn't really leave me.

Look honey, assuming you're not bullshitting me, then... I just don't know where to begin, I wrote. Should I turn to eBay? Amazon? Where the hell does someone start the quest for special powers?

I have an idea, you replied. Turn down the lights, relax and listen to this song. Just disengage from everything, clear your head of all thoughts, and we'll try to connect. To calm each other down a little.

I read your reply eight or nine times. Is this for real? I asked myself. What's he talking about? How did I get into this situation? And what's with that word "connect"? What's wrong with him?

There was a YouTube link at the bottom of the chat window. I clicked it. Pink Floyd's "Wish You Were Here" with the lyrics. Oh well, I sighed, tonight's ruined anyway, so go with the flow. Nobody's watching. Turn off the lights, listen to the song and lie in bed. How bad could it be?

I slowly undressed. I slipped between the sheets, naked, and put the laptop beside me. I closed my eyes and just listened, let the music caress me. I mumbled the lyrics to myself. I was surrounded by a really pleasant sensation, like a gentle tickle at my fingers and toes. I thought about you. Not anything specific, just… you. Your eyes when you talked about the little girl you were in love with, the smell of your kiss, the boyish smile that revealed a little of your fluster.

Then suddenly – and I have no idea how to put this – you were there. Not really, but something about your being was there in bed with me. I could feel you, your presence, and I found my breath quickening involuntarily. It wasn't like sex, it wasn't a fantasy, it was… I don't know what it was. I just knew we were there together, both of us, though it was just me. A gentle shudder wrapped around me and turned into a soothing cloud of unfamiliar emotion, and my breathing became heavier, more rapid. I didn't understand what the hell was going on, but I didn't really care. It was so good I didn't want to overthink and ruin it. About five minutes went by until my breath settled, the chill died down and I was engulfed by massive exhaustion. The next thing I remember is waking up the next morning and asking myself whether it was a dream again. But when I got up I saw you'd sent another message, only eight words:

Don't be scared, I'm with you. Keep trying.

Your presence accompanied me throughout the entire day. Every time the thought of "powers" came up, I looked around and tried to improvise something. Use my gaze to move a stubborn pencil on the table, make Erik trip in the hall, unlock my car without the key, but nothing worked. In the evening I helped Tom with his homework, and as he did his math problems, I shut my eyes and focused on making the Culture editor from Ma'ariv call me back, though he'd been screening me for days.

Mom, are you asleep? Tom asked, and I mumbled, no, sweetheart, I'm just trying to concentrate.

Are you trying to do things with the power of your mind? He asked naturally, as if asking me if I was making an omelet. I panicked. How badly had you messed with my logic? You reduced me to an eight year old boy's Harry Potter fantasy. Just so you know, if this was a joke at my expense, I'll wish I was dead. There's a good chance I'll want you to die too if I find out you've been lying to me.

When Tom fell asleep I went to my laptop to look for you on Facebook. On your wall I saw that you'd posted something only four minutes ago.

With thoughts like that, who needs enemies.

I panicked again. I don't like feeling like you're stalking me. It's like you've installed Big Brother cameras inside my head. I was offended too. I hate it when you make me feel like a scolded child. I wondered for a minute if it was just my paranoia talking. Was this just a coincidence? But two minutes later you started a chat.

I have a killer headache. Any idea how to make it go away?

Maybe you should take an aspirin and make it an early night, I replied. I didn't know what you expected me to say.

I waited for a few minutes, you didn't reply, and I figured you'd abandoned our chat. Did I offend you? Or did you just go to sleep?

But then another sentence appeared: You want to try something? Take a piece of candy, lie on your back, shut your eyes, suck on it, and as it dissolves in your mouth, imagine you're dissolving my headache.

I stared at your reply for about two minutes. Above all I felt so dumb. So incredibly stupid for engaging in this. I wanted to write - is there any chance that anything between us could be a little more foreseeable? But I went only with: What??

Just do it, you said. Stop thinking why not all the time. Just do it.

What candy? I asked, any specific kind? I think all I have is butterscotch drops.

You didn't respond.

I sighed and went into the kitchen. I found a little box of butterscotch drops in one of the drawers. I took one out, peeled off the wrapper and popped it in my mouth. Is he serious? I asked myself out loud. Then I quickly went to my laptop and deleted our chat. Last thing I need is for someone to find it one day and have me committed.

I was amazed at myself, at how easily I was playing along with all of your nonsense, but I pinned the candy to the roof of my mouth and started sucking it slowly. I climbed into bed, lay sprawled on my back, tried to relax, and thought about you again. A minute later I felt your presence surrounding me. It wasn't as tangible as the night before – it was as if only your shadow was there in bed with me. I sucked at the candy and thought about your head. I stroked your hair, my fingers combed it and massaged your skull, and I imagined the pain like in those aspirin commercials, a big large throbbing orange circle that slowly faded, until it disappeared. Then, without realizing what was happening, I fell asleep without brushing my teeth. The next morning when I awoke, I rushed to the laptop first thing.

Thanks for the date in the cosmos, you wrote. That's the second time you've made my headache go away.

Jesus, I thought, he's totally wacked, and went to wake Tom. Cosmos? I muttered into my morning coffee. Is that the unique sense of humor that only thought-hearing lifeguards understand? You seriously think a butterscotch drop will make me believe I made your headache disappear?

Before we left the house, I snuck a peek at my laptop, and there was a new status on your wall.

When you doubt your power, you give the power to your doubt.

No doubt, I muttered, especially in the cosmos, right? Then I shouted out to Tom, let's go sweetie! We need to start our day.

22:44 p.m.	No doubt you're a tough case.
22:44 p.m.	No doubt there's no one in the world who would believe you with such pitiful proof.
22:44 p.m.	You don't get it – I wasn't trying to prove anything, I was trying to show you. You're the one who's looking for proof, not me.
22:45 p.m.	Well, obviously, who wouldn't look for proof for this wacky theory?
22:45 p.m.	Yeah, but look at the way you think. If you decide it's wacky, you're not really giving yourself a chance to look for the signs.
22:45 p.m.	I don't know, Michael, you're acting as if it's the simplest thing in the world to live like a normal person for forty years and then one day just start living differently. Sometimes I think - what do I need this whole weird power stuff for? What was so bad about my life up till now?
22:46 p.m.	You don't need anything, Sheera. Who's forcing you? It's your choice. If you want, you can choose to leave it behind and go back to the phony life you've invented.
22:47 p.m.	Has anyone ever told you your answers are annoying? Can't you just explain like a normal person?
22:49 p.m.	OK, I hear you. Everything has to be logical with you. Didn't anyone ever tell you some things can't be explained rationally? I'll try to write you something tomorrow. Good night darlin'.

To: <softspoons@gmail.com>
From: <softspoons@gmail.com>
January 12, 2016 at 8:50 p.m.
Subject: Ella Cinderella

I can barely remember myself in fourth grade. I remember the class looked like a basketball court. Nobody in the world scared me more than the principal (who was 5 foot 2), and the teacher seemed about the size of King Kong (although slightly less hairy).

On the first day of school, the door squeaked in the middle of class. The teacher stopped talking and a tall, curly haired man walked in with a girl in his arms. She wore a red miniskirt and had a cast covering her entire right leg. Her face was buried in his shoulder, so all I could see was her long, fair-colored hair. I was the only one in class sitting alone. The man sat her down next to me and left, without noticing that the cast had left a white line of dust on his pants. He leaned her crutches against the wall.

During recess I asked if she wanted me to get her crutches. Right away I felt the need to do things for her. How wouldn't I – a princess who still got carried around at the age of nine. Ella Cinderella. I asked her what happened. She said she slipped, running around the pool. When class started I realized I forgot to bring my book, so she put hers in the middle, between us.

I don't remember much more. Childhood memories are like standing on shards of a mirror. Every once in a while I accidentally stand at an angle where the light suddenly dazzles me as it flashes from a sliver of a memory, but if I move just an inch - it's gone.

So I have a few slivers of her. During recess she would stay in the classroom because of the cast, and I had an excellent excuse to keep her company. The boys had fistfights out in the yard, and I wasn't so good at that. She taught me to play cards, but I had trouble concentrating because of the dimple in her left cheek and the little green-stoned ring she wore on her finger.

Funny how you reminded me of her out of nowhere, Sheera. You know how many years it's been since I've thought about Ella? I have no idea what she's up to these days. I haven't seen her since grade school. She had a small mouth but a giant smile and a soft face that was clean of all malice. She reminded me of that song... "Here comes the sun... doo doo doo doo..." We were best friends in fourth grade, but something kept bothering me.

She was the prettiest girl in class. I wasn't the only one who thought so. Everyone wanted to be her friend. I was drunk with joy but couldn't figure out why she was friends with me.

From the minute her father sat her next to me, I wanted to know what she was thinking, but it was too scary. So I stopped myself from listening to her thoughts. Tightened all my muscles, like you hold it in when you need to go to the bathroom. I learned how to block thoughts thanks to her, in fact. Until then I didn't know it could be controlled, even when I went crazy because my brain would be raped by tidal waves of chatter, when there were too many people around. But I was scared shitless she thought something bad of me, so I was able to block the hearing. I was afraid to tell her I wasn't normal. I only told her which of the girls in class were jealous of her, and which thought she was nice. She didn't ask how I knew, but I could see in her eyes that she believed me.

I held on for a few months, but eventually I caved. Began loosening my grip. Loosening the hearing muscles, you know? Like any trap, it started out well. She had a light, soft voice, like her hair. She thought I was cute, smart, not like the other boys. I felt like a king. I grew two inches just by listening to her nonsense. I became a little obsessive. Thought about her nonstop, even at night. I'd get so deep into it I could hear her voice as if she were next to me. One day she said something in class, and I knew I'd already heard it, in the same exact tone. I suddenly realized that at night when lying in bed I'd heard her thinking just that, from afar.

So thanks to her I learned how to focus on thoughts from a distance. Man, what a discovery. So one night I was tucked in bed listening to her with a stupid smile on my face, I got used to falling asleep with her in my head like that, when suddenly I got whacked with the exact thing I'd been terrified of. Story of my life. The worst punch is the one that comes when you're not ready for it. I was half asleep when she started thinking about me, and then came the thought that made me get what had been bothering me all along. I finally found out what she saw in me. She wanted me to keep trying to get her to like me, but only so she could feel pretty. She knew I liked her a lot more than she liked me, and that's just how she wanted it.

Believe me, nothing prepares you for a knife to the heart at the age of nine. I was a scrawny little runt, and I could barely take it. I was so shocked I couldn't move. And that was nothing. After I knew what she really thought I couldn't go on. I cut off our friendship right there and then. Without explaining.

Even as a kid it was all or nothing for me. I was willing to hang in the air for her when I thought I'd have it all, but now that I realized it would never happen, I preferred to have nothing. I was crushed, broken, and she couldn't understand what'd happened. Wrote me a couple of notes. After that she got insulted and stopped talking to me. Wouldn't even look at me anymore, and asked King Kong to move her to another seat.

I regretted it later, of course. I fucked up like a rookie. Didn't realize the hell I was getting into. Every night I'd toss and turn while hearing how much she hated me. Died every night, all over again. Couldn't sleep. I'd have done anything to go back to the cards, to the scent of her hair. I tried to recreate the thoughts she used to have, but her voice had already changed.

My mother sensed something was wrong and saved me from myself. You wouldn't believe the talks we had back then. I remember her face when she told me I had to stop listening to Ella's thoughts. She said I'd reached the edge, that it was "self-destruction". I didn't know what it meant but it sounded awful. I promised to stop. A few weeks later, she asked if in hindsight I'd choose not to know what Ella was thinking. I said yes, that I'd made a mistake. She didn't say anything, but then bought me a Sherlock Holmes book. I didn't see the connection, thought she was just trying to cheer me up. I only got it while I was reading, when one sentence stopped me like it was being engraved in my skin. Someone asked Sherlock how he'd cracked such a difficult case. So he said that most people rush to put their theory together before they have all the facts. I read it a few times – it's a little complicated for a kid to understand. Too philosophical. But do you get it? Sherlock was special only because he knew how to wait. Those who rush to decide want to reach a conclusion more than they want to reach the truth. They start looking for selective evidence to support their theory instead of developing their theory based on all the facts.

It took me a few good years to completely figure it out. At first I only thought I understood, and immediately decided I'd done the right thing with Ella Cinderella. That it's always better to know the truth. You can get over pain, but you can't get over a lie. There are two options – either the excruciating truth that stabs you only once, or a lie that causes you the constant dim pain of frustration, every day. Every day. It adds up.

When I grew up, my mother brought it up again. She said that when you love someone, sometimes it's better not to know what they're thinking. I asked why. She said that even when you love there's anger, sometimes even hatred, and some thoughts you're better off not knowing. I said I always prefer knowing. I was adamant. She looked at me without saying a word, she used to do that sometimes, just look at me quietly, so I wouldn't argue and just think about what she said.

Living is complicated. Today I'm not sure there's one sole answer. You know why? Because I already know what it's like listening to the thoughts of someone who loves you. It's better than Disneyland, trust me, though you never know when the punch will come. You need to know when to stop. But the whole idea behind Sherlock was that my mother didn't want me to reach absolute conclusions. She wanted me to keep on thinking, even when I'm sure I know, because tomorrow I could very well find out I was wrong. But Sheera, you never stop to think about this stuff, do you? You're too determined. Think for a second before you slam what I'm saying. You make up your mind in advance. You don't really ponder. Unwilling to see a different reality.

Now do you understand what I mean when I say you don't see the signs? You're a princess too. You see only what you want, cherry-picking the signs that suit you. Before you tell me that I'm an idiot, try to think when this happened to you. When something happened and you realized, in hindsight, that all the signs were screaming at you all along, but you preferred not to see them.

I hope I've finally explained it right. Can't believe the stories I'm fishing out from God knows where for you. It's not easy being your guide. Good night.

    10:49 p.m.   Michael... I admit you stopped me. I finished reading and I just had to go give Tom a hug. I promise to think about it without putting you down, okay? Thank you for the story, it's beautiful. I promise to try to think of an incident like that. And I'll come see you soon with a butterscotch drop. Good night.

11:52 p.m.	Are you still up?
11:52 p.m.	Of course.
11:52 p.m.	So, do you hear everything I think?
11:52 p.m.	No.
11:52 p.m.	When do you hear it and when don't you?
11:52 p.m.	When I decide to.
11:52 p.m.	Do you hear me often?
11:52 p.m.	Define often.
11:52 p.m.	Every day?
11:52 p.m.	Yes.
11:52 p.m.	More than ten times a day?
11:52 p.m.	No, are you crazy? I have a couple of other things to do.
11:52 p.m.	It's kind of troubling, you know?
11:52 p.m.	Yes.
11:52 p.m.	Oh, right. I should've figured you know that as well.
11:52 p.m.	Don't worry. I'm not stalking you. I'm not prying. I learned something from Ella Cinderella, you know? But if I want to guide you I have to know how you think. That's all.

To: <softspoons@gmail.com>
From: <softspoons@gmail.com>
January 13, 2016 at 8:50 p.m.
Subject: The story of what happened after our second date

I still haven't come up with an incident like you asked for, so meanwhile I'll keep reconstructing our story, okay? I also have a question I wanted to ask you at the time and forgot, but I'll get to it in a minute.

So where were we? When you informed me I'd made your headache go away with a butterscotch drop, and I, to say the least, found it hard to believe you. The morning after, I got a reminder from you – Keep trying. That morning stretched out like a sticky piece of gum, nothing went smoothly. I couldn't find my car keys before we left the house, then Tom forgot his math book and we had to go back in, and then when he ran back to the car he tripped and twisted his ankle. He insisted that I put a hand on his ankle the whole way to school, so I drove with only one hand on the wheel, wondering whether something had really happened or he just needed attention, and after I dropped him off I got stuck in this crazy gridlock at the entrance to Ramat Hachayal. The cars inched forward in an everlasting line, and I tried to understand what really happened that night. You already told me that I'd made your headache go away once, when we were at the boardwalk, so why would you make up something like that? I didn't really think you were some kind of a con artist or a fraud, but was this your way of trying to create a dependency between us?

I was twenty minutes late to the staff meeting. Moni was really irritated. He sat there pale and grim and didn't even bother to say hi. What's with the boss, PMS? I texted Avi, who sat facing me, his knee jiggling restlessly.

Don't know, he says he sprained his neck, Avi shot back.

Did I miss something important? I asked.

Only my whining about the shitty advertising market, he texted, you didn't miss anything.

Moni started describing the pros and cons of a second season of "The Human League" – he has this thing where he makes his decisions up front, and only pretends to consult everyone to make them feel valuable. He looked in everyone's eyes and asked whether we should make changes and air another season or jump ship. Erik barged in saying he's sure that with upgraded casting and the new writer he recruited, it would be a fatal mistake not to air another season. I quietly sneered, because Erik always thinks that anything contrary to his opinion constitutes "a fatal mistake".

I had a feeling Erik and Moni had already made up their minds before the meeting, and he too was just playing his part in the act. It really pissed me off – "The Human League" had originally been Erik's idea, and he would do anything to avoid being associated with a failure, even when everyone knows it's a flop and wants to move on. His tactic is to pull on for another season and assign it to somebody else on the team, so that later he can assign the blame as well. Sometimes I can't understand how Moni keeps this despicable creature in such an important position – he's VP Content for Christ's sake! Moni registered my expression out of the corner of his eye, but didn't say a thing; he just gave me that look that says – gimme a break, even if you're right, let it go, not today.

So I kept quiet. I felt sorry for Moni, but on the other hand – I couldn't totally not be me.

Erik attempted to dominate the meeting as I became increasingly dominated by irritation, so Avi and I started texting each other like two finalists on the who-hates-Erik-the-most contest, but suddenly it hit me – wait a minute, if I'd really cured your headache last night, does that mean I can uncramp Moni's neck? Hmm.... If I loosen up his neck he won't be as cranky, and we'll all be able to talk more freely and make Erik shut his big mouth, right? Why waste the entire meeting talking about a second season that nobody really wants?

So I rummaged through my bag and found an old mint, peeled its wrapper and tossed it into my mouth. I placed it in a good spot between my tongue and the roof of my mouth, and slowly sucking on it, I looked at Moni's neck. I'd never noticed before how bulgy his neck muscles were. For a moment I thought I felt a tiny spasm of pain on the left side of my neck, but it came and went. I tried to focus - as much as I could in a conference room full of people. I took deep breaths, but Moni asked me how we could sell "The Human League" as "same but different", and I had to give a somewhat intelligent response that would present my very clear position but wouldn't sound like a personal attack on Erik.

When I was done talking, I started sucking the candy again, but then Erik gave me that sneering look of his and said – how hard is it to launch a campaign? We had pretty good media coverage during the first season.

Oh, please. Somehow, my job always seems so easy when you're not the one who has to do it, I said sarcastically, and "good media" must be a matter of definition, because I was under the impression that everyone hated us. Then for Moni's sake, I restrained myself and said nothing when Erik muttered - You can't get so worked up over every review, our job is to hold a mirror in the face of society, obviously not everyone likes what they see.

The meeting was long and tedious, and when it finally ended Moni asked me to stay for a second and finalize a press release I had to issue at noon, about the launch of a new and totally unnecessary drama series I can't stand. How's your neck, I asked casually, and he carefully turned it right and left and said – a little better than this morning, thanks for asking.

I left his office wondering how to interpret his answer. What does "better than this morning" mean? Was it me, or would he have felt a little better by now anyway? Was he even telling the truth? Maybe he just didn't want to sound whiny. How could I know?

As usual, I left with more questions than answers, and above all, more doubts. Look what you're dealing with instead of focusing on work, I scolded myself, do you realize what'll happen if you keep this up instead of nipping this insane adventure in the bud?

But then suddenly I remembered Tom's ankle. Why had he asked me to keep my hand on it the whole way to school? It'd been years since he'd stopped believing in kissing and making it all better.

I texted him, how's your ankle?

What ankle? He replied.

Didn't your ankle hurt this morning?

Oh yeah, it's okay now.

Great, I replied, and Michael, I have to admit that for a moment I believed that it was my doing, and I was filled with this bliss – Wow, I made my son's pain go away. For a few seconds I felt like a hero, but that feeling quickly vanished and I just felt stupid again. Why would I even think that it had anything to do with my hand? Maybe he was just being dramatic because he needed a little attention. And if we're already on the subject of "connections", was it my special connection with Tom that made him sense I'd started searching for my "power" and decide to let me try out my new skills? In fact, why am I using this strange terminology while talking to myself? It's amazing how quickly you infected me. Luckily, no-one but you can hear my thoughts.

There wasn't much choice but to ask you. I didn't have much time to waste, I'd wasted too much of it on this nonsense as it was, and I'd soon create a horrific bottleneck of work if I didn't get my ass moving. So I texted you on the way to my office, telling you what happened, and asked if you thought it could've been me.

Of course it was you, you replied.

But how do you know? How can you be sure?

Redefine your expectations, you replied in your obscure way. You expect straight out answers, but no-one will give you a seal of approval that something you did worked. It's not a video game and you don't score points. You just know. The problem is that you don't believe in your power and therefore you "don't know".

Great, thanks for answering. I had so many meetings to prepare for and so many phone calls to make that I couldn't allow myself to linger on the subject. It was only much later on my way home that I thought about it again.

Okay, so let's say I loosened Moni's stiff neck, at least partially, and let's say I made your headache go away, and relieved Tom's imaginary sprained ankle. Is that my power? Being an Advil? That's my forte? I mean, it's nice to know I made three people in my life feel better, but honestly – I couldn't really see how this could be useful in my day-to-day.

Maybe I have this inexplicable ability to alleviate pain with butterscotch drops, but what was I supposed to do with it? Adopt spiritual sayings like the Dalai Lama? Take a Reiki class and open an incense-reeking clinic in some dump downtown? Leave the television industry and spend my days working at a hospital? Because if that's what you think – let me tell you – you're wrong. I was never into all that therapeutic bullshit, and yes, I still wasn't sure any of this was real. So even if I did have some sort of "healing power", I couldn't see how it worked, why there wasn't some kind of user manual for it, and most of all - why me.

I called Tom and asked if he wanted McDonald's for dinner. Yes! He squealed, while mentioning that I was the best mom in the world. I wondered if my secret power was being too lazy to cook something decent, feeding my child fried gook and still making him believe that I was a serious candidate for the Mother of the Year award.

I stopped at McDonald's and got a burger, fries and a coke, and even decided to supersize it. As I waited Rona texted me: Where do I find people who will talk about their relationship?? Ideas?

Maybe on Facebook, I suggested. But you know I have a Facebook phobia, she complained, and I found myself paraphrasing you – Stop being so stiff, do something you've never tried before, dare a little.

Are you trying to agitate me even more or do you want to help? She snarled, so I abandoned your new age approach and promised to send her an idea for an enticing Facebook post, something along the lines of "Big Fear", that would get everybody's juices flowing. Don't worry, I wrote, everyone wants to be an insta-celebrity, and besides I'm the number one expert on communication problems and failed relationships, you're lucky I'm your adviser.

Just before I parked, Erik texted me, postponing our meeting with Gaya the next morning. He had a terrible stomach ache, probably a virus. Well, I thought, maybe there is a God after all. No problem sweetheart, I texted back, feel better.

I grabbed the brown takeout bag and locked the car with its familiar chirp. When I walked in, Tom was almost as happy to see me as he was the bag from McDonald's, and when I hugged him I asked if he was sure the ankle was all better. Sure, he said, as if I was grasping the obvious, you made it go away like you used to when I was little.

I stood there for a moment, feeling a little dizzy. So why don't you ever ask me to do it anymore? I asked, and he just shrugged, squeezing the bright red ketchup out of the little white packet and spreading the thick sauce on the hamburger.

I looked around. The house was a mess, it's incredible what this child can do if left alone for one hour. When he finished eating, he pretended to help me clean up, then tried, as usual, to argue about showering, and by the time he got into bed I was beat. I lay next to him and he moved restlessly. I have a stomachache, he grumbled, and I put Harry Potter aside, slid my hand under his pajama shirt and placed it where it hurt. I could feel his rigid abdomen gradually melting into my touch, with each breath. I shut my eyes and tried to imagine, skipping the butterscotch drop this time, and in less than two minutes he was sound asleep. Did I really melt his pain or was he just regressing and wanted to go back to those childhood moments when he believed that my touch could fix anything?

Before walking into the shower I deleted tomorrow's meeting from my calendar, and thought about Erik's stomach pains.

Don't even think about it, I imagined myself telling you angrily. If you think I'm going to play angel and try to cure that revolting asshole's pain, you've got another think coming. Special power or not, I'm not touching Erik, not with a ten-foot pole and not through the air with a hundred butterscotch drops. He can drop dead for all I care.

So you see why I still don't get the whole concept? Because that was my first, authentic, instinctive response. I'm not the type who would care if someone's pain went away. Obviously, if it's someone I love I'd want to help, but it would have to be someone like Tom, or you, or Moni. So why would a person whose default is to ignore other people's pain have the ability to cure pain, for God's sake? The whole concept is still beyond me.

9:17 p.m.	Think about it for a minute and you'll see the logic. Same thing happened when you preferred to get mad at the bartender that night instead of understanding him.
9:18 p.m.	But that's exactly what I'm saying.... I have no patience for stuff like that. That's my nature, and I don't understand how it goes with this ability.

9:18 p.m.	Humans are complex creatures, Sheera, things don't always color-coordinate. You have the ability to heal pain, but you can't heal pain if you don't want to see it. Try to understand your contradictions, the reasons. You really think your destiny is to become Florence Nightingale? You crack me up sometimes, I swear.
9:19 p.m.	We can laugh all you want, but you don't realize how disturbing this is. When everything becomes surreal, you have no idea what makes sense anymore. Anything becomes plausible.
9:20 p.m.	Don't give me that bullshit. You're stuck on seeing yourself as you always have, instead of getting to know who you really are. You already know damn straight that you have this ability, you've used it enough times, but you don't feel like admitting it because God forbid someone might tell you you're weird. Notice what your true motives are?
9:21 p.m.	It's not bullshit. You have no idea how distressing this is.
9:21 p.m.	Lucky you have me.
9:21 p.m.	Yeah, right. I can always count on you to distress me a little more.
9:22 p.m.	It's all about what you choose to see. I, for one, was never guided with such patience. I had to figure out most of it on my own.
9:22 p.m.	Really? So how did you do it?
9:23 p.m.	The hard way. You don't know how easy you have it. You complain that I'm condescending because I'm your "guide", because you don't feel like seeing that I'm your gopher. I try to be understanding and I have endless patience for all your exhausting doubts. Everything on a silver

	platter. I had nobody to complain to when I was little, totally alone and no-one to ask why I'm so fucked up.
9:23 p.m.	Wow.
9:24 p.m.	Do me a favor and spare me your wows. I'm telling you so that you understand it could be much harder. Stop complaining and start acknowledging your gift, start falling in love with it. You don't know how to love, Sheera. A talent is something you're supposed to love. Why this and not that. You're driving me nuts. I don't even know if you even realize what you're doing.
9:25 p.m.	Why are you so mad at me?
9:25 p.m.	I'm not mad. Just telling you. Good night.
01:05 a.m.	Are you still up?
01:06 a.m.	Yes.
01:06 a.m.	Why aren't you sleeping?
01:06 a.m.	Just got back from Jerusalem. My father decided to visit this afternoon, so I got on the motorbike and brought him here with his car, then took him back.
01:07 a.m.	Your father came to see you today? While we were chatting before? Why didn't you tell me?
01:07 a.m.	I'm telling you now.
01:07 a.m.	But why did you drive him instead of calling him a cab, like a normal person?
01:08 a.m.	Because I'm not a normal person, and I can't send my father back home to Jerusalem alone in a taxi.
01:09 a.m.	Listen sweetie, if I'm capable of sucking a butterscotch drop and curing imaginary head-

	aches through the air every night, I think you can get over your limitations and call your father a cab.
01:10 a.m.	Come on, you of all people should understand as an only child. Who else has he got? If something ever happened to me, no-one would even drop by to see how he is.
01:10 a.m.	Okay, sorry, I was just kidding.
01:11 a.m.	I know, but look at you. You're full of doubt. Curing my headaches but calling them imaginary. What good is all this practice if you weaken yourself with that talk? Even Muhammad Ali wouldn't have knocked anyone out if he didn't believe that he could. You know what faith is? You need to believe rock solid. One hundred percent, all the time. There's no way around it. How do your friends at work put it? Faith is not like the cable company, you can't just unsubscribe whenever you like. You have to believe all the way.
01:12 a.m.	Let's agree that I'll believe all the way the minute I see a spoon bend.
01:12 a.m.	Stubborn as a mule. Can't you see it's the other way around? The minute you believe, the spoon will bend as well.
01:12 a.m.	The real question is what I'm supposed to do with all these bent spoons, anyway.

To: Sheera and Michael <softspoons@gmail.com>
From: Sheera and Michael <softspoons@gmail.com>
January 14, 2016 at 8:38 p.m.
Subject: Listen, Guide, can I make a suggestion? For efficiency purposes?

If I keep getting stuck with the inability to believe all the way, why don't we think of some task that will prove beyond any doubt that I have these "powers"? Something that'll help me understand what exactly I'm capable of? My logic says everything will be simpler that way. Why do we need this documentation with all the details? Why are we doing everything the long, hard, complicated way? Maybe we should take a little shortcut. What do you say?

8:41 p.m		Sheera, do you understand what it means to believe? It's absolute knowledge. When you believe, you don't need proof. Do you see the paradox? You're asking me to spare you the road you need to walk in order to believe in yourself. If you don't believe with all your heart, you won't be able to max out your power anyway. Stop fiddling with shortcuts and start asking yourself why you still find it so hard to believe.
8:43 p.m.		Do you know the famous story about placebos?
8:43 p.m.		What story?

8:44 p.m.	One of the funniest studies about the incredible power of placebos - they took five groups of people with arthritis, okay? One group was given real medicine, and the four others were given placebos. But the first group got the placebo from women in regular clothes. The second - from women in white nurses' uniforms. The third group got it from men in regular clothes, and the fourth group – from men in doctors' scrubs. And the results? The last group reported the highest relief from the symptoms. Even more than those who had received the real drug.
8:45 p.m.	Incredible.
8:45 p.m.	We ran a documentary on it.
8:46 p.m.	But you understand what that means, right?
8:46 p.m.	Sure I do. Do you?
8:47 p.m.	Of course. That's the power of faith. That's what I keep trying to explain.
8:47 p.m.	No, I understand something entirely different. That if you believe in something, it doesn't have to be true in order to work. And then, when you find out the truth, you feel pretty stupid.
8:48 p.m.	Let me ask you something: if something works, is it true or not?
8:48 p.m.	It's true until someone clarifies that it's not, and that it's all in your head.
8:48 p.m.	But how can anyone clarify that something isn't true if it works?
8:49 p.m.	Look sweetie, I realize you're trying to build up my confidence, but what you're saying has the opposite effect. You're actually saying that even if I believe I have powers but it's all going to be in my head and not real, I'll be able to use them. Or rather, I won't *really* be able to use them, but

	because I'll *believe* I can do all sorts of things with them, I'll be sure that I am.
8:50 p.m.	You're crazy, my love.
8:50 p.m.	You started it.
8:51 p.m.	Listen. You have powers. They're absolutely real. But you have to believe in them to make the most of them. Why are you so keen on not believing in yourself?
8:51 p.m.	I'm not! I want to believe in my own way. Through logic. Through doing and seeing.
8:52 p.m.	Faith has nothing to do with logic! Look at all the people who achieved the greatest things in history. Were they logical? When Herzl dreamt of founding a Jewish state smack in the center of the Middle East was that logical? He didn't need logic, because he was a believer. And because he believed – he made it happen.
8:52 p.m.	I love those romantic arguments of yours. But they don't convince me. I need proof. Why don't you just flow with me for a change?
8:53 p.m.	You know the sad thing? When I love someone, I believe in them completely. Blindly. Without a doubt, without suspecting that they're conning me. So what am I supposed to make of all this proof you need from me?
8:53 p.m.	Oh come on, Michael. Don't trap me. Why do you have to mix it all up and confuse everything?
8:54 p.m.	I don't have to. It's mixed up anyway. And you know what's messed up about your placebo study? You didn't have a control group that received the real medicine from men in doctors' scrubs. Faith works even if there's no real power, and real power is weakened when there is

no faith. But what about a combination of real power and faith? That's what you should aspire to, my Song of the Sea. You see what I mean? That's the real deal.

To: Sheera and Michael <softspoons@gmail.com>
From: Sheera and Michael <softspoons@gmail.com>
January 17, 2016 at 8:29 p.m.
Subject: And this time – the story of how you stood me up

But first I need to tell you something. It's kind of a confession.

Sometimes I really envy you.

Sometimes I look at you and think – why can he do it and I can't? I envy your special ability, even though I don't completely understand it. I envy you for believing in it and I envy you for knowing how to use it. But more than anything, I envy your ability to overcome the shame. With me, the shame is always present. Even here, when I write to you with complete honesty such as I've never shown to anyone in my life, it's still there, the shame, as if hiding underneath the blanket. It pokes its head out only when it needs to warn me of something urgent – no, no, don't say that, that's the kind of thing you need to keep to yourself. Maybe it has to do with how I was raised. My father was so judgmental because he himself was always terrified of the critical eyes of strangers. We lived in constant fear of what other people might say. He was even afraid to admit it, as if the mentioning in itself entailed some curse that was only waiting for him to slip and set it free.

But you're not ashamed to step out of the lines. Time and again you say something completely surreal, even though you already know I'll be skeptical and find it hard to believe. You just take me by the hand and start to walk, as if you know that I'll trot along even when you've crossed a line into an area that I consider no man's land.

That's what happened on the day that Erik cancelled again, remember? I awoke to a hazy morning and a message from Julia saying that Erik was really sorry, we had to push the meeting with Gaya productions again. I don't have time for his stupid manipulative tactics, I cursed silently, I have no tolerance for his attempts to keep me away from the producer, and no patience to fight about every little thing with this unnecessary man.

My mood coordinated wonderfully with the weather. The phone wouldn't stop grinding even before eight a.m., and all I could think about was how I hated the TV industry, in which I probably wasn't cut out to ever make it. I flipped impatiently through the morning papers as I waited for Tom to finish his breakfast, restraining myself from yelling at him when he slurped the milk from his cereal bowl complete with irritating sound effects. Meanwhile I saw the terrible review on the new drama series we'd aired the night before, and although it didn't surprise me, it managed to further fray my nerves.

On my way to work Avi called to complain that he couldn't sell any commercial time for the new drama series. Obviously, it has such an annoying concept, I said. It's totally inauthentic and the message is too self-righteous and just doesn't come through. I don't think that's the reason, he waved me off, you're too poetic, the lead actress is not as sexy as we thought, that's all. I promised to see him about it as soon as I got to work, and he said he'd try to see if Erik had any ideas about how to improve the lead's image, which immediately made my blood boil. Why Erik, I cried, he's been telling everyone he's sick, haven't you heard? Besides, these things should be decided between us two, he just gets in the way, we need to get him out of the picture and keep him away. Okay, cool down, Red, he said, get yourself over here and we'll hash it out face to face.

I'm not a redhead, I'm a chestnut brunette, I had to have the last word, and only then did I notice that my hatred towards Erik had been worse than ever in the past few days. For a moment I thought we'd reached a truce, but I guess I was wrong. What you said back then also pissed me off, about him getting partial ownership of the program. Great, I muttered, if he ever lets me do my job, I'll bust my ass and he'll get rich. Well, I hope he gets to spend it all on meds, that creep. I had no doubt that all these cancellations were part of his strategy to demand a larger share.

Just before I parked my phone vibrated.

Why are you angry?

I smiled. I asked myself if I'd ever get used to the way you know things without being told.

Nothing, just life, I texted back. And how are you this morning?

Not great, I guess I caught it from you. We're connected, you know.

What do you mean? I pulled up the brake abruptly.

You feel me and I feel you, don't you know that yet?

Are you serious? I asked with that instinctive childishness that always accompanies my questions whenever you say something I'd be really ashamed to say if I were you.

Don't look for logic, you wrote, there's no logic in our nightly encounters. They connect us on another level.

I stopped for a minute, trying to digest what you said.

Does that mean that at night, with the b-drop in my mouth, when I feel your presence, you think about me as well? I asked.

Not only do I think about you, but at the exact same moments and the exact same thoughts.

I never know if you're shitting me when you say stuff like that, I answered.

Has anyone ever told you that you're hopelessly suspicious?

Yeah, I had this guide who used to tell me that all the time.

We really need to talk about that, you wrote. Can you meet me tonight?

For a moment I didn't know what to say. I was a little surprised, a little glad, but I wasn't sure of the meaning of the unexpected proposition to drop the butterscotch drops and meet face to face. Does it mean I found my power? Or are you planning to drop another one of your Land of Oz bombshells on my head?

After my parents agreed to babysit, we decided to meet at your place. I was a little excited to finally find out what your apartment was like, to find out something more about you, to be alone with you... I guess there is no end to my naivety, because for a moment I thought I recognized a normal progression in our relationship. Yeah, right.

In the elevator I found myself drifting into daydreams. You texted me an address on Shenkin Street, and I tried to imagine what your home looked like - an old building, high ceilings, paint peeling at the edges, Bauhaus balconies flooded with flocks of flowery pots, a wooden railing along the stairwell and an ancient red button doorbell you had to press at a very particular angle for it to actually ring. You open the door into a spacious apartment with dim lights and soft music, there's an awkward moment when I walk in, you're a little hesitant but I make a move and come closer and...

Oh, I'm glad you're here! Ruthie's teacher-like tone sounded so off-tune all of a sudden. Moni needs to see you, would you step in for a minute? She tossed over her shoulder as she walked by on the way to the bathroom, bursting the little fantasy bubble I'd so carefully blown in the elevator.

What's up? I asked Moni cheerfully as I walked into his office, but his news melted away the little excitement I had left. He asked whether I'd seen the news item saying that Gaya was in negotiations with our competitors to produce the Hebrew version of a new American series, while she was supposed to become our exclusive in-house production company and devote all of her energy to my Masterpiece. I didn't see it, I said, feeling the blood drain from my face, while he pressed his speakerphone button and jabbed impatiently at the buttons. Maybe it's just a rumor, it doesn't make sense, I said as Gaya's scorched voice crackled out through the speaker and filled the room. Hello?

Moni quickly picked up. What am I supposed to make out from what I've been hearing about you? He said, dispensing with the polite introductions. He just listened and gazed through the window with frozen eyes for about thirty seconds, then uttered a small "okay" and put the receiver down. She says it's bullshit, but I'm not sure there isn't anything behind it, he looked at me, expecting an answer. I thought maybe she'd also had enough of Erik's games and cancellations, but to Moni I just said – let me find out.

On my way to Avi's office I called my favorite reporter, who'd become a good friend, and asked what he knew about the rumor that Gaya would produce the series for the competition.

According to my sources it's entirely true, he said. I cursed silently and made a note to check with someone else as soon as I could. Before entering Avi's office I managed to peep into Hanna's office in Legal, and ask her how the contract with Gaya was coming along. They've kind of disappeared in the past couple of days, she said, although we don't have any more serious disagreements.

Avi was really stressed, and we barely managed to scrape together a few ideas to boost commercial sales for the tepid drama series nobody wanted to watch anyway. I asked him to sniff around his sources about Gaya and whether she was really negotiating with the competition, and at that very moment you texted me: Relax, you're too worked up again.

What's going on, am I going to have to apologize for every random mood? I grumbled, but texted you only that I had a feeling Gaya was about to stab us in the back.

You disappeared for a minute and then wrote – is she the sole decision maker at her office?

Yeah, it's just her, why, do you know anyone there?

Sort of, you replied.

I wondered what "sort of" meant, but immediately went back to my demanding and endless to-do list.

That afternoon, just when I was about to wrap things up and head home, Hanna called to say the paperwork from Gaya had arrived and we needed to go over it one final time and sign. I didn't get it – did you hear Gaya's thoughts or what? How the hell did you do that?

On my way to the parking lot I texted Moni and Avi, and we agreed that Moni would sign overnight and send the papers to sickly little Erik who would sign them at home, and that we'd issue the press release the next morning. I was glad and relieved, but it drove me crazy to think how you affected everyone in the industry, although anybody who I mentioned your name to frowned and said "never heard of him". My suspicion was aroused once again, and I decided to cross examine you that night, just you wait. Enough, it's time you told me more about what it is that you do. I was tired of the over-the-top secrecy.

My parents were having dinner with Tom when I arrived, the smell of scrambled eggs was in the air, and my mother pointed at the fourth empty plate on the table, and said in a sing-song voice, sit down, Sheera'leh. I kissed everyone, lingering on Tom and sniffing his soft smell, apologized for not having time to join them and went straight to the shower. I used my favorite soap, smoothed on my best lotion, wore my favorite jeans, a white lace bra and a supposedly-casual t-shirt that had just the right cleavage.

My dad gave me an irritated look when I went out into the living room. What's up, I asked, and he said - No news, which is his code for "leave me alone, I'm not in the mood". Usually I play along with the codes, but this time, for some reason, I didn't feel like doing so.

Is something wrong? I tried again.

Nothing, a bit of a back pain, he said. And then something pretty strange happened.

I'd never done this before, but I just came up to him and asked – where does it hurt? He tried to explain and I started to feel his back with my fingers, slowly working my way up from the center to the shoulder blades, pressing gently, scouting and asking, here? Right there, he moaned. Wait a sec, I said as I went to the mess drawer in the kitchen, fished out a butterscotch drop, came back to him, placed both hands on the exact spot, closed my eyes, breathed deeply and tried to focus. For a minute I thought I felt some pins and needles in my own back. What are you doing back there? He investigated, but I wasn't listening. I concentrated on my breathing, deep and slow, and on the strange tingling sensations that flowed from his back into my fingertips. I imagined his pain slowly melting until it disappeared, along with the remains of the candy. When I opened my eyes I saw that his eyes were shut, and asked quietly, how is it now? He slowly opened his eyes, moved his head left and right, shrugged his shoulders, wiggled around carefully, turned to me, his eyes glazed over, and in a soft voice he murmured – It's crazy. Nothing like this has never happened to me, it's completely gone. What did you do?

I smiled awkwardly. It was a strange moment, with too much information to process at once. What did I do? I had no idea. I just did it, without thinking, without expectations. I certainly hadn't expected a reaction like that. I have to tell you that at that specific moment, I totally believed you. I believed everything, but instead of answering my father, I just said I had to get going and made my escape.

Alone in the elevator, I looked at my face looking back at me from the mirror, and said out loud: I can make pain go away. I heard myself say the words, I heard them echo in the little metallic chamber, and it was the first time I knew for a fact that it was true. My father would never just say anything like that for no reason. If anything, he's a pro at grumbling and complaining and downsizing me about how I'm just not good enough. His reaction caught me off guard, but also convinced me that there was no better proof that you were right – it really works.

But what does it mean? Is this my power? And if so – what else am I supposed to do with it? Can I relieve anyone's pain? Or can it only work on those who were close to me like you, or my father or Tom or Moni?

Through the haze of thoughts I glanced at my phone, and saw that sometime in the past fifteen minutes I'd missed a message from you.

I've been attacked by a crazy migraine, you wrote.

No problem, I'll come over and fix it for you, I immediately responded, all riled up and full of confidence after my unbelievable success with my father's back.

No, darlin', you answered. You can't come near me when I'm like this. I don't want to take you down with me. I'm really sorry.

I felt as if you'd slapped me across the face. Why did everything sound like a lame excuse? I stood there in the lobby of my building, feeling pathetic, all made up and perfumed for nothing. Why were you such a tough nut to crack?

My phone buzzed and startled me. Listen, you wrote, leave the house, go to the boardwalk, to our bench, and when you get there, think about me and make my headache go away.

Okay, so now I had a mission, and I'm good at missions. Focused on my task, I headed right for the car, and drove to the beach. I'd make your migraine disappear, or your headache, or whatever it is, and then I'd be able to go back to your place and back to plan A. All right – I could live with that.

I reached the beach, parked my car, and on the way to our bench stopped at a kiosk and bought some mints. Could we use mints? Why not, actually. It's even better, because butter "clogs" and mint "opens", I thought and immediately shook my head, embarrassed at myself. I'd begun sounding as kooky as you did with those stupid thoughts. I continued towards our bench, and when I sat I was immediately filled with the memory of the feeling back then, on that first night with you.

I listened to the soft rustle of the waves, and looked at a woman who stood there struggling with a screaming baby writhing in her arms. I considered moving to another bench so they wouldn't distract me but figured there was a significance to this specific one, so I just pulled out a mint and did what had to be done.

I placed the mint in the little dimple in the roof of my mouth, shut my eyes and started to slowly melt it, stroke it with my tongue. At first the baby's crying distracted me, but the harder I thought about you, its yowling faded away into the background. I thought about your migraine, and placed you opposite me on the bench in the dark night, cross-legged, eyes shut, your hands in mine. I shuddered at the intense sensation, I could almost smell you. I ran my fingers along your forehead, stroked your nose, your eyes and your cheeks, brushing away the pain. From there my fingers moved to your head, burrowing into your hair and raking out the troubling chaos, until the mint dissolved and disappeared.

I opened my eyes carefully, unsure of how much time had gone by, and was relieved to see that there were other people around. The woman with the baby was sitting right beside me, leaning back, the empty stroller beside her. She didn't even look at me, her eyes stared out into the distance of the waves, and the baby was fast asleep in her arms, his little head resting on her shoulder.

I noticed the inexplicable serenity that washed over me as well, just like it did on that first night, when nothing could bother me although everything was so strange. The aggravations of the day had all disappeared. I felt as if we'd met after all, even if it was in some parallel universe. I texted you, what's up?

I kept sitting there quietly by the woman with the baby, and ten minutes went by before you answered. Sorry, I fell asleep, you wrote. And your head? I asked. Much better, you said, but I want to be sure that it's completely gone before we meet, otherwise I'm putting you at risk. We're connected, even though most of the time you don't acknowledge it.

Your response made me smile but at the same time depressed me, because somehow I believed you but simultaneously thought you were callously lying.

I realize you're disappointed, you wrote, so I'm sending you a special email, okay?

Jesus, what's wrong with you, I thought. Who needs your emails?

Feel better, I texted, and suddenly I felt so hungry and thirsty and didn't know why. I drove home with a heavy heart, trying to comfort the emptiness with the emergency candy bar I keep in my purse for Tom. But when I got home I put on an indifferent face so as not to arouse my parents' suspicion. My father scanned me with invasive eyes and said - You came back quickly this time. Yes, I replied coolly, thanks for that profound observation. My mother smiled, reached out a hand and gently touched my cheek. Her touch was cold and unpleasant, but I tried to smile back. Good night, she said softly, in a voice that tried to be and not be at the same time. My father hurried her along, and just before they left she snuck another look my way.

I kicked off my shoes and peeled off my jeans, changing into a ratty pair of sweatpants. I went into Tom's room and just watched him sleep, half of him in the dark, half in a yellow rectangle that the hall light threw on the sheets. For a moment it hurt so much that he'd fallen asleep without me. I missed him terribly though he was right there beside me. I lay carefully next to him, at the edge of the narrow rectangle of light, trying to steal a few moments at the end of the day. I kissed him and stroked his sweet silky hair. I indulged in the smell of the room, soft and engulfing like a hammock, the smell of clean children who hadn't argued before showering. I scolded myself for spending so little time with him recently, kissed him again, contemplated for a moment whether it was all right that his hair was getting so long, and then got up carefully and tiptoed towards my laptop.

I opened my mailbox and found the email from you.

Ten thoughts I wish you could hear, you wrote.

1. I love you.
2. I love having your smell on me after you touch me through the air.
3. I love smelling it on myself and fantasizing about you.
4. I think you are sexy beyond belief.
5. I love how you run out of words when you have an orgasm.
6. Every once in a while, you accidentally hit the wall when you have a very intense one.
7. I know how to make every one of them very intense.
8. I love hearing you. Even when you're not talking.
9. I love reading your voice in the words that you write me.
10. But I love most of all when you run out of words.

9:08 p.m.	You know, it wasn't exactly mine, the thing I sent you that evening.
9:08 p.m.	What do you mean?
9:08 p.m.	I was inspired by someone.
9:09 p.m.	Really? Who?
9:10 p.m.	You.
9:10 p.m.	Oh, be serious.
9:11 p.m.	I'm serious. When you touched me on the bench, I heard a whirlwind of words coming from you, words you wanted me to say to you. Maybe it's something you would write yourself, if you overcame your shame. Or your pride.
9:11 p.m.	What..? Every time I start getting used to your foggy explanations, you take another step into the Land of Oz and make me wonder if I'm living in the right universe.

9:12 p.m.   It's not that complicated. When our connection is strong, I can hear subconscious thoughts you aren't aware of. It's never happened to me with anyone before I met you.

To: Sheera and Michael <softspoons@gmail.com>
From: Sheera and Michael <softspoons@gmail.com>
January 18, 2016 at 8:40 p.m.
Subject: You know what the next chapter of the story is, right?

Actually it's not really a chapter. I just copy-pasted my reply to that email you sent me, and then your reply, and mine, and so forth, that night.

- Michael... Those are some interesting thoughts you've been having.
- You make me fly when you touch me with that healing touch of yours. You thought I'd drugged you once too, remember?
- Truth is I haven't thought about it at all... about what you feel when I do it.
- It's not just when you do it. Don't you know how I feel about you?
- I don't know anymore. I'm reading the stuff that you wrote here and I don't get it. We could've seen each other today.
- No, we couldn't. Why don't you trust me when I say that?
- Because every one of your explanations sounds more and more elusive and enigmatic, so why are you so surprised?
- I'm elusive? You haven't even told me if you want me to be your guide. That's what I wanted to tell you today, that you have to decide. For now you're just going with the flow, toying with the

idea, toying with me. I wasn't kidding when I asked you. It's a commitment. Meanwhile, like an imbecile, I started guiding you when you didn't even say if you want me to.

- Commitment to what? To you? Are you serious? We're not even dating... and you keep changing your mind without explaining anything. And what does that even mean, being my guide? Don't you understand that nobody talks like that? It's not normal... There are too many contradictions in your behavior, so why is it so hard to grasp that I find it confusing?

- I mean you haven't committed to the process. I'm waiting for you to agree to come with me and figure everything out, together. If you don't agree to commit, nothing's going to work because you don't really believe me. I don't understand everything either, but I put myself in your hands when you do whatever it is you do, no questions asked. So why can't you trust me?

- It's not the same thing.

- Sheera, look, I won't be able to explain anything if you don't trust me. Even about that bonehead Erik, whom you insist on seeing as your rival just because you're used to it. Erik could've been your ally if you only wanted it, do you know that? He's threatened by your influence on Moni, and instead of being friendly and making him feel safe, you're cultivating his intimidation, can't you see it? Erik is crazy about you.

- Erik?? Crazy about me? That's a good one... You're kidding me, right? Erik likes obedient women with big lips and small brains, like Julia. At least give me credit for knowing him a little better than you do, and trust me when I tell you he's always hated me.

- Would you knock it off already Sheera? I hear what he thinks, you forget that whenever it's convenient. Erik likes strong women. Like you, like Gaya. You have no idea how badly he craves your respect. Try to understand what's really going on instead of complaining about how much money he makes or his need to impress Gaya, who cares? Focus on your goals, not his. You're so into this rivalry you won't even stop to consider if it could be different. Erik is just an example, I'm pointing it out because if you understand this, you'll understand the whole idea. You focus on the wrong things. With your powers as well. You're preoccupied with the doubts. You think "Did it work or didn't it? Did I affect Moni or was it a coincidence?" Instead of thinking, "How come I denied my power until now? What made me do that?" There are reasons. You need to understand yourself if you want to use your power in the right way.

- Okay, okay, suppose that's true. But Michael, forget that for a second and tell me the truth, did you really have a migraine today? Or a headache? Or whatever it is you want to call it today?
- Of course I did, didn't you feel that you made it go away? Migraine, headache, what does it matter what I call it, it just hurts. I told you that hearing too much is no picnic. I'm not tricking you or twisting reality for you. You twist it so well on your own, you don't need me for that.
- So if your migraine is gone, why didn't you want to get together tonight?
- See, I can't manage to make you understand that either. How can I explain it? We had a strong connection earlier when you were on the bench – don't tell me you didn't feel it. I don't completely understand what it means either, and we have to be cautious, trust me. Our connection is not just plain attraction. It's complex. We're not entirely normal, Sheera. Accept that. We both have extra-sensitivity and extra-power. It's dangerous. The intensity of our meetings is not some coincidence. It's stronger than us. Once we get physical, we won't be able to stop it. That's why you need to know what you're doing first. Otherwise the emotions will go wild, and you're not going to know how to control your power. It'll be a snowball. We'll have no way of stopping it without crashing into something. We have

to make sure that when it starts rolling, we both know how to roll it in the right direction.

- I'm sitting here, reading your Tibetan monk sermon, and I've got to admit that I'm wavering between completely believing you and thinking you're even more screwed up than I am when it comes to relationships.

- You know what? It really is too much to take in. Go to sleep, and when you get up read this again, without getting offended, but in order to understand it differently. Different from the way you're used to. Can you do me this one personal favor? Please?

- Fine, fine. You know, you keep saying that I refuse to understand, but it seems like you're the one who refuses to understand. Of course I have doubts, I have no idea what I've gotten myself into. All that "guide" stuff. I'm not into mysticism. Why does everything have to be so bizarre?

- Mysticism?? What do you think, that I have a crystal ball, or a deck of cards? You have to learn how to feel, that's the whole story. Without feeling, you can't use your senses. I think you're missing the whole point because you're overloaded with information. I don't know how to clear things up for you. How about if you tried to write it all?

- Write what?

- What we're doing. Look, I have an idea. Start a blog. Or even a Gmail account. After you set the username and password, send them to me. Don't use it for emailing, just use it as a place to document everything, like a journal, by sending emails into the mailbox itself. Only you and I will be able to log in and read them. As you write everything that happened, it'll be like those slow motion replays on TV. I think it'll work. You'll finally be able to see everything you missed when you watched it the first time around.

- I don't see how that would help anything. Besides, do you really think I have the time to start writing essays? I don't know, Michael, maybe we should think of something else.

- Alright, forget it. You'd object to anything right now. Let's go to sleep. We're both tired.
- Okay, we'll go to sleep. I don't know why you seem so angry at me for not understanding. I guess I'm not so great at this power stuff.
- What are you talking about, Sheera? Who's angry? Do you even remember how this started? I just didn't think you'd react this way the first time I told you I love you.

9:15 p.m.	You see how even after that you still didn't give me a straight answer, if you wanted me to be your guide or not? Plus you didn't set up the email account either. You're the one who hung *me* out to dry.
9:15 p.m.	I didn't realize we had to rush it.
9:16 p.m.	I thought you were the one who wanted to rush it. But you still haven't written me about an instance where you didn't see the signs and only saw them later. Even though you promised.
9:16 p.m.	I actually thought of something. Busy days, though, haven't gotten around to it yet.
9:17 p.m.	Right. You needed more time then, and you need more time now. But eventually things happen at their own pace.
9:17 p.m.	At their own pace? Come on, Michael, seriously. If things continue to move forward so slowly, I won't be able to handle it. I won't be responsible for my actions.
9:18 p.m.	Don't say things like that. Delete that last line.
9:18 p.m.	I don't feel like it.

To: Sheera and Michael <softspoons@gmail.com>
From: Sheera and Michael <softspoons@gmail.com>
January 19, 2016 at 10:10 p.m.
Subject: Reading the signs

I've thought a great deal about those "signs" of yours. About the existence of things that I don't want to see. When a sensitive person enters a room, he sees not only the people in it - he picks up on the vibe, the temperature, the glances, the smells. But is seeing something we choose to do? People see what they see. At least that's what I thought, until I did remember this one time that I'd somehow refused to read the signs. All of them, down to the last billboard.

It started with the way I'd found out that I was pregnant. The whole pregnancy thing caught me off guard. I was thirty one years old yet acted like an ignorant teenager who doesn't realize sex could culminate in conception – like those girls who suddenly find themselves giving birth in the toilet and almost flushing the baby down. I'd reached the end of the first trimester and somehow the mere possibility hadn't even occurred to me. I didn't see any of the signs, I didn't even notice my period was late, maybe because at the time I was buried in work and detached from everything else.

Strange, but once I found out – everything was crystal clear. I didn't hesitate for a minute. In retrospect it seems to have been one of those decisions that make themselves, after which the thoughts are arranged to just validate the instinct. I'd never even wanted a child, and as for the father - it was pretty clear to me that we were no longer anything, that it wasn't just some kind of "a break". I was heartbroken and couldn't picture myself ever getting married, but the moment I found out I was pregnant I was overwhelmed with such a tremendous and unfamiliar emotion. All at once I truly wished to be a mother, and not just any mother, the mother of this very specific baby. The feeling was so powerful it curtailed and diminished anything else I felt.

I had no way of predicting the near future as I sat on the toilet, staring at the home pregnancy test and its two flashy blue lines. I could barely bring myself to stand up from within the pulsing tornado of excitement and fear. I tried pushing it all aside like some heavy curtain, preferring to keep it to myself until I got it confirmed by a doctor. I didn't know what I'd say either, because telling the truth was as viable an option as blaming the holy spirit. I knew I had to create a good cover story, so I just sat down and wrote a flawless tale, preparing myself for any possible question – how I'd made the decision, what I'd worn when I went to the sperm bank all trembling, what the receptionist looked like, how I'd chosen the right donor, the cold hands of the doctor who inseminated me. I investigated, invented and polished all of the details for two weeks until it was perfect.

When I tested it on Rona she was stunned – she stared at me dumbfounded for about ten seconds until I started to sweat, then asked me a couple of hesitant questions, but quickly pulled herself together and got into her practical mode. You don't really need a man, it's much more important to find a good nanny, she ruled. One of many weights was lifted off my shoulder. I knew that if she bought my story, anyone would.

I was afraid of motherhood, labor, afraid that something was wrong with the fetus, but that was nothing compared to the fear of my parents' reaction. How the hell would I tell them? I imagined myself in a sitcom scene, waltzing into their living room – hey, Mom, Dad, guess what? I'm going to be a single mother! And the canned laughter as my mother's jaw dropped and my father passed out and collapsed on the carpet.

That inevitable conversation weighed on me like a ton of bricks. I put it off as long as I possibly could, but I finally cracked at the end of the fourth month, when I was there for Friday night dinner. Sheerie, you've put on weight, my dad declared as my mother and I cleared the dishes. Oh stop it, my mother scolded him with a little slap on his hand. Then I just looked at him and said – I'm pregnant, Dad, I'm not just putting on weight.

My mother froze, the empty salad bowl in her hand. For a moment she beamed at me, seeming to realize she was about to become a grandmother, but then her face fell as she remembered that I'd skipped an important step of the process, as there was no husband around. Wait, so what are you going to do? She asked.

Have the baby, I said.

But why on your own? My father asked, how will you manage?

Don't worry, I found myself soothing him about my biggest dread, my salary is good enough.

My mother resumed washing the dishes in the sink, faster than usual and spraying lots of soapy detergent around, and suddenly I couldn't hear anything but the flush of hot water. I switched the kettle on but could feel the furrows in my dad's brow even with my back turned to him. Then we all focused on the steam rising from our tea cups, and for a moment it seemed there was nothing more important than deciding whether the tea had cooled enough to sip without burning your tongue. I thought that was the sign that the conversation had ended, with the usual long silence, but then my dad had to add – I don't know why you always have to be so odd.

As the pregnancy progressed, so did the degree to which I wrinkled my nose every time I looked in the mirror. I really wanted a perfect little tummy, with no other visible changes, but I was clumsy, tired, irritable. What did you expect? You get fat when you're pregnant, Rona would wave me off, and I didn't want to burden her with my whining, she was swamped between her job and her husband and two little girls of her own.

I completed all of my prenatal tests, and my baby grew bigger every day. I could swear I was hearing his flesh coming together in there. Sometimes he would kick my ribs so hard I would choke, as if to remind me that the clock was ticking and I needed to get things done. At work I kept up a strong front, smiling through the nausea, but once I got home I was so exhausted I'd fall straight into bed. I slept like a log at night, but startled myself awake every morning, covered in a cold sweat.

Well, have you found anything? My father would call to ask every day, and I'd lie – I'm considering a few apartments, haven't decided yet. I avoided him because I couldn't stand the anxiety, like thousands of ants running a triathlon on my skin. I wanted the perfect apartment – with a spacious room for the baby, a well-lit kitchen, and a nearby playground – all for a decent price. I began to develop a terror of being fired. I have to be good, not just good but the best, I'd mumble at my stomach when I was alone in the elevator, we can't have Moni thinking he can get rid of me after you're born, understand?

I finally found an apartment when I began the eighth month. The landlord wanted me to enter two weeks after we signed, provide guarantees, wouldn't negotiate the rent, and I was too stressed so I agreed to everything. My father started bugging me with new questions - Are you packed? Do you need help? I appeased him by saying that the house was constantly full of friends who were helping, but the truth is I did it all by myself. Rona gave me the number of a moving company that did all the packing, but when I heard the price I preferred to save the money. I filled boxes, threw out loads of old junk, bought some new things. I haggled with a cheap renovator I found, and eventually we agreed that he'd only paint the walls. I painted the doorsills and kitchen cabinets myself on one romantic weekend, just me and a can of acrylic paint. I felt heavy, bloated and tired all the time, but I put off my regular checkup because I had no time for the signs. There was too much to do before the baby came.

I remember the dark feeling that gripped me when the movers finished unloading and left me there, alone. A large mirror that was leaning against the wall forced me to look at myself. I was astonished at the woman I saw in there, a stranger with broad shoulders, a huge stomach and a double chin, standing breathless amid the chaos of dusty boxes and furniture wrapped in blue Saranwrap. Why didn't you arrange for someone to help you? I scolded myself wearily. My dad wouldn't stop calling, I screened him but eventually cracked, and he asked – well, how's it going?

Great, I said, but there's too many people here right now, I'll call later, okay?

The smell of damp cardboard filled the apartment, and I was lost among the boxes, with no clue where to begin. I walked into the bedroom, tore the blue wrap off the bed, arranged the closets, filled the drawers, pulled out some sheets, and about two hours later my stomach began to ache but at least one room was done. I was trapped in my insistence on doing everything alone, but at that moment I couldn't think of anything but my desire for a clean and perfect home. Rona called in the afternoon. I don't believe it, are you there alone, you psycho? Before I could even say anything she informed me that she was sending someone to help me clean up. An hour later she arrived in her jeans and perpetual All Stars, accompanied by her cleaning woman, and when they walked in I was sure I could see transparent wings sprouting out of their shoulder blades. I had zero energy left. I felt the blood pounding heavily in my veins, and I was so tired even my eyesight was growing weak. Rona rescued me. She made some tea, and I sat down on the sofa for a minute and couldn't get up anymore. At some point I put my head against the armrest, ignored my black fingers, and just fell asleep in my dusty clothes. When I awoke it was dark outside and my whole body hurt. I was alone again, but when I turned on the light I discovered a spotless house. How grateful I felt for having Rona in my life. I dragged myself into the shower and crawled into bed. I was an alien in the apartment, foreign to the scent of the sheets, estranged from my body. Before falling asleep, I found myself tearing up at the sight of the midnight news without knowing why.

The next morning I awoke with a strange feeling – there was a new life beating inside me, but I'd never felt death hovering around me so clearly. Everything hurt as if someone had replaced me with a faulty model that should be quickly recalled off the shelves. On my way to work I had this grave premonition, I could smell it, but I ignored everything. Even the worried expression on Moni's face when he asked me if everything was okay.

That afternoon I went to the doctor for my routine checkup, which I'd postponed for over a month. I wore black maternity tights, a huge button down shirt and the only shoes that still fit – flip flops. When I got on the scales, they insisted I'd gained 24 pounds since my last visit, which was a little odd given I wasn't eating much at all. The doc raised an eyebrow and started his checkup, and as he ran the ultrasound scanner over my stomach, he leaned slightly against my hip and I yelped as if bitten by a snake.

What's wrong? He asked, befuddled. No, it's nothing, I mumbled, it's just this swelling, it kind of hurts.

Edema in your thighs? He asked, as if I were the doctor. Yeah, I said, I thought it was normal, just part of the whole pregnancy deal. He asked me to lower my pants and looked intently at my thighs. I swear he grew pale, his eyebrows scrunched together, tiny beads of sweat were forming on his forehead, and that's when I started to panic.

Is everything all right? I asked, and he didn't respond, just wrapped the blood pressure monitor sleeve around my arm. What's the score, I asked, remembering I had a sense of humor once, but he remained silent. Wait a minute, he said, and went out to the receptionist.

I began shaking, it was uncontrollable. What's wrong? What had he seen? God, what have I done to the baby yesterday by insisting on unpacking on my own? The doctor came back with a plastic cup filled with water and told me to drink. What's happening? I asked, trying to sound like a good sport despite my cracked voice. There are signs of advanced toxemia, he said, I've called an ambulance. You need to get to the hospital right away.

Toxemia? The last drops of my strength drained at once. Damn, that sounds bad, I said, but what the hell does it mean? The presence of the placenta is causing disturbances in your body, he said, I don't understand why you didn't call, you didn't say anything. I didn't get what I should've called to say, or what's wrong with the presence of the placenta, but I didn't care about that. I asked him how this affected the fetus. Your fetus is fine, he said, we need to monitor him, but right now he's not the reason I'm worried, okay?

I wanted to just drive to the hospital but he wouldn't hear of it. I was worried about the car I left at the parking lot for 20 shekels per hour. Will you come with me? I asked so quietly I could barely hear my own voice, and he said no, but not to worry because he's making sure they'd be waiting for me. I considered begging him to come, but two paramedics burst in and put me on a stretcher. I could feel the baby going wild as one of them asked me a zillion questions on the way to the ambulance, while the other stuck a cold needle into my arm. What's that? I asked. Don't worry, he said, it's a magnesium IV, it will protect your brain. You need it because your systolic blood pressure is over 180.

My body disintegrated into a thousand humming particles. The magnesium may have protected my brain, but the icy fear and the cramped smell of the ambulance swirled in my gut in waves of nausea and uncertainty. I put a hand on my stomach and tried to calm the baby, who was storming inside me relentlessly. I didn't know what was keeping all of my pieces together, or how I wasn't oozing out of my frame. I trembled, breathless, unable to think of the possibility of losing this baby.

Will my baby be okay? I asked the nurse who drew blood from my arm in the emergency room after a doctor checked me, and she immediately berated me – Why did you wait for the last minute instead of coming in earlier?

I didn't know, I apologized, I only just found out. I could barely see who I was talking to, the magnesium had totally blurred my senses, and she looked like kaleidoscopic fragments of a nurse. Let's hope it'll be fine, she said while picking up the phone and dialing. Zina, I have a pregnant woman with advanced toxemia, send someone to take her to an emergency C-section. I felt as though all the blood had left my body at once. C-section? Now? I hadn't even finished the eighth month. Where's your husband? She turned to me, and out of my incontrollable shaking I murmured – I don't have one, I'm alone. It was the first time I could see a glimmer of empathy on the nurse's face, who'd been replete with emergency cases. Is there anyone else, she asked, siblings, maybe your parents? No, no, I cringed, I'll call them later, and in my heart I whispered, no, please, just don't call my parents, I can't take them when I'm like this, I can barely deal with myself.

I was so knocked out by all the medication, all I have left is shreds of memory. The smell of rubbing alcohol. The incessant jolts in my stomach. The brief dilemma of whether to call Rona and the decision that I'd go through it alone. The bald orderly who pushed my bed down the hall with the dripping magnesium IV and the fluorescent lights passing over me like they do in those hospital series.

The operation went quickly. Ironically, it was the easy part, and I can barely remember anything. I couldn't understand from the staff what was going on with the baby, "he's fine", they said, and "you need to rest now". I spent an entire day in recovery until my blood pressure stabilized. At a certain point I could no longer swat away the nurse who asked about my family – I asked her to get my things, and when they arrived in a tiny plastic bag, I took out my cell phone. As if a reflection of me, the battery was on its last bits of power, nearly empty.

I couldn't recognize the fingers that pressed slowly on the keys. They were so bloated that for a minute I wasn't sure they were mine. When my mother answered I said four words – Mom, I had it. She was swept with excitement and started shooting questions in a hysterical volley, but I couldn't find the energy to respond. I just asked her to come to the hospital, but without Dad, and go see how the baby was.

I craved sleep, but the light in the room was too harsh and I was surrounded by the sounds of moaning women. I couldn't just switch myself off like I'd switched off the phone. About thirty minutes later the nurse approached. Are you transferring me? I asked. Later, she said, but you have a visitor. Your father's here.

Oh no, my heart sank into my torn uterus. I explicitly told you, I whispered to my mother who wasn't even there, I can't, his presence will kill me now.

Michael, it was an awful moment. You know how sometimes you're aware that you're in bad shape, but you don't realize just how bad until you see yourself through the eyes of someone who knows you? In spite of how zonked I was, I understood the meaning of his terrified look. I couldn't see how I'd be able to stand on two feet again, or how I'd reached such a terrible physical condition, like a cripple. Out of habit, I tried smiling despite my dad's anxiety, as he stood there staring at me, holding back tears. I tried to pretend everything was all right. For a minute I thought it would work, after all - my dad and I are used to this game, I hold a cool façade and he believes me and unwinds. We tried to play our usual roles, but this time it was clear to us both that it was just a charade.

Is mom with the baby? I asked, and he nodded. He was born a bit small, he said, and I wanted so badly to ask if he was all right, but my father wasn't the right person to ask. When he left, he took the last remaining crumbs of my energy with him. The cruel light beat down through the dust on the fluorescent bulbs like in an interrogation room. I just wanted to faint in peace. To collapse into myself. To lose consciousness and disappear. I was living on the fumes of something, and I didn't even know what it was.

The nurse tried to be nice. At some point she brought my mother, who beamed while wheeling a transparent plastic crib towards me. You don't need to feed him yet, I just thought you'd like to be with him, she said. I looked at the drowsy baby. I managed to feel happy about the fact he didn't need to be in an incubator, but suddenly I wasn't sure he was even mine. His face was scrunched up and ugly. My mother picked him up in a movement that was entirely natural. Do you want to hold him? She asked, but I didn't even have the strength to sit up. Who is that boy, I asked myself. It was such a frightening moment. I was glad he was alive, he seemed fine, but I didn't know him. I felt so detached from the strange little creature, and it shocked me how I didn't feel anything towards him. I could suddenly relate to those desperate women who left their babies in trash cans by the hospital, who only wanted to escape their fate and have no idea how, and then I was even more freaked out by the fact that I could even have such thoughts. What's happening to me? I gave birth too early, had acute toxemia, and I didn't love my baby. God, what have I done? How would I manage? Everything was collapsing around me as I realized it wasn't so simple to just impulsively jump into the cold water of motherhood.

The next day they put me in a regular room. I slept some, recovered, my swelling went down, and that afternoon I was already walking slowly down the pale green halls to get Tom from the nursery. He was tiny, so quiet, wrapped in a bundle of magic. For a moment I thought someone had replaced the ugly baby from the recovery room. It was like meeting a whole other baby. I picked him up carefully and held him in my arms, and he warmed up my body and hummed like a tiny generator. He opened a pair of honey-colored eyes and gave me a look that planted me in my new reality. He had his father's eyes, they returned to me from a past life that suddenly reincarnated and surprised me. It was a moment of finding your true love, of being swept away into euphoria. For a moment I thought I was done with the fear forever, that my life had changed into happily ever after. The fears came back in new forms, of course, they're still here when I'm not sure I'm doing the motherhood thing right or when I'm worried about money or about the future. But at that moment when our eyes met, I felt something else. It was like a sudden cure for all ailments, for all worries, and I just knew that everything would be all right, simply because I had no choice and I'd have to make it somehow.

I don't know if anyone's ever told you about toxemia, but it goes like this: the pregnancy develops, the child grows, but the body just doesn't play along. It resists. I read a lot about it later when I was on maternity leave. Toxemia is actually a kind of response to something that's in your body, that can start at any point and send your blood pressure sky high while crazy amounts of liquid accumulate everywhere. My skin had almost cracked with the edema, as if the water had no more room inside the cells. It felt like everything was gushing over from the inside, like an irritating stream buzzing quickly through my veins and trying to shove me out of my own body. I'd felt all of this, but I decided it was normal. I just didn't want to see the signs.

Life became pretty intense once Tom entered it, and I never really took the time to figure out how it all happened. It wasn't that I didn't care – I was addicted to "What to Expect When You're Expecting", but I was only interested in the fetus. When I finished my prenatal tests I focused on all the chores and tasks, and all I cared about was the weight gain – I didn't stop to think about how I was feeling. But it wasn't even fat that I gained, it was all water, humming allergy water, which I peed out over four days after he was born. When I could finally stand on my legs and get on the scales I discovered that the pounds had all gone down the drain. I couldn't believe it, but I was one of those annoying women who had actually lost weight during their pregnancy.

I insisted on believing that everything was normal, though every cell in my body was screaming that it was anything but. I didn't want to listen. There must be things that I'm too scared to feel. Sometimes the emotion is just too strong, so I do what I can to detach from it in order to gain back some control. I told myself I'd jump right in, and that somehow I'd make it. There wasn't a glimmer of hesitation in my mind about having the baby, but my body somehow resisted.

Maybe it was the part of me that needs freedom, that has to be independent. That needs to be capable of doing whatever it wants at any given moment, that needs the option to rebel and shake off the shackles. If I'd thought about it before and realized the price I'd have to pay, maybe I would have passed on the whole thing. I had to move through that whole period with blinders on or my doubts would've eaten me alive. So I went through it so blind I almost died, but in return I got Tom.

He's not even nine yet, but I bought him a special sized bed two years ago so we'd both have enough room. At bedtime when I lie down gently beside him, we connect into this kind of embrace which brings us back to that moment when we met in the nursery. A soft and perfect little click of mother and child, alone in the world. A click that always recharges me no matter how tired I am. Maybe that's the real meaning of family. Small, reduced, lacking, and naturally you can't really compare, but if I could, I'm sure I'd find that the connection is just not as strong between other kids and their "regular" mothers.

So why don't I read the signs, you ask? Maybe I prefer not to see when I want to get around myself. When I want something with all my heart and know that I might surrender if I consider all the facts and think too much about it. If I realize the price up front. That's how I made the decision to have Tom. I just made it. On the way I ignored a lot of important signs, but it was the best decision I've ever made in my life.

10:39 p.m.	You had a lot of conflicting desires. But eventually your strongest will triumphed. You got what you wanted most of all.
10:39 p.m.	Tom?

10:40 p.m.	Exactly. Hey, do you feel the power you put in your words?
10:40 p.m.	Does that mean you liked the story?
10:41 p.m.	Actually that wasn't a compliment. I asked if you can feel the power you put into your words.
10:41 p.m.	I'm not entirely sure what you're asking.
10:41 p.m.	Never mind, forget it, not all at once. Just try to remember you have a tendency to ignore things. To avoid feeling them. It's important.
10:41 p.m.	Look, maybe it isn't part of your guidebook, but I think the world won't end if you say something nice about what I wrote. I put a lot of time into it.
10:41 p.m.	Sorry... I like everything you write me. I thought you knew that.
10:41 p.m.	No, I can't hear thoughts, remember?
10:41 p.m.	Lucky for you. Come on, you're getting really close to the end, to the night you figured it out. Finish your reconstructing and we'll move on.
10:41 p.m.	Okay, Guide.

To: Sheera and Michael <softspoons@gmail.com>
From: Sheera and Michael <softspoons@gmail.com>
January 20, 2016 at 9:58 p.m.
Subject: The story of how we met – the part before last

So where were we in this reconstruction of yours? On that night, about two weeks ago, right after you sent me that hot list of thoughts I only wish I could've heard. I lay in bed awake for hours thinking about our long, twisted chat, but I couldn't figure out what you'd meant. What's so dangerous about my power? What's the big deal about an aspirin-like affect I seem to have, for God's sake? Is that really the reason you're keeping your distance, or is it something else that you're hiding? Fragments of words from your list kept coming back and flashing in front of my eyes, inciting feelings I'd forgotten existed. But at the same time – I knew something was too messed up with the communication pattern between us. How did we end up arguing after that beautiful thing you'd written? I scorned myself for completely ruining the moment, desolate about our twisted way of handling things.

The next morning I woke up late. As if to make it even more difficult, Tom was all over the place and just couldn't get it together. I had to take him to the bathroom, dress him, sit with him as he chewed his cornflakes with his mouth open. You've got to learn to get ready faster in the morning, I said, and he just drowned his eyes in the milk puddle at the bottom of his bowl and didn't respond. Before we left the house I got a text from Julia: Sorry, Erik needs to postpone the meeting again, he's really sick and won't be in today. I texted back "Fine" although I was really getting furious. Jesus, how long is he planning to mess with my work by carrying on like this?

Mom, why are you so angry all the time? Tom asked me as we got into the car. I'm not angry, I answered impatiently, I just don't like being held back.

I don't do it on purpose, he said, his eyes burning with pain. His lower lip trembled a little, setting all my guilt loose. No, sweetie, it's not you, it's someone from work, it has nothing to do with you, I answered, immediately groveling. That's not true, he said, on the verge of tears, it is me. I suddenly hated myself so much, my impatience, my short fuse. I ruin everything without even noticing. We spent the rest of the way to school with me trying to explain Erik and his cancellations, and for a moment I thought he was satisfied, but when we arrived he immediately opened his door and rushed out into the yard, denying me the option of even thinking about a kiss goodbye.

When my gloom and I continued to drive to Ramat Hachayal I dialed Julia's number and then pretended to care, hoping my act would slip right under her rusty radar. So what's the matter with Erik, is he all right? I asked sweetly, trying to sound concerned. I have no idea, he sounds like shit, she said while chewing her gum profoundly, he's totaled, can't get out of bed, must be some killer stomach flu.

I didn't buy it, but Julia sounded completely convinced. Something smelled funny. I wanted to hang up, but Julia suddenly pulled out a question of her own: Hey, can I ask you something personal?

Sure, I answered without even thinking.

Me and the girls had a little bet here, she giggled.

What about? I was curious, so she just came out with it: Are you seeing someone new?

I fell silent for a moment. Why do you ask?

I don't know, she stammered. It's just... something about you lately. Your behavior, I don't know.

It's complicated, I said, and I have a journalist on call waiting so we'll talk later, okay? And then, trying to buy some time, I hung up. Before I could even think about what to say, the phone rang again and I took the call impatiently.

Yes?

Who bit your ass so early in the morning? Rona asked.

No, nothing, I'm just swamped with calls, I said.

Okay, I've got some hot merchandise for you, are you listening? Your Facebook post was a hit, everybody wants in, and even The Predator was aroused by the amount of confessions. We decided to take only rough stories so it won't be too sticky sweet, and not only did the idiot promise me a cover, we're splitting up the survey into sub-topics and making it a series feature on the Death of Relationships, so get this - until further notice I'm going to have a cover story once every four weeks!

That's great, I said, apparently not enthusiastically enough. Remind me who The Predator is? The editor of the magazine, come on, what's with the solemn grief? Did something happen? And before I could deny anything she added: Hey, you haven't told me what's going on with that guy in a while.

What guy? I played innocent.

That guy, you know, the Stranger. Are you still seeing him?

Oh, no, I blurted without thinking. It didn't really work out.

When I got to the office I stopped by Julia's desk, supposedly to see about the meeting. She sat at her computer in a grey mini-dress, horrifically made-up to the last detail and meticulously combed, and looked up at me, a little embarrassed. Gaya hasn't come back with a new time for the meeting yet, she said, flashing her gleaming white teeth in an enormous smile that she usually reserves for male celebrities such as Rafi Hadar. I leaned over and said in a low voice: By the way, about what you asked earlier, I've started this new behavioral therapy thing, maybe that's why you think something's changed. And then I added: But keep it to yourself, okay? Hoping that once I asked for discretion, it'd be all over the office in ten minutes. I don't know if she bought it or not, but it's much easier to admit you need a shrink or a shaman than to tell people you're involved with someone who thinks you have special powers and will only meet you in the cosmos.

I went into my office, my angst only increasing. It wasn't just Erik's antics, or my aversion to the gossip racing through the halls. After spending the entire morning lying to people about your existence, I suddenly understood why I've been feeling so alone since we met. I'll never be able to tell anyone about you, and not only people at work. Obviously I can't tell my parents, and not Tom either. Even my best friend wouldn't be able to understand what's happening to me lately. I've been swept into something that I don't have any real ability to judge anymore. If I could only tell someone rational on the outside, someone I can trust, maybe I'd be able to understand how it could be possible that I'd lived for so long without knowing. What does it mean about me? That I'm totally obtuse, or just plain stupid?

I called you around noon to get a sense of just how badly I'd offended you with my screwed up response to your declaration of love the night before. I told you about Erik and asked if you thought I was a terrible person, because the last thing I wanted was to help that revolting man even if his stomachaches were real.

You're focusing on the wrong things again, you said. You really think that's what I think about you? It's the exact opposite. Better to put aside your self-judgement if you really want to understand yourself and what you're capable of.

What do you mean judgement, I asked, trying not to sound cynical this time. I tried, but I couldn't put a finger on what kind of mood you were in.

Don't label everything as good or bad, even Erik, you said. You're wasting your energy on guilt instead of focusing on the signs.

Focus on the signs, I thought, what are you trying to imply? You sounded kind of distant, but I wasn't sure. Are you feeling all right? I asked. You sound a little moody. I kept feeling around in hopes we'd set up a new date, maybe even for the next evening, which was December 31, though I usually hate going out on New Year's Eve. I wanted to see how badly I'd ruined that sexy moment that suddenly sprouted in you the night before.

I'm actually in a pretty good mood, you said.

Good, me too, I answered, and suddenly I realized that the morning gloom had disappeared.

We're connected, you said, get used to it. We copy each other's moods, so when you have a certain emotion it affects me as well. Only today it's the other way around. I felt your down in the morning, so I tried to change it.

But we didn't even talk, I said.

I watched an old Seinfeld episode, you said casually. That always helps my mood, so you got it from me.

And yet another wacky thing I'll never be able to tell anyone, I thought to myself, will this ever end? I decided to be direct and asked: so after George Costanza cheered us up, you want to get together tonight?

I'm not sure, you said. Your mood is swinging, maybe better to practice from a distance for now.

I said nothing, but it was clear that I'd indeed succeeded in ruining the beautiful moment we had yesterday, thanks to my exceptional powers. I'd castrated you. I felt so stupid. Is it just me, or are there any other forty year old women out there that still have no idea how to behave with men? But then it struck me – wait a second, if we're connected and affect each other like you say, maybe I can affect you and somehow put you back in yesterday's romantic mood again? Because I liked it a lot better.

At night, after Tom fell asleep, I took my butterscotch drops and placed them on my night table. I shifted between utter satisfaction from my brilliant idea and feeling so utterly pathetic I wanted to kill myself. A woman who hasn't had good sex in at least a decade, willing to believe in supernatural phenomena and communication through candy, in a desperate attempt to score some sort of a relationship. But I was determined to move forward with my scheme. I took a slow shower and prepared for my connection with you as if getting ready for a date. I realized that the more attention I paid to the details, the stronger my sensations during our sessions. So I applied my best lotion, brushed my hair, wore a short little black camisole with see-through lace panties, dimmed the lights, put on soft romantic music, and slipped between the sheets, armed, of course, with a butterscotch drop.

I began thinking about you. I imagined you at the entrance to my building, recreating that night when we stood there vigilantly. The cool night air, my sexy dress, the intense look in your eyes. But this time I changed the script. You closed your eyes, and when I pushed my body against yours, you didn't resist. I reached out for the back of your neck, and shivered with the warmth of your breath. The image was so vivid I could actually see your face, your expression. I felt through the entire outline of your skull as I raked out the pain. I slowly drew closer to you and gave you a long, sweet, dizzying kiss, and you kissed me back. It was so captivating, so real. The passion inside me increased as the words from your list of thoughts came back and beat inside my body, stirring me. My hands left your head, traveled down your shoulders, stroking your neck, your chest, undoing your belt. For a moment I was convinced I could really feel your flesh at my fingertips. A tiny moan escaped my lips. You're beautiful, you whispered, and my eyes stung with tears.

Suddenly I felt a tiny unexpected touch that spooked me out of my total concentration. I gasped and opened my eyes, petrified, without a clue as to what was happening. I couldn't decide whether to be even more startled or to relax when I saw Tom at my side, holding his Harry Potter book, rubbing one eye and looking at me, confused. I hugged him and he asked – Mom, what are you doing?

Nothing, meditating, I mumbled. He sat next to me on my bed. Why did you make that sound, are you sad?

No, sometimes sounds like that come out when you meditate, I said as I felt my cheeks flushing in the darkness and wanted to die. He asked if he could have a piece of candy too. You can't go to sleep with candy in your mouth, I said, it ruins your teeth, and he asked – so how come you can?

I took the butterscotch-drop out of my mouth and made a show of chucking it into the waste basket in the corner. Why do you eat so much candy? He asked. God help me, I thought, nothing escapes this child. He has the eyes of a hawk, and I sometimes forget he can be a little dangerous. My throat's been aching a little lately, I lied, and these drops help. He got under the covers with me, holding his book, and asked if we could read a little. When I said it was too late he snuggled against me and suddenly asked, Mom, we're not allowed to lie, right? And I paused for a moment before saying yes, it's always best not to lie. That's why I hate Harry Potter's mean family, he muttered, they lied to him about his parents.

I hugged him again, my heart still pounding, wondering why he felt the need to say that and what exactly he'd seen when he came in, what he'd noticed and if he bought the strange meditation story.

I can't sleep, he said, cuddling into me under the covers, can you comb out my thoughts? I started stroking his head and he fell asleep pretty fast, but I kept lying there awake, mussing his hair absently, wondering at what age I was supposed to tell him that sometimes, when there's absolutely no choice, it was okay to lie. When I awoke in the morning there was another message from Julia: Erik is in internal intensive care, he was hospitalized last night.

10:28 a.m.	Why didn't you ever tell me that Tom walked in on you?
10:28 a.m.	Don't worry, he's already forgotten about it, and since then I always lock the door before I

	connect with you. BTW, haven't *you* ever been caught? Come to think of it you never told me how this all started for you. Who told you. And how you reacted. And what you did when it happened.
10:28 a.m.	I wasn't exactly surprised. I always knew I was different.
10:29 a.m.	And...?
10:30 a.m.	And that's it. I always thought I was the only one in my family, until one day my mother told me she was different too, and she became my guide.
10:31 a.m.	Seriously? Your mother is your guide? She can hear thoughts too?
10:31 a.m.	Not exactly. It's a long story. I'll write you about it when you're done with the reconstructing. But that's not the point, Sheera, I told you because it's important you understand our stories are not identical. Each of us has a different story. The one about the girl who doesn't know, who needs somebody to appear one day and tell her – that's your story, not mine.

To: Sheera and Michael <softspoons@gmail.com>
From: Sheera and Michael <softspoons@gmail.com>
January 21, 2016 at 10:21 p.m.
Subject: The end of the story of how we met

On the night Tom walked in on me, I had a dream about an old lady.

She was wrinkled and blind, and she sat at a sewing machine in a dark, suffocating chamber. She sewed incessantly, with the kind of skill you develop only by doing something every day for your whole life. She didn't even look at the needle or the cloth, just automatically stepped on the pedal, quickly running the cloth under the needle, occasionally replacing the spool of thread. How can a blind woman thread the needle? I asked. It takes perseverance, she toothlessly mouthed the answer with her dull, visionless eyes magnetized to the cloth. I stared at the heap piling up at her feet, picked one swath and looked at it closely. I couldn't see what it was, what she was sewing, except for the fact that it was cut with great precision, sewed tightly with accurate, almost invisible seams. I asked her what she was doing. I'm doing the only thing I know, she responded, I'm sewing quality excuses.

The whole time I'd been sure that Erik was making excuses. Excuses not to play along, to keep me out of the loop, to make me fail. So when the text message from Julia came through that morning I was momentarily shocked. God, how did this happen? Intensive care? I was sure he'd been overdramatizing, pretending. I wasn't sure how to digest this information. I did manage to hate him a little less, but notwithstanding, I realized that even if his illness was real, I was still stuck, and so was the show's progress. So I just texted Julia: if you're sending flowers, add my name on the card, okay?

I wanted to write you something quickly about Erik before waking Tom, but when I picked up the laptop I saw a message waiting for me on chat. It began with the words: "You're beautiful", which immediately swept me back to last night's rude interruption of our erotic date. I smiled to myself, but my smile faded pretty fast. I could feel you so strongly last night, you wrote, but you need to know that when you try to ease my pain out of a desire to sleep with me, it doesn't work very well.

I didn't know what to make of that comment. Truth is I was offended, but I wasn't sure I understood so I just wrote - Excuse me?

It's a little complicated, you replied.

Give it a try, I responded.

Try to be focused, to know exactly what you want to do, you wrote. When you want to heal someone's pain, you need to be in a state of mind that's free of anything but the desire to ease the pain. When you do it like a trade-off, it weakens the effect.

I was even more insulted, but just wrote: Oh, I didn't know. And the truth is I held myself back from writing that it's hard for me to imagine touching you without wanting you. What are you, a moron? Did you really need someone to explain this to you? Besides – what about that list of thoughts, and why were you allowed to think about me in any way you wanted to?

Don't get offended, you wrote. That's just the way it is. When you touch me I can get carried away because I don't need to do anything except submit. But when I want to focus on your thoughts, I push my personal desires aside. Emotions come in packages, so you need to unravel and separate them carefully, and leave only those that do the job.

That's a nice image, I said, but seriously, how do you separate them?

You focus, you wrote, without getting annoyed or bitter or agitated. You do it with love or you don't do it at all.

I'm not sure I get it, I wrote. The sharp transition between spiritual platitudes and stale Hallmark card couplets didn't exactly clarify anything.

What's to get? You asked. Don't you know how to love?

Is this where you start with your Buddhist questions?

I'm serious. What do you think love is? Come on, bear with me for a minute.

Love is an emotion, I answered. Or maybe a sensation. Something that sweeps you away and is beyond your control. It wraps itself around you and takes you for an extraterrestrial roller-coaster ride, and doesn't really ask your permission before it does so.

I think love is the desire to do something without expecting anything in return, you wrote.

I read your response at least three times before answering. Where does he come up with those answers, I muttered. What does he want? Sometimes I think he's this Tibetan monk pretending to be someone from around here.

Look, dude, I typed, that really does sound lovely. But you know that nobody really thinks like that. Clichés from movies from the sixties don't really cut it in today's world.

Do you want to feel what it's like to really affect someone? Before you heal someone's pain, ask yourself why you're doing it, you continued to explain, completely ignoring my sarcasm. Start doing it only once you know you're doing it only for yourself, because it makes you feel good, because it's what you want to do now, and you aren't expecting anything in return. Not now and not later. You will not believe the difference it'll make.

And when I was too shocked to reply you continued – You understand that thinking about sex is wanting something in return, right?

I felt as though you'd slapped me. Do you realize how arrogant that sounds? Who the hell do you think you are?

I was so hurt, I didn't even respond. I slammed my laptop shut and went to wake Tom. Fuck you, asshole, I'm sick and tired of this wacky relationship. I've had it with all these stupid rules, your patronizing. Every time I bend to adapt to your mad desires, you're still unhappy. Has anyone ever told you that you're crazy judgmental? You keep criticizing me, demanding like a baby that can never be satisfied.

Rona called when I was on the way to work. Did you see my Facebook page this morning?

I didn't get a chance, I said, impatient.

Someone wrote this insane story, I think I'll do the next article in my series about emotional abuse, maybe I'll call it "Enemies, a Love Story", what do you think?

Tell me about it, I blurted.

What's with you lately?? She asked.

No, I just meant that things are crazy with the show, Erik and Moni are driving me nuts, I faltered.

That's totally unlike you! She scolded me. Come on, get a grip on the reins. It's just men, you know how to manage them.

And suddenly it hit me: I should really start thinking differently. Why am I acting like the ultimate female victim? How did I sink this low? Why was I letting you dictate the rules?

And that's it, it was at that moment exactly when I made my decision.

It was Thursday, my parents' regular babysitting night, and incidentally it was New Year's Eve, for which I had no plans, as usual.

When I got home they were making omelets, and I kissed them all and sat down with them although I wasn't hungry. Tom gave me a funny look, and when I asked him if something was wrong, he just said - nothing.

He's all stressed because we said we'd play cards after dinner, my father said, and winked at Tom. I asked if it was all right if I went out for a while. Parties? My father raised an eyebrow. No, of course not, I said. I'll be back early, just some quick coffee with Rona.

I showered and wriggled into some jeans, threw on a button-down shirt and put on my boots. I didn't put on any makeup or perfume, didn't want you thinking I've come to seduce you or something. A short, friendly, informal visit, where you wouldn't be able to avoid me any longer. I want to know what this "guiding" thing is and what kind of "commitment" you expect. It's time for you to explain yourself like a decent human being, and after you've done so I'll decide if it suits me.

I didn't feel like looking for a parking space, so I hailed a cab on the street and when I got in I told the driver: 23 Shenkin St. Once again I was amazed at myself: I've had your address for a few days, how come it hadn't occurred to me to just show up? I've never been so subservient, it wasn't at all like me. Besides, I need to see your face. Something about your behavior just wasn't adding up. Once I see you, I'll know if there was really anything to worry about or it was all in my head. I promise not to set any huge snowballs in motion. We'll just have a quick cup of coffee and clear up any misunderstandings.

I got off near the Carmel Market. Your building was newer and in better shape than I'd imagined. Clean lines, painted white, with a dark wooden door frame and a big mirror in the lobby. I climbed the stairs to the second floor, and instead of the old red doorbell there was a heavy metal security door. But at least it had a small Armenian style tile pinned to it with the name "Eden" on it. Oh well. I ignored the chill of fear that gripped me and knocked on the door. Pretty determinately.

I could hear footsteps behind the door. They were a little slow, kind of dragging. The door opened a crack, and your beautiful eyes appeared only they seemed a bit dim, and I was mainly worried by the fact that they were stuck in the wrinkled face of an old man. My heart started pounding. Hello, he said. I began to stutter. I asked if you were there. He opened the door wide. It was Michael Eden, but with thin white hair, a little shorter and a lot older. I didn't need to ask if it was your father. It was obvious. Come in, he said with a slight frown, he's sleeping.

My heart blundered with slow, thick beats. I hesitated, suddenly regretting coming. The old Michael was wearing baggy brown pants and a slightly worn black sweater, and there was something a little odd about him. Maybe because he didn't smile at all. Is it possible that he doesn't like me? In any case, I made an effort to be really nice. He was wearing some old-fashioned cologne, maybe Old Spice? Maybe. He turned his back and went inside, dragging his feet. I don't know why he's asleep at this hour, he mumbled, so he's got a migraine, so what.

I followed him inside, and a wave of compassion suddenly washed me. Why were your migraines going so crazy? I got a little dizzy as we passed through a small hall leading to the living room. At the end of the hall was a large wooden counter with three bar stools, indicating the boundary of the small open kitchen, which was entirely white. Everything was very neat. Minimalistic. Pleasant looking. But something in the air was heavy, and it burdened me with a huge exhaustion. I fantasized about just lying there on the rug and shutting my eyes for a minute. I felt a thin sense of nausea and couldn't understand what was happening.

Despite my sudden fatigue, I tried to take in as much detail as I could. A light colored shaggy carpet. The wall was covered by a dark bookcase, and on one of the shelves was a little paper lamp bathing the books surrounding it in a golden light. A pair of black speakers sat on the floor on either side of the bookcase, and a large television screen was silently settled in the middle. In the corner was an old piano, its keyboard shut, without a bench or any sheets of music. An open book lay on a low wood table, face down. The Girl with the Dragon Tattoo. There was a little box of pills beside it, reading Tramadex. Who was taking it? You or your father?

Wait here for a moment, I'll go and wake him, your father pointed at the yellow sofa. He turned and started walking towards the hall. No, I reached out to stop him with my hand, which suddenly hurt. It's fine, I was just passing by so I thought I'd say hello. I'll talk to him later, he's better off sleeping if he has a headache.

Are you sure? He asked. Yes, absolutely sure, I responded, trying to ignore my growing sense of vertigo.

By the way, I'm Sheera, I said, and held out my hand. He took it with the firm grip of dry, weathered fingers, and pulled his hand back pretty quickly, and I felt a sudden jab of pain in my jaw and neck. The kitchen window was open, but I had trouble breathing, couldn't fill my lungs all the way in. A cold sweat covered the back of my neck. Could it be the smell of his cologne? I couldn't explain it, but although I liked the apartment, my legs were shaking and my heart was beating irregularly.

Just before I turned to go, my eyes fell on a large world map hanging on the wall above the sofa. It was a beautiful hand-drawn map, marked with tiny red circles. Something like an artistic war-room. I smiled at your father again, but he didn't smile back as I said goodbye and walked heavily towards the door. I had to get out of there, and fast. It was only when the door shut behind me that I could breathe again. When I reached the lobby, my nausea disappeared. As I stepped out into the street, my wooziness vanished. I stood out there like a pillar of salt, not knowing what to do. What the hell was going on? It was as if someone had pulled out a bucket of information and splashed its entire contents on my face. I had to stop for a moment and process it all.

Who hangs a world map in their living room? Clearly everything about you just had to be weird. I thought about your father. What was he doing there? Why had he come without your mother? Do you see each other often? Do you have any brothers or sisters? And what's the deal with your migraines? I was a little helpless. You were really worrying me, and I didn't know what to do.

A taxi approached from up the street, and when I raised my hand to hail it I was shocked to see that it was trembling uncontrollably. What happened to me up there? Why did the encounter with your father affect me that way? Does he have special powers too? And if so, what does it mean that I felt that way around him? That he didn't like me? It was really impolite to come in and leave like that, without talking to him at all. But I just couldn't stay in that apartment, really. I had to leave as soon as I could, and I couldn't explain why.

I got into the cab, and as I told the driver the address I felt like saying, please take me home. I was overcome with worry. What's wrong with you, Michael? Why does it seem like it's only gotten worse lately, if I'm healing you? What am I doing wrong? I had to ask you. Or maybe… it seemed too sensitive. You can't ask somebody how to cure their own illness. On the other hand, if I couldn't ask you, who could I ask?

When I got home my mother was sitting on the couch watching TV, and Tom was in his pajamas seated on his bed with my father, in the middle of a game of Rummy. I kissed them both, but they were so intent on the cards that they barely looked my way. I said I was giving them ten more minutes, and went out into the living room and sat at my laptop. First thing I did was to Google "Tramadex". I didn't know whether to stress out or calm down when I saw it was a strong pain reliever, so I just moved on. I started frantically looking for articles on headaches. Most of them said there was no telling what really caused migraines, but some referred to tension, imbalance, or overstimulation of the nerves. I suddenly remembered the book "Dot and Anton", which I'd loved so much as a girl, where Dot's mother was always suffering from terrible migraines. I went to the bookcase, looked for my old copy, and started thumbing through it, and when I found the word "migraine" I stroked it with my fingertip, folded the corner of the page and put the book back in its place.

The television show ended, a noisy commercial break began, the Rummy game ended in a crushing tie, my parents got up to leave and I got into bed with Tom.

Mom, are you angry again?

No, sweetie, I'm just tired.

Are you sure? He asked, and I nodded, trying as hard as I could to really calm down. I wrapped him in my arms, feeling him melt into me. I listened to his breathing, which became deeper and deeper, and knew exactly what I was going to do the minute he fell asleep.

When I was totally sure he'd fallen asleep I carefully extracted myself, changed into my pajamas, brushed my teeth, thinking about how eventually my teeth would fall out if I kept brushing them and falling asleep with candy in my mouth, and consoled myself that at least it was sugarless. Before sitting in bed, I stopped to pick up my perfume. I opened the bottle, inhaled its scent and dabbed some on my palms and fingers. I breathed deeply for a few minutes to make sure I was totally calm, and then remembered that Tom might wake up and ask questions so I got up quietly, locked the door, sat on the bed and asked myself, in all honesty – what do you really want to do right now?

I waited a few seconds, and the answer was entirely clear. I'm worried about you. I want to heal that harsh pain of yours. To rescue you from the migraine. Other than that, I don't really care about anything right now.

I shut my eyes and slowly began to suck the butterscotch drop. My imagination took me back to your apartment. I recreated the hallway, the living room, the shaggy rug, the bookcase and the map on the wall. This time I moved in my thoughts towards your bedroom and opened the door. I pictured you laying on a large bed covered with white sheets, in a room that was dim but pleasant. I walked up to you quietly, sat beside you and massaged your shoulders with my perfumed fingers. Then I wrapped one hand around the back of your neck and placed the other on your head, and started breathing along with your, long, deep breaths. I thought about tranquility. Balance. Physical balance, psychological balance, the balance of scales, financial balance, the balance in a spirit-level. I imagined breathing your pain into me, melting it into the candy, swallowing it and perfuming you with a pleasant scent. I don't know how long it took but when I finished I opened my eyes, slowly got out of bed and went to the bathroom. I stood at the toilet, looking into it. Sorry darling, but you're fucking history, I said to your migraine and flushed the water noisily.

The next morning I woke up very early, made sure Tom was still sleeping, and when I opened my laptop there was a message from you waiting.

It worked perfectly, you wrote. Be advised that last night was the first time you performed real magic. By the way, you've got a new fan. My father thinks you're gorgeous. And your scent... I can still breathe it in from my sheets.

I read it again and again, unable to take my eyes off the words. I tried to remember what I did before coming over to your place, and I could've sworn I hadn't put on any perfume before leaving the house.

There was something simultaneously familiar and foreign about the feeling that filled me. It wasn't happiness, more like a quiet contentment. Without making a fuss, without analyzing it, without being a wiseass or resisting or agreeing, I'd just made everything okay. It had even been easy.

Don't get used to it, I wrote, once is okay, but you don't actually expect me never to think about a give and take relationship with you, do you?

Allow me to tell you the most important thing my mother ever taught me: how to do something out of love, and not in the Hallmark sense. Try to understand beyond the cliché. You already know the feeling – from your son. When you do something for him, it's no sacrifice. You're not doing a favor, or calculating what could be in it for you. You do it simply because you want to. Now transfer that to your work. Isolate your desire, because the rest is just noise. You won't believe how many things will just fall into place when you work like that.

You're delusional, I answered. Nobody lives like that, and it's hard for me when you expect the impossible.

I expect only one thing, dammit: a clear decision on whether you want me to guide you. Yes or no, just make up your mind. Do you want to know what else you're capable of? Because this is just the tip of the iceberg.

I inhaled deeply. Of course I do, I wrote.

Then give it a chance. Believe. Commit. Start up that email account we talked about and start writing everything down, retelling, reconstructing everything that happened. As you write you'll notice what you've missed, you'll find it out on your own. And never say "impossible". Your goal is not to bend spoons, but to bend the definition of the word "possible". To soften it. To make things happen.

When I read the words "make things happen" I suddenly remembered the dream about the old lady. For a moment I blanched. That old lady was not Erik, it was me. God, I'm so damn good at saying "no" to everything. Give me a few seconds, and I'll find a great excuse for every refusal. I say "No, that can't be true," or "Not now, I'm in the middle of something," and that old lady, she always has something perfect and readymade to give me, and it sounds more persuasive each time. I have a kid, I've got a job, it's my parents, the market is competitive, there's rent to pay. There's always something more important. But what happened yesterday is that somehow, for a few minutes, I stopped fighting.

I want to quit the excuses, I mumbled to myself. I want to know if you're right, and if you are – I want to know who I am.

Before waking Tom, I managed to log onto Google and create a new email account. I called it "soft spoons", softspoons@gmail.com, and the password I chose was "makeithappen". I texted you the account details, adding "Yes Michael, I want you to be my guide."

Although everything still seemed surreal, vague, incomprehensible and frustrating, I decided that somehow I was actually going to do it. The next stage of "Big Fear" started airing the next evening, and the twelve contestants who passed the auditions were moving on to compete in head to head duels. Forty percent of the households in Israel were glued to the screen, but at my house the TV was off, because I sat on the living room sofa with the laptop on my lap, and started to write to you.

10:40 p.m.	You know you really saved my ass that night, right?
10:40 p.m.	Really?
10:41 p.m.	I swear. Everything changed since then. Your motives were one hundred percent real. Nothing stood in your way.
10:42 p.m.	Truth is I also had a totally different feeling that night. I could feel it working. Something different was happening.
10:42 p.m.	Have you already figured out what happened when you came into my apartment?
10:43 p.m.	What do you mean?
10:43 p.m.	Why you had to leave and why you felt so sick.
10:44 p.m.	Because even through your sleep and migraine, you wanted me to leave?
10:44 p.m.	No, man, I can't believe your crazy conclusions sometimes. I told you – when I feel bad, you can't get anywhere near me. You felt my pain from up close, and you couldn't stand it. You understand

	what would've happened if we were in the same room and you touched me? You'd collapse.
10:45 p.m.	Fuck. Are you serious or are you shitting me again?
10:45 p.m.	When have I ever shitted you?
10:45 p.m.	Listen, sweetheart, I can't take all this surreal stuff. It just gets weirder every time.
10:46 p.m.	Stop calling it weird. You've realized you have a power, right? So instead of belittling it, start understanding it. Start mastering it.
10:47 p.m.	BTW, what's the story with that huge map on the wall?
10:47 p.m.	I took it when we sold the start-up. It was on the wall in the conference room.
10:47 p.m.	And you just put it in the middle of your living room? What's it supposed to stand for?
10:48 p.m.	The world, I guess.
10:48 p.m.	Come on, I'm serious.
10:49 p.m.	I don't know. Maybe it's a reminder of how crazy the world is. That at any given moment you could get the air knocked out of you, and you still have to land on your feet. Not to give up even when it seems impossible. Believe in love.
10:49 p.m.	Has anyone ever told you that you're a hopeless romantic?
10:50 p.m.	Only that I'm a spineless romantic.
10:51 p.m.	You?! Spineless? Then what am I? I follow you around like a sheep.
10:52 p.m.	You're not spineless, Sheera. If anything, you've got too much of a spine. You know what my mom told me about that? That a strong character doesn't have to become the cage of the soul. You can't let it rule. I always think about it when

	I want to do something for you. Sometimes you want to do something and your character resists, gets in the way, you know what I mean? But because I love you, I can always find the strength to bend the bars of that cage.
10:52 p.m.	Spoons, cages, what's the deal with all this bending?
10:52 p.m.	Try seeing your character as something you can bend a little, because if you do, your soul will have more room. Shame for it to be caged up like that. And the opposite just won't work. You can't follow your character blindly no matter what, and expect your soul to change.
10:54 p.m.	I've never thought about it like that, but now I think that's exactly what happened that night… I just wanted you to be okay. I wanted it so badly that I managed to bend the bars of the cage. So… what do you think? Is it possible that I've fallen in love with you as well?
10:58 p.m.	Michael? Are you still there?
10:58 p.m.	I needed a minute to recover. I've heard you think it a thousand times already. But it feels totally different now that you've suddenly agreed to reveal it in writing.

Part Two

To: Sheera and Michael <softspoons@gmail.com>
From: Sheera and Michael <softspoons@gmail.com>
January 24, 2016 at 10:08 p.m.
Subject: How I lost three fingers and then got them back

When I got in to the office this morning I knew I only had an hour. You know those days when your schedule is timed to the minute, but right from the start nothing goes as planned? It began with crazy traffic that held me back for at least ten minutes, and then when I turned my computer on it wouldn't start up. In light of my rich experience, I immediately checked whether it was plugged in and if all the cables were connected, but everything seemed fine. I called Zadok, the building super, and begged him to come ASAP. Meanwhile I logged into my email from my phone to at least get something done, because at ten I had to leave for a chain of meetings around town. Then I suddenly saw the envelope… just lying there on the mail pile, as if quietly waiting for me to notice. A plain white envelope, with an address carefully printed on it in thin green handwriting: "For Sheera Leitner – Personal".

When I first opened the envelope it seemed empty, until I saw the delicate bracelet hiding at the bottom: a tie-on hand-knotted bracelet made of colorful string. I smiled. I don't know how, but I knew it was from you. As soon as I saw it, it felt as if you burst out from the envelope and warmed up my office with your presence. I tied it onto my right hand, immediately liking it. So I just texted you – thanks.

A few minutes later I had my answer: a little something for completing the great reconstruction of events ☺ are you moving on with me?

Yes, Guide, I replied, what's next?

I expected some astounding answer, another eccentric idea you'd come up with. But you only asked me to continue documenting. To play back everything that had happened at the end of each day, and kind of write a daily recap.

Before I could reply, Zadok emerged through the door, took one look at the computer and said – your screen is off. He pushed the tiny button at the bottom and turned on the screen, and I was a little embarrassed and smiled in a technologically-challenged kind of way, but at least I could start working. Zadok stayed for another minute or so to make sure everything was okay, and asked – do you leave the computer on when you go home?

No, of course not, I said, and he asked – are you sure? When the cleaners see a computer left on in the evening, their instructions are to turn everything off right away, the screen as well. I thought that's what happened.

Zadok went away and left me with a disturbing feeling I couldn't put my finger on. I texted Tom and asked if everything was all right. Even after he answered, my strange notion wouldn't budge. For a moment I thought I'd forgotten to do something important regarding the final round of "Big Fear" that started last night. Time flies, and in three weeks the season will already be over. I checked my to-do list just to make sure, and then quickly scanned my emails again before leaving. But I didn't see anything out of the ordinary, except for an email from Julia saying Erik was feeling a little better although still in the hospital. I didn't understand what was bugging me, and you said to develop my consciousness – remember? I thought maybe it had to do with what Zadok had said. Did I leave the computer on before when I left the office? I didn't think so, but who knows. Maybe someone had tried to poke around. But who would do such a thing?

Somehow I didn't think it was the competition. Even if they did manage to break into our building, there were much more interesting computers to go through. Could it be someone on the inside? Strange. I didn't think I had anything to hide from anyone inside the station. Unless it was something personal. Like my correspondence with... you. That suddenly got me all agitated. I thought I'd been careful, but maybe I'd written you something from work and forgot? I decided I'd check when I got back, but a bubbling anxiety fermented in my stomach all day.

On the way to my last meeting, I passed by my old apartment. It's not very far from where I live today, but it's tucked away in a tiny street I rarely pass through. I lived there for over three years, the whole time I was with Ziv. Or rather - the whole time I wasn't really with Ziv, because he didn't really want me.

Yes, I know, I still haven't told you about him.

You've already realized that I like things to be clear, and Ziv was very unclear. For three years, I couldn't understand what he was after, what was his thing. We were both young and didn't fully know what we felt, but we did know that every time we were together, there was something unique about it. Something that reminded me of that childhood feeling I had when I built a tent in the yard with Tal, the neighbor's son. It was a tiny tent improvised from a shabby army blanket and two sticks, and we sat cramped inside for hours, folded up like two puppies. For some reason we were so happy in there that it became one of those memories that never fade.

My apartment had been tiny. It had a nook that pretended to be a kitchen, a staggering fridge, a bathless bathroom, and a bedroom that could barely fit a bed. We'd meet about once a week, and only at night. At least half of the lightbulbs were burnt out, so the weak lighting concealed the peeling walls and the dust, and when Ziv stayed the night we'd always hold each other in our sleep.

Rona never understood why I continued to see him. He was a musician, so she called him "The Poet". By then she was already married to Eyal, whereas I refused to grow up. He's a classic one-night stander, she'd say about Ziv, you'll never have a normal relationship with him, I can smell those "can't commit" guys from miles away. But ironically, over time, Ziv's lack of commitment became something I could count on. He'd appear out of nowhere and then disappear into thin air, and almost never call. On the other hand, he never refused when I suggested we meet. I didn't know if there was anyone else in the picture, and his lack of initiative was very frustrating. I always wondered how he really felt about me, I didn't know how to define our relationship. I waited for it to change, and sometimes when I had trouble sleeping I'd write pages and pages of passionate letters to him. I was so bold at night, suddenly expressing my true feelings, describing exactly how I wanted it to happen between us. But the letters remained in my drawer. When morning scattered the night away, somehow my courage to send them would disappear as well. I was afraid he would say he didn't want anything beyond what we had. I loved him, but he was a free-spirit kind of guy, very anti-establishment.

He never had a steady job. Sometimes he had no gigs for weeks, and he'd stay up all night and expect me to stay up with him, as if I too didn't have to work the next day. He wrote songs and composed for some artists, and we'd go see them perform at clubs with sweet strips of marijuana smoke hanging in the air. Sometimes when he had to make a living, he'd write jingles as well. One morning, after a pretty wild and sexy night, I left him a note before going to work. I tried to maintain my dignity while hinting that we could have more nights like these, that he didn't have to always wait for me to call. I hesitated whether to simply say it straight out, but eventually only mustered up enough courage to sign "crazy about you". The note was gone when I came back home, but he never said a thing about it.

After three years I'd had enough of this impossible routine of uncertainty, and decided to launch a scientific experiment: I stopped calling him. Two, three, maybe four weeks went by, until I realized I'd spent three whole years on this elusive guy. I laughed, I cooked,

I put on perfume, I seduced, I dressed up and undressed a thousand times, only to discover he was never going to abide.

I fell into a deep depression. Every day I almost called, my fingertips would hover over the phone keys of their own accord. I missed him terribly, but held myself back, couldn't stand the humiliation of actually dialing. I was so surprised when he suddenly turned up at my apartment one day. He may have been challenged, but he'd finally understood that if he didn't make a move, he'd simply lose me. I opened the door, and without saying a word he drew closer and hugged me. We stood there, entwined for several long minutes, holding each other timidly, touching, caressing. At some point we started kissing and couldn't stop, frantically got rid of our clothes and had sex right there by the door. I remember the cold floor that contrasted with his warm skin, the heavy breathing, the feeling of urgency that burned through me, my cries and his hand that covered my mouth so the neighbors wouldn't hear. The tears that blended with the sweat and the lustful honey that kept rippling out of me. At some point we left our clothes there and moved to the bed in the tiny room, still too starved to think about sleep. I was already hurting everywhere, it burned when he entered me, but I wanted more, I couldn't get enough of him.

We fell asleep after dawn, and I woke up at eight and rushed off to work, bleary-eyed and happy as a child. I didn't wash my hands for the whole day so I could feel his remnants on my fingertips. When I got back that night he was still there, naked on the bed, surrounded by a cloud of that tempting musky spice, just as I'd left him. I threw my bag on the floor, and he slowly undressed me and whispered, so how would you feel if I moved in here with you? I smiled and kissed him, very slowly. His smell was driving me crazy, his touch, I wanted him so badly but I didn't know what to say. He kissed my stomach, my thighs, slowly taking off my panties and starting to lick me. As I moaned, he mumbled, what've we got to lose, let's give it a shot, it's about time, don't you think?

I was floating on air. I couldn't believe it. There, it's happened. It took three years but when I let go of the reins, I'd finally got him.

It was hard to admit it back then, but I really loved him. We were alike, always laughing together in perfect timing, like brother and sister. At night he would mumble these broken melodies in my ear before we fell asleep. I loved touching him, unveiling his body, feeling his nudity. I loved having sex with him, not because he was some virtuoso in bed, but because of the connection we had.

Two or three weeks went by, and all I did was go to work in the morning and return to the bed at night, the bed which had become the primary meaning of life and the center of the little apartment. He barely worked, but I said nothing. I was used to it, I knew that it was a matter of ups and downs. We agreed that in a few days he'd move all of his things to my apartment.

One day I bumped into Simon, a close friend of his. We chatted for a while, and I waited for him to ask about our sudden couplehood, but he didn't say anything. That surprised me, and just before we said goodbye I asked – hey, have you talked to Ziv lately?

Sure, all the time, he said, and then looked right into my eyes and said – you know he's in debt, right? We need to figure out how to help him.

I didn't say anything, just nodded, but his words turned into a clump of black pins that prickled too many conclusions into me. Not only did Ziv not feel any need to tell his friends about us, but my old-new boyfriend was keeping secrets from me. The timing, then, had nothing to do with my new strategy, but with the fact that he suddenly needed me. Three years of hope crumbled inside and piled up in a pathetic heap. I couldn't go back home, and I couldn't go to work. I walked around aimlessly for hours. I was lost. At some point I collected the pieces of myself off the sidewalk, walked into a café, and called to ask him to join me.

The breakup was unbearable. Every cell in my body rebelled but I knew I had no choice. I remember that little café on Bograshov

Street, with the old floor tiles and iron tables, the lone flower in the vase, the waitress who was pretty but too skinny for my taste. I can't remember what I told him, I just remember that my voice trembled constantly. I didn't say "you used me" or "you lied" because I didn't have the guts, I just made up some excuse, something along the lines of "I've thought it over and I'm not sure anymore." I drew every bit of strength I had, clenched every muscle so as not to fall apart, not to cry.

He didn't argue, didn't ask why, just looked at me like a little boy, saying nothing. We went out into the night and just stood there between two streets, right on the corner, wondering what to do next. It's an odd moment, that moment right after you break up. You still love but you can no longer show it. It was cold and dark, and as he gave me a quick hug before turning away, my throat clenched so hard only a tiny painful stream of air managed to slip past into my lungs. My heart couldn't let him go, but my brain was determined, as if it knew there was no choice, and that someday I'd get over it.

From there I had to go to some work thing, a premiere at the hottest club in town. I needed to muster up my phoniest smile. It was crowded and hot, so I stood beside a vent in the wall. My breathing was shallow and I put my hand closer to feel the cool air, unaware that there were fan blades whirring around inside. At once my hand was flung back with a sharp pain, and I looked at it, petrified, but it was dark and I couldn't see what had happened. I went out into the street, and stood trembling under a streetlight. All I could see was chunks of blood. I asked someone coming out of the club to drive me to the ER. A short little doctor with a narrow nose and glasses sewed me up, and was impressed by the fact that I didn't faint. The blades had pulverized three fingers. It looked awful, like a whirl of meat. You're lucky, he soothed me, there's no irreversible damage, it's an area that heals well.

I got home at four a.m., my right hand bandaged. Ziv was no longer there, his toothbrush was absent from the glass in the bathroom and the jeans he'd thrown on the chair the night before had disappeared. All I could feel was my heart throbbing in the battered fingers, and I smiled to myself instead of crying. I slowly laid down on the cold floor, by the door, in the spot I was sure we had blindly loved each other only weeks ago.

A few days later, persuaded by the channel's legal consultant, I decided to sue the club. He must've been intimidating enough for their insurance company to compensate me to the tune of 200,000 shekels, and he didn't even take any fees. For the first time in my life I started a savings account. It was the only money I had, and a little over six months later, part of it became an advance payment for a long-term lease on a new apartment. The apartment which Tom was born into.

After the injury I was supposed to rest, stay at home, but I couldn't be there alone. I went out walking for hours, with aching fingers in the pockets of my trench coat, trudging through the entire city, staring at the sidewalk. When I got back to work I felt disabled. Till then I'd never realized how much I liked the feel of healthy fingers dancing freely on the keyboard. Work suddenly seemed boring, and I had a constant feeling of numbness. I couldn't even write the sadness to myself, just to ease the soul.

I continued to dream about Ziv now and then, but I never responded to the only message he sent me after that night. As expected, he quickly gave up and stopped calling. He wasn't the kind of guy who knows how to fight for a woman. At first I kept obsessing about our moments in bed, yearning for them and dredging them up in my mind. But over time they soured. They were no longer passionate or thrilling, my memory transformed them into defeated farewell fucks.

Why had I met his friend on that day, of all days? I asked myself that question over and over again. I've never run into Simon again. Sometimes fate creates interesting encounters, don't you think? Random, but totally not random. I met Ziv only once since, a few years ago, also by chance. I was overcome with confusion, my heart stuttered. We didn't even embrace, I just gave him a little smile, and all I was capable of saying was "what's up". He said he was on a brief visit, he'd moved to New York where he was working with some artists. You look great, he said, and for a minute he had that look, like the one on the bed in my apartment. I ignored the compliment, tamed the wild horses that were stomping in the stables of my chest, told him I was still working at the same place, and then hesitated for a moment, but eventually didn't mention that I sometimes see that same look in the eyes of the son I gave birth to.

The decision not to keep in touch when we split up was hard. But the really bad part came two months later, when I decided not to tell him anything about the pregnancy. To contain the truth alone without rupturing. To lie to everyone, even to Rona, to lie to Tom about his father when he was still a sweet helpless toddler. I had a few crises along the way, but the whole time I knew it was the right thing to do. I knew that Ziv couldn't be counted on, he was the kind of person that always disappears somehow, and Tom was better off living without him than having to deal his whole life with the constant pangs of rejection that were beating me up inside. There's a luscious taste to someone you love, but a God awful taste when that someone disappoints you. This metallic taste, like a corroded battery in your mouth, which you can't get rid of no matter how often you brush.

But since I met you I've suddenly begun to wonder. Not just about Tom, but in general. Could I have been mistaken then, making that decision?

I chose to take what his friend Simon had said at face value, without question. I didn't consult Rona, I didn't tell Ziv the truth, I didn't even give him a chance to explain. Suddenly I'm not sure – maybe I just didn't want him to convince me to stay. Something inside me wanted to continue being alone, as always. I blamed him for his inability to commit, but maybe it was me. Or maybe the fate that brought Simon to the street I was walking on was actually related to the fate that kept me single, so that one day I'd meet you. I don't know, it's strange to write this all down after so many years. You're the first person I'm telling. I just knew that in those few weeks he lived with me, I was terrified of sharing my life with him. Today when I went by that old apartment, I suddenly had a flashback of that fear. I really felt it again for a few minutes.

I'm scared with you as well, if you want to know the truth. Among other things, of the fact that you're in my brain listening to every thought. Sometimes I ask myself if you're sane, if everything that's happening between us is real. We only meet at night, through the air and the butterscotch drops, me in my bed and you in yours. When I think of it like that I get really freaked – how did I end up in this situation? It scares me that we don't meet, even if there are exceptionally good reasons for it. I'm also afraid of that moment when we'll really be together. That maybe somehow you'll realize I'm not the one for you.

I really want to believe that with you it'll be different. Ziv was a three-year long dream, and only when he was suddenly mine did I begin to see him for who he actually was. I was afraid of a future with him, a future of uncertainty and too many problems. Over time I knew I wouldn't be able to be the only responsible adult who has to care for two babies.

For two years I continued to miss him. Even after Tom was born. Not all the time, it would hit me occasionally and all at once I would fall, tumbling down, unable to latch on to an available branch to prevent my crash into the abyss of loneliness. I was furious at him. Why hadn't he been clearer from the start? I was angry that I'd developed hopes and expectations, that he hid his true situation from me. I guess any choice in which we leave the heart behind is not really a complete choice. But the anger subsided over the years, the feelings faded, and the love that had been there eventually died. Suffocated.

I don't know why all this stuff resurfaced. I had such a weird day. When I got back to the office in the late afternoon, I immediately went to the computer to see if anything had arrived in the internal mail, when I suddenly realized how stupid I was. Why hadn't I realized that someone could hack my computer during the day? Anyone who wanted to could snoop around when I was out and the computer was on. Anyone who knew that Julia has all the passwords in her emergency drawer. But why would anyone want to do that?

I've never written to this mailbox from work, so I searched through my regular email and Facebook to see whether I'd left any incriminating correspondence with you. There was nothing special there, but just be sure, I deleted all the evidence. That was also weird, you know? When I turned off the computer and was about to leave, I suddenly felt a dull pain in the fingers of my right hand. When I looked at them they seemed totally normal, but it felt as if they were swollen again. At the time, by the way, they really did heal quickly, even before I discovered I was pregnant. But tonight it was like my body was trying to warn me about something, like a traffic signal. It was reminding me of a retired pain that's still hiding in there, an old pain that's been hibernating.

10:36 p.m.
1. I love you.
2. I don't like your exes.
3. OK, I hate Oren.
4. And now I hate Ziv too.
5. I love reading you.
6. It's hard for you to release the truth.
7. But when you do, you fly like a butterfly.
8. I hate your fear of me.
9. I don't eavesdrop on you. I listen a little every once in a while.
10. And if there was only one thought I could plant in your head, I'd make sure you realize how much I love you.

10:38 p.m.	When you say things like that it actually does get the job done... and by the way - I really love the bracelet.
10:46 p.m.	You know you didn't just get it for no reason, right?
10:46 p.m.	I'm sure I'll have to pay for it somehow.
10:46 p.m.	Have you noticed what it's done to you?
10:46 p.m.	Was it supposed to do something?
10:47 p.m.	Can't you feel it? You've passed a level. A stage.
10:47 p.m.	I didn't know there were levels... why am I always the last to know everything around here?
10:48 p.m.	Don't you feel that your ability to heal pain is growing stronger?
10:48 p.m.	Really? Good thing you told me.
10:48 p.m.	My head has been perfect for two weeks. Nothing hurts.
10:48 p.m.	Wow... but how can I feel an ability? Hey, when you pass a level do you finally get the user manual?
10:49 p.m.	No, when you pass a level you realize that you're the one writing it.
01:23 a.m.	Michael, are you awake?
01:23 a.m.	Yes.
01:23 a.m.	You keep strange hours.
01:23 a.m.	So do you. Why are you up? Could you feel me thinking about you?
01:24 a.m.	Maybe... I don't know. Actually I'm lying in bed with my laptop and it suddenly occurred to me that you've never told me anything about your previous relationships.

01:24 a.m.	What's to tell. You think I'm some kind of Casanova?
01:25 a.m.	It's not the quantity that counts.
01:25 a.m.	People who hear thoughts don't fall in love very often. But when they do, it happens fast. I fell in love with you right after we met at the bakery, the minute I started listening to you.
01:25 a.m.	And that never happened to you before?
01:25 a.m.	Before you there was only one love.
01:25 a.m.	When?
01:25 a.m.	It ended nine years ago. We were together for a little over a year.
01:26 a.m.	And why did it end?
01:27 a.m.	She left me.
01:27 a.m.	Why?
01:28 a.m.	Good question. It was a long time ago. And since meeting you I've forgotten there was a time when I still looked for an answer.

To: Sheera and Michael <softspoons@gmail.com>
From: Sheera and Michael <softspoons@gmail.com>
January 25, 2016 at 9:56 p.m.
Subject: A WTF discussion with Moni

I was pretty pleased when I awoke this morning. I must have been excited by the fact that without knowing, I'd passed some invisible level or aced an obscure test. I looked at the bracelet, and for a moment I felt something strange – it was on my right wrist, but I could've sworn I could feel it on my left wrist as well. What's this, I said to myself, did he give me some kind of an enchanted bracelet? And why do I feel it on both wrists, like handcuffs? Is it something kinky, or just that basic urge for control that comes with all men?

Tom was a little preoccupied this morning, I tried to milk him for details, asked if something had happened, but all I got back was a determined "nothing". We were silent all the way to school, and he insisted on keeping his backpack on when he got into the car. It bothered me, but I didn't want to fight, knowing the endless bickering that gets us stuck for hours in stupid arguments. So I tried ignoring the little body scrunched uncomfortably into the seat beside me, and distracted myself by thinking about other things. What did that mean, that I'd passed a level? For a few weeks now, I'd been falling asleep with you and the b-drops almost every night, you say my strength is growing, but the truth is I have less and less of a clue where all this is headed.

Tom was quiet, clumsily strapped into the seat beside me with his backpack, and suddenly I knew exactly how he felt. Sitting on the edge in an impossible position, waiting for the ride to be over, exactly the way I've been feeling since starting this mailbox and documenting everything with you. I mean, I'd finished reconstructing, and as far as I could see, what I was doing at night was working. You said I had to find my power and from there we could move on, so I think I've found it, haven't I?

Tom and his giant backpack got off pointedly by the school gate, and made their way to class without looking back. As I headed to work on my own, you called.

You realized it's working because I told you it was, but you have to learn to feel it on your own.

So that's what I have to do now? That's the next level?

You could say that, but it's not the only thing.

So would you start answering my questions? I've got too many piled up. Like, I don't understand how you make people change their minds. What did you do to people at the station? To Erik, to Moni?

You want to rush things, but you need patience, you said again, like a broken record.

Why can't you just tell me? I was beginning to get annoyed.

Because it doesn't work that way, you said. You learn from trial and error. If I tell you exactly how I work, you'll instinctively try to imitate me instead of searching for your own unique power, don't you get it?

I was silent. Sometimes I really hate your answers.

You've found one ability, and you have another very important one. The bracelet is supposed to accelerate the process, to help you find it. And you'll see that when you combine the two, you'll understand more about the first one.

Another one??? Good thing the light had changed and I stopped, as I needed a moment to process. So do you also have another ability besides hearing thoughts?

Yes.

Are you serious?? I quietly wondered what was coming – maybe you had x-ray vision and a bionic leg.

You laughed. You think I'm a character from a comic book you read with your son? What you have is not a superpower, my darlin' Sea Song, it's senses that are overly receptive, and they're related to each other.

So what kind of overly receptive sense do you have besides the thoughts? I asked, barely believing we were having this bizarre conversation.

I can feel when danger is coming, you said.

What does that have to do with anything?

It'll only confuse you if we talk about it now, okay? One step at a time.

So can you at least tell me what's going on with the bracelet? I asked impatiently, and your answer fit beautifully with the annoying traffic jam I was in: try to figure out what you feel.

I didn't answer, but everything felt stuck. Is this what things are going to look like from now on? I'll be the challenged one trying to follow directions, and whenever I make any progress, you'll be the one to send me looking for another ability?

You're just driving yourself nuts, you said, would you relax? Disengage for a minute. Stop that assembly line inside your head. You overthink everything, and it kills your intuition. Chill out, believe me, you're close.

Fine, I spat, and the call ended. There was an endless line of cars on the road. I suddenly realized that it wasn't only you. Erik was still absent and that meant I was stuck with the show too.

Enough, I decided, I have to start pushing things along on my own, at least with the show, and come to think of it - all I need is a silent nod from Moni. Since the car was practically moving at snail speed, I used the time to finally think up a Hebrew name for the show. I couldn't keep the name "Masterpiece" because that was too close to the competing channel's "Master Chef". Besides, a show about writing in Hebrew should have a Hebrew name. I thought about words derived from art, creativity, expressing the soul, fear of exposure, desire to convey the truth in a way that had never been done, and by the time I reached the hot and cramped parking lot, the best name I could come up with was "The Write Stuff". I wasn't sure it was perfect, but it was definitely good enough as a working title.

When I reached the office I didn't even stop at my desk to put down my things. I headed right to Moni and asked Ruthie to find me ten minutes in his schedule. You're in luck, she said, he has a few minutes right now, go right in.

Moni sat at his computer with a furrowed brow. After all these years I know him so well – the nuances, the little expressions, the entire spectrum of moods – and exactly how to behave in order to get what I want in the shortest time possible. When Moni is preoccupied with something, you need to speak quietly and use short sentences, and then there's a good chance of getting a quick yes because he doesn't have the time for petty issues.

I won't waste your time, I said, standing at the door. I just thought that because of Erik's unexpected sick leave, we should move the development ahead without him. When he gets back we'll fill him in. It'll be better for everybody.

I expected him to say "no problem" and get back to his screen, but he just gave me a long icy look, which got me really stressed, and then quietly said – sit down for a minute. A cruel little chill grappled me. On those rare times when Moni isn't one hundred percent on board with me, something just makes my blood freeze. What is it? I asked in a low tone and sat on the couch.

I want to tell you something, as someone who's looking out for your best interests, he said.

Of course, I said, and inside I thought, shit, this really doesn't sound good.

Maybe I'll start with a question, he said. Do you have some sort of outline of how you want the show to look in Israel? Ideas? About structure, setting, casting, budget? Have you done anything?

I sat there, dumbstruck. Moni never talks to me like that. I'd come in to work out a minor manipulation and found myself being scolded. A tiny speck of dust got stuck in my throat and I couldn't swallow it. Look, I coughed, I have plenty of ideas, I've even got a pretty good idea for a name, I just haven't put them down on paper yet.

So let's start by you putting them down on paper and sending them out to everyone relevant, including Erik, and we'll go from there, he said.

Sure, I said in fake nonchalance, while practically gluing my knees together to keep them from trembling. I gathered my things coolly, as if nothing had happened, told him he'd have something by the end of the day, forced a smile and left.

My heart was pounding like crazy, as if reconsidering its competence for supervising the circulatory system. I'd never been so frightened by something Moni had said to me, and realizing this scared me even more. When I reached my office, I shut the door behind me and just stood there for about five minutes, my back to the wall, trying to restore my breathing. True, it was an unpleasant conversation, but what had gotten me so terrified? The back of my neck was covered in cold sweat and my whole body was shaking. At some point I felt the weight of my bag and the papers I had in my hand, so I went to the desk, put my stuff down and began pacing back and forth, my knees weak, striving to regain control.

What the hell happened that made me feel this way? Am I missing the signs again? Maybe Erik had spoken to him, said something, made something up, trashed me. I stopped for a moment, dialed Julia's number and asked her how Erik was doing. He's a little better, she said, but he's still in the hospital and I don't know when he'll get out.

Okay, I had to admit that my theory was not very solid. Even Erik would have trouble conspiring from a hospital bed. Could Moni be angry about something else? Does he think that I'd been neglecting him lately? I tried very hard for him not to feel that way, but maybe it wasn't working. Recently my mind wasn't as focused on work, because I'm focused on you, and those spiritual verities about consciousness and intuition and feelings and God knows what else. You slip into my thoughts at every free moment, distracting me, diverting me. Maybe Moni feels that I'm not all there like I used to be, and that it's because of the show. Maybe he's afraid that if I dedicate my time to developing the show I'll have to neglect my primary responsibility?

I glanced at the clock and realized how late it was. I sat down, fired up the computer and began running through my messages, but my hands were still shaking. I stopped for a moment and logged into Facebook. You were online. A sharp stab sliced into my back, and some vague sense of sadness filled me, like something bad was happening, and I didn't know what. I wrote "Hey, baby" with a smile emoji in the chat window, and your immediate response was – What's wrong?

Can't I send you a smiley without you thinking that something's wrong? I asked.

Get on with it, you wrote. I know that this is the busiest time of your day and you're not here for nothing. Just say it already.

I couldn't tell if you were angry or if I was only imagining, because I'd left all of my cool in Moni's office, under the couch. I told you about our brief meeting and asked if you had any idea what he was thinking about me. You disappeared for a few minutes, and then wrote – don't be afraid. Moni loves you. He has no hidden agenda. You caught him at a bad moment, but just between us, he's right.

You've really been taking your time, so just do what you do best – start writing down what you want to do with the show.

Then you added – and don't forget - when you write something, it's not just a regular document written by a normal person, alright?

What? You left me with a finely chopped salad of emotions. On one hand you were calming me down about the Moni situation, but on the other you were always saying these things I couldn't understand. I called Gidi, head of the promo department, who draws out his Helloooo like secretaries in old-fashioned movies, and asked if there was any chance he could put together his most creative copywriters to brainstorm ideas for the show. He covered the phone with his palm and I heard a blur of dim shouts, after which we set up a four o'clock meeting. That's it, I said. Enough with the bullshit. Today I begin working.

Suddenly I was much more efficient. I finished up everything I had to do pretty early, and even had time to take Avi to lunch. We started talking about "The Write Stuff", about angles that could work well with the commercial side. Think marketing content, he said, chewing his hamburger, you can't go to the supermarket with authors, so bring me ideas that'll go well with sponsorships.

At four o'clock I met Gidi and his copywriters that call each other "my brother" and love calling me "sister", and we agreed that first off, we need to encourage intrigues among the participants. Maybe we should go with the message that the pen is mightier than the sword, I said, and Gidi made a barfing sound and said that with all due respect for the message, the celebrity is mightier than the pen. We started throwing around ideas for a host that would bring in the numbers, and decided to include not only authors but famous actors on our judges' panel as well. We agreed that during the auditions we'd choose those who have the most active Facebook accounts in order to push the shares on the social networks, we laughed a lot, and I left them ninety minutes later holding a laptop bursting with ideas. That's it – I had enough for a preliminary proposal.

I went into my office and began to put it together. I glanced at the clock, it was six. Damn, I'm such a shitty mom, I thought, I was supposed to be home by now. I called the babysitter. Tom was in the middle of a game on PlayStation with a friend and didn't have much patience for me, which calmed me down. When he says "fine" about everything, it means he's busy with something he likes. To ease my conscience even further, once again I played the junk-food card, immediately becoming mom of the year as I promised to be home in an hour and a half with McDonalds' meals for both of them.

I turned my full focus back onto my document, laying it out in immaculate headers and bullet points, explaining why the Israeli viewer needs a more colorful version than the Italian original (instead of admitting we needed a few changes for the sake of the ratings), concluding with a grandiose wording of our aim and vision, just the way Moni likes it, as if this program is so important it would save Israel from impending doom. I headed the document with a huge title - "The Write Stuff", and at 7 p.m. on the dot, sent it to the entire management.

On the way to McDonald's the babysitter called to say she really had to leave and I said it was okay, she could go because I'd be there in ten minutes. But when I arrived it turned out that Tom's friend had gone home too, and a wave of guilt sloshed over me when I saw him sitting alone on the sofa in front of the TV, bouncing a little ball on the floor. Why did he deserve being the son of a single mom who was unwilling to give up her career for him? I hugged him fiercely, fighting back flickers of tears. You're a very special boy, I whispered. I'm not special, mom, stop saying that already, he grumbled, extracting himself from my arms. I didn't say anything. I thought he was just mad because I'd come home late. We sat at the table, dunking our fries in a pinkish goop of ketchup and mayonnaise, and without meaning to, I ate his friend's entire soggy hamburger.

After Tom fell asleep I was drawn here, as always, to write you. Strange how I've gotten used to this new routine. So now I'll pause for a minute, trying to "figure out on my own" why I feel so glum. What you said keeps echoing through my head – that even when I write some ordinary document it's never ordinary and never normal. I logged on to my email account to see whether anyone had responded to my paper, but nothing. Maybe it's not as good as I thought it was, did I put it together too hastily? I don't know why I'm suddenly filled with such insecurity. It's probably the overload. Maybe we should start thinking of a new system, Michael. I'm not sure I can discover my other ability on my own, if I want to function properly at work and at home.

10:31 p.m.	All of your stories are about how you respond to reality. Has it ever occurred to you that maybe you're the one creating it?
10:31 p.m.	And all of your feedback is full of patronizing comments. Has it ever occurred to you that maybe you could say something nice? Like about how I got my act together after my talk with Moni and finally started working?
10:32 p.m.	I'm proud of you. I'm just not sure you understood what happened in his office.
10:32 p.m.	Why, what did I miss? Are you implying that you know that Erik did talk to him about me?
10:33 p.m.	Erik's in no condition to talk to anyone. Do you realize what it means to be in the hospital for two weeks? Sometimes I really don't get you.
10:33 p.m.	What, it's that bad?
10:34 p.m.	Erik's out of the game for the moment. Listen, something's screwed up with your interpretations. You misread what Moni was saying too. He meant stop investing all your energy in this rivalry with Erik. Do you really not get that it's hurting you?

10:35 p.m.	No, it's you who doesn't get it. That's exactly what I just wrote you, so why do you feel the need to criticize me all the time?
10:36 p.m.	Who's criticizing you? I'm trying to show you something. You're addicted to conflict. It's what fuels you. When you're in a power struggle, suddenly life has meaning. You can't do without it. You fight with Erik because it turns you on. You want to beat him more than you want the show. You want Moni to choose you over him. It's important that you acknowledge that part of yourself, you understand what I'm saying?
10:36 p.m.	Why is it so important?
10:37 p.m.	Because it's connected to your ability. If you realize how it magnetizes you, you'll be able to control it. You have to identify the bomb before you can defuse it.
10:37 p.m.	You're totally exaggerating. It's not a "bomb" and I'm not "addicted". Right after the talk with Moni I shaped up and forgot about Erik.
10:38 p.m.	Yeah, you put your favorite toy in the closet. Let's see when you get the urge to take it out again.
10:38 p.m.	Michael, do me a favor, try talking to me without being so condescending, can you do that?
10:39 p.m.	Who's condescending? I just gave you an example, relax. Maybe we should talk about it some other time.
10:40 p.m.	Yeah, of course, always some other time. This time you don't have a headache for a change, so you've found another excuse.
10:41 p.m.	Listen, you're on the edge. And I don't feel like fighting. Can we let this go and pick up again tomorrow?

10:41 p.m.   And what if I say I don't feel like picking it up again tomorrow, will it matter? Are you even waiting for my answer? I've had it up to here with the way you try to dominate everything.

To: Sheera and Michael <softspoons@gmail.com>
From: Sheera and Michael <softspoons@gmail.com>
January 26, 2016 at 7:18 a.m.
Subject: I don't mind fighting every night if this is what happens after...

How did you do it...?

I didn't know that on top of everything, you have a special ability to make up with me from a distance.

It was just after I got in bed last night, still pretty pissed at you.

I set my alarm clock and put it on the night stand, and suddenly I was so scared, almost like that time Tom came in and interrupted in the middle of my candy. All at once I felt you there, so close, as if you'd entered my bedroom through the walls and just jumped on top of me, playfully, like a kid, totally ignoring how angry I was.... I've never felt you so strongly, Michael. Is it possible that I really sunk into the mattress because of your body's weight on mine? I don't get it, how could there be such strong sensations but no real contact? For a moment I thought I was hallucinating, or having a dream about an alien attack, but you were so sweet... it felt like you were kissing me.

I awoke very early this morning, still shrouded in you. So I took advantage of that lost time before the sun rises, when the small creatures of the night are tired but still haven't returned to their caves. That abandoned time when anything can happen and you can do anything you like, such as reaching out blindly for the nightstand drawer and pulling out a butterscotch drop. I hope my massage removed any memory of the headache that I thought came back to you last night...

07:20 a.m.   What's this, have you suddenly developed a sixth sense? I like the way you've started to feel things.

07:20 a.m.   I can guess why... I've decided to spare you the more pornographic details, but just so you know, I could feel everything you were doing there.

07:21 a.m.   That was my intention. That's what I wanted you to feel. You have to learn to separate... sex is one thing, and work is another. No need to mix them. Multitasking is for wimps. When you focus on one thing only, it enhances it.

07:21 a.m.   When you explain it like that, like last night, I can understand... you just need to give me more tangible examples of all those dazed rules of your ab-normal world.

07:22 a.m.   Why don't you write me why you want to be a normal person so badly?

07:23 a.m.   Why, is there anyone who doesn't want to be normal?

07:24 a.m.   I don't know. I'm just asking you to write about it. Try to understand yourself. It's important, I swear.

To: Sheera and Michael <softspoons@gmail.com>
From: Sheera and Michael <softspoons@gmail.com>
January 26, 2016 at 9:54 p.m.
Subject: Not exactly a normal person

Is it possible that the bracelet you gave me reminds me of things? I don't know what kind of witches weaved it in what sort of dark caves, but sometimes I think it's a spell-binding bracelet that yanks at my memory cells and draws out forgotten events. Not that I needed anyone to remind me, as this is a story you can't really forget, though it's the kind of story that you pack carefully in a sealed box and store on a deserted shelf in your attic and try not to poke around it too much after that. Come to think of it, what I'm about to tell you didn't just happen on one particular day, and I'm not sure I remember how and when it began. I only remember that at some point it became clear to me that my father is not exactly a normal person.

At first it was still within "reasonable". Apparently he was just overprotective, ever since I can remember. When I was twelve, for instance, he still wouldn't let me cross the street on my own. At some point I began lying, it was impossible to live with that rule. Any outing became a battle. This still went on when I was a teenager – I did manage to receive a street crossing license after a series of strict exams, but new decrees came along every day. He wanted to know where I was at any given moment, and whenever I left the house, at some point he'd go out to roam the streets looking for me. One time I was cramming for a test at Rona's, and suddenly her mother walked in and said – your father's here. I thought he was in the living room, but turns out he was standing on the street, across from their house. He'd been there for hours until Rona's mother suddenly recognized him through the window.

I'd shrug at my friends and say, "it's part of being an only child, your parents are crazy overprotective," but at home I had to fight for my right to breathe. I asked him why he did it, I was furious with him. I didn't know where you were, I was worried, he'd say. But I told you! I'd fume, and could never understand why he couldn't remember what I said. It took me a while to realize that he was simply lying. I'd yell at him to stop, that he was embarrassing me, and when I tried talking to my mother, she'd look at me helplessly and say, you know your father, when he sets his mind on something there's nothing you can do to stop him.

I thought that it was just hard for him to accept my growing up. What's with your dad? They'd ask in class, and I despised them for it, despised myself even more. I filled an entire teenage diary with ferocious entries about how I hated my moonstruck, deranged, lunatic of a father, because there was no one I could tell. I wanted to be just like everyone else, to shake him off, to be left alone. At some point I just stopped going out, I was so scared of those unexpected surprise visits of his.

But just when I stopped going out, his wandering became even weirder. I remember waking from a dream this one night, getting up to go to the bathroom in the dark, a little scared, and on the way back, peeking into my parents' bedroom. My mother was sleeping there alone, and the sheets on my father's side were all bunched up and stray. I waited in bed, awake, and after an hour or so I heard him walk in and head straight for the bedroom. A few minutes later I tiptoed to their room to have a look, and there he was in his pajamas, asleep beside her. The next day, I asked my mother where my father had gone last night, and she looked at me blankly and said – what do you mean? Nowhere. I was afraid to say anything, and it occurred to me that he might be cheating on her, though it didn't really seem logical. Not only was I incapable of picturing my father in a romantic position with a mistress, he'd never have gone to see her wearing flannel pajamas with bunnies printed on them.

Another time I was at the supermarket, juggling a loaf of bread, some bananas and a carton of milk as I made my way to the register, and I ran into a friend of my mother's. How are you, sweetheart? She asked in a saccharine voice and pursed her pink-painted lips, her eyes looking me up and down as if I were naked. Before I could say anything, she said loudly, as if it was important that everyone hear - your father called us last night at 1:30 in the morning to ask for the name of the guide that did our tour last year, can you believe it? She gave me a lengthy stare and I began to stutter. When she realized I had no idea what she was talking about, she let out a short artificial titter. Never mind, just say hello for me, and tell your mom she should check if the clock needs fixing. She turned her butt to me, packed into a tight striped skirt, and wiggled on her way, pushing her overloaded cart towards the cashier.

Did you know Dad called Miriam and David in the middle of the night? I asked my mother when I got home. She looked at me and frowned. Don't go believing everything Miriam says, she sneered, taking the bananas from me and muttering "witch" under her breath.

One day when I was climbing up the stairs as I got back from school, the second floor neighbors' door opened. Tell your mom that your father paid us another visit this morning, the neighbor grumbled at me. I didn't understand, and when once again I found myself in the role of the courier bearing the message to my mother, she locked herself in the bathroom for a long time, and I couldn't hear anything but I knew she did it because she didn't want me to see her crying. Turns out there'd been a few incidents where my father had knocked on the neighbors' door at five a.m., asking politely if he could borrow a cup of sugar, as if the sun was shining and it was the middle of the day. When they said something about the time, he got annoyed and called them stingy.

Dad, you've got to stop this, I said in the gravest tone I could muster, when he got home from work.

Stay out of it! He shouted. I'm the parent here, you understand?

Quietly, in the kitchen, I told my mother she needed to take him to get some tests done. Are you nuts? She almost stabbed me with her petrified eyes. Don't you know you can't tell your father what to do? How am I supposed to take him to the doctor against his will?

A few days later, when he knocked on the neighbors' door at 4 a.m., they called the police. When I startled awake from the loud yelling it was still dark out. I tried opening my room door, but it was locked from the outside. Mom! I pounded the door again and again as the yelling from the stairwell continued, but nobody came. When she finally returned and opened my door I asked where my father was. He needs a little rest, she stammered, he went away for a few days. She was so disheveled, her hair was tied back but a thousand strands were going wild around her face. Her appearance scared me. I stood in the hallway, finally free, but frozen and mute. She looked at me for a moment, her eyes glazed, turned her head as if trying to decide where to go, then simply walked into her bedroom and shut the door softly. I stood there for a few minutes, staring at the closed door, then went to the living room, sat down, got up, sat down again, and then paced back and forth in the apartment wondering what would happen now and what my father meant when he always told me I was an oddball, until it was time to get ready for school.

Later it was just… strange. Our house had always been quiet, with barely a word said at dinner, but my father's sudden absence brought on a different kind of silence, empty and piercing. Every time I asked my mother where he was, she said – don't worry about him, he's in a health sanatorium. She never looked in my eyes, and I never said a thing but I despised her in those days, mostly because she was such a terrible liar. After about two weeks I overheard her talking on the phone in an extremely low voice. I waited for her to finish, then walked determinedly into their bedroom. She sat on the bed, folding laundry. I looked at the two piles of underwear slowly growing beside her, instead of the three I was used to.

What's a psychotic breakdown? I demanded to know. She looked at me, shocked, and then collected herself and said that it was none of my business and don't I dare ever eavesdrop on her conversations again. A wave of rage rose in me. I want to visit him, I said, trying hard not to scream. They don't allow children in there, she responded, staring at the laundry. I'm fourteen and a half, I yelled, I'm not a child. She continued folding determinedly, carefully, and I looked at her furiously, loathing her lame answers, and suddenly I noticed a streak of grey hairs sprouting at her temple. How long had that been there without me noticing? I could swear that she hadn't had a single grey hair the night before. I stopped and just stared at her for a moment, her pale lips, her crouched back. Suddenly I was afraid she'd start crying again.

What should I say when they ask me where he is? I asked quietly. She didn't look at me, just mumbled that it was best to say he was on rest leave because he was worn out from work. I stood there like a mummy, not knowing what to say. Up until that moment I hadn't realized that she really didn't know what to do. I sat quietly on the edge of the bed, and placed my hand on hers. We sat there for a few minutes in total silence, and then she put her other hand on mine and smiled and said – you've got golden hands, Sheeri'leh. I didn't know how that had anything to do with anything, so I just asked if she wanted me to make her some tea and finish folding the laundry for her. That was the longest conversation we ever had about the subject, and then I stopped asking, because what's the point in asking someone who's more lost than you are.

You know the old joke about the guy who tells his wife he's going out for some cigarettes, disappears and comes back a year later? He sits in his armchair and flips through the paper, and his stunned wife asks, where the hell were you? He's so focused on the paper he doesn't even look at her. What do you mean where was I, he says, I went out for cigarettes, I told you.

That's how it was with my father. One day he just came back. When I got home from school he was there in the living room, in his armchair, reading the paper. He raised his eyes, looked at me and asked how was school, as if nothing had happened. I looked at him and wanted to ask, when did you get back? What did they do to you? But the words had abandoned me. For a whole minute I just stood there, unable to move or pronounce a single syllable. He went back to the newspaper and raised it to conceal his face, his pale fingers trembling slightly as he gripped the edges. I quietly went to my room, as a sharp pain spread through my throat like an infection. I put my school bag down, took a deep breath, but the air wouldn't come in, as if there was no room in my lungs. After a few minutes I came out, pretended to be on my way to the kitchen, went over to him and gave him a little kiss on the cheek. He cringed and forced a tiny, almost polite little smile. What's going on, Dad? I managed to ask softly, although the pain in my throat was getting to be really bad.

No news, he said, in a voice nearly identical to the voice he used to have.

He was a little bit thinner, but other than that he hadn't changed. Maybe just something in his eyes – there was less anger or something, I couldn't really say what it was. Nobody needed to tell me that it was best not to question my father. He made the rules in the house, and if he didn't volunteer information, there was no point in trying to get him to talk.

Later, as the three of us sat down to dinner, I noticed that the old silence had returned – the silence I was used to. I tried to listen and decipher it, to understand how one silence could be so different from another. At some point my father looked at me gravely and said: I hope you're old enough to understand not to discuss what happened with anyone.

Yes, of course, I said, the salad serving spoon trembling in my hand.

I've never argued with him about anything since then. At some point I discovered the bottle of yellow pills that became part of the permanent design of the kitchen, hidden behind the kettle. Whenever I'd boil water for coffee it would calm me, give me a sense of security, as if as long as it was there, nothing would happen. And since then, everything really did work out somehow. I wondered whether he'd always been like that without me noticing, or if one day he'd just flown over the cuckoo's nest. How does something like that just happen to someone? But the questions sank in my stomach, unanswered, and meanwhile he even found a new job, and none of us talked about what had happened any more.

The next part of my story took place about a month before I completed my military service. Rona called me all excited one morning, to say she'd seen an ad in the newspaper announcing a short story competition. This year we're doing it, she announced, and that very day she sent in a story she wrote when she met Eyal, about a physicist who tries to crack the formula for finding the person that completes you. I said I didn't have any ideas, but promised to try and think of something. As an only child I was stationed at Headquarters, near home, I had the night shift, it was boring, so I grabbed some stray papers and wrote a story.

I called it "My Sanity Went Out for Some Air." I wrote it in first person, a monologue narrated by a man who's sure he's completely normal and cannot see what is eminently clear to everyone else around him. I didn't try to change the facts or disguise the source of my inspiration, just invented a different ending. My protagonist was also committed, but unlike my father he never got out. I hesitated about sending it in, I wasn't sure I liked what came flowing out of my pen that night. I let Rona read it and was surprised when she liked it. I thought she was just trying to make me feel good about myself. Where did you get the idea? she inquired, and I just shrugged, adhering to our family code though it was clear to me that she knew. That night I also let my mother read it. She always liked the poems I wrote, there were even one or two that I dedicated to her, and I needed a second opinion. We sat at the kitchen table, she dove into the words and I waited patiently as she read it through seriously. When she finished, she took off her glasses and just looked at me with a hollow gaze. Why are you doing this? She finally asked.

I started to stutter. I didn't know what to say. Do me a favor, she said, please tear this up into little pieces, okay?

No need to make such a big deal, I muttered to myself, who would be interested in such a stupid story anyway. That night I went up to the rooftop with a box of matches, and let the pages go up in flames. I stood there among the ashy scraps that fluttered in the wind around me, and couldn't understand why the hell my eyes were burning so bad.

Rona was shocked when I told her I'd decided not to send it in. You've got to lose your virginity and get something published or you'll never be able to write, she ruled. I didn't argue, nor did I tell her what my mom had said. I did have second thoughts for a minute, but it was too late – I'd burned the final copy as well as all the drafts.

A few weeks later I was discharged, and while applying to university I waitressed at a little café. One night when we were about to close, my eyes fell on the worn out remains of the daily paper. The headline on one of the inner pages defied me – winners of the short story competition. I drew up my courage and peeked. Rona's story had come in second place, and the winner was also a love story. My heart sank so fast it physically hurt. I knew that when I got home I'd find an ecstatic message on my machine from her. Envy burned my eyes even worse than the smoke on the rooftop when the fire seared my words. I have to focus on serious stuff, I told myself fiercely, I'm not cut out for this, who would ever want to read stories about insanity? I thoroughly crumpled up the paper, aimed for the wastebasket, and swished in the ball of its remains.

You know, it's strange when I think about it now. Why did I give up so easily? How did I even give in to what my mother wanted? I can dig in my heels till they bleed when I want to, and truth is my mother never knew how to insist on anything. For years I was sure I was being considerate. I didn't want to hurt them, those parents, who were the only family I had in the world, the people I loved most and hated at the same time. I could've changed some of the details, masked the identities, maybe even sent in the story anonymously. I chose to burn all those syllables on the rooftop, to turn my back on the ashes. After she won, Rona was offered a job as a journalist, and I went down a different road.

My father was worried that if anyone found out, he'd be fired from the new job he'd managed to find. He'd always taught me there were things that just shouldn't be said. I couldn't adopt my mother's pathetic lies, so at first when people asked, I'd say he had surgery and made up some illness. But the questions died down over time, and meanwhile, whenever I made coffee, I'd exchange secret looks with that bottle of yellow pills. To this day, when my dad makes trouble now and then, my mother whispers, let it go, you know he's not exactly a normal person.

By the way, I didn't tell you yesterday, but when I sat down for dinner with Tom, I was still bothered with what he'd said the night before. So in the middle of our French fries I asked him who in his opinion was a special boy, since it was obvious that he isn't. There's lots of them, he said. I asked if he could name any.

There's this kid in India, he said.

India? I asked, surprised. How do you know about kids in India?

I saw it online.

And what's special about him?

He has this little Siamese twin coming out of his neck.

Damn, Michael, do you get it? I suddenly realized that the more I insisted on telling Tom he was special, I was actually making him feel he was different, and not in a good way.

We used to have offensive names for kids with problems, nowadays they call them "children with special needs". It may seem really nice to us, but that's because when we were kids, there was a different meaning for the word "special". With our own kids, "special" has transformed from a compliment into something you just don't want to be. Kids want to be like everyone else. Especially a kid like Tom, who doesn't have a dad, which already makes his "special" status feel like a heavy millstone around his neck.

At night I lay beside him, inhaling the scent of his long silky hair.

Hey, I whispered, besides special kids, are there special moms too? Yeah, he said. And what kind of mom am I? I asked.

You're a regular mom, he said, and then hesitated for a moment and added: except for sometimes. For a minute the night he surprised me in the middle of the b-drop flashed through me, but I didn't say anything. I kept stroking his hair until he fell asleep, but a tiny anxiety pestered me inside. I think this kid can see and understand more than I can grasp. You know what I mean?

10:23 p.m.	You're surprised that Tom doesn't want to be special? Neither does his mom.
10:23 p.m.	But you don't tell me I'm special, you say I'm not normal. Maybe you should stop saying that.
10:24 p.m.	You want me to sell you lies, Sheera? Your sensitivity isn't normal. It's got nothing to do with your dad. Your father is unstable and needs pills, but you're not normal in a completely different way. A girl that's come into the world with senses that are extremely exposed. Who can feel me going down on her when she's in her bed and I'm in mine.
10:25 p.m.	Stop it, Michael... I'm serious, don't deviate me now. I don't understand how I never felt those exposed senses until now.
10:25 p.m.	Because you shut them down. Locked yourself up. And now it's strange to reopen. It'll all work out in the end, trust me. You have to get used to it, my Sea Song. Readjust your definition of "not

	normal", and maybe then Tom will also agree to be a special kid.
10:26 p.m.	Everything is always the other way around with you.
10:26 p.m.	With me? Start getting your definitions straight. Like, how would you define what you write here? Have you thought about that?
10:27 p.m.	I document everything that happens. I don't get your question, wasn't it your idea?
10:27 p.m.	Yes, but you're creating something. You're putting your energy into detail, validating the words. What's your intention? What do you want to make happen?
10:28 p.m.	I want to find my power. I thought it was obvious.
10:29 p.m.	A person needs to know what he wants. You know most people don't get what they want out of life, right? There's a reason. They think the world is cruel, but the reason is they don't really know how to define it. Definitions and words have power. Especially yours.
10:30 p.m.	Are you trying to imply something?
10:31 p.m.	I'm not implying, I'm telling you. Haven't you noticed that whatever you really want, happens?
10:31 p.m.	What?? It's the other way around, if anything. I've noticed that what I want doesn't happen.
10:31 p.m.	Maybe there's something you want even more and that's what's standing in your way. Have you thought about that?
10:32 p.m.	Fine, you want clear definitions? Then I want our relationship to change. I want this whole guiding thing to stop. If we really love each oth-

	er, I want to feel it in real life. You understand? Not only in your "cosmos", and not only in this mailbox.
10:32 p.m.	I want that too, Sheera. I'm dying to say "fuck it" and just go wild with you. But I have to watch us. So please do that too. Pay attention to your words. And if in a week or so you realize that you got something wrong, go back and change it. Change the words.
10:32 p.m.	There's nothing to change. I thought it through before I told you.
10:33 p.m.	Sometimes you get it wrong even when you think it through. Everyone makes mistakes. Especially when it comes to love. It's the simplest and most complicated thing in the world. My mother says that the worst human fear is not of war or death, but of true love.
10:33 p.m.	Sounds a bit over the top. Why would she say such a thing?
10:33 p.m.	I don't know.
10:34 p.m.	So is that why you're also afraid to love me?
10:34 p.m.	There's no love without fear, Sheera. Think how long it took you to be able to say you love me, although we both felt it very fast. And you think it's easy for me to love you? You're constantly suspicious. Kissing and then kicking. It's scary. Like at any moment you could get up and leave.
10:34 p.m.	Are you really afraid of losing me?
10:34 p.m.	Above all I can't believe you're still capable of asking me such things.

To: Sheera and Michael <softspoons@gmail.com>
From: Sheera and Michael <softspoons@gmail.com>
January 27, 2016 at 8:41 p.m.
Subject: Okay. I have a confession to make. I saw you today

I was at lunch with this asshole, Israel's biggest douchebag of an agent, who pretends to be really nice, peaches and cream, but if Moni hadn't asked he'd never have taken a meeting with me. As it was he set up the meeting and then canceled, and then at the last minute said he could make it, and I had to drop everything and get there in twenty minutes. Nor could I say anything because that's just the type of guy he is, and the thing is he doesn't even have to try to change his shitty personality because everyone needs him. Anyway, one of the actors he represents would be perfect to host "The Write Stuff". So I had to drag myself downtown in the middle of the day with all the traffic and parking to meet him at that new restaurant on Ehad Ha'am St.

To make a long story even longer, we sat at a corner table, and naturally, being the gentleman that he is, he stuck me in the less comfortable seat right behind a pillar, and we started looking over our menus – meaning, I pretended to read it but was actually planning how I'd incidentally slip what I needed into our chat, so he wouldn't think it was the reason for the meeting and immediately make impossible demands. And suddenly, in the middle of my scheming, the door opened, and everything stood still as you casually waltzed in. For a minute I wondered if you knew I was there and had shown up deliberately.

You couldn't see me as I was behind the pillar, but I saw you perfectly. You walked in your catlike steps, running your fingers through your hair to smooth it out, and beamed when you came up to a young blonde who sat at the bar, legs bare, tanned, crossed, armed in huge sunglasses as if a thousand invisible spotlights were gleaming right at her.

You kissed on both cheeks as you placed your hand on her lower back, a bit too close to her ass if you ask me, mumbled something incomprehensible, I couldn't hear it, I just saw you smile, and before I could collect myself and use both hands to catch my heart which had started bouncing all over the place like a deranged rubber ball, she got up, took her purse, and you both started walking towards the door. You let her exit first, because unlike Agent Asshole you really are the perfect gentleman, and I have no idea where you went from there. I hope you went to another restaurant, or even to hell for all I care, as long as you didn't go to your apartment.

You disappeared outside, and I looked at the agent and felt dead inside, as if you'd shot me in the chest and left with my punctured soul. The world could have come to an end right at that very minute as far as I was concerned, but unfortunately it didn't. I realized I'd missed at least three sentences and that I had no idea what he was talking about. I just pulled together the little I still had left in me to manage to fake an authentic-looking smile, as he stared at me, looking pretty baffled.

Look... I'm willing to put up with a lot of shit from you, as you've noticed. I can flow with your crazy ideas about this power shit and all these stupid rules, but there's a limit to what I can take. And I'm not talking about how the entire meeting got fucked. Or about the fact there's no chance in hell he'll give me the actor I want unless Moni or Erik step in. I can't believe I'm saying this, but I'm actually waiting for Erik to get better and come back, because I can't see how I can fix what happened without his help. Yeah, I'm in that deep.

Throughout the entire meeting I made a huge effort just to stop myself from doing the only thing I wanted to do – getting up and dashing out into the turbulent streets of Tel Aviv as if I were being chased by a pack of wild starving hyenas, running all the way home, ripping the sky apart with my bawling till my lungs hurt, my mascara streaming black rivers down my face.

Michael, my whole body hurt. Nothing like this has even happened to me. I felt like I was disintegrating, really coming apart at the seams. I needed all the energy I had left to hold it together, or I'd scatter with the wind. It was fucking scary. I shivered the whole way back to the office, couldn't keep my foot on the gas pedal. When I finally got into the parking lot I lay on the back seat of the car and couldn't get out. And just between us, the agent is nothing. Thing is, I can't do this anymore. I can't have you keeping so many secrets, not letting me into your life even a little. I want to know who she is. And I want to know what's going on between you. I want the truth, and I don't care how bad it is.

8:49 p.m.		You're killing me.
8:49 p.m.		You killed me first. So spill it. Speak up. Shoot.
8:54 p.m.		You're crazy. I met Maya today. A serial wantrepreneur. Only thirty, and she's already got two start-ups under her belt. She's now on her third. It's always "the Uber of" something. I invested in her second one two years ago. A convention registering app that identifies participants at the entrance by a 3D photo, but in zero time and for zero money. Never mind. The idea was good, she's a brilliant enthusiast, but she can't follow through. At some point she always finds a cooler idea and abandons. I knew that when I put in the money, but I thought development would be faster. So then there were problems, she quit, the money evaporated, the start-up shut down. Now she wants me to invest in another idea. She's cute, but no chance. Sometimes I meet

	people even when I know nothing will come out of it. The restaurant was packed and she forgot to book a table, so we went somewhere else. By the way – she's a lesbian.
8:54 p.m.	Are you sure she's not bi?
8:55 p.m.	Bipolar?
8:55 p.m.	Bisexual, moron.
8:55 p.m.	I'm sure. And even if she was, it wouldn't matter. Trust me already, dammit. You're the one I love.
8:55 p.m.	You swear?
8:55 p.m.	On my mother.
8:55 p.m.	You actually promised to tell me about your mother, and you didn't of course. Why doesn't she ever come visit you with your dad?
8:56 p.m.	Because she's dead.
8:56 p.m.	Oh... I didn't know. You keep talking about her as if she... doesn't matter. I didn't know. I'm really sorry.
8:56 p.m.	It's OK, it's not your fault. And it happened a long time ago. But you're a drama queen from hell. You have no idea how you killed me with that story.
8:56 p.m.	Neither do you. With all due respect to jealousy tantrums, I swear nothing like this has ever happened to me. Not even close. I was shaking for hours like I had a high fever. I couldn't control it.
8:56 p.m.	I think it's part of the side effects. You're picking up more sensations, even if you're not entirely conscious. And the bracelet intensifies it.
8:56 p.m.	What do you mean intensifies?
8:57 p.m.	There's a reason you can feel it on your left

	wrist too. There are two bracelets – one on your right hand, one on my left. We were connected before, but the bracelets intensify it so you can feel deeper layers. The emotions between us are strong, and when they connect, we both feel much more of our surroundings as well. The idea was to increase sensitivity so it'd be easier for you to develop awareness of what's happening around you. You wanted to move faster, remember? If you suddenly feel an attack of emotions, you have to understand it's probably related.
8:57 p.m.	Now you tell me?? Jesus, Michael, I really thought I was losing it. Or having a panic attack. It only got worse after you left. I was sure you were having an affair and my intuition was warning me. You told me to look out for the signs.
8:58 p.m.	You're not even close. It's good that you're trying to be aware, but your interpretations are way off. It'll probably take some more time. Maybe trying to speed things up was a mistake.
8:58 p.m.	So that's what you do all day? Meet bare-legged start-up babes?
8:59 p.m.	Not all day. Only when I come across a good idea. But you knew that already, didn't you? I don't see why you're so surprised.
8:59 p.m.	Because you never tell me exactly what it is you do or about the women in your life.
9:01 p.m.	Sorry to disappoint you, but there's only one woman in my life. And I haven't had anyone since that story that fell apart nine years ago.
9:01 p.m.	Get out. No-one? Nine years? That just doesn't make sense.

9:01 p.m.	Not everything in life makes sense.
9:02 p.m.	I don't know how to explain it... it just hurt so much to see you with someone else today. I want to believe she doesn't really matter. But you meet her for lunch, right in the middle of the day, and you don't meet me. You touch her, and you don't touch me. I know it's childish but I'm not just trying to be dramatic. It really crushed me.
9:04 p.m.	I don't know what to say... sensitive people always hurt more. That's the way it is. But it's a story you invented. It has nothing to do with reality. I swear. We went to another café, a few feet away, and I wasn't feeling too great, so after about 15 minutes I made an excuse and I've been home ever since.
9:04 p.m.	Migraine?
9:05 p.m.	Horrific. Are you calm enough to meet in the cosmos?
9:05 p.m.	I am now. I think. But don't bring along any start-up babes. Not even the lesbians.
9:06 p.m.	Fine, I'll only bring the bi's.
11:45 p.m.	So you really haven't had any sex in years?
11:45 p.m.	I didn't say no sex. I said there was no-one.
11:45 p.m.	Is it me or do you keep changing your story?
11:46 p.m.	Sheera, stop trying to catch me out. I'm not lying. I haven't had anyone for years. Now and then there was sex, because I needed sex. Because otherwise you go crazy. And since I met you, that hasn't happened either. I'm incapable of being with anyone else but you.

11:46 p.m.	So tell me... honestly. How can you stand all this endless foreplay?
11:47 p.m.	Let's just say I use my imagination and my hand pretty freely.
11:47 p.m.	Hmm... so is that what you were doing before, after I finished practicing on you with the candy?
11:47 p.m.	You felt it too, you wiseass, so why ask instead of trusting your instincts?
11:48 p.m.	Because it's so weird... when I have such tangible thoughts about you, I can feel you so strongly it seems like I'm delusional. I don't get it. What is it, am I feeling your imagination?
11:48 p.m.	I told you, our connection is strong. Lately even more. When our thoughts mix, the fantasies grow stronger. Or maybe they merge into one fantasy. I don't completely understand it either. But our connection is outlandishly powerful.
11:48 p.m.	I don't know what to say... I really want to believe it.
11:49 p.m.	If you really want to, just believe it. Tame your fear. You have to calm down.
11:49 p.m.	I want to calm down but this is too much for me, all this long distance guidance thing. It doesn't really have to be this way. It's exhausting.
11:50 p.m.	Let's just agree that you'll try to calm down and I'll try to explain it to you like it was explained to me when I was little.

To: Sheera and Michael <softspoons@gmail.com>
From: Sheera and Michael <softspoons@gmail.com>
January 28, 2016 at 8:38 p.m.
Subject: An afternoon with mom in the kitchen

My father had a business. That's what he called his carpentry. He built my mother the nicest kitchen in the neighborhood. Modern, white with red accents. The height of fashion back then. The cabinets matched the table and the chairs were padded in faux leather. He'd bring customers home to see what he's capable of, so if anything got scratched, we'd go into emergency mode. We were disciplined like workers at a nuclear reactor, but at least the kitchen was perfect.

So one day my mom is at the sink with her dishrag. Ladylike and graceful. Even when washing dishes. Her back straight, hair pulled back, serene smile. Most of the time she'd speak with her eyes, not her mouth. I reached her waist maybe, standing there with a crocheted towel like some girl, putting the dishes away. Good thing my father didn't see it – he would've disowned me right then and there. He thought I was a wimp. I'd only help with the dishes when he was out, so he won't send me off to a military academy. There were still some dishes in the sink but suddenly my mom turns off the water, wipes her hands on her apron, stands facing me and grabs both of my hands. Her hands were cold and I didn't get what she wanted. She sat me down on one of the chairs and sat facing me without saying a word, and I could hear her thinking – you're different because of me. It's because of me.

What's different? Who's different? I got so nervous my head started hurting. And she's smiling at me silently, shutting her eyes and goes on thinking instead of speaking. Do you understand you're different because of me, Mikey?

You need to understand – my mother had never acted that way. She was a regular mom. Hanging laundry, cleaning up, screaming at the sight of cockroaches, worrying that I'm not eating enough. The situation was very peculiar. I didn't understand if she was thinking instead of talking to me, or what she wanted. After we sat there a few more seconds she thinks it again - do you understand that you're different because of me? And opens her eyes and looks at me. So I nod like an airhead though I still didn't understand anything, and she keeps thinking: don't be scared, I'm not a normal person either, Mikey. We're different but alike, and alike because we're different. I'm quoting it exactly as she said it. My memory may not be a hit, but that's a sentence you never forget. You get it, Sheera? That's the way my mother spoke to me when I was nine, in Dr. Seuss riddles, and you complain of how unfairly you're treated because I don't know how to explain. I swear, there's no justice in the world.

But I was a good boy, so I didn't complain. I thought she could hear thoughts, like me. So I'm sitting there thinking up a question for her – how are we different? And waiting for her to answer with a thought of her own. But she just looks at me, not thinking anything. Total silence. So I ask out loud – how are we different? Then she finally opens her mouth and says – you can hear my thoughts but I can't hear yours.

You get it? That's how she chose to tell me, she wanted me to figure it out by myself. To feel it. Instead of saying it she thought it, so that I'd understand that she knows I can hear her, and then she cleared all of her thoughts so I'd hear silence and understand that thoughts can be controlled.

Once I got the message, I ask her out loud – so why did you say we were alike? And she answers out loud – I also know what other people don't know, but in a different way from you. Get it? Good, because I didn't get it either. I was nine! But as I said, I was a good boy, so I kept quiet. I waited for her to go on, and then she said – my power is different than yours.

Power? I have power? I was sure I was the weakest kid on earth. But she asked if I wanted to know how to use my power. I nodded again like an imbecile, and she said she could teach me how to truly know myself because that's how you use power. She said she had a guide that showed her how to do it when she was little. And I sat there listening, with no clue how to react. Couldn't get what was going on. She asked if I wanted her to be my guide, so I said yes. You can probably relate to that – even if it sounds like Chinese, it's one of those offers you can't refuse, right?

That whole conversation felt like a mind fuck. On the one hand, for the first time in my life I understood what I was – not just a regular freak but someone who hears thoughts. Great. Straight to the circus. Before that I didn't know it had a name, I just heard. But I didn't know how my mother knew things, if she couldn't hear thoughts. How did she know what I was? And why hadn't she said anything all this time? I couldn't figure out why I'd never heard her thinking all this, how her thoughts about me had slipped from my ears. But she did manage to spark something. Curiosity. All this was happening during the Ella-Cinderella nuclear meltdown. I was down in the gutter. My mother hadn't planned on telling me until my Bar Mitzvah, but she saw what was going on and couldn't keep it from me anymore. She was right. I lost Ella but I got her, and it hoisted me out of the sewer.

She warned me not to tell anyone, especially my father. She didn't have to explain, trust me, that I understood. My father's the kind of guy you want to spare words with. We agreed that she'd guide me only when we were alone.

Our home routine was tough. Breakfast at seven, lunch at one, dinner at six thirty. On the dot. Dad would come home late from the carpentry. Mom would finish tidying up and wait for him in the living room with her knitting. The faint click of needles, the door creaking, the remains of his thoughts about the business. Those are my childhood memories of him. He'd walk in heavily, asymmetrical steps. Sometimes he'd come into my room to see if I was awake, like a huge shadow blocking the light from the hall. I'd pretend to be asleep, wasn't one of those kids who run to daddy. We had strict rules – no getting up after lights out, and he always came home after. The upside was that it gave me and my mother a lot of guide time together.

The first time we did it she said – I'll teach you to get to know yourself so you can do magic. Magic? I was stunned. Let me remind you – I was nine. I started getting excited. I was sure I could make Ella-Cinderella like me again, or make the kids I hated disappear. But she just sat me on the carpet with my legs crossed, told me to shut my eyes and taught me to meditate. You get it? I was waiting for the legendary David Copperfield show and she gave me Mahatma Gandhi. I didn't understand a thing, but I wasn't rebellious like you. I did what she said. At the end of each session she'd allow one question. Exhausting. But I kept waiting patiently until the next time. Realized there was no choice.

Once or twice a week we'd sit there silently, sometimes she'd agree to put on Chopin's Nocturne no. 2. A soft harmony. Clean. It helped me focus.

I asked her why we were different. She said that's just the way it is, there's nothing we can do about it. I asked if we were the only abnormal people in the world and she said no, there were others who feel everything too strongly. Hear too much, see too much. I asked who else was like that, and she said – you'll know when you grow up. I asked her who her guide was, and she said she'd had a neighbor like us, who was a little bit like a grandmother to her and taught her everything. She said we were lucky because we're different but in the same family, and she was the only one in her family. I asked how come it wasn't hereditary, and she said sometimes it was and sometimes it wasn't, just like any human trait. I asked how her neighbor even knew they were alike, and she said it was something you just know. That people like us always find each other. You meet the person you have to guide, because you can't be like us and go through life completely alone. Fate somehow brings us together, the strong senses are attracted to each other without knowing why, and when it happens – you just know. I didn't understand, I asked how you know, and she said – everyone knows in their own way. I asked if I'd know someday, and if I'd guide someone, and she said I would, that there were plenty of surprises in store for me. She was right about that too.

I'm giving you the special TV industry executive summary, you get that, right? These are questions I asked her over three years, maybe more. One at a time. At first I knew nothing, and she just taught me how to silence the thoughts. Not only to block thoughts, like I learned to do on my own because of Cinderella, but to totally detach myself. She said a person needs to know how to put himself in a state of detachment from the world, especially people like us, who feel too much. So I learned to clear my head, completely, of everything. At first it scared me shitless. I was used to hearing constant noise, the silence seemed unnatural. Like the end of the world. But I learned how to control it. Like a "mute" button, all at once everything would be calm. Or maybe what calmed me was the discovery that there was someone else like me and I wasn't the only screwed up freak in the world.

For more than two years I wanted to know what my mother's special ability was, how she knew things without hearing thoughts. I asked a few times, and she always said she'd tell me but not now. If you only knew how long she dragged me along like that, with practically no answers. You'd blow a circuit. She said first I had to practice, that you learn only through practice, and then I'd figure it out on my own. So I practiced, like you practice with the candy at night. But I also practiced my patience. If my patience was as thin as yours I wouldn't know anything to this day.

She was right about that too. You know how much practice I got? I became an expert at disengaging. At first I'd be able to detach for only a few minutes, but I reached a point where I could be completely out of it for a week. After I knew how to detach myself, she taught me to hold hands and connect with her. To her feelings, her thoughts, sometimes her dreams. That's how I figured out her way of knowing. She didn't have my hypersensitive hearing, she had hypersensitive vision. Actually we both had two kinds of thoughts. The regular thoughts normal people have, and along with them, another kind of thoughts. My other kind was thoughts I heard, the thoughts of other people. Her other kind of thoughts were fragments of the future, which she'd seen. Sometimes it would be clear images, other times blurry pictures. Sometimes it was a sequence lasting a few seconds. How can I explain? She had flashes. Visions. My mother knew what was going to happen before it did.

It took time until I learned to distinguish my regular thoughts from the thoughts of others, but after I learned I could also distinguish her thoughts. If I connected with her and concentrated hard enough, I could hear what she was seeing.

Some processes can't be shortened, Sheera. I'm not exactly a poster boy for patience, but she taught me to overcome my eagerness. She said I had to take it step by step, there was no such thing as understanding everything at once. She wouldn't say much. She always left room for me to think and complete the picture on my own. I trusted her, so I agreed to take it slow. She opened the doors, but allowed me to walk through them alone.

I know you, you'll probably want examples. You'll say "what do you mean 'open doors', explain it!" So here's an explanation. Sometimes a door opens, and it takes years until you figure out how to get in. My mother loved dancing to rock-n'-roll songs from the 50's, and she taught me the moves. She'd put on a record and we'd go wild. Sometimes we danced careful waltzes. She wanted me to know how to distinguish between the types of energy I had. Energy of chaos versus energy of order. Energy of fervency versus quiet love.

One time in the middle of a slow dance she asked if I felt anything special when she and I embraced. She told me to remember that feeling, so I could search for it inside when I was alone. She said that love is the strongest raw material in the world, it could turn everything I do into magic. She had a lyrical soul too. She promised me I'd get anything I wanted if I did things with love. I believed her. It captivated me as a child, before I grew up and thought I knew everything and that she was too naïve.

Once she held this multi-colored ball of yarn, and said that every person is a jumble of string. You have to unravel it, untangle the knots and separate the threads. She spoke in brief sentences I didn't want to forget. I did anyway, but since I met you it's been coming back a lot. Sometimes I write her quotes on Facebook, but then you get pissed at me for speaking Tibetan. It took me years to figure out that sentence, "to separate the threads". She meant I have to separate what I want to hear from what I'm really hearing. To separate the dry facts from my interpretation. Interpretation contains feelings, and feelings stop you from seeing the facts, you understand? She taught me not to be afraid to recognize my fears. It sounds stupid, I know. But I've learned not to be afraid to recognize my hatred, my desire for revenge, my jealousy. Nobody wants to see their own negative emotions, but she explained that that was the trick, it was the only way a person can get to know himself. She said if I wasn't ashamed of my feelings I'd be able to see them, identify them – and then push them aside and see what remains. She said that what remains after you separate the emotions is the truth. It's hard to understand, I know. It takes time and the learning never ends.

That's how it went for a few years. As a nine year old, you don't argue. You're told that's the way it is, and that's that. So I waited patiently although I had a hundred questions. About her neighbor, for instance, I knew practically nothing.

But when I grew up the anger started. I didn't want her to teach me anymore. I stopped asking. I cut it off, all at once. I told you, all or nothing. I don't remember exactly when it began. Maybe when I was fifteen, maybe a little later. I could hear all her thoughts, but I could no longer understand her. How could she know what was going to happen, and still end up with my father. Didn't she see what would happen to her with him?

I hate talking about it. You'll probably want examples now too, and I have many, but I'll give you only one, just so you can understand. Something that happened even before Ella-Cinderella and the talk in the kitchen. Do you remember Camp David? The peace treaty with Egypt? You were young, maybe you don't remember, but everyone in Israel was sitting in the living room and watching it on TV – and those who didn't have a TV went to watch it at their neighbors'.

So I'm six years old, we're watching TV, but I can't tell what they're saying because my father is giving us this endless speech, talking with his hands, like a sports commentator. I realize that something big is happening though hardly anything is happening on the screen. And then they shake hands and the cameras click, there's a wave of excitement in the room, and my mother suddenly blurts out – one of them will pay for this with his life. Everyone fell silent. It wasn't a regular sentence. Her voice sounded weird. Suddenly the air grew cold. All at once my whole body began aching. I started crying. My father pounded the table with his fist and got up angrily. Look what you're doing to the boy! He walked over to my mother and stood over her, barely containing his rage, face red as a beet. I was so scared I stopped crying. He put his finger next to her face, holding it in the air, trembling, and his thoughts at that moment – I never knew he was capable of such violent thoughts. Eventually he just muttered – you're not bringing your dirty witchcraft into my house. He went to the bedroom with his uneven syncopal steps and slammed the door so hard it cracked the doorjamb. The crack remained there for a long time, like a warning signal. When I was old enough I fixed it myself. I couldn't stand seeing it.

Her abilities scared him. Especially when she saw something bad was about to happen. So he mocked her. He took pleasure in proving she didn't know anything. Sometimes she'd say something and he'd look down at her and say – yeah, is that what you think, genius? Like you thought they'd kill Begin? He was sure it was hilarious. If I didn't laugh along with him he'd wave me off, say I've got no sense of humor, just like my mother. She'd never respond, the most she would do was retreat to her bag of yarn and start knitting miles. But that wouldn't stop him. He'd follow her and keep spitting his poison at her, and I'd look at him like a loser and burn inside, but say nothing.

When Sadat was assassinated and no one at home dared breathe a word, I was still young but understood that my father wanted to always be right, and the facts didn't matter. He rewrites his own memories. There's no point in arguing with people who don't know how to unravel the yarn. They see only what they want to see.

You probably know that song – *"When the house is empty at night, it doesn't matter who was right."* It reminds me of her. My mother knew what was going to happen, but she conceded her power. She knew what she was giving up, but that's what she wanted the most - peace at home. When we sat on the carpet, she explained what I'm trying to explain to you. A person needs to get to know himself, without any shame. To admit what they're not so comfortable admitting.

So eventually they were both my guides. My father was always right, but didn't know himself and learned nothing. A life of make-believe that fell apart the minute she died. My mother was never right, but knew herself inside out. She made a conscious choice when she gave up her power. But that choice ruined her.

I bet you think it's just another story about a domineering man and a submissive wife. It used to happen a lot. Today not as much. People like us experience the same things normal people do, but everything happens to us in extremes. More painful. And the ramifications of any trauma or disease are especially harsh.

But forget about that, it's beside the point. I'm trying to tell you that my mother guided me, but I figured out most of it on my own. That's how it's supposed to work. If you know yourself you can control your power, but you understand the power only through experience. You have to feel it. So you see why I want us to walk this road together? Trust each other? You get annoyed when I don't tell you everything right away, when I don't give you the answer you expect. Maybe you think I went to some guide school and I know everything, and I'm doing this on purpose. But you need to figure out things on your own. That's how it is. You try, you practice without knowing anything and then there's this moment when it all suddenly clicks. My mother had a really good way to explain it. One day it'll all come together, you'll understand everything. I know because that's how I learned. I may not be the best guide, but please at least believe me that everything has a reason.

8:58 p.m.	If you only knew how much I love reading what you write especially for me.
8:58 p.m.	If you only knew what you bring out in me. The soap operas I write you. I'm usually skimpy with words. Generous only with thoughts.
8:58 p.m.	But why didn't she tell you from the start?
8:59 p.m.	She was afraid of my father. When they got married, she promised not to practice her witchcraft anymore. That's what he called it. But when she was pregnant, she realized the kind of baby she was going to have. She must've panicked. She planned on telling me when I reached thirteen, thought I wouldn't be able to keep a secret before then. But when Ella dumped me, she cracked.
8:59 p.m.	I want you to tell me more…
9:00 p.m.	I knew I shouldn't have started.
9:00 p.m.	Seriously, Michael, I'm curious. What was the deal with her neighbor?

9:01 p.m.	I don't know much about her. I didn't get to ask, I was allowed only one question at a time. I know she'd knit and crochet and there was something special about her craft. I was a kid, so I imagined her as that arts and crafts lady on TV, let's see what I've made. My mother kept a lot of her old stuff. Our bracelets, for instance. But her story is not that important. What's important is that we're part of a chain, Sheera. Me and you both. At some point in life it just happens to people like us. There's a guide and someone who's being guided, and they meet because they need each other, they need to keep the chain going. It'll happen to you one day too. I'd pay a lot to see you in my shoes, squirming as you try to explain. Remind me to get front row tickets for that one.
9:02 p.m.	Wait, are you serious? Cool! When do I get a trainee I can torture?
9:02 p.m.	I don't know when. When you're ready.
00:07 a.m.	You awake?
00:07 a.m.	Yes.
00:07 a.m.	You never sleep.
00:08 a.m.	Cause I know you'll have another question soon.
00:08 a.m.	Come on, I'm serious. Have you always had insomnia?
00:08 a.m.	No. But that's not what you wanted to ask, is it?
00:09 a.m.	No, I just wondered if you eventually figured out why your mother married your dad.
00:10 a.m.	I think she was like us. We're too exposed. We go through life looking for protection. I think

	she didn't feel as vulnerable with him around. Strange, isn't it?
00:10 a.m.	I don't feel exposed. And I'm not looking for protection.
00:11 a.m.	You're only just starting to feel again, Sheera, wait. I told you it wasn't always a picnic. My mother didn't like feeling that way, so she married a dominant man. She thought it would protect her. Maybe she was right, what do I know.
00:11 a.m.	But regarding that "trust" thing... you realize it's a bit different, what happened with you and your mother and what happens here between us, right?
00:12 a.m.	Of course I realize it. I'm not as dumb as I look. But those are the cards we got. So we deal with it.
00:12 a.m.	Easy to say. You're actually trying to dominate me as well.
00:12 a.m.	Me?? What are you, kidding? Do you have any idea what a domineering man means? I'm fucking submissive. You're just stubborn and constantly itching for a fight. You want to know everything now, instantly, without learning.
00:13 a.m.	Oh come on, Michael. No I don't.
00:13 a.m.	Aren't you tired of contradicting everything I say? I'm on your side, don't you get it yet? Come on, let's move on, Sheera, surrender to the search, you're almost there.

To: Sheera and Michael <softspoons@gmail.com>
From: Sheera and Michael <softspoons@gmail.com>
January 31, 2016 at 8:31 p.m.
Subject: Have you seen my special power? Cash reward promised

You know how sometimes you have to step outside of your body and look at your life from the outside? I think it happened to me today. Or maybe I just managed to unravel a little knot in the jumble and separate a couple of threads.

Erik got out of the hospital. At our morning roundup, Moni told everyone. I couldn't decide whether I was happy or sad, but I felt a little uncomfortable so Julia and I said we'd go visit him on our lunch break. Erik lives pretty close, and Avi said he'd join us. So we got some takeout pasta from the Italian restaurant downstairs and drove over to Erik's. The scent of focaccia saturated the air in the car, I felt like tearing off a bite but was afraid of the faces Julia would make, and Avi went on and on about the show. Any progress with a host? He asked, and I avoided the question, so as not to reveal the disastrous meeting with Agent Asshole. But Avi wouldn't let it go. Come on, move it up already, once Moni gives me a green light I'm all over it with endorsements. Avi is really cute, and I do love him, but I always have to remind myself that if he needed to, he'd not only sell his soul to the devil, but toss his mother into the deal, as in buy one get one free.

When Erik opened the door I was shocked. For a minute he didn't seem like the same person. It looked as though he'd lost at least 20 pounds. His pants bunched up around the belt that was struggling to hold them up, his eyes looked sunken, he was barefoot so he suddenly seemed smaller, and for the first time since I'd known him, he wasn't trying to inflate his chest and was just standing there normally.

When we went inside, I was struck by a sharp sour smell that hovered in his apartment, and held back a wave of nausea. Actually, it was more than just nausea – it hurt, as if someone had punched me in the stomach. And another weird thing happened. When I saw him like that, I really felt sorry for him. As if all at once I realized that when he lay on the creaky hospital bed like a rotten potato, I kept thinking business as usual. I was sure he was pretending and imagined him standing in front of me with all his antagonism, feeling that I had to fight back with everything I had. But there was nothing to fight against. His entire being radiated weakness, as if he'd left himself somehow, releasing all hold. I've never seen anything like that in him before, and it really confused me. It was supposed to have made me feel good, but it really didn't. I have to admit I prefer him strong and irritating and jumping at any chance to say something condescending. I wanted to grab him by the shoulders and shake him, asking – who are you, and what have you done with the Erik I love to hate? He shook Avi's hand, gave Julia a hug, and hesitated for a moment before giving me a quick friendly kiss. The pallor that took over his face was so pasty I could feel it sticking to me, partially remaining on my cheek.

We tried to ask what was wrong, and he said it was still unclear. They thought it was a virus, they thought it was appendicitis, they thought it was an infection, but according to all the tests, other than strong incessant pain, he didn't have anything. So they put you in the hospital because your tummy hurt, Avi joked, and Erik smiled politely, lowering his gaze and said – people say "the pain is killing me" about every little thing, but do you know what it means to really feel that way? Have you ever passed out because the pain was so strong?

We all fell silent for a moment, and then I asked if the pain was gone now, and he smiled and said – still hurts but much less than before. Turns out he'd undergone a zillion tests, but some of the results weren't back yet. The word "cancer" crossed my mind, an obvious association, and I wondered if he really didn't know what he had or if he knew and didn't feel like telling us. There was an oppressive heaviness in the air, my stomach ached and I asked if I could open a window for some air. I got up and went towards the window, and when I reached out to the handle, I froze. It really was a kind of illumination – a chill ran through me, like a frost inside my body, because I suddenly understood what I was feeling.

I felt Erik's stomachache, Michael, like I felt the migraine back in your apartment. I looked out into the street, to the grey sidewalk, stunned by that sudden, strange realization, and quietly admitted to myself that I really hoped he would pull out of it. Get better. The whole time I knew he was sick, I never imagined him looking so bad.

We sat in his minimalist living room, a massive brown leather sofa, a colorful rug and a glass and chrome plated coffee table. A cellophane wrapped chocolate cake from the coffee boutique on Nachmani St. rested on the table, revealing that someone was quicker than us and had already visited. Julia trotted to the kitchen and brought plates and forks and knives, but Erik wouldn't touch anything. The sour smell overcame the scent of focaccia, and I noticed that his lips were pale and cracked. I asked if he wanted something to drink. I'm dying for a cup of tea but I'm too tired to get up, he smiled apologetically. Julia went to the kitchen and put the kettle on, and I exchanged a look with Avi while wondering since when Erik, the guy from "make me a mean espresso, Julia", drank tea like some old man.

How's it going? He asked me, and I said – actually I'm stuck, I'm really waiting for you to come back, and suddenly I didn't know if it was a polite lie or the truth. He looked at me, confused, hesitating with a smile, but then Avi saved us from the awkward moment by slicing the focaccia and handing out pieces while giving Erik an update on the ad market. At that moment, you won't believe it, but an idea suddenly hit me. I said I was going to help Julia and went into the kitchen. I told her – leave it, I'll make Erik his tea. She leaned against the counter looking at me slightly suspiciously, but didn't argue. I went through his cabinets and found some chamomile tea, like my mother used to make me whenever I had a stomachache when I was little.

I put the teabag into a glass mug (I wanted a transparent mug so it wouldn't block my intention). I poured in the boiling water slowly, intently, recalling how my mother would make this tea for me, its moist gentle scent spreading through the kitchen and my complete childish faith that this was a magical remedy. I added two spoons of sugar and stirred it in gently, slowly. As the granules melted into the warm liquid, I imagined Erik's pain dissolving and disappearing.

I went back to the living room and put the steaming mug on the table. I smiled at Erik, and he looked at me uncomprehendingly.

Drink up, I said, this tea always used to make me feel better when I was a little girl. He took a small sip of the piping hot liquid and his eyes closed. It's really good, he said, and I smiled and joined the conversation, but out of the corner of my eye I kept looking, making sure he drank it all down to the last drop. It's one of the strangest feelings I've ever had – with each sip he took, I felt my stomachache slowly disappearing.

When he finished drinking, Erik tore off a little piece of focaccia and started chewing on it. Why aren't you eating? He asked, and only then did I notice I was sitting there like a mummy and just staring at him. There was something so lagging, so defeated about him. He listened patiently to everything, waited a few moments before responding, and he was so matter of fact, as if he couldn't spare any energy for games. It was like he'd deposited his boots along with his arrogance with the receptionist when he was admitted into the hospital, and by the time he got out she couldn't remember where she'd put them. Something was still bugging me, so when Julia got up to put the dirty dishes away I was so relieved, I immediately joined her to help. I wanted to get out of there already, free myself, breathe some fresh air. I hadn't expected it to be so hard to see him. When we stood at the door, Avi suddenly said, I think our visit did you some good, you're not as pale as you were before. Erik smiled. Truth is I'm feeling a little better, he said, maybe you should come back tomorrow, and we all laughed politely. Just before we left he called out – the proposal for "The Write Stuff" looks great, Gaya liked it too, I let her read it when she was here yesterday, why don't you set up a three-way meeting so we can push things forward when I come back. He had a strange look on his face. I'm pretty sure I made the rest of his pain go away with that spellbound tea, but his eyes were still dim, and it seemed for a moment that he'd lost not only his arrogance at the hospital but also the desire to live. I smiled at him cautiously, and we agreed to talk about everything when he returned.

I left there with a vague, unclear feeling. As if something in my life had forever changed, and though I didn't know exactly what it was, it was obvious that whatever it was, it would never be the same again.

For some reason it took me back to the moment I found out I was pregnant with Tom. It felt like I was standing on some sort of boundary, or imaginary line. Have you ever been in Greenwich? You know that copper line planted into the ground, marking the mean time for the rest of the world, making it tangible? Something like that. The feeling you get when you capture a specific moment in life, and you can recognize it as the border between today and yesterday. Even if you have no idea why or how, you know that it's the platform upon which you stand to part from your old life and sail on, waving goodbye and brushing a tear from your eye.

When I made Erik the tea, without thinking too much, I succeeded in parting from the nagging doubt. I just did it, like I did it after my surprise visit to your apartment. I didn't resist, I didn't think about why it wouldn't work, or about how stupid I was for believing such nonsense. I focused on what I wanted to do. Only this time I really wanted to make Erik's pain go away, completely ignoring the fact that I'm supposed to hate him.

Yes, no doubt something about Erik changed, something about our whole dynamic. It saddened me but also made me glad, like an emotional milkshake. I went back to the office, logged onto Outlook, trying to regain my focus on work. An email from Rona captured my eye. She'd sent me a draft of her feature story to read and tell her what I thought.

My stupid predator says that somewhere down the line in this series we need a melancholic celebrity on the cover who'd confess about his fucked up relationship. Notice how I've converted from a serious journalist to his writing whore? A little lower every time, may he die today and forever rest in peace, she wrote.

Something in her words irked me, and I didn't know what it was. I was still shrouded in what I'd been feeling in Erik's apartment. Feeling someone else's pain is weird. It's different from feeling your own pain. It's like a diluted ache, kind of dull, an imitation to the real thing. So how had I suddenly felt his pain? What had I unraveled there, in that crazy jumble? I think it was the first time I looked at Erik, isolated from what I thought of him. He looked so sickly so I couldn't maintain my usual reaction, and that's how I managed to separate and put aside what I felt about him. And once I wasn't obsessed with how much of an annoying loser he was, I could suddenly feel his pain. I saw him as he was. Could that mean I've moved up one more level?

Before I went back to work I took a few minutes to Google the word "pain". Among the thousands of painkiller ads there were all kinds of articles. Did you know there was a pain disease? It's called fibromyalgia. Some kind of severe chronic muscle ache that doesn't show up as a specific problem on any test. In extreme cases it could reach a stage of total dysfunction requiring long hospitalization, because the pain makes it impossible to move. For a moment I thought that's what Erik has. I'd never heard of it before.

But it wasn't only the pain. He was so pale and scrawny, and there was something really frightened about him. Life had hit Erik really hard, and only one thing pleased me about it: the fact that I felt no need to gloat. So that's it. Without making too much of a big deal, I took away Erik's pain today. Can you believe it?

9:17 p.m.	Sure I can. It's your most basic ability, nobody can take it away from you. But do you know why you felt Erik's pain? Why you still don't feel other people's pain?
9:17 p.m.	That's not accurate. Sometimes I can feel your headaches too.
9:18 p.m.	Exactly. Love gets confused with hate... you're connected to me by a powerful emotion, and to Erik as well.
9:18 p.m.	Wow, I never thought of it that way. Kind of gross, actually.
9:19 p.m.	Let's agree that Erik's a scumbag, but there's much worse scum in the world.
9:19 p.m.	Someone should start a reality talent competition. Once and for all – let's find out who's the world's biggest asshole.
9:20 p.m.	Remind me not to sign up as a judge.
9:20 p.m.	You can be a judge on "The Write Stuff". We really need a lifeguard on the panel.
9:20 p.m.	Good thing you reminded me, I wanted to ask you. What would you really like to do with that show?
9:21 p.m.	I'll send you the proposal I wrote.

9:21 p.m.	No, I'm not talking about the proposal. I asked you a question in Tibetan, like my mother used to ask. If there were no limits or restrictions, and you could do anything at all with that show, what would you choose to do?
9:21 p.m.	What I'm doing. To be responsible for the whole thing, from the concept to the grand finale.
9:22 p.m.	You're shooting from the hip. Think before you answer. You wrote that something was bothering you, something didn't feel right. Read everything you wrote here, and try to give it another interpretation.
9:23 p.m.	Oh, come on... If I knew I'd have to reread this stuff again I wouldn't babble so much.
9:24 p.m.	Cut it out, crybaby. Read it again, it'll be interesting. And one last thing – about your investment account.
9:25 p.m.	What do you mean?
9:26 p.m.	I need to tell you something about your investment account.
9:26 p.m.	How do you know I have an investment account?
9:27 p.m.	Any more bright questions?
9:27 p.m.	Okay... I still have trouble adjusting to the fact that you know everything. So what is it this time? You want me to empty it out and wire all the money to your Swiss bank account, no questions asked?
9:27 p.m.	No, you paranoid freak, but it's heartwarming to find out what you think of me. Maybe someday you'll get used to me knowing everything and I'll get used to you not trusting me for shit. Ask your banker to invest in a company called Fire Island. Put ten percent of your money in it,

	and when you see it going up, after about a thirty percent increase, ask them to put all of your money in it.
9:28 p.m.	Everything? Why? What kind of company is it? Are you invested in it?
9:29 p.m.	No, I'm not invested in it. Would you just trust me and do what I ask?
9:29 p.m.	I don't understand why it's so hard to just tell me. You see how dominating you get sometimes?
9:30 p.m.	I'm not dominating. I just can't explain right now. You'll understand soon enough.
9:30 p.m.	I promise to consider it, okay? Good night.

To: Sheera and Michael <softspoons@gmail.com>
From: Sheera and Michael <softspoons@gmail.com>
February 1, 2016 at 10:12 p.m.
Subject: Houston, we have a problem

My day started off with a phone call from the school secretary – she asked me to come in for a meeting. I admit I was a little startled. I didn't know what had happened. I went into the bathroom, and stood behind Tom as I watched him brush his teeth through the mirror. Do you have any idea why the principal wants to see me? I asked. He leaned forward to spit the gooey paste into the sink as he asked, what do you think I am, a mind reader?

On the way to school I tried to milk it out of him, and it turns out that the day before he'd been in a fight. Who hit you? I asked, concerned. He swallowed hard and said – it was a girl.

And what happened? I pressed on.

Nothing, he said indifferently, she started it, so I hit her back.

As soon as I stopped the car he opened the door, threw a tiny "bye" over his shoulder and ran into the schoolyard, ignoring the huge weight of his backpack, and I found myself walking into the principal's office alone like a scolded child. Please sit down, she said, pushing her dark glasses higher up on the bridge of her nose. When I sat down on the hard wooden chair she asked, is everything all right at home?

Yes, everything's fine, I said, why?

I assume you're aware that I personally handle each and every case of violence at school, and Tom has been showing some signs of violence lately, she said with a frozen expression, but even with the best intentions we cannot tolerate any sort of violence, you understand that.

I really don't, because he's not a violent boy, and at home he's perfectly fine, I said, and she just gave me a thin smile and said she's yet to meet the parent who would admit his child was violent. Inside I hated her viciously for being so condescending, but I continued to pretend to be mom of the year.

I realize the situation at home is… unique, she said.

What do you mean, unique? I tensed.

You're certainly aware of the fact that boys who grow up in a fatherless environment can develop a great deal of rage, she went on, in her tone of feigned authority.

There are no rules for those things, I responded, you can't determine in advance whether someone is supposed to develop rage, and besides, Tom has a very loving and supportive family.

I suggest you look into it, she said coldly, maybe some more tranquil activities at home, and I have an excellent child therapist if you need a referral. We wouldn't want this to lead to a suspension.

You have no idea how pissed I was when I left her office. Beyond her being a disgusting prejudiced woman, I suddenly felt all shaken up, disconnected from my own son. As if we'd detached at some point, like an engine that keeps moving down the track without noticing that it's left the train cars behind. A terrible sense of failure closed in on me. How could he be going through all of these things without me even knowing? How deeply had I delved into our story without noticing what was happening with Tom?

On the way to work I got a phone call from Rafi Hadar. I had to pull myself together and take it. What's new, have you told the kids yet? I asked, as his divorce confidante. Not yet, he said, she doesn't want us to say a word until we finish the arbitration, and I'm still unsure what's best to tell the press.

What are you undecided about? I asked, and quietly wondered what kind of a father he was, about to break up his family and all he cared about was the media coverage.

I'm afraid they'll flip me around like a hamburger, but I have to say something to the public, don't I? And the minute he said it, the idea sprang into my head. Once he agreed, I called Rona right away. Where've you been? she yelled. Just don't tell me it's some guy, 'cause I'll hang up and call you an ambulance.

I was busy finding your interview cover story, I said proudly.

Who?? She asked, curiously, and after making her swear on her children not to say a word, I told her that the heartbroken celebrity who's leaving home will be Rafi Hadar.

Yes! My queen! She screamed in my ear.

Relax, I'm not your queen, just tell your Predator in Chief that it'll take a little time, and you have to promise me that he's going to come out smelling like roses.

Dammit, you get a divorce already and you do your story and leave me alone, I grumbled to myself, but the minute I ended the call Avi called to complain there wasn't enough media attention around the guy who was turning out to be the star of "Big Fear", some douche with a filthy mouth whom I couldn't stand. I grimaced and promised to take care of it as soon as I got back to the office. I have a scoop for you, he said, Gaya wants "The Write Stuff" to air twice a week instead of once, and Moni's considering it. How do you know? I asked, and he answered impatiently – me and her secretary get along, what do you care how I know, the question is if it airs twice a week will you be able to run the show and still do your regular job? I cursed softly and made a note to talk to Moni about it when I got in. But what will I say? I didn't know what I wanted anymore.

So you see what my days look like? And all this before I even got to the office.

You said I should surrender to the search, but real life isn't a sci-fi movie, I can't continue running the marathon while searching for hidden abilities. I'm not a nine year old child helping mommy with the dishes, and I'm starting to fuck up, I'm losing my grip. You don't know how strong my connection to Tom was over the years. Nothing could happen to him without me knowing about it.

The grimy residue from the talk with the principal didn't leave me. All the way to work I had flashbacks from those first days when I was a brand new clueless mother who didn't have anyone to share her new status with. I walked into the house with my new baby bundle, and didn't know where to put him, what to feed him, how to hold him or what to do if he suddenly stopped breathing. I stood there panicking, and then suddenly realized this is it. It's just him and me, and I need to learn really fast how to take care of this oversized Chia pet I'd brought home from the hospital with me.

I had no choice, and somehow I grew into it, but it was like donating my body to science. My entire life shrunk down to this menial never-ending care, and the growing fatigue wore me down into dust. Life continued without me, I was trapped at home in an incessant dance around a demanding little baby, so tiny yet insistent on devouring me whole. I had such bad breakdowns, there were moments I even considered calling Ziv, telling him everything and begging him to help me. You talk about surrendering, but do you even know what it means to give yourself over like that? It was total devotion, and it tore me apart.

So now I have to do tranquil activities with Tom. What the hell is a tranquil activity? Meditation on the carpet while listening to Chopin? I'm sorry but that's just not me.

I tormented myself the entire way to the office. Maybe I'd made a mistake leaving him home with a nanny, who worked in shifts with my mother so I could go back to work after three months?

I had to make us both a decent living, I had no choice but to run back to my previous life. Maybe now I'm paying the price for that decision. I don't know. But is it possible that without noticing the changes, I'm raising a kid with aggressive tendencies?

When I was in the elevator I suddenly remembered a giant art book someone had given me as a gift. Tom and I once sat looking through it for hours. I was never a big art fan, but I was drawn into the images and colors with his enthusiasm. I tried recalling the last time I'd seen Tom sit down and draw, but couldn't. When the elevator stopped I pushed the button again and went back down to street level, slipped into the office supply store and quickly bought a pack of watercolors and a pad of art paper. That's it, that's what we'd do together in the afternoon.

When I picked Tom up to go home, I told him about my conversation with the principal. That's not fair! He kicked his backpack. She didn't even tell you the real story.

What's the real story? I asked.

That girl said something mean, he said.

Why do you even care what she said? I asked.

I don't, he grumbled, you're the one who cares, what's the big deal? Something in his tone suddenly reminded me of my father, and a small wave of nausea rippled through me.

I didn't know what to say. I took out the paper and watercolors, but he just looked at them without saying a word.

You feel like painting? I asked.

No, he said. So I spread it all out on the living room floor and started drawing on my own. He walked to his room dramatically, but a few minutes later came back and stood there watching for a long while before saying – that's not how you draw the sky, it's too blue and it doesn't look real. I shrugged and continued to paint. He sat beside me and took a clean sheet and brush and dipped it in the cup of water.

I finished my painting and just looked at him. So fixated on what he was doing – it's been a long time since I'd seen him that way. Studying the colors, his movements slow and focused, trying to get the best out of each and every brushstroke. I remembered you told me that if I wanted to find my primary power, I should look for it in what I love doing most. Tom loves to draw and paint most of all, and as I watched him I suddenly realized what you meant. But what was it for me?

Tom painted a lava-orange sky, tar-black mountains and gushing red rivers. One of his paintings had a pile of unidentifiable parts, with a round face on top of them. What's that? I asked. It's a person that fell apart, he said. See, Michael, it's not just me and you, my son knows something about parallel universes too.

I hung the paintings to dry on the laundry line outside the kitchen balcony, and Tom sat down for dinner, truly calmer. Why hadn't he painted in so long? How easy it is for him to distance himself from what he loves doing the most. I too sometimes do that, decide against my nature, clamp down my emotion, suffocate my instincts. That's what I did when I broke up with Ziv. That's what it was like on those first days when I left baby Tom and went back to work. It was the right thing to do, but dead against what my body wanted.

Don't listen to stupid things that other kids say, I whispered to him just before he fell asleep.

I froze for a second when he said – it's just a stupid girl who thinks she can say whatever she wants 'cause her dad is famous.

I knew exactly who the girl was, her parents were actors. I wanted to ask if she'd said something about him not having a dad, I'm always worried he'll get teased about that, but I didn't want to wake sleeping dogs. What did she say? I asked carefully.

That I can't draw, he said, and I was so relieved.

You draw wonderfully, I whispered to him, that's your basic ability, and no matter what anyone else says, nobody can ever take that away from you. Tom smiled with his eyes closed, goose bumps rising on his skin at the sound of my whisper. Something about your words, coming at him from my mouth, calmed him down. I made a mental note to beware, because without noticing I'd started sounding like you. Must be contagious.

After Tom fell asleep I lay in the dark room staring at my hands. I use them when I take your pain away, even if it's only imaginary. But what else lies in them – what kind of powers? I don't even remember what it was, that thing I once knew I really loved doing. And maybe that's the problem. Maybe I've distanced myself from what I wanted most of all, but the passion hasn't really died down. It just erupted in other places, spilling over the rim. It became anger, power struggles, frustration, rabid whims.

On the other hand, look what happens when I surrender to the search. I lose contact with my son. I lose contact with life. "Surrender to the search," you have such a way with words sometimes, you make everything sound like strawberries and cream. What exactly do you expect – you want me to drop everything, quit working, give up the new show, dump Tom in a boarding school and dedicate my life to the search?

It's getting too hard for me to continue this documentation, this never-ending search. It throws me off track and it's not going anywhere. And yes, I also want to see you already.

    10:50 p.m.   Calm those waves, Sea Song. You're feeling everything on a stronger level, and it's hard because you're not used to it. Your body's picking up signals and you still don't know how to decode them. Play with the pieces of the puzzle. Solve it like a riddle.

    10:51 p.m.   I'm tired of playing.

    10:51 p.m.   As someone who's so addicted to work, don't you want to figure out your true calling?

10:52 p.m.	I want to, but I've had enough. I'll continue my search when things between us are clearer.
10:53 p.m.	But you're so close to understanding everything, Sheera, don't turn the distance between us into an excuse for ditching everything.
10:53 p.m.	It's not an excuse, Michael. I'll go a little further but you've taken it too far. The further we go, the more I get this growing fear that we're in a destructive relationship.
10:54 p.m.	Pay attention, my love. Pay attention to the words.

To: Sheera and Michael <softspoons@gmail.com>
From: Sheera and Michael <softspoons@gmail.com>
February 2, 2016 at 4:12 pm
Subject: Michael, where are you?

I tried calling a few times and you're not picking up. Not answering messages either. I'm sitting like a moron in my car in the office parking lot and don't really know what to do. Or where to go. I can't go home like this, I'm on the verge of a nervous breakdown. Call me if you see this email, I really need to talk to you.

To: Sheera and Michael <softspoons@gmail.com>
From: Sheera and Michael <softspoons@gmail.com>
February 2, 2016 at 4:48 p.m.
Subject: Just to let you know everything's falling apart

Well, you're still unavailable for some reason, and I have to tell someone what happened, but there's no one I can tell except you, so I'll just start writing until you do me the honor of getting back to me from your oh-so-busy schedule. I'm still sitting in the car in the parking lot like an idiot... Jesus, I don't know where to start. Maybe in chronological order. Actually, this whole day got off to a bad start. I could barely open my eyes. I don't know what's with me these past few weeks. Why am I so tired? Through the fog of my sleep, it took me a minute until I realized I'd missed the alarm clock. Shit, seven forty five, I can't believe it.

Tom! I yelled to the other room, sure it would take us hours to get ready, and suddenly he came into my room, completely dressed, holding a glass of chocolate milk. My sweet prince, I whispered, surprised, why didn't you wake me? He looked so big that for a second it seemed he'd grown six months overnight.

You looked tired, he said with a serious expression, so I decided to walk to school.

No, baby, there are too many roads to cross, I'll get up and take you, I said, throwing the blanket off. But it was as if he'd anticipated my response, as if he'd walked in with all that anger stashed in his pockets, just waiting for the opportunity to draw and fire it at me. Stop it, Mom! His face grew red, I'm not a little kid anymore, I'm walking alone today, goodbye! And he turned his back and marched out like a soldier. I leapt out of bed, stumbling, still woozy, and stopped him in the hall with a firm hand on his shoulder – wait two minutes, I'll get dressed and take you.

I don't want to! He flung my hand away angrily, everyone laughs at me for coming with my mom every day like a baby. I didn't feel like having that argument, so I just said "oh please", locked the front door so he couldn't leave, and took the key.

I didn't expect his reaction. He just raised his hand and hurled the glass onto the floor. I'm sick of this! He screamed as the glass shattered. I wasn't the only one shocked by the spray of brown drops on the wall, he must've shocked himself too and he immediately froze. An awful silence hung through the house, the kind of silence that makes it possible to hear the fearful galloping of the heart. We both stood there, staring at the shining shards of glass in the chocolate puddle. I had no idea how I was supposed to respond – and suddenly a thought came out of some mysterious fold in my body – that everything would've been different if he had a father, who would now be dressing in the bedroom, and I'd go to him and say – what's going on with that boy? I'm really worried, you talk to him.

I took a deep breath, holding out my hand, and out of some genetic habit he held his out too, and we walked carefully around the broken glass and I sat him on the sofa. I looked into his eyes and asked, Tom, what's going on with you? Clear little pools welled up in his honey-colored eyes, and in no time he was crying. Really crying, wailing with sobs and moans and snot, and my heart shattered like the glass just did. I held him really close, and we just sat there like that for about five minutes, breathing and focusing on the slowing of the beat, ignoring the clock that obtusely continued ticking, and the mess that needed cleaning up on the floor. I just kept holding him and kissed him in that soft spot I love so much, right by his temple, until he calmed down. At some point I got up, ran a mop over the floor, scribbled a note with one hand and got dressed with the other, afraid of what the principal would have to say about his tardiness and the "unique situation" at home.

On the way to school it turned out there was only one boy in class who walked to school on his own, a big American kid who teased Tom for being a "mama's boy". I offered to talk to the teacher but Tom was horrified at the idea and made me swear not to intervene. When we were almost there, he asked me to drop him off before the turn, so he could walk the rest of the way alone. So I stopped and let him play out the façade for his friends. I guess not only do I want to be the perfect mother I'll never be, he too wants to be the perfect boy, independent, mature and strong. I watched him until his giant backpack disappeared around the corner, and made a mental note to talk to him about what happened, and about everything he was going through. When I continued driving, I asked myself how well I really knew him, my own son. Is it possible that he was ashamed of me? Allegedly I know every pore in his body, every movement, like only a single mother can know her only son. On the other hand, I too was an only child, and the last thing I can say about my parents is that they knew me well, or understood me. Was I just like them, without realizing it?

Why weren't you at the morning meeting? Julia asked me as we rode up in the elevator together, her manicured hands holding a cardboard tray of coffees and sandwiches from downstairs. A hold-up at home, I mumbled, did I miss something important?

Erik's back, all skin and bones, she said, so I've decided to put some meat back on him, until he recovers, you know.

I forced a smile. Instinctively, the word "Erik" still brings a lump to my throat, like some incontrollable gag reflex, though after what happened at his place the other day, the reflex was much weaker than usual. I decided to be nice and walked by his office before going to mine. He stood at reception in his cowboy boots, surrounded by a small posse of admirers. He really did look sickly skinny, and the skin on his face was transparent and waxy.

I went to him and kissed him hello, an action that required me to stop breathing for a moment. So glad you're back, you look great, I lied through my teeth.

Erik smiled out of the pale desert of his face, a little weaker, a little less arrogant, but Erik nonetheless. Let's have lunch later, he suggested without asking if I was free, we'll talk about the show, see what you've accomplished without me. We scheduled for one at the Italian place, and I walked to my office with a strange feeling of relief –my familiar punishment was back.

At the restaurant we asked for a side table, but were constantly interrupted by people we knew from the industry. They were all over Erik, wanting to know how he was. He basked in the attention and I found myself wondering if he wasn't getting back to his old self a little too quickly. Well, how was it without me? He asked, waiting for me to say it'd been unbearably horrible.

We managed somehow, I said with a half-smile, and politely inquired whether there were any new results for all the tests he had undergone.

He moved in his seat uncomfortably and then said – not yet, it's still inexplicable.

Have you ever heard about fibromyalgia? I asked cautiously, and he gave me a surprised expression and said that one of the doctors had actually suggested that possibility, but his symptoms didn't really fit, it was a disease that usually breaks out after a trauma, develops over time and doesn't disappear so quickly. Hey, I decided to ask him, though we've never had such personal talks, did it really make you start thinking differently, going through such an experience?

He gave me a look that was a little hollow and said – Yeah, it's kind of inevitable. When your whole life flashes in front of your eyes you can't avoid it – it makes things surface.

What kind of things? I asked, giving him a look that was supposed to mean that I'm both profound and interested.

Thoughts about life, he said, and after a momentary silence added – you suddenly want to get everything done fast.

I nodded, though I didn't really understand what he meant by "done".

Look, you and I both gave up having normal family lives, he suddenly said, which made me flinch in my chair, offended at his nerve for even comparing himself to me. I didn't give up anything, I'm five years younger than him and I have an eight and a half year old son. But I didn't respond, just swallowed hard and asked, so what are you trying to say, that this lifestyle is no longer right for you?

Erik stared at some spot in the air for a second, sipped at his soda and said – I had a lot of time to think, obviously, but you know how it goes – you get back to work and there's no more time for soul-searching.

I raised an eyebrow. His honesty surprised me, even if he hadn't really disclosed anything. To be truthful, I wasn't really sure what I expected to hear, and if it were up to me, what I'd prefer – that Erik would stay or leave. Who knows who his successor might be. No doubt, sometimes it's better to live with an old familiar enemy.

But then something happened that just turned me to stone. He suddenly put his cold hand on mine and said – Sheera, I know you don't like me.

It was completely out of the blue, as if someone had patched in a scene from a different movie. I was so confused, I just sat there staring at him, not knowing what to say, only wishing he'd take his hand off me. Luckily the waiter appeared, full of ambition, bearing a tray of pasta for me and clear broth for Erik, who's still trying to watch what he eats. After he'd served our meals and walked away, I asked – why do you think that?

Erik lowered his gaze, tasted his soup, paused for another moment, and then looked right in my eyes. I don't think, I know. He put such an emphasis on the last word it gave me chills.

How do you know? I asked, and he said – it doesn't matter, I just wanted to say it doesn't have to be this way.

Of course not, I said quickly. I couldn't understand what he wanted. We changed the subject, but throughout the entire meal I tried to figure out what was going on, why he felt the need to say that.

I'm so naïve, Michael, not to mention a total idiot, because when we got back to the office I was still wondering if the change had anything to do with what happened at his apartment. He'd always managed to push my fury button and bring out the evil in me at full force. So which one of us had changed – him or me? I couldn't grasp how you could loathe someone so fiercely, and then one minute later think they weren't really so bad. You did once tell me that he liked me, and after the restaurant incident it suddenly didn't seem as far-fetched.

On the way to my office I poked my head into Avi's room and asked – hey, did you say something to Erik about me?

What do you mean? Avi frowned at me.

Did you ever mention something about me not liking him?

Avi looked at me, hurt, and said dramatically – Are you for real, sister? I'd never talk about you behind your back with Erik, I can't even believe you're asking.

And then he added just before I left - But I wouldn't be surprised if he figured it out on his own, you know, from your behavior.

I went back to my office, my head buzzing with thoughts. I already thought you may have been right, that sometimes I hate just because it's easier. After breaking up with Ziv, for instance, I constantly shifted between dying from a broken heart and hating him with a passion. The emotions kept interchanging so quickly it made me dizzy, but ironically, when I hated him I somehow felt stronger. At some point I admitted to myself that I preferred hating him. When I felt the love, there was nothing I could do with it but plunge head first into this despair that just crushed me. But when I hated him it injected an evil force into me, and when you want to regain control over your life, you grasp any sense of power over the helplessness and vulnerability.

So I was sitting there immersed in my silly ponderings, and suddenly Zadok's head poked through the door, and he just stood there, smiling.

What's up? I asked politely when I realized he wasn't leaving.

I just wanted to make sure you remember to shut off your computer at night, he said. Of course, I smiled. And suddenly, all at once it felt as if the temperature had dropped ten degrees. Erik's words echoed in my ears: I don't think, I know.

Fuck, I can't believe I hadn't thought of it! The minute Zadok left, I attacked my computer and started going through all the emails, including those left in the trash folder. It was impossible, the amount was endless, so I decided to filter them. Who could I have sent something bad I'd written about Erik? Actually it was only with Avi that I ever let myself loose and totally trashed him.

I started going through my entire history of correspondence with Avi, and the more I read, the more I felt I was drowning in mud, until it seemed as if the entire world had gone dark. I started shaking, shuddering from the cold. Almost every email I'd sent to Avi contained something disparaging about Erik, whether badmouthing, cursing, or just plain despising. There was so much incriminating evidence, that I couldn't decide what scared me the most. I felt so stupid. Why hadn't I deleted this stuff? I never imagined Erik would see it.

Reading everything through his eyes was awful – I'd written that Erik was a loser, a worm, a useless idiot, full of hot air, a shitty scumbag that only got in the way. There was an infinite amount of venom and smearing. In one mail I proposed that Avi and I collude to reject "The Human League" in the next meeting, because Erik is just an egomaniac and a failure who'll bring the entire channel down. In another mail, on what seemed to be a particularly moody day, I wrote that Erik deserved to suffocate and die a slow, agonizing death. The letters flickered in front of me, suddenly they seemed so awful. Yes, I wrote them in a moment of anger, but if Erik really had seen them, it was the end of me. There was nothing left to say.

With a trembling hand, I dialed Zadok, trying to sound extremely casual. Hey, I asked, have you ever seen anyone go into my office when I'm out? I don't think so, he said, maybe just our people, like Julia, or Erik who sometimes needs something from your computer, but when I warned you I meant there were tons of producers, agents, advertisers, actors wandering around, they come in for meetings, and who knows what they're looking for and who they give the information to later.

I put down the phone and really wanted to die. He saw it, there's no doubt. He saw everything. How stupid I was - leaving evidence around. He came into my office when I was out and read it, and now he was probably plotting his revenge. Trying to soften me up, pretending to be friendly, so he could catch me off guard once I lower my defenses.

I highlighted all my correspondence with Avi and deleted it, emptying the trash as well. I wanted no reminder of my stupidity. As I began to rack my brains figuring out how to behave at our meeting with the producer that afternoon, Julia called. Erik's first day back had exhausted him, and he went home early. He'd like to push the meeting with Gaya to another day. I ended the call, not knowing what to do. It was clear that he was planning something against me, that his change of approach was not real.

I texted you, but you didn't reply. I wanted to write you, but was afraid to write from the office. I don't trust anyone here, I don't know who could be going through my stuff. I suddenly realized that nothing was certain anymore, that although some people think I was molded into the foundations of this building, maybe my days here are numbered. How will I feed my son? A dark tsunami washed through my soul. Tears came streaming from me eyes, and I didn't want anyone to see me like this so I quickly got up to shut the door. Look what's become of me. You said I'd get used to the bracelet, to this over emotion, but I've never cried at work. Ever. At some point I regained some control, snatched my things and ran out of there.

In the elevator the fear began turning into rage, which swelled inside me like a huge tidal wave. On the way to the car I looked at the dirty walls in the parking lot, imagining myself shoving Erik against one of the moldy walls and with a menacing squint, shooting three bullets into him. The nerve, the audacity of that asshole. I tried calling you, but you didn't answer. I cursed softly. Erik has a lot of power at the station, and I had to think how I'd defend myself. I considered calling Rona for advice, I thought of calling Avi, but decided that for the time being it was best to keep it to myself.

I sat in the car, started the engine but didn't know where to go. So I'm still here, hating myself and what's become of my fucked up life. If this was a normal relationship I'd drive over to your house right now, unannounced. You'd open the door with a look of surprise, slightly disheveled, day-old stubble on your chin, and before you'd even realize I'm there, I'd opt to talk later, and unload this entire storm on you. I'd bite into the intoxicating silkiness of your lips, pin myself to your body, slam the door behind us with a kick and just… crash into you. But nothing is going right and this is anything but a normal relationship, and I can't go home in this state, so I'm just sitting here with my pathetic laptop, writing you from the car.

Look, I don't know what Erik will do now, if he's going to pretend we're good friends but try to block my every move, or if he's actually thought up a real plan for my total annihilation. What was his goal in this vendetta, getting me fired? That lame son of a bitch, can you believe he calls himself a man? Fighting single mothers who have to make a living. Do you realize what's happening to me, Michael? Every single part of my life is falling apart. With Tom, at work, and, let's face it – everything's falling apart with you as well.

4:55 p.m.	Sheera, calm down, I'm here and I'm reading you. I'm in the middle of something and couldn't get back to you. But Erik's not tricking you and not trying to destroy you. Trust me, it's not what you think. You're misreading again.
4:55 p.m.	Fuck it, Michael, would you stop with that bullshit already?? I'm telling you he read everything I wrote about him, don't you get it?? And what are you in the middle of that's so important you can't talk for so long – another emergency meeting with some start-up whore?
4:56 p.m.	Stop it, Sheera, you're getting yourself all riled up over nothing, listen to me! Even if Erik saw your emails, he's not conniving against you. You're letting your fear get the better of you, and you're completely missing the essence of your power – with Erik, Tom, and me too. I can't talk now, but you've got to calm down and believe me!
4:57 p.m.	No Michael, I can't do this stupid email thing anymore, I've had it up to here with this shit! Let's face it – we failed. Nothing's working right. It's not funny, it's no fun, I'm really not enjoying any of it. I've played along, tried my best, but baby, there's a limit to everything, and we've crossed that line long ago. It's time to stop. I'm exhausted. The more time goes by, the less I understand. Why is everything so clear to you when I can't see a thing? Why can't I find my primary power, when you always knew, ever since you were a little kid? What's wrong with me? And this unconsummated attraction is also driving me nuts, I'm sick of constantly holding back. I'm drowning in fantasies, I've never had so much imaginary sex in my life, it's driving

me crazy. I can't function, we're in a destructive relationship, can't you see it? If we ever do end up together, how the hell will it be after all this insane build-up? We've overstretched the foreplay so long we've ruined everything before it's even begun. I can't take it anymore, Michael, I'm sorry. Either leave, or come already. Snowball, landslide, I don't care anymore. Just not this, not for one more minute. I don't want to keep searching. I don't get this power stuff. I'm tired of missing you, I'm sick of this distance. What are you waiting for, you want me to get down on my knees, tear my clothes and beg you to take me? That's it, I'm out. The ball's in your court. Either leave me alone, or tell me what my fucking power is and we'll get it over with.

To: Sheera and Michael <softspoons@gmail.com>
From: Sheera and Michael <softspoons@gmail.com>
February 3, 2016 at 9:58 p.m.
Subject: Agent A – the Sequel

When you fall for someone, you can't really grasp how deeply you've plunged, until that certain moment when you're suddenly forced to acknowledge how much you've changed since you've met them. Throughout that time you cross one line, and then another. You break some outdated rule, concede another old vow. Little by little you get carried away until all logic is lost, and you can no longer explain your actions or even recognize them as your own. At some point you look at yourself and admit that you've already walked quite far down this senseless road. How do I go back from here? You wonder with a furtive look over your shoulder, but can't make out the spot where you started, and realize that there's nowhere to return to.

I couldn't write you last night, I needed some time for the dust to settle. I was so distraught when I wrote you from the parking lot. The weird states I find myself in since I met you. I didn't want to go home like that, the morning events with Tom still hovered in the background, so I just shoved my laptop into my bag and started driving. At some point I decided to go to the beach, just to walk, breathe some air, wind myself down. I put the car in one of those highway-robbery parking lots, got some takeout coffee, went to our bench on the boardwalk and sat down.

I tried to decide what to do with Erik. I felt sick just by thinking that I'd relieved his pain only to make it easier for him to get his revenge. I wish I could take it all back. But what should I do now? Should I say something about those emails? Confront him? Rat him out to Moni? I'm ashamed to even tell Moni anything about it.

My blood boiled and the storm in my stomach wouldn't subside, so I got up, tossed my barely touched coffee into a trash can and started pacing down the boardwalk, trying to tame my stress. I think it was more or less at that moment, just when it felt like I'm about to implode from the accelerating revolutions of my brain, that you surprised me from behind, placed a hand on my shoulder, and my heart was so startled it grew wings and fluttered out of my dress.

I was so surprised I didn't even recognize you at first. I hadn't seen you in so long, it was as if I'd forgotten what you looked like. You stood there, mulling the stem of a flower with your fingers, half smiling at me. Come here often? You winked. I stood there frozen, waiting for the pigeon that flew out of my heart to return to its coop.

What are you doing here? I mumbled. Your hair was mussed and there were dark circles under your eyes, but when you held out the flower and gave it to me your eyes were so clear, pools of emotion. I almost stumbled into them. Your mere presence turned the shade of the sea into a deeper blue. The breeze was so gentle, it caressed my face, soft and undemanding. Gold speckles of sunlight danced across the water, everything changed the moment I saw you.

As if to make sure this was really happening I slowly reached out to your cheek, touching the velvety stubble. Our strange set of rules baffled me, I didn't know what to do. You took a small step closer, and hesitated for a moment before embracing me. A faint dizziness swamped me as I inhaled your scent. I feared the moment this would end, didn't know how I'd manage to break away from you. You looked into my eyes as you slowly loosened your grip. I melted at your touch as you stroked my hair, my face, your finger lingering on my lips. You put your hand on the back of my neck and then you caught me completely off guard, just when you did the most obvious thing that you should've done long ago – you pulled me over and kissed me. After an infinite amount of imaginary kisses, you gave me a real one. I was so surprised that this simple reality seemed a lot more far-fetched than any fantasy I'd ever had about you. You kissed me with such sweet passion, and your taste was so familiar I could have sworn this had happened before. Only the intensity of what I felt proved that it hadn't. Drugged, I was sucked into your heartbeat, and warm streams of energy pulsed through my organs. I shut my eyes and for a moment it felt like I'd lost all muscle control; that I was simultaneously flying and drowning. At some point you broke away slowly, and we just stood there, dizzy. You took my hand, lacing your fingers in mine, and without a word we began walking towards our bench. Your steps were measured, and when we sat down you looked so tired. A little pale, maybe thinner. Baby, are you all right? I asked, and you took my hand and pressed it to your lips.

I'm here because there are things you just don't get if I don't look in your eyes when I say them, you said. So look into my eyes and listen carefully – Erik is not out to get you, he's not pulling anything, he really does want a different kind of relationship, I'm telling you this with the utmost certainty.

Something in your expression put me at ease, but still, it didn't make sense. Then what did happen? I asked.

You were silent for a moment and then said – I need to ask you something important, okay? Don't write me anything you don't really mean.

But I meant everything, I said. I don't know what was more jolting – your evasive behavior or this whole surreal "power" thing.

Your face suddenly darkened. What the hell are you talking about? Evasive? Me? You really think you have to fall on your knees? Don't you get what's going on between us? How can you describe me like that, so impenetrable? Seriously, Sheera, do you even see who I am?

The pain that spewed from your eyes stopped me. For a moment I thought I could see a glisten of tears. Seeing you like that, it crossed my mind that maybe I'd overreacted a little. Maybe it's the bracelet that keeps throwing me off balance. I reached out to touch you, but it wasn't like before. Like a child, you were wrapped in resentment.

I'm sorry if I said some things I shouldn't have, but look, I really can't do this anymore, I said quietly. So we're both here right now and we can finally talk about everything, why don't you just tell me?

You shook your head and looked out at the waves. I don't get you, I swear, you said. You don't have the tiniest bit of patience. You just want to get there. So here, here's an instant insight, just the way you like them, because I don't have any more patience for arguing either. Actually if you'd read what we wrote, you'd see that I already told you. You have power with words, Sheera. Words. That's my primary power too, but in a different way. So instead of arguing with me, try to figure out how you influence things with your words. Which includes the bundle of accusations you threw at me when you were at the height of your meltdown.

What...? Again I didn't understand.

You know what your problem is? You still insist on thinking you're normal. Cross the line already, accept the fact that you're not like Rona or those wise-asses around you. They don't care, but you can't afford not to! You get it? You can't play innocent, because your words have power. And you have no choice but to find it on your own. There are some things that nobody else can do for you, not even me.

But what do you mean that we have power with words? I persisted, I thought you said you hear thoughts, that we're different.

Right, we're different but alike, alike because we're different. Sound familiar? You have to find the rest on your own, so leave me alone and dig deeper into your words and figure out how you influence things. You're making me insane, seriously.

Okay, okay, don't go insane. Can you just explain how your power is related to words?

I'm not even sure I can explain anything to you anymore, you looked away. I don't know why we can't communicate, it's like a short circuit.

I didn't know what to say. A little ball hardened in my stomach, maybe because I knew you were right. Something in our communication was off. You buried your face in your hands, rubbed your eyes. You looked distraught. We sat there silently for a few minutes. I waited for you to look at me, say something. I knew that this time I had to leave with some answers.

But then you just got up and held out your hand. You asked where my car was, and we started walking towards it.

We walked in complete silence. I threw the occasional glance your way. There was something stiff and slow about your gait. I wanted to say – you don't seem so well, Michael, why don't you tell me what's wrong? We walked hand in hand but you seemed a million miles away and I knew it wasn't the right time to ask. We reached the car, you sat beside me, I placed the flower you gave me on the dashboard. You asked me to drive to a small café in the center of the city. I turned on the radio, no questions asked. We were quiet the whole way, and most of the time you just listened to the music with your eyes closed.

When we reached the café it took me a while to find a parking spot. When I finally did, I cut the engine and quietly asked, shall we? You opened your eyes and gave me an unfocused look. Your Agent Asshole is in that café right now, you said, so listen to me and just do as I say, okay? I looked at you, but couldn't make out what you wanted or what to say.

Get a grip, you said, you're going to walk in there, as if by total coincidence, and pretend to be surprised when you see him. You're good at faking it, right? So fake a good mood, be chipper. Walk up to him with a huge smile, kiss him on the cheek, chat him up, laugh, and tell him you're sorry you weren't so well when you met, but it doesn't matter because you've found someone else. And that's it, go sit down at some table and I'll join you in a couple of minutes.

I looked at you, confused, but your eyes told me this wasn't a good time to ask questions or argue. Thing is, I was suddenly overcome with the sense of adventure, and decided to play along. I gave you a huge fake smile, and asked – like this? You put on a theatrically grave expression and nodded dignifiedly. I opened the car door and walked towards the café, feeling like the lead in some bizarre play. I walked in, scanned the place with my eyes, and spotted Agent Asshole at a table with a famous actress. I skipped the part where I'm surprised that you knew all this and went straight into the role you'd written for me. I put on a huge smile and sauntered over, flowing with cheerfulness. Benny! I called out, totally over-friendly. I walked up, kissed him on both cheeks, noting his surprise at my enthusiasm. How are you? I asked, and before he could say anything I said – you look great! As he mumbled something I turned and held a hand out to the actress sitting with him, and introduced myself. By the way – I turned back to him and recited the line you fed me in the car – I'm so sorry about that lunch, it was such a bad day, but we've found someone else, so it doesn't really matter anyway. He nodded, somewhat confused, forced half a smile and asked – who? But I didn't reply. I just smiled, said we'd be in touch, and sailed on to another table.

I sat down, my heart pounding, not daring another look in his direction. I pulled out my phone and pretended to be busy with emails or God knows what. Out of the corner of my eye I saw you come in. You walked over and held your hand out for me to shake as if we were on a business meeting. You sat down facing me, your back to Agent Asshole. You winked and I suppressed a laugh. Well, what now? I asked quietly as you held back a smile. I started enjoying the game. A waitress with a perky ponytail handed us menus. Now look at the menu, you said, and at once you grew serious, and casually shut your eyes. I continued to look at the menu as if nothing had happened. The waitress appeared again, and I ignored her curious expression at the sight of you sitting there sleepily, and just ordered two cups of coffee. She walked away and you continued to sit there with your eyes closed, and at some point you mumbled that I should pretend to be talking to you.

About ten minutes later the agent and the actress got up to leave. He hesitated for a moment, then came up to us. Unlike me, he wasn't polite and simply ignored your existence. Sheera, he said, if you haven't signed yet, we might still be able to talk. I'll call you tomorrow. I was a little confused, but recovered quickly, smiled and just said okay.

When he left, I looked at you and burst out laughing. Would you please explain how you did that?

I love your laugh, your tired eyes smiled at me.

And…? I asked.

Look, you said, thoughts are made of words, right? So I can hear those words. But the hyper hearing is just my sensitivity, it's a sense that's too exposed. My power is the ability to affect what I hear, you understand?

Not really, I said, you're going to have to explain in more detail.

I hear too much even when I do nothing. The thoughts just gush into my ears if I don't stop them. But my power is not what I hear, it's what I do with it. I can change people's thoughts, influence them. If I focus on someone, I can separate each thought into single words, then focus on one word and pull it out, like with tweezers, and then I slowly dissolve it, and the thought changes. Sometimes I don't remove anything and just rearrange the order of the words and the whole meaning of the thought changes. I can move words inside someone else's head, you get it?

You're not shitting me, right? Is all I could say.

You look at the world through your inferiority complex, Sheera. That agent of yours needs to find work for his actors. After your meeting, he thought you were desperate and wanted to bend you.

When you walked in so confidently today you confused him. He immediately thought – maybe I was wrong. I heard his hesitation, and tightened his thought. I dissolved the word "maybe". Then I connected it to another thought, to a rumor he heard about you, how well-connected you are in the business. He's unaware of what I did, as far as he knows he changed his mind completely on his own.

I sat there, mute. How did you expect me to come up with such a dazed explanation on my own? If I hadn't seen it with my own two eyes, there's no way I'd have figured someone could do something like that.

The agent will call tomorrow, you said, pretend it's really hard for you to turn things around now, bring down the price. You'll get the actor you wanted.

I didn't know what to say. We sat there silently for a few minutes. I sipped at my coffee, which was already pretty cold.

You want to tell me I can do stuff like that too? I asked.

No! You said, appalled. That's exactly what I was afraid of! You don't know who you are because you've spent your whole life trying to imitate others, so don't try to imitate me now. Your power is different. Look for it inside yourself – not in me.

Okay, I promise not to imitate, but answer a few more questions, I insisted on clinging to this momentum before you disappeared again. What did you do that morning when we chatted for the first time on Facebook? How did you influence the ratings? And how did you get Moni to give me the show? How did you turn his thoughts around?

I didn't. You can't turn someone's thoughts around from black to white. At best, you can just move them a little. But even a little five degree nudge can cause a big change in behavior.

So what did you do? I persisted.

I heard Moni thinking that the competing channel was looking for content people, and I just added your name to that thought, you said casually, as if it were obvious. That made him suspect that maybe you'd already received an offer and that he'd lose you if he didn't do something. You live in fear that Moni will fire you, but you have no idea how afraid he is that you'll leave. That's another thing you don't see.

Really? I mumbled. I wish I could believe that Moni's scared of losing me. The waitress suddenly appeared with another cup of coffee, put it in front of me and left. I looked at you puzzled, and you reached out and took my hand in yours, and a sudden softness radiated from your eyes. I noticed your coffee was cold, and from behind your hair looks exactly like the hair on the woman at the next table, it's a little confusing, you winked. You tightened your grip and a gentle warm flow streamed up my arm. I couldn't take my eyes off you. You leaned towards me over the table and said – it was easy with Moni. A walk in the park. Kind of like with the waitress. And with Erik too. Would you understand already that they like you?

So who was it hard with? I asked.

You shook your head and released half a smile. You know what it's like to try to change a thought with someone who's locked? Think about a person who's got nothing to lose. There are people like that, Sheera. People who are even capable of killing, positive that killing is a good deed, because they believe in some God. Can you imagine the kind of determination you need to actually go and do something like that? Fierce determination, meaning crammed thoughts, completely locked, that ignore any other option. But even the most locked person in the world can suddenly experience a tiny crack in consciousness.

Wait a minute, I stopped you. Why are you speaking Tibetan again? What's a crack in consciousness?

You sighed and leaned back. It's hard to explain, Sheera. Hard to explain to someone who can't hear thoughts. You can feel it, if you use your imagination maybe you'll understand. When someone's determined, their thoughts are rigid, hard as a rock, but there's always something that can crack it. When I concentrate, I can actually hear that tiny screech when a crack opens in someone's mind. It can happen through the most random things, like a song on the radio that distracts and reminds you of something, or a waft of familiar smell, or some unexpected behavior, like with the agent when he was confused by your sudden over-confidence. A person can be totally locked-in but when a different emotion suddenly bleeds through, that's the crack. And inside that crack there's an opportunity to change someone's mind.

I suddenly realized I was sitting there listening to you with my mouth hanging open, so I closed it. As always, there was some degree of sense in what you said, but it still sounded implausible, unfounded. I could feel my pulse throbbing in my temples, my shoulder blades, my neck. The waitress passed by and you motioned for the check. Does your head hurt? I asked. You looked at me and the dark patches of fatigue suddenly stood out on your pale face. I wondered if it was a good time to ask you what was going on, if you'd finally tell me, but the waitress arrived with the check and you quickly pulled out a credit card.

Outside it was dark, and the pavement was bathed in the gold streetlamp light. You naturally wrapped your arm around my shoulder, as if we always walked this way. It felt so good, despite your measured steps, and I wasn't sure if your breathing was a little heavy. When we got to the car I stopped you. I gently pushed you back to lean against the car, put my bag down on the dirty asphalt and closed my eyes without saying a word. I reached out and raked through your hair. My fingertips massaged your roots, and once again I marveled at the tremendous difference between what I'd imagined so many times and the intense sensations I felt in reality. An electric cloud surrounded us, there was something so intoxicating about it, but I made a huge effort to control myself, to set aside your sweetness, to disregard my attraction. I focused solely on the pain, on your temples, your neck, your shoulders. When I finished you opened your eyes and I stumbled into your clear gaze again, sinking into it. I was surprised when you put your hands on my ass and pulled my body to yours. Have you ever noticed how you're turned on by power? You asked. Your heart beat so hard I could feel it thumping all the way down to my feet. What do you mean? I smiled and wrapped my arms around your neck. I hate these circus performances, but they really get your juices going, you said, pulling me even closer, just before softly squashing my lips with yours. Your body swayed back and forth, in perfect sync with mine. I was absorbed into you, and instantly forgot everything – the agent, Moni, even Tom. My hands acted as if of their own accord, feeling their way under your shirt, blindly reaching into your pants. Your realness was so sweet on my fingers, my tongue, my skin. He's mine, he's mine, I whispered to myself again and again in disbelief. Why don't we go to your place? I said softly. You kissed me again, but something loosened in your grip. All at once my passion collapsed and gave way to my worry. Don't make me be the only one here trying to stop this, you whispered into my neck, I just can't, this time I won't be able to do it.

I took one step back. Only then did I realize that it wasn't over, this strange arrangement of ours. I tried to settle my breathing. Scolded myself for naively believing things had finally changed. How did you get to the boardwalk? I asked. In a cab, you said. Come on, I'll take you home, I said, and forced myself into the car.

Are you feeling okay? I asked as you heavily sat beside me, wondering why you hadn't come on your motorbike.

Much better than before, you managed a smile.

Is it just me or are you getting more migraines recently? I finally asked. Sometimes they get worse, you said.

When did it start, these headaches? I asked. When I was born, you laughed, headaches are a built-in feature for people who hear too much.

Strange, you know, sometimes I can feel your pain in my shoulder blades, my arms, my back.

We drove silently. I had no idea what I was feeling. A mixture of so many things. I was worried about you. I suspected there was something important you weren't telling me, and I didn't know what it was. I also knew you were right, because what you showed me at the café only confused me and didn't bring me closer to understanding anything. But I was also wrapped in a kind of happiness, or maybe a quiet satisfaction, just from being close to you, from cracking your great wall of China and actually tasting you.

You closed your eyes, leaned your head back and placed your hand on my thigh. When we stood at the red light I looked at the flower laying there in the shadows on the dashboard, then looked at you.

So is this what you do with your power? I asked. Somehow, even after all the demonstrations, I still felt I hadn't solved your enigma.

No, you said, and opened your eyes. It was a just small demonstration, especially for you. No big deal, really. If I could only show you how I persuade people who are really extreme. Totally locked in. Sometimes I have to listen to one person for days. You wouldn't believe the focus you need to penetrate that tiny crack in consciousness, at exactly the right moment.

So why can't you show me?

Because it doesn't work like that. I'm not a performer, I don't do live shows. It all happens inside my head. No-one has to see and nobody needs to know.

I was silent. Your answer frightened me. I didn't know what to think. I'd seen how your power worked, but still had no idea how it was connected to me or to what I'm supposed to do. I remembered what you wrote to me earlier – how I get carried away with my fear and lose sight of the essence of my power. But what was I missing? What was I incapable of seeing?

When I got home I decided that this time I was going to do my best to see beyond what I was used to. My father was half asleep, the shadows of the TV news flickering over his face. My mother sat at the table with a cup of coffee, hunched over some magazines. Tom was focused on the computer and didn't even think about coming for a hug, just raised his head and looked at me for a moment with Ziv's eyes. What's up? I asked nonchalantly, to mask the tiny shiver I always get when he gives me that look, but I was even more shaken as he answered in perfect chorus with my father – no news. Something about the perfect family portrait without me made me rift a little inside. As if that's the way it was supposed to be. Two adults and a child.

Where were you? My mother asked without raising her eyes from the papers.

At work, I answered without batting an eyelid.

My father looked at me dubiously and then turned to Tom and said – well, your mom always had her secrets, and gave him his challenged version of a wink. He doesn't really know how to wink so he shuts both eyes hard and pretends it's a wink.

Oh please, I tried to keep cool, Tom and I have no secrets, we tell each other everything, don't we, Tom? And just as the words came out of my mouth I felt the lie slithering down into my gut, ugly and oily and grey.

So maybe I did see something differently, because I suddenly realized that they were onto me. There are so many things I keep to myself, that I can't tell, but meanwhile, my life goes on without me. When I'm not around the three of them talk about me, and the worst thing is that I only thought that Tom didn't have a father figure, because my father filled that vacuum, apparently.

I'm sitting here by the light of the laptop, looking at the peculiar flower you brought to the beach, alone in the narrow vase, only starting to open up. So wild and so delicate at the same time. I'm still trying to understand, Michael, but I'm so tired. I have no idea what the hell "power with words" means, or how I'll ever be able to do anything similar to what you did with the agent yesterday. I have no idea when I'll see you again, if I'll ever regain control of my life, or if Tom turning my dad into a role model is a good thing or a bad thing.

And yes, on top of everything I'm trying to figure out the answer to your question. I haven't forgotten. I thought about it all day and I'll find the answer, I promise.

When we reached your house I stopped the car by the entrance. You were still right there next to me, but I started to sense the hollowness of your absence. I wasn't sure what was supposed to happen now, if I was just going to start missing you again or if our visitation rights had changed. An inexplicable fear flashed through me. It was so hard to say goodbye.

You turned to me quietly and put your hand on my nape. There was something sad but also soft in your eyes.

The man who can make anyone do anything, I murmured, kissing your hand. A tiny smile escaped your lips as you said – not quite.

I looked at you questioningly.

I discovered a bug in my system, you said, taking a deep breath. It works on everyone, except for one person. I try to be patient, moderate, explain, and you refuse to believe, get angry, and can't take it anymore. I don't understand, is this what it's supposed to be like? I've never loved anyone like I love you. Our communication is supposed to be the best of its kind, first-class, crystal clear. So why are you the only person in the world I can't persuade to change her mind? I always answer all of your questions, how about for once you find an answer to one of mine.

I didn't know what to say. For a second I wanted to apologize. How did you wind up with such a stupid trainee? Dark misery began to spread over my insides like tar.

I hate it when you call yourself stupid, you said. Instead of apologizing, think of the reason. Why it's so easy for you to believe in my power but not in yours. Instead of seeing your influence, you prefer to get furious, go crazy and ruin everything. It's like you'd do anything to avoid believing how strong you are.

10:04 p.m.	Did the agent call today?
10:05 p.m.	Yes. We signed the actor I wanted. Look, I really wanted to reconstruct everything that happened yesterday, but I want to stop writing for a few days. Until I get it. Until I have an answer for you.
10:05 p.m.	Fine. I'll be patient. Catch up on my porn or something.
10:05 p.m.	There's just one more thing I have to ask you before you do that. That first night on the boardwalk, when you opened up my HBO channel or whatever it was, before you set me on this road of no return, did it occur to you to even ask me if this is what I want?
10:06 p.m.	That's a complex question.
10:06 p.m.	I have time for a complex answer.
10:07 p.m.	You're forgetting I could hear your thoughts. I knew you weren't happy. And... I had no choice.
10:07 p.m.	Why?
10:08 p.m.	I couldn't just leave you like that. You had an OK life, maybe it wasn't simple but you could handle it, and suddenly I came and messed it all up. But you couldn't have gone on with your normal life even if you hadn't known. Something would've changed.
10:08 p.m.	What?
10:10 p.m.	I told you. An ability is not an option. You're not just born with it. You can choose not to use it, but there's a price.
10:10 p.m.	What do you mean? That if I'd continued not knowing something bad would've happened?
10:11 p.m.	I don't know how to put it, Sea Song. But I'll try. Everyone has an ambition living inside.

	Not some childish urge that becomes worthless when we achieve it. A real desire, a reason to exist. If a person follows that ambition, they get where they're supposed to, for better or worse. But if they ignore it, it doesn't disappear. It finds a crooked way to come out. In frustration, in bitterness. It's self-destruction. That's how people get sick.
10:12 p.m.	Wow. It would've never even crossed my mind.
10:12 p.m.	I know.
10:12 p.m.	I've got to ask you... does that have anything to do with your headaches?
10:13 p.m.	I was actually referring to my mother. We all have different ways to self-destruct. She tried to suppress her powers and barely used them. Trust me, you don't want that.
10:13 p.m.	Is that why she died?
10:13 p.m.	After being sick for many years.
10:14 p.m.	But what was her ambition?
10:14 p.m.	I'm not even sure she knew. But her sensitivity was seeing flashes of what was about to happen. So if she'd used her power, maybe she would've been able to affect the future. Her own future too.

00:24 a.m.	Michael.... Are you awake?
00:24 a.m.	Yes.
00:24 a.m.	I'm reading it all again, I really intend to get it this time so I can give you a serious answer. I only have one more question. You told me about how you influenced Moni and Erik, but you didn't say how you affected the ratings of Big Fear that morning. What did you do?

00:25 a.m.   Nothing.

00:25 a.m.   So how did it happen?

00:25 a.m.   Sheera, if you believed in yourself you'd understand that it happened simply because you're good at what you do.

To: Sheera and Michael <softspoons@gmail.com>
From: Sheera and Michael <softspoons@gmail.com>
February 7, 2016 at 8:48 p.m.
Subject: Hey Michael, are you okay?

I know I promised to think and not to write until I had answers. But I just want to know how you are.

8:49 p.m.	Good to hear from you. I missed you.
8:49 p.m.	I miss you too… I'm so used to yacking away here every night. What are you doing?
8:50 p.m.	Nothing. Thinking about you. Watching the news in the dark on mute. They stopped a suicide bombing attempt in Thailand.
8:50 p.m.	Boring.
8:51 p.m.	Yeah, just some people's lives saved. Too bad, but it really is boring.
8:51 p.m.	Does it have anything to do with you? With what you do?
8:52 p.m.	Not everything is about me, Sea Song. But I always wonder whether it's a good thing or a bad thing, how no one really knows what they've been spared. What could have happened.
8:52 p.m.	That's not entirely true. People always play "what if".

8:53 p.m.   No, I mean like when an accident is prevented, or a catastrophe that could have even killed someone – if that person doesn't know, he just goes on living his life, depressed about all sorts of nonsense, because it's impossible to appreciate something when there's no way of knowing it could've happened but didn't.

8:53 p.m.   You mean me?

8:54 p.m.   No. But it's also related to you. To the fact that you have trouble appreciating your power because you're unaware of your influence. You have to pay attention to your choice of words. When you write me only about what you don't have, you give it power. It's like when you focus on making my pain go away and then it happens – it works the other way around too, when you keep putting all of your power into what's wrong.

8:55 p.m.   You make me sound like a spoiled brat, but you don't understand what I've been going through since we met. I'm going crazy. It's like I'm living in the dark, searching for a match to light so I can see something. Your secrecy also stresses me out sometimes. Like that investment account thing. Or where you were when I called from work and you didn't pick up. You want me to trust you, but I need you to talk more without my having to nag and ask all the time.

8:56 p.m.   Are you sure you want to know what's going on with me? I had a lousy day. Tedious conferences with Yanky and the partners in the VC fund he started after we sold the start-up. I work with them sometimes. Yanky is my only real friend, but on days like today I have no patience for their bullshit. Their priorities. They spend hours shooting the shit about the Three Commas Club while thinking about the secretary's ass. Wannabe success stories. I'm dead tired. My brain hurts. The kind of day where all you want to do is sit on the couch in your underwear and watch football. If only I loved football like they do, right? But all I love is you.

I love listening to you. I hear the tiniest strands of meaning behind every word you write. Like a symphony. Funny you think I don't talk to you enough. I've never talked so much to anyone in my life. And despite what you think, I've never lied to you. But you're so caught up in wanting me to tell you more, you don't acknowledge what you already know. No offense, but you're ignoring the signs now too.

8:57 p.m. So why do you love me if you think I'm so dense?

8:58 p.m. You're not dense, you're stubborn. And you're not entirely honest with yourself. And speaking of honesty, you actually caught me at a moment when I want you like crazy. I can't stop thinking about you since we met. Especially now... I'm dying here. You probably felt it and that's why you wrote, right? I'm lying here on the couch, Norah Jones and her sexy voice in the background, and you all over my mind, pinned against me as we stood there by the car, with all your softness. And your mutiny. And your hair, and your smell... you're right on time. Hey, how about a little power struggle? In the bedroom? That's what turns you on, isn't it? Think of me, laying here on the couch with the music... write me something dirty, what do you care. I've got my bracelet hand in my briefs, waiting for you.

8:59 p.m.   Michael... I can't stop thinking about it either. Can't stop thinking about you. And if we're being totally honest, then the truth is that yes, I could totally feel you thinking of me that way.

To: Sheera and Michael <softspoons@gmail.com>
From: Sheera and Michael <softspoons@gmail.com>
February 7, 2016 at 10:02 p.m.
Subject: My fantasy is simple. No props, no leather, no garter belts, no role playing. Just being with you. Just being.

It smells like kisses here, doesn't it? A warm, wet smell, that tastes like soufflé. The taste of our meeting is still with me, hasn't faded out. I promised you I'd do some thinking, but something's happened to me after the other night, I can't concentrate on anything. All I want to do is go back and feel that closeness we had. It almost hurts, I've never missed you this much. Do you think our connection has grown even stronger? Jesus, I've started to speak in Michael-talk, but I swear I could really feel you before. So I lay back slowly and shut my eyes, wondering – is he touching himself right now? Because maybe when you touch yourself and think about me, your sensations drift out the window and start making their way to me, over all the buildings in Tel Aviv and through all the busy streets, until they seep through the microscopic holes in the thin fabric of my panties, stroking me in the dark, in that twilight zone of ours where time or place have no meaning. Is that what you mean when you say we share fantasies?

I don't know what your fantasy is, but after all that restraint in real life, my fantasy is simply... to stop stopping. I imagine that moment when you asked me to help you stop, only this time instead of begging me to hold back, you beg me to come to your place. You allow it to happen, to rise and take over as we start to undress each other with uncontrollable urgency, finally letting go of the brakes.

I slowly open the door to your apartment, walking right into the soft Norah Jones lyrics wafting through the living room. You're lying on the yellow sofa, bathed in the last light of the day as it slips through the slits of the shutter. Bracelet hand in your pants, eyes shut, you're drawing me near, merely by thinking. I move silently towards you with bated breath, and when I'm beside you I lift one leg to straddle you. At the very last moment I gently pull your hand out of your pants and sit myself down on the exact spot where it was. You moan a small smile and move your pelvis a little, stiff and throbbing against me. I press my silent lips to your eyelids, one and then the other, breathing in the scent of your skin, placing my hand on your nape, pulling you up towards me. Hey, I mumble into your neck, any chance that at least in my fantasies you finally get rid of your clothes?

I hear your smile spreading sweetly in my ear, it's like warm honey dripping into me. I help you take off your t-shirt and throw it aside impatiently. You undo my shirt buttons and give me that melting look, while running one finger underneath my bra strap, and then you lean forward to kiss the soft cleavage tiding out of it. I clench my thighs against your body, pinned to you like a needle to a magnet. No point in resisting, it's stronger than me.

My body's so thirsty for your touch, my lips drink you up as if my life depended on it. Your taste from real life flashes back at me and rushes right to my head like narcotics, invading my blood and coursing through my veins. My hands yearn to touch you and don't know where to begin, your back, your face, your arms, your chest. We've yet to decide which one of us will submit and which one will take the lead.

The last strips of daylight fade into a thick darkness, and we're blinded in the shadows, hungry and lost, hastily clutching and tasting like two kids left alone in a candy store.

You whisper two words, my love, and they softly dissolve into my ear, but like a drop of water on parched lips, they also carry a certain sting. You turn me around, I'm on my hands and knees as you undo my hooks, and your chest is so hot on my back as it presses against me. For a moment I'm unsure, is this happening for real? I can genuinely feel you, you breathe into me and my heart slams wildly like some hysterical child. Kiss me, bite me, be gentle, be ruthless with me.

Your hands reach forward, my bra is flung away and I whisper something even I can't understand. Your hand disappears into the soft valley between my breasts, and I lose my breath as your other hand hovers down over my stomach, and shiver as it quietly infiltrates my panties. I'm fused to your touch, losing control, reaching behind me to grab hold, my head dropping back on your shoulder, tiny ripples of ecstasy crashing through me.

You're right against me but I miss you, I want to feel you on my back and still be able to see you. I want you wrapped around me from all sides, filling all my cracks because I'll never have enough. I want your flesh, your bareness, your control, your surrender, I want to feel you melting in my hands. My fingers feel back, searching for you, undoing your pants, pushing into your underwear. When I touch you a moan slips out of your mouth and bleeds into my skin, flickering through me. You're hot and hard and pulsing in my palms. You're gentle and cruel, smooth and rough, I discover more mystifying scents with every breath, another piece of you with every touch.

Kiss me baby, let me bite your soft lips, interrogate me with your tongue and I promise to tell you everything. Your beautiful groans wound me, you jerk my panties off with one quick pull, you're out of patience and the anticipation is dripping out of me as well. I spread my legs and when your hand touches me I thrust forward with a small shout. I can't wait anymore, I'm aching, don't play with me, fuck me, I whisper, come inside me already. I lean forward toward the armrest, my knees trembling, my arms gripping frantically, I have to hold on so I don't fall. You hold my waist and as you enter it feels as though you've penetrated my soul. I've lost everything at once, all life disintegrated around me and all I can hear is you murmuring, oh God, I'm dying. Don't stop, just don't stop, I whisper, as I can feel your excitement growing, your movements getting faster, stronger. I shudder in waves every time I hear you groaning, your heartbeat accelerates, pounding through me. I cry out, yes, go on, keep going until this tsunami drowns me in unbearable pleasure, pulling me deep into the sea, and then tossing me back onto the shore, dazed and confused, so much pleasure, I can't contain it all. It pours out of me as I beg you for more, I can't remember anything, not even my own name. Don't stop, Mikey, you're so deep in my being, my organs, my cells. I sink into the whirlpool, sucked in, twisting, dissolving in our miraculous blend.

10:11 p.m. My woman.
My love.
My princess.
My slave.
I surrender. I'm yours.
Give me room, let me link to your soul. Fill you all the way up to your throat.

To: Sheera and Michael <softspoons@gmail.com>
From: Sheera and Michael <softspoons@gmail.com>
February 8, 2016 at 9:18 p.m.
Subject: Something a bit unexpected

This morning I got up totally drunk. Last night was so strange. What was that? I've never had such a fantasy, it was utterly different. Had a life of its own. As if God took some time off from all his other business, came down and kissed it.

Something already began to happen when I wrote you. The room was pitch-black, only the light from the laptop and its warmth on my stomach. I lay on my back in the dark, slowly moving on the bed at the memory of those words, then suddenly it began. The strange thing is I didn't do anything, I didn't even touch myself. There's no subtle way of saying this. I felt you... really strong, between my legs. I found myself flinging my hands behind me to grab the headrails, panting, wriggling, moaning, baby, yes, more, harder my love, fuck me hard, my breathing came faster as my pleasure increased, and suddenly... it happened. I came. Not very intense, but it happened just through the power of the mind.

I felt so relieved when it was over, that my whole body collapsed onto the sheets. A tremendous exhaustion covered me, my eyes were as heavy as old theater curtains, and sleep just kidnapped me into it.

When I awoke, the first thing I felt was guilt. Jesus, what was happening to me? How loud was I? Most importantly – had Tom heard me from the other room? I quickly got up and woke him. He wasn't in a great mood, but he got ready for school pretty fast and didn't say anything.

I was a bit relieved, but on the drive to school I asked him if something had happened, because he looked kind of edgy. I don't know, maybe it's the dream, he said.

What dream? I asked.

I dreamt that something bad happened to you.

What was it?

I don't remember, he said as we stopped, but nobody was helping you and I couldn't save you either.

I gave him a fierce hug, though he locked his limbs and resisted me. Don't worry, I said, I don't need help, I'm always looking out for you and nothing bad happened to me. I was so scared he had heard something, even in his sleep.

After I dropped him off I texted you. Hey, did we fuck last night or was I imagining it? You texted a smile. It was a little scary... I wrote. Interesting, I didn't feel any fear from you at all, you replied. But what was that? I asked.

It's the power in your words, silly. Are you starting to understand?

Good thing I'd just pulled into the parking lot and had to stop because otherwise I'm not sure I'd have been able to keep driving. That's exactly the kind of thing you say that I never understand, but this time I could feel it, Michael, and I know I wasn't imagining or dreaming. So that's how it works? I spoke the words out loud to myself – I used my imagination to create a fantasy, I wrote the words down to the tiniest detail, I sent them to you, and then, it... became reality?

My heart thumped hard, startling itself.

I switched off the engine and took another moment to sit there, trying not to think about anything. I scooped up my bag and got out towards the elevator. When it arrived, empty, I walked in, looked at the pale face in the mirror and asked – so that's what I was supposed to understand? That what I write is what happens later? But that's impossible. And I'm not only talking about the cosmic likelihood of this fairytale. I'm talking facts: I've written thousands of things that never caused anything to happen. No, that can't be it.

My theory deflated. I exited the elevator and started walking pensively towards my office. On my way I ran into Erik, who looks great by the way, I smiled at him and he winked as he said good morning and kept walking down the hall, his boots echoing behind him. I entered my office, still in a turmoil, because after all I hadn't really cracked the riddle yet. What had my power unleashed last night, and how did it make the words work?

I turned on my computer and logged onto my email. Dozens of messages began pouring onto my screen. My eyes stopped on one from Avi. He'd replied to an old email he'd probably saved, about that drama series I didn't like which he couldn't sell. I opened the email and there was only one line, which he sent last night at eight thirty, probably just before calling it a day. The season is almost over and you still haven't helped me solve the advertising problem, he wrote.

I scrolled back. He was replying to one of the emails I'd deleted a few days ago.

Listen to me and listen good, I'd written to him once when I was really pissed off. Never, ever involve Erik in anything that has to do with my work. He just wants to ruin everything, that poisonous snake that slithers down the halls, I could strangle that repulsive reptile with my bare hands and watch him suffocate and die in agony, real slow.

I read it and the color drained from my face. With a trembling hand I picked up the phone and called Julia. She answered with a fake cheerfulness that forced me to be excessively nice. Tell me, sweetie, I said, sounding the least hypocritical I could, when Erik was in the hospital, did he have any trouble breathing?

I don't think so, she said, it was something in his stomach, why? I was so relieved I didn't even notice I wasn't answering, but just before I could say thank you and end the call, she suddenly said – oh but wait, in the ICU he was on this machine. What machine? I asked. You know, that machine, what you said, a ventilation machine.

I felt all the color draining from my face like prickly petals of ice. I silently put down the phone. My pulse was so loud it shook through my ears, every beat so heavy and strained as if it were squeezing an entire ocean out of my heart. Other than the dizziness, my head was completely blank. A thin buzz filled my ears. A minute or two went by until I began to recover. Could that be even remotely possible? Or was I finally losing it? Could it be possible, that my writing that crap about strangling Erik made him end up in respiratory distress in the ICU?

Shut up, you're delusional! The little responsible voice shouted inside. Get up, go to the bathroom, wash your face and snap out of it!

I obeyed. I went to the bathroom, twisted the faucet, cupped the clear water in my palms and threw it into my face, accidentally spraying some drops on the mirror. I looked at the little droplets as they started to trickle down and then at my face. I was very pale. I reached out blindly for the paper towels and took a couple of them, but kept looking in my own eyes instead of drying my face. I'd written a sex fantasy and had an orgasm without anyone touching me, myself included. I wrote Avi, wishing that Erik should suffocate and die in agony, and he'd almost turned into a corpse on a hospital bed.

I remembered that afternoon when you surprised me on the boardwalk. When you said that even if Erik had read it, his response was different from what I thought. But no, that's impossible. It's a coincidence. It's not that. I must have taken it too far. As usual, even if I see the signs I read them wrong. It doesn't make any sense. I'm always joking with Avi, and I'm sure that I've written him at least once that he should drop dead or something, and nothing ever happened to him. See? This is what happens when you tell me to think things through on my own and don't give me any clues. I start to make up b-rated horror movies.

I got it together and went back to the office, trying to forget about it and somehow get through my day. But I was suddenly very careful. I walked on eggshells. Just to make sure, I went over every stupid email I sent at least three times.

At this rate, with the weird theories I've started to develop, the next step will be to ask my parents to adopt Tom and have me committed. So please write back as fast as you can.

9:33 p.m.	Wow.
9:33 p.m.	Don't "wow" me. I need a decent reaction.
9:34 p.m.	Can I answer you with a question?
9:34 p.m.	I think you just did.
9:35 p.m.	So here's another one. What did you feel when you thought you understood?
9:35 p.m.	What did I feel? I don't know. Like I was riding on a bullet train and someone had suddenly yanked the emergency brake.
9:36 p.m.	And have you ever felt that way before, when we talked about reading the signs?
9:36 p.m.	No.
9:36 p.m.	So?
9:36 p.m.	What are you trying to say, that I've finally hit the bullseye? Just when I had the weirdest thought I could imagine?
9:37 p.m.	You're still not entirely there, but you're totally in the ballpark.
9:37 p.m.	Oh come on, you're killing me. I don't understand a thing.
9:38 p.m.	Then start asking. I'm the man in your life

	whom you can ask anything.
9:38 p.m.	I don't even know where to start…
9:38 p.m.	Start slowly.
9:38 p.m.	Are you trying to tell me that I was the reason Erik went to the hospital?
9:39 p.m.	Yes.
9:39 p.m.	Are you kidding me?? Because of that stupid little email I wrote Avi? Is that how my power works?
9:40 p.m.	No. Not because of that.
9:40 p.m.	Then what do you mean?
9:41 p.m.	Not only that, but that too. Chill down for a minute, I can feel your stress. Sit down and listen for a second, but openly, without fear, and without judging yourself. Can you do that?
9:41 p.m.	Let's say I can.
9:42 p.m.	Listen, Sheera. You have the ability to relieve pain. So just like any other gift, the important question is not whether it exists, but what you do with it. My mother used to say that a talent is a blessing and a curse. Your talent has to do with pain, so you can make pain disappear but you can also intensify it. And this ability multiplies its strength when you express it in words and combine the two abilities.
9:43 p.m.	Are you a total moron? Why didn't you just say so from the start?
9:43 p.m.	Would you have believed it? Come on, you barely believe a word I say as it is.
9:43 p.m.	You could've tried!
9:43 p.m.	I told you, there are things you have to find out on your own. You only gain a deep understanding of them when you feel them happening.

9:44 p.m.	But I still don't get it... what does it have to do with what I wrote in the email? You know how many times I texted Avi in meetings, writing "I wish they would choke" but nothing happened?
9:44 p.m.	Baby, don't get so defensive on me, OK? Separate yourself from the guilt, or you won't be open to understand.
9:44 p.m.	Okay, okay, just go on. How does it all add up?
9:45 p.m.	A word is just a shell. Like a slingshot without a stone, or a gun without a bullet. You can jokingly write "I wish they would choke", and then nothing will happen. But you can also load the gun. You can focus on a certain feeling, or some desire that burns in you, for days. Weeks. Months. It piles up inside, sharpening itself, gaining precision and meaning. Intensifying. And then there's so much passion and power when you write that one simple word "strangle". The phrasing doesn't matter, your power is in the intention. I'm trying to tell you that this time it worked because you really meant it.
9:46 p.m.	Oh God. Wait a second. I need some air. I'll be right back. I'm going to get some coffee.
10:03 p.m.	Okay, I'm back. I'm trying to take deep breaths and understand what I've caused. Michael, I'm shaking all over and I can't stop it. I'm trying to find some reason to this madness. So it's all about passion? Like in the fantasy I wrote, where I felt the passion, and then later I felt the sex with you as if it were real?
10:04 p.m.	Passion is important, but the thing is first of all to recognize your true intention. Sometimes your true intention is to hurt someone. There

	are thousands of ways to say a word. Ironically, boastfully, cynically, humorously, reluctantly. So the question is what you really wanted, and how precisely you expressed your desire. The intent is at the base of it all. Then there's the passion with which you wrote it, and passion is like gunpowder, it thrusts the intent forward. So you realize what you did? You rammed full force into Erik. With all of your power.
10:05 p.m.	But those were just words. Words that people around me say all the time. It doesn't make sense... look, I read some more about fibromyalgia.... Maybe that's what's wrong with Erik after all.
10:05 p.m.	There's nothing wrong with Erik. You said it yourself – he looks great. Get this into your head, when you feel such hatred, such a strong intention of hurting someone, or getting back at them, you can cause tremendous pain even to someone who doesn't have any illness.
10:06 p.m.	But how do you know he doesn't? Just by hearing his thoughts?
10:06 p.m.	I'm telling you he doesn't, OK? If on top of everything he had some kind of pain disease you would've finished him.
10:06 p.m.	Do you really not see how any other explanation would seem more normal than the one claiming my intentions put someone in the hospital?
10:07 p.m.	You keep forgetting you're not a normal person, Sheera. You have power, and you can say it doesn't make sense until you're blue in the face, but it'll still work. Especially on people who care about you. Erik really cares about you. You affect him, I've already told you. So what if people

around you say words like that. If you have thick skin you can avoid them. But there's no defense against what you write. Your words have power. They penetrate everywhere, right through the cracks, with all their might.

To: Sheera and Michael <softspoons@gmail.com>
From: Sheera and Michael <softspoons@gmail.com>
February 9, 2016 at 2:58 a.m.
Subject: I don't understand how I'm supposed to suddenly stop hating someone I can't stand

Michael. I can't sleep. It's 3 a.m. I keep tossing and turning. Look, I don't know what to do. Really. I don't want to be responsible for this kind of thing, even if it's someone I can't stand. I keep running thoughts and memories through my mind, about things I did or didn't mean. What I wrote, what I didn't write, I write millions of words every day. I have this sudden fear that I've hurt other people. I can think of all kinds of annoying people that I wished would disappear from my life. And the truth is I've picked up quite a few along the years. I'm scared shitless. You've brought me to a state where I'm just afraid to think. I'm afraid it'll slip into something I write without my being aware of the meaning. I can't be so calculated all the time. My thoughts have a life of their own, they don't really ask me before popping up – what can I do? How can I not feel stuff like that? Everyone hates someone, we all get pissed off and sometimes fantasize about killing someone, making them disappear. How can I stop feeling hatred? How can I never say anything bad about anyone? I'm not a saint. I'm not an angel. I'm fucking human. My emotions have always been intense, but I managed to contain them. It's just that ever since the bracelets the emotions carry me away… they're like a raging river, so how is this shit supposed to work? How do you control it?

03:02 a.m.	Don't freak, Sheera, it's really simple. It works exactly like it is on the inside. Without faking it, without lies, without denials. Just as it is. That's why I said that in order to control your power, you have to really get to know yourself.
03:02 a.m.	Simple? It's crazy complicated! Look, the more I think about it, the more it seems that I'm just not cut out for this... I'm totally serious. I want you to help me. How can I shut down those channels? Can I opt out? Unsubscribe? Talk to Customer Service? Who do you call if you just want to turn off your special powers? I'm not kidding, baby, I'd really like to go back to being a normal person. I'm not good at this. It's over my head. So don't be upset... but I really think it's best that you help me shut it down or give it to someone else who can grasp it.
03:03 a.m.	Are you for real? I don't know if I should laugh or cry.
03:03 a.m.	Why?
03:03 a.m.	Your childishness. You crack me up. You make me sad. You captivate me. All at once. So I can't decide what to do either.
03:04 a.m.	Why childish?
03:04 a.m.	Can you hear yourself? First of all, I'm sorry to inform you that I'm not God. I don't give or take special powers, nor do I lend them with interest. I'm human. Just like you. The power to take away pain is yours. So is the power to create reality with words. You were born with it and ignored it until now, all I did was draw your attention to it, I didn't give you anything. You can't shut down a power. You can't exchange it or get a refund. I can't believe I have to explain

	this to you. It's like a singer asking to give away his singing talent. It's in your soul. No matter what you decide to do, first of all you should understand, Sheera. It's your power. You can't give it back.
03:04 a.m.	So I'm fucking stuck with this for life? Michael, I'm not kidding, this is not for me. I can't stop feeling the things I feel. What do you expect me to do, to stop getting angry? To never get annoyed? Not to say or even think one bad thing about anyone because it might send them to the hospital??
03:05 a.m.	I don't expect anything from you. I told you.
03:05 a.m.	Yeah right, you don't expect anything. I'm a total disaster. Everything I do gets screwed up somehow. I've never felt so clueless in my life.
03:05 a.m.	It only seems that way now. It's not true.
03:05 a.m.	Yes it is... I take away your headaches almost every night, but they just get more frequent. So assuming they're not an excuse to avoid seeing me, what are you afraid to tell me? What am I doing wrong?
03:06 a.m.	Actually you've become much better at making pain go away. But other things develop simultaneously. It's complicated.
03:06 a.m.	Yes, I get it, I also have this power with words that I don't know how to use. I'm still shocked that you wanted me to figure it out on my own, in that roundabout way. You're a total idiot. Why did you refuse to explain it?
03:06 a.m.	I wish I could explain. I wish I knew why people have trouble understanding without experiencing the pain on their own flesh. Trust me, I don't want it to be this way. But that's the way

it is. My work is to prevent things. To stop what really shouldn't happen. People listen to news broadcasts every hour, but they never get told what didn't happen. There's no way they can know what was prevented, but if they were to see death flash in front of their eyes, they'd appreciate life a lot more. You get how crazy it is? At first all I cared about was the lack of recognition, that nobody knew what I was doing, but that's bullshit. That goes away when I remind myself that I'm actually doing it for myself because it's what I want to do. The worst thing is the futility. When something doesn't happen to you, you have nothing to learn from. If nothing happened to you, and you don't even know it didn't happen, how can you draw conclusions?

03:07 a.m. So that's what you do? You prevent things from happening? Why did you tell me you're a start-up investor?

03:08 a.m. I didn't lie, Sheera. You think you're the only one going crazy and that I don't get you, but nobody understands you better than I do. When you have this intangible gift nobody knows about, you can easily lose contact with the world. But startups are tangible. You can see them. You can talk about them. Sometimes I get up in the morning and I don't know if what I did the day before really happened or it was all in my head. That maybe I'm inventing my own life, or the tragedies. I need something to hold on to, and business is tangible and sane. It's the only reason I still do it. I don't need the money anymore, and as time goes by I take less interest in it. But it's my link to the world. To a job normal people can understand. There's no name for my real work.

03:08 a.m.   Great, and mine has a name. Spokeswoman. But what good does that do me?

03:09 a.m.   Look, it's a catch-22. You're a different kind of person but you compare yourself to normal people. It's a trap you've been stuck in all your life without knowing, and now you're sniffing around outside and wondering if you should get out. There's no way you can compare yourself to Rona, for instance, without getting frustrated. You're not like her. But that's all you know, which is why you cling to it. You can't let go of what's normal, because that's how you define yourself, but that definition is wrong. I understand, believe me. I know what it's like when people ask you – so what do you do for a living? And you have to keep lying. What do you call what I do? Am I good at it? Am I bad at it? Those are questions I've stopped asking, because there's no way to answer them without failing. I don't know how I rank, and I don't even know what list I'm on.

Everything I say about myself is always a lie, because what can I say? At startup meetings I call myself an angel, because it's something people can grasp. On Facebook I call myself a lifeguard, as a joke, but that's not really true either. I'm a preventer. When I succeed – nothing happens. I have no one to give me feedback, nobody I can compare myself to or exchange stories with. I only have you... have you ever thought about that?

03:10 a.m.   This conversation is making it hard for me to breathe. What kind of things do you prevent? Please tell me.

03:10 a.m.	Don't get mad... I promise to tell you. But not now. It's complicated, and not for emails. You can figure out some of it on your own. It's not that complicated. I live here, so I prevent disasters that can happen in Israel. But as time goes by, I realize the futility, because clearly I don't have the ability to control everything. There are so many people here with desires, and conflicts, and memories. It's never-ending.
03:10 a.m.	Not for emails, but God knows when we'll meet again. Michael, you scare me. I don't know how you can live like this. There's no way I can. What good does it do to understand that my hatred can be lethal, if I don't know what to do about it? How the hell can I totally stop hating people?
03:11 a.m.	You can't stop hating people, but you can control it. You know what you feel when you hate someone, don't you? So when you recognize the hatred, step away. Stop yourself and don't spit it out at people. Take it out some other way or try to accept reality as it is.
03:11 a.m.	But that's just it. I don't want to live that way... don't you see?
03:11 a.m.	I do, but you'll get used to it, I promise. You're in limbo. The confusion will go away. And it'll help if you find your true destiny instead of fighting it. Cross those lines already, admit you've been walking in the wrong direction for too long. When someone does what they're destined to do, they're at peace with themselves. So they also feel less hatred.
03:12 a.m.	Great, so what are you telling me? That I'll only be at peace with myself if I write this hippie mumbo jumbo about light and love? That's not who I am! The mere thought of it makes me

	want to jump off a cliff. I don't want to. You're wrong, this is not for me.
03:13 a.m.	Cut the bullshit, OK? You don't know what you're destined to do, but you're very close. Don't worry, when it comes, you'll feel like I did when it happened to me. You'll be overcome with a sense of calling. It'll burn inside you. Everything will change. You're not going to want to do anything else.

To: Sheera and Michael <softspoons@gmail.com>
From: Sheera and Michael <softspoons@gmail.com>
February 9, 2016 at 9:09 p.m.
Subject: Whose life is it anyway

At the end of our conversation last night I really didn't have anything left to say, I'd worn myself out, and at some point I fell asleep for like an hour, half sitting half lying on the living room couch. I awoke when too-bright, too-cruel rays of sun suddenly pierced in through the window. Reality hit me all at once. I'm not a normal person, but I think like a normal person and I can't stop my thoughts. I need to watch my words and I need to figure out what's going on. To learn to read the signs. Dammit. Why me?

Tom.

The thought of him made me leap from the couch. I rushed to his room. My sweet boy slept there like a little angel, sprawled across the wrinkled sheets, but he didn't seem calm. His breathing was too heavy. What's wrong with him? I sat next to him on the edge of the bed. I put a hesitant hand on his chest. He started shifting uncomfortably, as if having a bad dream. Is that how my touch affects him? Is it me causing this? I took my hand off and got up quietly. He rolled to the right and then to the left, and then it seemed that he was calm again. I walked to the bathroom. It felt like my legs were in shackles. I never knew how exhausting fear can be. I turned the faucet and put my face under the cold stream. The coolness pricked my skin as it brought me back to life. But whose life was this? Over these past months you've really managed to convince me that I don't know who I am. I'm doing something really wrong, but can't interpret what it is. All of my instincts, all of the insights I've gathered, all the rules – everything suddenly seems wrong. If I can't understand this new world I'm in, and have to let go of what I know of my old world, what can I trust? What can I lean on?

I got dressed, made coffee and went to wake Tom. He woke up startled, but when he saw me, he softened a little. I hugged him, and for a quick moment he seemed little again. Skinny and fragile and so dependent on me. What time is it? He muttered into my neck. It's seven, I said, you gotta get up. I'm tired, Mom, he said. So am I, I said wordlessly, and stroked his head.

The drive to school was silent. He put on his seatbelt with the giant backpack still on his back. I turned on the radio. We listened to the news, but he didn't ask me to explain anything, just asked me to turn it off. I didn't argue. I looked at him. I smiled. He just said, Mom, your eyes are really red. Grandpa thinks you don't get enough sleep.

Grandpa isn't always right, I said, and he looked at me angrily and said – no, Grandpa knows what he's talking about.

There's something strange going on with me and Tom. For the first time since he was born, I feel like I don't entirely know how to handle him. His clinging to my dad, the anger, the violence. Suddenly I'm not sure of anything. It's not just these fucking powers, it's also my motherhood.

On the way to work I got a message from you – when you feel like this, just remember that you affect everyone.

I didn't answer. I didn't want to say that I can't decide what to feel, that I can't get up one morning and resolve not to ever be sad again. I didn't want to tell you that you should watch a Seinfeld episode or something, because I can't live like this, the way you expect me to. Tears stung my eyes. I wanted to tell you to leave me alone.

Tom spent the night at my parents'. I called my mother and wanted to tell him good night, but she said he was in the middle of a game of Rummy with my dad and didn't want to talk. That's never happened. I was going to end the call but then she asked, Sheerie, what happened the other night? Did you have a bad dream? I felt my pulse quickening.

I don't think so, why? I said, and I felt so terrible, like a terrible mother.

Tom said something, he heard you shouting at night. I asked if you had a friend over, and he said you were alone but that sometimes you sleep with the door locked.

I was silent. All of the words desiccated in my mouth.

Sheerie, Dad asked me to ask you if you were seeing someone, she said.

No, Mom, I said as the lie noosed itself around my neck, you can tell Dad there's no one.

There's something different about you, she said, Dad's been saying so for weeks, that something about you has changed and he can't put his finger on it.

Everything's fine, Mom, I said, trying desperately to hide my choked voice, kiss Tom for me before he goes to bed, okay?

Michael, what should I tell them? The three of them keep talking about me, and I don't know what to tell them. What should I say, that I've been carried away like an infantile teenager? That since I met you I have no idea who I am and my life is falling apart? Maybe I'm not really lying when I say I don't have anyone. Let's face it, you're never really here. I am so utterly alone with this crap.

9:31 p.m.		Enough, Sheera, go to sleep. You're wearing yourself out.
9:31 p.m.		Enough??

9:32 p.m.	We'll talk about it tomorrow, after you get some sleep.
9:32 p.m.	There's no way I'll be able to fall asleep. Could we please stop these idiotic chats and go have a drink somewhere? I need to see you, to talk.
9:33 p.m.	I'm not feeling so great.
9:34 p.m.	Michael, what's going on? What's wrong with you? Would you tell me already? Why are you only drifting further away?
9:35 p.m.	Stop it. I can't take this resentment.
9:36 p.m.	What? What are you talking about?
9:37 p.m.	Lying won't help. When you hate me I feel it. I wanted you to figure it out on your own but apparently that's never going to happen.
9:38 p.m.	Hate...? Are you crazy? I love you.
9:39 p.m.	Stop it, Sheera! There's no way you don't understand, I don't believe you anymore. I've barely gotten out of bed the whole week because of your lies, and like a blind person you keep up this act of how hurt you are, and now you complain that I don't want to meet you. That's your love? Is that how you love me?
9:40 p.m.	You haven't gotten out of bed in a week? Why don't you ever say anything? And why do you think I'm lying? I really do love you!
9:41 p.m.	The fuck you do! You have no idea what love is, Sheera, and all the emails in the world won't help, you don't learn a thing! I've told you a hundred times, think about what you do, what you're creating here, you don't need to defend yourself against me, damn it, I'm on your side! I'm not your fucking kickboxing coach!

9:42 p.m.	Mikey, calm down for a second... have you taken your temperature? You sound completely out of focus. It's impossible that you've been in bed for a week, I saw you a few days ago...
9:43 p.m.	Listen to what I'm telling you already! I'm not delusional, you are!
9:44 p.m.	Baby, I'm on my way over to take you to the ER.
9:45 p.m.	No, I don't need a doctor! And don't you dare come over, how many times can I explain? Can't you see that when your feelings go wild, I can't stand your thrashing even from a distance? You write that you love me, you come at night and melt away my pain, but then you get up in the morning with those fucked up thoughts about me not wanting you, about me ruining your life. You send the pain back a hundred times stronger with your resentment. You think I don't know what's going on? I can hear and feel your subtext so loudly you have no idea! I thought that after our meeting you'd realize how much I want you and you'd calm down, I dragged myself out of bed with painkillers strong enough to knock out a horse, but even after you found out about Erik you're still kicking, so what kind of doctor are you thinking of? It's you, you're making me sick, can't you see that?
9:48 p.m.	Mikey, I don't understand... It's true that I hated Erik, but how can you even compare?
9:50 p.m.	Look, I can't do this crossed wires thing anymore. You're just like my father, you refuse to see reality. I can't live like this. You're wrecking me physically, I can't take it anymore. You've brought me to the edge. Let's stop. It's best if we just cut this off. There's no choice.

9:50 p.m.   Mikey, you're not serious, are you?

9:51 p.m.   I can't handle this. You've crushed me. You don't want to trust me, but have you ever thought about how the hell I'm supposed to trust you? I'm your other half, aren't I? So why is my other half killing me? You hypnotize me with your storms, and then you explode all over me with your crazy fears. Acknowledge your power already! You're fucking causing pain, you have power in pain, in words, own it already! Forget it, you don't even need me. Just keep reading everything you wrote here until you understand. All the answers are here in the words, screaming out to you! I have to go, Sheera, I'm sorry. You've finished me off. It's too painful.

10:03 p.m.   Mikey, I keep calling and you're not picking up. Let's just leave it, okay? Get some sleep. Calm down. I'll calm down too. We'll think everything over and talk in the morning, okay?

To: Sheera and Michael <softspoons@gmail.com>
From: Sheera and Michael <softspoons@gmail.com>
February 10, 2016 at 2:58 p.m.
Subject: Mikey, are you all right?

Without my even touching it, the bracelet you gave me fell off my hand yesterday as if someone had cut it with a knife. I know it's a sign, but I don't know what it means. Please tell me what's going on with you... your phone is off, and I'm worried sick.

To: Sheera and Michael <softspoons@gmail.com>
From: Sheera and Michael <softspoons@gmail.com>
February 11, 2016 at 11:15 p.m.
Subject: Baby, just show a sign of life. Please. I'm so worried.

To: Sheera and Michael <softspoons@gmail.com>
From: Sheera and Michael <softspoons@gmail.com>
February 12, 2016 at 6:34 a.m.
Subject: Mikey, I think I get it. Let's talk, please.

This morning

An entire percussion band set up camp in my head

To prevent me from looking out the window

At the sickly sun that stumbled through the pine needles, to find me half dead.

I crawled to the kitchen for coffee,

The radio is still on from yesterday, I forgot to turn it off,

And Leonard Cohen reminds me that you loved me once, A thousand kisses, a headache, a cough.

A dirty black cloud has come through the window

And sat down on the empty chair, as if to say it will never give up.

Listen, I said, some people depend on my mood

So I can't be your friend anymore,

And on your way out bring me the milk from the fridge if you don't mind.

Meanwhile, the radio sent out a sound that trembled in my chest,

If I'm not mistaken it was an old song

That twisted and rose like vapor, with the chance of surviving this day.

To: Sheera and Michael <softspoons@gmail.com>
From: Sheera and Michael <softspoons@gmail.com>
February 13, 2016 at 7:58 p.m.
Subject: Mikey. Just so you know that although everything is falling apart, and despite everything you think, I do. Always remember that I really do love you.

Part Three

To: Sheera and Michael <softspoons@gmail.com>
From: Sheera and Michael <softspoons@gmail.com>
February 15, 2016 at 2:58 p.m.
Subject: Start over without me, Sheera.

February 16, 2016 at 11:18 a.m.: Oh baby... I just came in here and saw.... How could you? Why did you do it, my sweet Mikey?

To: Sheera and Michael <softspoons@gmail.com>
From: Sheera and Michael <softspoons@gmail.com>
February 23, 2016 at 9:04 pm
Subject: I want to know what happened to you, but don't really want to know

My mind will be flooded with disaster scenes if I start imagining what happened to you, why you haven't answered your phone in two weeks, and why this mailbox is so silent and empty.

Why my words are suddenly echoing back at me.

Are you that mad at me? Did you delete everything we wrote here because you don't want any memory of what you had with me?

To: Sheera and Michael <softspoons@gmail.com>
From: Sheera and Michael <softspoons@gmail.com>
February 27, 2016 at 10:10 p.m.
Subject: I don't know what this is, Doctor, I think it used to be my heart

At first it was like a slap in the face. Cruel, stinging and dry.

Then, for a minute or two, I was gripped by sheer terror. Nothing is coincidental anymore, everything has a hidden meaning, even the password I automatically type to get in here. I'm a terrible student who causes unbearable pain because there's power in my words, but I have no idea how to read the signs. Maybe I misunderstood your meaning again. Why should I go on without you? What happened to you? What have I done now?

Then I stopped.

Because no matter how angry you are, if you came in here and deleted everything, does that at least mean you're all right?

I don't know. It definitely means that you're capable of typing a password, and five words, and pressing control-A and delete.

I was a little relieved, because up until that moment I wasn't entirely sure you weren't dead. And believe it or not, even if you never want to see me again, I'd still hope you were alive and well.

I've been coming in here a few times a day for the past week, just to make sure it wasn't a dream. I hoped it was some strange cyber bug, or that you really did delete everything but then had a change of heart, maybe wrote something, or recovered our correspondence. But it always stays empty in here.

I've grown used to living in this mailbox with you, and now it's like coming home and discovering that everything's gone. The furniture, the carpets, the stuff in the closets, the memories, the smells. I can't get used to being here with only the ceiling and walls. When you listen to this cold silence, you can't help but think that maybe there never was any real love here at all.

But I know what I felt here, Mikey. I just don't know what happened to you, especially after that night. You haven't replied in a long time. I stopped calling. Could it be that you don't even know about that crazy night? It was a few days after you left, maybe you're not even aware that it happened.

If you do know, don't worry. I'll get over it. Just give me some time.

Hey, is this what you meant when you said one day I'd wonder whether my power was a blessing or a curse? Because I think I've shattered. And that place where I always felt one big sense of longing for you, well now it's like thousands of tiny broken longings. Thousands of shards.

There's probably a really good reason for everything, and someday I'll know what it is, right? I'll know what it is and maybe even shake my head and laugh about it.

To: Sheera and Michael <softspoons@gmail.com>
From: Sheera and Michael <softspoons@gmail.com>
March 3, 2016 at 9:34 p.m.
Subject: Suddenly I remember

Strange, because ever since you left, when I get up in the morning I remember. I never forget anymore. I open my eyes and immediately know that you're gone, and I remember what happened to me afterwards. I also know that the person I used to be is not who I am any longer.

I wake right into that knowledge, and it's so frightening, it spreads over me like a heavy blanket with no beginning or end. I've never felt incapable, or unable to handle things or know how to get by. Suddenly I can't trust myself, I have no idea what I can or can't do, and all I want is to count on myself again. But everything inside is shaking, my kidneys, my liver, my lungs.

So I get up quickly in the mornings, as if there was something to get up for. I go to the bathroom and brush my teeth, spit the white snail of toothpaste into the sink and look in the mirror. For a second it soothes me a little and I can swear it's that same woman from back then. What have you done? I ask her, and instead of replying she just imitates me. God, she's so dumb.

You know, after you told me that first time, I couldn't stop wondering how someone else would react in my shoes. If suddenly one day someone appeared in their lives out of the blue, showed them the burning bush and said – okay, listen up. You have powers you're not aware of. And now, if you don't mind, move your ass and start using them. Well, what are you waiting for? Wasn't I clear enough for you?

You kind of freak out when you're told such a thing. You start calling to mind every single sci-fi movie you've ever seen, and you can't decide if it's a dream or it's a scam and you're a total idiot. Something inside you is just dying to believe it, but you hold back on it because you know it's impossible, come on. It takes a while until you figure out that it's possible simply because it's not what you thought. It's nothing like any movie you'd seen. Takes some time to realize that your "power" is entirely human, after all, any idiot can cause pain. And of course all words have power, even if we don't acknowledge it. So you too have these human traits, but they're warped – they're ten times stronger, or a hundred times stronger, or God knows how many times. It takes a while before you realize that you're not about to see any magic tricks, and you're very far from what anyone would call "a hero". That only if you try very hard you might spot that quiet whispering spell that's crawling underneath our lives, and cannot really be explained. A spell that works in very unpredictable ways, and if you don't understand it, it goes wild and suddenly turns into a snowball that crushes you at the bottom of the slope. You were right, Mikey, there really is no way to explain it. Some things can only be understood through the flesh, through the bones.

I never told you, but after that quirky conversation we had by the entrance to my building, when you told me "you don't know who you are" and I was sure you were nuts, I asked around a little. I'd pull it out in the middle of conversations, pretending it was a hypothetical question – what would you do if one day you found out you had a power you didn't know about? I wanted to know how others would react. I also wanted to check, maybe it hadn't only happened to me, maybe it had happened to someone else who was also ashamed to talk about it.

When I asked Rona, she gave me a slightly astounded look, which soon became a slightly worried look, and then when she smiled hesitantly, I grabbed the opportunity to back out and said – just kidding.

When I asked Gidi from the Promo department he looked at me somberly and said – it isn't funny, I really do have powers. My eyes were almost ripped open when I asked – Really? What kind of powers? My intuition is insane, and I can read people like that, he snapped his fingers right in my face. It startled me a little. At first I was surprised by his answer, but then I realized he wasn't actually reading anybody, and it annoyed me to think that some people could be so full of themselves that they had no problem believing in their power, even if it doesn't really exist.

But Avi was the funniest. When I asked him what he would do if somebody told him he had the ability to remove pain, he thought about it for a moment, then said he would stick a fork in people's arms, and then immediately try to take the pain away to see if his power really works. After a while I'd probably lose interest and ditch it, he winked, like those new apps that keep coming out. I laughed so hard at his response. But then I understood that we all define powers differently, we've all been influenced by different movies, which is why Avi is certain that "special powers" mean explosions, flying objects, and open wounds that just magically heal within seconds. Avi and I are also different but alike. Different because I'd never have thought of reacting like him, yet alike because we're both infected by the same disease. Excited by new things, we try them out, get addicted, but quickly get tired and abandon them, looking for the next new hottest thing. Neither of us has patience for lengthy processes. Isn't that exactly what happened to me with you? What was I doing the whole time, if not trying to shorten the never-ending paths that were supposed to lead me to you?

I'm alike yet different because I'm one of those crash-and-burn types, apparently, so Avi's evident advantage over me is that he takes things lightly. But maybe that's exactly it – the fact that you have twisted powers screws you up in more ways than one. So there's no point in asking anyone else what they would do if one day they found out. No matter what they say, it's completely irrelevant, because even if one day they did find out, their reaction would obviously be different from mine. Everything that happened to me is my unique story, for better or worse, and everything is somehow related inside me – all of the emotions, the memories, the inhibitions and reactions and self-deceiving lies, just as you said. The power is only part of that jumble, and within it lies also the reason why I chose to ignore my power and deny who I am. There's a great reason for it, I'm sure, too bad I still haven't found it.

Earlier, I lay on the couch in the living room, and Tom came and laid next to me. Since that night he's suddenly become my little boy again, taking every opportunity to curl up against me. I held him and asked – so what would you do if one day you found out you have special powers? He didn't find my question odd and his response was entirely serious: I'd try to get more life. What do you mean? I asked. Like in digital games, he explained patiently, you have to get life points to gain more strength. So I'd try to get more life. What for? I asked. More life is better, he shrugged, it's just good to have it.

Maybe I too should try to get more life. I haven't been to work in three weeks. I'm recovering from all the incidents. Moni asked someone at our PR firm to fill in for me, my mother has moved into the sofa in my living room, and I pretend to still be the adult in charge of raising Tom. I told people at work that I have mono, and it's also the official excuse for why I'm not returning Rona's calls and why I said she can't visit. I just can't tell anyone what really happened. Not only what happened with you but also what happened one crazy night three weeks ago, a few days after you left. It's become the best-kept secret since the yellow pills behind the kettle. Tom knows nothing of course. My father is barely speaking to me since, probably because I gave him too much of a shock, and my mother doesn't talk about it either. Well, she's used to it, you know, there's nothing like family experience. To appease her, I went to a few sessions with a therapist, but yesterday I told him that I don't see the point in continuing. He said he thought I was making a mistake and that a person in my condition needed to talk to someone. A person in my condition. I lingered on those words for a few moments, then asked him if he thought I was crazy. You? He looked at me, surprised, and then laughed. That's the last thing I'd say about you.

That settled me, but on the other hand, what does he know? I didn't actually tell him anything. That's why there was no point in "therapy". I mean, I told him what I did that night, and about the constant internal tremor that won't go away, but I didn't say a word about you. Not a word about my mornings that start off with the obituaries to make sure your name isn't there, and not a word about how I Googled Yanky's VC fund but couldn't work up the nerve to call and ask him if he knew what was happening with you. Naturally, I didn't mention anything that even sounded like "special powers". I don't think he'd take it lightly, and it didn't seem like a good idea to tell him and then realize I'd been committed and send my mother to tell everyone that everything was all right and I was at some health sanatorium.

My head can't stop thinking about what you're up to, where you are. What you know or don't know about all of this. I'm really trying not to think about disasters, but I have no way of knowing what happened to you. Since you disappeared I can't feel you at all. Or maybe it's since my bracelet fell off. I kind of hope you don't know anything and that one day we'll meet and you'll ask what's going on and let me be the one to tell you.

To: Sheera and Michael <softspoons@gmail.com>
From: Sheera and Michael <softspoons@gmail.com>
March 6, 2016 at 8:56 p.m.
Subject: Do I have someone?

Today I had a reciprocal visit from Erik.

Remember when he was released from the hospital and we went over to his apartment? Yes, that time I felt sorry for him and cured the pain I didn't know I'd caused him in the first place. So today I was sitting on the couch, totally immersed in Rona's next cover story – she sent me the final draft right before it was published. The first two features had been great, and this one was dedicated to confessions by couples who had completely lost interest in each other. I was so wrapped up in it that when the intercom buzzed I jolted back. I got up to see who it was, and turns out the entire entourage was there, in full force but with no prior notice, and armed with warm Chinese takeout, that released an odor that made me a little queasy.

How are you, sweetie? Kiss kiss. Jesus, you've lost weight... heroin chic seems like a good look for you. Got a few germs left for me?

Erik sat down, and Julia sat next to him with a tight smile, crossing her slender legs. Avi positioned himself on the opposite couch, and I was anxiously anticipating the moment they'd start grilling me and I'd have to come up with lame answers like Erik did at the time. I brought plates and glasses from the kitchen and we spread out the food. Are you alone? Julia asked as I inserted myself in the small space between them. Yes, I said, Tom's not back from school yet. I didn't tell them that in the morning I'd asked my mother to go out to get some air so that I myself could breathe, but to come back at night because that's the hardest time for us all. Is it hard for you too at night, Mikey? You never could sleep normally.

We started rattling knives and forks, opening bags and taking off lids. The house was immediately filled with fumes of noodles in peanut sauce. I got up to open the window, wondering if my house had that same sour smell Erik's apartment had. Maybe that's the smell people give off when they're falling apart. So I opened more windows and promised myself that later I'd spray some perfume all over the house.

First Erik, then you, Avi joked, everyone's asking me if Super Pharm is now our chief sponsor.

Julia smiled, as did I, but Erik's face remained frozen. Come on, get better already, Avi grumbled, come back, we need you.

Don't worry, it's no longer contagious and I think I can come back next week, I said, though the very thought made me tremble. How could I go back to the salt mines and do everything I did before this happened? How would I be able to function at that place which I couldn't care less about anymore? I breathed deeply and remembered something the shrink had advised in our first session – don't think forward because it's just too much pressure. Take one day at a time, that's more than enough.

What's happening in the ad market? I pretended to take interest. Nothing much, Avi grimaced, so I turned to Erik. What's new with "The Write Stuff"? I asked. Gaya went wild with the budget, he said, so I'm arm wrestling her to make it more profitable.

Julia, would you email me updates when you get the chance? I asked her.

I'm always sending you updates! She opened her huge blue eyes at me, haven't you seen them?

Oh, there was something wrong with the network this week, I stammered. I couldn't tell them that for the past three weeks I'd only been checking our mutual mailbox, and other than that I'd been too zonked out to check my work email even once.

Avi complained that my replacement wasn't cutting it, and he felt sorry for her because it always looked like she was about to fall apart. When they got up to leave, he paused for a moment, waiting for Erik and Julia to exit into the stairwell, and put his hand on my shoulder. I felt a strange sensation, as if his pressure was flowing into me through his touch. Either stop screening me or give me a call, he said quietly, you've taken this sick leave thing a little too far. I nodded silently. Okay, talk to you soon, he said impatiently, you coming back next week? Promise? His words were a delicate oxygen tube that connected me back to my life. I started to realize I have no choice. They need me. I have a place in the world, even if I feel completely left out.

I shut the door behind me, relieved that they left without putting me through the third degree. I listened to the cold silence of my apartment, and suddenly understood what Julia had meant when she asked if I was alone. She didn't mean here and now, until Tom came home. She was attempting to find out if I had someone in my life. Like that day when I called her and she asked if I was seeing someone – she was trying her luck again.

What do you think, Mikey? Good question, huh?

I stood there in the middle of the house and said out loud, as if she were still there – yes, Julia, technically you could say I'm alone. Then I remembered what you said right before the end. That even if it doesn't seem so, I'm always getting what I want. That when I think I'm not getting what I want, it's only because there's something else I want even more. And that's what happens even when I'm sure there's nothing in the world that I want more than being with you. So what the hell is it that I desire so much? God only knows.

I've been waiting for you all these years, Mikey. You weren't the only one who recognized my smile in Ella Cinderella's face, I've always searched for traces of you in other people. My childhood neighbor Tal had your deep pool-like eyes, and Ziv had that same sweet lopsided smile that echoes yours. I've searched all my life without knowing you were the one I was looking for, but when you finally came and I had the chance to get the real thing, I didn't know how to do it. So according to your theory, it wasn't my cruel fate that determined I had to live this way. It was my own concealed decision, and there's nobody else I can blame.

I can see that now, though it's a little too late. Is this really the end, Mikey? Is it over between us? It seems impossible. It scares me to even think about what will happen if I really allow myself to believe it's the end. You've completely disappeared and erased everything that was here and you're not responding anywhere, but still - I just can't believe it.

To prevent myself from getting caught up in those thoughts I took the laptop and opened that proposal I'd written for "The Write Stuff". Something did manage to awaken me today and make me feel that despite everything I'd lost, I still had a life. People were waiting for me. Commitment is a burden but it's also a lifesaver, and I truly want to pull myself out of the ocean I've been floating on since my raft drifted away. I began reading, hoping to work myself up a little, but the paper I wrote only depressed me even more. Everything seemed so shallow, boring and meaningless. I couldn't understand how I could've been happy with this program only weeks ago.

You said that when I write something, it's not just a normal document. I didn't realize what you meant back then, and now I knew even less. There's nothing more ordinary than the document I wrote for the program, it was so trivial, a collection of celebrities and gimmicks that might bring in the ratings and make a small profit, but nothing beyond that. I recalled our first conversation on the boardwalk, when you said they didn't make monumental movies anymore, and I suddenly realized that it wasn't because talent was becoming extinct. People are still trying to change the world, but their motives have changed. Everyone still makes an effort to impress, to dramatize, to provoke or frighten or amuse, but their primary intention is to become famous. Changing the world is just a secondary goal, if any.

Disgusted, I closed the document, and then deleted it childishly, as if that changed anything. I'd sent it long ago and everyone had already read it, and there really was nothing I could do about it – that's what the television industry is about and that's what I do for a living. For a moment I considered checking my work email, but the mere thought of it increased the tremor I keep feeling inside, and the fear that my downtime is running out. But how would I be able to go back to my old routine without even knowing what happened to you, or where you are?

My hand reached out for the phone. I scrolled through it, looking for Yanky's office number, which was in my contact list already. But once again, I just sat there staring at the screen, frustrated that there's no one I can ask what's going on with you except for him and your father, longing to dial but unable to. But suddenly an idea hit me. I played around with it for a few minutes, and then before chickening out, I decided to just do it and stop thinking about why it wouldn't work.

Hello, is Yanky there? I asked in a shaky voice when the receptionist answered.

He's in a meeting, who's calling? She asked in a polite monotone, as other phones rang in the background.

Oh, I'm an entrepreneur working with Michael Eden and I haven't been able to get hold of him for a few weeks, I managed to say with practically no stutters, I thought maybe Yanky knows if he's changed his number or something.

I'll leave him a message, the secretary said coolly, and after taking my phone number she asked, who shall I say was calling?

My heart started pounding. I was silent for a minute, but eventually just said – Maya.

To: Sheera and Michael <softspoons@gmail.com>
From: Sheera and Michael <softspoons@gmail.com>
March 7, 2016 at 10:25 p.m.
Subject: Decaffeinated coffee, De-passionated Sex

After the delegation from work had been here I couldn't keep holding Rona off by saying I was still contagious. She arrived in the afternoon holding a huge pot that trailed a scent of rice and cranraisins, and with the drumbeat rhythm of the outside world. She paced from the kitchen to the living room and then back again, her red Converse sounding quick little squeaks on the floor. I'm making some decaf, she shouted from the kitchen. As she put the mugs down in front of us she ran back to get some sugar, then sat down and immediately jumped up, having forgotten the spoons, and then got up yet again and came back with a plate of cookies. I just sat there staring at her, amazed at the gap that had yawned open between us. I suddenly recognized the slow-mo I'd grown accustomed to since leaving work.

For a moment I missed us, how we were in the past. I used to be just like her, with my foot planted firmly on the gas pedal all day. I had never carried such a heavy load of buried secrets, secrets that had become walls between her and me. In our high school days we'd sit cross-legged on the carpet, notebooks on laps, chewing on pencils, writing juvenile poems about love and telling each other everything. As I looked at her with the realization that those times had ended long ago, a tiny drop of sadness invisibly trickled from my eye and absorbed into my t-shirt.

She opened a window in the living room, saying the apartment was stuffy. I hope you realize I didn't buy your lame mono story – she didn't even look at me as she breezed around. My internal trembling immediately increased. For a second I couldn't tell if she was kidding. Maybe I'm so scared someone will find out what really happened that I've lost all my sense of humor, because I used to be able to understand her with one word, one look. She came back and sat facing me on the couch, looked into my eyes and said – talk to me.

What do you want me to say? I asked. I could feel the defensiveness hardening in my stomach, the sting in her skeptical look. I was so scared that she knew something, and at the same time I had a tremendous urge to spill out the whole story to someone who knew me, someone sane who could offer another perspective, another opinion. The amount of concealed information was swelling, pressing against my walls from the inside. But I couldn't tell her only pieces of the story, like I told the therapist, so I chose to stick with the mono version. It didn't require much explanation, as I do look pale and thin and lifeless (and it's also much more credible than my father's former excuses).

Sheer, I know you, Rona was as straightforward as a guided missile. You've fallen for someone, it's written all over everything you say and do lately. I tried shaking my head in disagreement, but it didn't really work. Tell me who the bastard is, she said, come on, it's me, what's the matter with you. We exchanged little smiles, but the shadow of insult in her eyes didn't escape me.

I was silent. The false denial was stuck in my throat, and I remembered your method of dividing humanity into three kinds of liars. Maybe I lie to myself less as time goes by, but I find myself lying much more to others. So if I need to lie to others in order to tell myself the truth, what kind of liar am I?

Rona joined my muteness, and the silence in the room became a bit too heavy to bear. I really liked your article about the couples, the lonely pairs, I changed the subject, it was the best of them all so far. Yeah, your idea to solicit confessions on Facebook was a smash, she said unenthusiastically, we'll see how the interview with Rafi Hadar goes in two weeks.

Aren't you happy about this? I asked, surprised.

Scoring cover stories is great, she raised an eyebrow, but I've become a third-rate reporter with this lowbrow beauty-parlor crap. What's next in my career, interrogational tell-alls on mani pedis?

I forced a smile. Strange that we think love is a lowbrow subject, isn't it?

Oh please, spare me the deep philosophies, she said impatiently glancing at the clock.

I looked at her for a second, suddenly realizing that the heaviness I felt was not mine but hers. I'd been trying so hard to hide what was going on with me that I'd completely overlooked what was up with her.

Enough about me, why are you in such solemn grief? She looked at me, smiling at my choice of words, as I don't usually use her sarcastic jargon. That article left me in solemn despair, she said, can't you see I wrote it about myself?

Oh, I mumbled, now that you mention it... but then she started talking so fast she didn't even stop for air.

The irony of it all is that Eyal was the only one who ignored this. We spent the entire weekend at his parents', then at my parents', fussing around the girls, and the whole time my phone was bursting with all these comments – on Facebook, on WhatsApp, I've never received so much feedback on something I wrote in my life. I waited for the deaf-mute to throw me some polite remark, but nothing. I started getting all stressed that maybe he was offended, maybe he sensed it was about him and me, so I decided to shut up and pretend nothing had happened. Finally the weekend ended, the girls fell asleep, I took a shower and got in bed with some mediocre book. He laid there on his back in the same underwear he wore yesterday, flipping through the channels, occasionally scratching his balls. At some point I mumbled an indifferent good night. I turned my back to him, hugging the blanket, when suddenly I felt his hands on me. I wanted him as badly as I wanted to fuck a sea turtle, but we're at that stage when once in a while you just have to, you know? It's like a credit card payment that keeps charging every month, on a purchase you made long ago and can't even remember why. So I started moving a little, hoping to recall that I once had a libido, but all we could muster was another boring, lifeless, de-passionated screw, where you agree to take off your underwear, rub against each other a little, and in the end he does me a favor by hanging around till I manage to come. The whole ordeal was over within four minutes. I couldn't take it anymore, Sheera, I lay there in the dark, tearing. This wasn't supposed to happen to me. The autistic rhino didn't feel a thing, of course, he just said good night and turned his back. I couldn't hold it in so I said – doesn't this remind you of my article, just a little bit? And he muttered, half asleep – what article?

You get it? He wasn't offended because he never reads what I write! I forgot that I stopped arousing his interest long ago. So I lay there, trying to recall the exact point in time that he changed into this... *man*. There's nothing between us anymore but a couple of kids, a joint checking account and a few administrative issues. That's how you maintain a cardboard marriage. That article was good because it was about us, I wrote about myself, and for dessert I swiped my credit card for the monthly sex payment so we could go on pretending we're still a couple.

At first I didn't know what to say. The force of her words pushed against my chest, and all I could say was "Wow" like some high school girl. It's not that Rona has never complained about her husband, for years that's practically all she ever says about him, but still, this time it was different. As if something was cracked for a long time and now it had finally broken. I remembered that old story she wrote, the one that won a prize, suddenly realizing what a "normal relationship" was and what I'd been trying to avoid all this time.

Do you think that's what would've happened to us too if we had become a couple, Mikey? Maybe we're lucky, because the passion between us can never fade. Unused passion doesn't fade away, it always continues to burn. Though I cannot simply call what we had "passion", it was so much more. There's something that feels like home in the person you love. You want to move in, live inside them. You're willing to make any deal, exchange internal organs at any given moment. You recognize something familiar in their face, pieces of yourself. I can't imagine that sense of belonging I had with you would have eventually ended.

The question is if you really have to accept it, I said to Rona.

You think I have the energy to get a divorce and then screw up my girls with some new blended family? She frowned at me.

That's not what I meant, I mumbled.

Then what did you mean? She asked.

I don't know, I said carefully, remember that once you believed he was "the one"? The one who completes you?

Yeah, she said disdainfully, but eventually I realized that he only completes the Sports Channel.

I smiled and hesitated a second before saying – can you try to remember what you loved about him once, at the start?

She let out a short laugh and said, seriously Sheera? I thought you'd advise me to go find myself some Wasabi on the side.

Something on the side is not love, I said.

She looked at me, confused.

Someone on the side is a deal of give and take, a tradeoff, I said, and when she continued staring at me, expecting me to explain, I mumbled – we want love without realizing it means doing something without expecting anything in return.

She kept staring, mouth agape, and then shook her head in disbelief and said – a little more of that talk and eventually I'll believe you really are sick.

After she left I was overcome by guilt. If Eyal wasn't enough, now she'd been hurt by me as well. She knew I'd been screening her, and to top it off I'd pulled out your mother's Tibetan phrase and had been no help at all.

I sat alone on the rug with a notebook and pencil, a little like high school. I recalled that book on the Art of Love we were so taken with back then, and started writing some stuff, erasing, jotting down thoughts. We thought that love was something that happens passively, that one fine day you just fall into it. We were so sure the only problem was finding the object of love, and that love itself was easy, something that comes naturally. So we invested all our effort in other things, in our kids, our social circle, our work. But in the end we both lost our love, and the only difference was that I lost it all at once, whereas she lost it slowly over the years.

I tried to remember what Rona had loved about Eyal back when they first met. Surely there was still something there, some remnant of that fragile glue that attaches two people.

What was our glue? What was it about you that was so captivating? I wondered if it was your somewhat childish posture, the dimple, maybe the way that you looked at me. But it wasn't one detail or another, it was the entire package. My connection with you. Only you could provoke such intense feelings in me, like roller coaster rides or snowballs rolling downhill. Or maybe it was your ability to see things in me that I could never see on my own. At certain moments it seemed that no one in the world believed in me as much as you do.

My mother was with Tom throughout the afternoon and I continued to scribble my thoughts until evening fell, and at some point I considered putting it all in order and emailing it to Rona. Suddenly the phone rang, shattering the silence. I jumped up as if bitten by a snake. Could it be Yanky? My heart started racing wildly. When

I realized that it was Tom's school principal I only trembled more. I wanted to hear how you were doing, she said sweetly, Tom said you were ill. I stammered a bit, waiting for her to complain about something, but she had nothing bad to say, and she even told me she didn't know how I'd handled things with Tom, but it was really working. What's with her? For a second I suspected that this change of attitude had something to do with you. That magic you do, maybe you dissolved some words, like you did with the agent. But that went away soon enough when I remembered that it was impossible because you were no longer around.

Tom went to bed, and my mom's getting ready for another night on the sofa, alone, since my father's been avoiding coming here lately. I offered to give her my bed, but she said no. So I'm here, writing you from my bedroom, and sleep seems light years away. I miss sex with you, the best sex I've ever had, although we never really had it. I miss feeling you, your warm skin, your touch that instantly melts all the stiffness in my body. I miss that helpless expression on your face when you're inside me, seeing you up close, absorbing the enticing echo of your moans. I miss the inexplicable urge to touch your face and make sure you're real, though you're not really there, yet you're more real than anything I know.

You were always gone from my life, but I knew exactly where you were. Since the bracelet broke I can't feel you. What are you doing as I sit here at home, trembling at the thought of going back out to the world? Are you in Israel? Are you okay? Are you sleeping at night? Since you left I don't even know what I should hope for.

To: Sheera and Michael <softspoons@gmail.com>
From: Sheera and Michael <softspoons@gmail.com>
March 8, 2016 at 10:45 p.m.
Subject: How my voice disappeared

The phone rang this morning when I was in the shower. I tiptoed out to the living room in a towel and saw the display reading "Bank". My stress level immediately increased in compliance. There's no real reason for fear, but ever since this happened, I'm constantly afraid, every little thing tips me off balance. What if this shakiness won't go away and keep me from returning to work? After you left, the fear just exploded in me like a stun grenade, and the smoke won't clear. I can't keep pretending that I'm normal, but I just don't know how else to behave. Without your crazy explanations, how can I read the signs or decipher what I'm feeling? I'm so stuck with this scary power. In the mirror I seem exactly the same, but I know that inside there's nothing, nothing to hold the shell together. All it will take is for someone to give me the slightest nudge and I'll crack and collapse into that void.

I haven't checked my bank balance for a month. I had no idea why they were calling, so I just screened them. I'm on sick leave, aren't I? I'm allowed to be unreachable. But the decision to ignore it didn't really put me at ease. What the hell do they want? Am I overdrawn without noticing? Because if I am, I'm not even sure I want to know. So I made some attempts to distract myself. I took my laptop and clicked the Outlook button hesitantly, and hundreds of emails began cascading into the mailbox like a waterfall. My eyes automatically scanned them for your name. Who knows, maybe you sent something to my work email after all. I went over each and every one. Newsletters, press clippings, group emails, people who reply to each other and argue and eventually decide all sorts of things that suddenly seem so petty and low. But there was no trace of you in that swarm of words.

In the early afternoon, when my mother brought Tom home from school, he dumped his backpack on the floor, ran over to cuddle with me, and said - Hi Mommy. How was school? I asked. Gross, as usual, he smiled. I suddenly remembered that boy who teased him, the one who walked to school alone, and asked if he was still bothering him. No, he said simply, we're friends now. Really? I was surprised, and he nodded, and for a minute I wondered whether it was simply the fluctuating emotions of childhood, or if this was the kind of thing you quietly fix without anyone knowing. Tom suddenly raised his head and asked, Mommy, how come you suddenly lost your voice and now it's back but different?

It was probably because of the mono, I lied. Funny, until now I'd been sure it was just my imagination, but my voice did sound a little different to me as well. I didn't want to tell him that when a barrel of fear explodes inside your chest – you scream with all the force you've ever had chained up inside, and the fear just gets worse when you realize you cannot stop. I didn't want to tell him that at some point you completely empty yourself, like a burnt out battery, and collapse into unconsciousness because there's simply no other alternative.

I held him, and the tears began to threaten me. He's turned into such a good boy since that night. He's also filled with fear since then, fear of losing me, and it kills me. I forcefully held back the tears. Any mood of mine immediately affects him, and I have to rebuild his confidence. So I shut my eyes and submerged into our cocoon, thinking of all the love that was packed in one embrace, especially if you just stop everything else and let it be. You won't believe it, Mikey, but not only do I understand that now, I've begun to see better with my eyes closed myself.

When we finished lunch I realized I wouldn't be able to escape it. I picked up the phone and dialed voicemail to see if there was a message from the bank, but suddenly I heard an old message I must've missed. Hello Maya, it's Yanky Rosen's secretary, he'd like to tell you that Michael is on vacation and unreachable, and suggests you try again in a week or two, unless it's urgent and then you can call Yanky on his cell phone. I choked.

I played the message again. I was so mad at myself for missing that call. How did it escape me? And what did unreachable mean? Is that why you're not picking up? What was I supposed to understand from this?

Obviously, I didn't call Yanky's cell. My abilities as an Oscar winning actress were limited, and it would be really awkward if he were to find out who I really was. I took a deep breath and called the bank, directly to my personal banker. Sheera, she said, you've accumulated quite a lot of money in your investment account, would you like to keep holding Fire Island or sell?

At first I didn't know what she was talking about. It took me a few seconds to come to, I'd completely forgotten. How much is there? I asked. When she told me the number, for a moment I thought I was being pranked, but then realized that made no sense as I was the one who called her. I was silent. I didn't know what to say. I don't know if it's going to keep rising, she said, so I wanted to ask you what to do. I said I needed a moment to think about it and I would get back to her. I ended the call, took a pencil and paper and began to scribble some numbers. Mikey, there's enough in there to keep Tom and me living well for at least two years without even having to work, and that's without the interest. The numbers I scrawled lay there casually on the paper, and I suddenly noticed that some of my worries had wilted and flopped over as they sank to the floor. I have money, I thought. You've set me up with a nice sum. The financial anxiety left the picture in quiet, catlike steps, and the troublesome trembling softened a little.

All at once I was awash with love for you, and hatred for myself. I had so many suspicions about you, regarding everything, even this. I hated your bossing me around, didn't get what you wanted. Suddenly I'm so ashamed for not having trusted you. I didn't like your nosy intervention. When you told me to invest, to transfer, to wait, I felt stupid for taking orders without understanding, without any explaining, it seemed chauvinistic and condescending and I was not only mad at you but at myself as well. The conversation with the banker today brought all those feelings back in a flash, immediately waking a flurry of questions from their deep hibernation.

Did you know this would happen? Did you predict my breakdown? Did you know I wouldn't go to work, and did you plan that the security in having money would help me reassemble myself? Or did you plan something entirely different for that money, and I still don't understand? I can never tell with you. But in some strange way, I suddenly didn't feel so alone. As if you'd knocked on the door and stopped by to say hello. For one fleeting moment I even hoped you might still love me after all.

I called the banker again, smiling at her through the phone, and said – sell it, and put it all in a short-term savings account. Mikey, maybe I understand a little more every day, but I'm still not sure I'm seeing the whole picture. Did you just want me to get rich? Is this even legit? Isn't it insider information or something?

The fear softened its grip with that surprising phone call, but some of it still remained. Apparently the feeling that the earth is crumbling under your feet does not disappear in a day. Or maybe it's something else – before we met I was blocking so many emotions, shoving them aside and ignoring their existence. Now I tremble all the time, because I'm simply incapable of feeling so much. You told me that the choices we make accumulated into who we really are, so what do my choices say about me? I think I'm just afraid of touching emotions. Maybe you were right about that too, because strong emotions make me feel weak. So over the years I've given the death penalty to so many emotions, telling myself I'm strong and independent. But I was lying to myself, just so I wouldn't have to admit, God forbid, that I was avoiding everything I truly loved because I was a coward.

Mikey, it's been almost four weeks now. On Sunday I go back to work, that's it. Back to the pressure, the chaos, the snake pit, the shallowness, the ratings. Back to Erik, to everyone who will sweetly ask how I am while inwardly gloat about my trouble. Back to the hypocrisy, the judgment, but also to the familiar world I'd learned to live in. Back to the option of escaping who I really am, so I can be a pro in an industry of lies. So I can be swept along with the crowd and say "that's life and there's nothing I can do about it", and continue to follow rules that maybe I should be the one to break. If you were here maybe you'd say that next week I go back to everything that seems possible to me, but only because I got stuck with too many spoons that I just never learned how to bend.

I reread the long email I began writing Rona, but I'm still unsure about sending it. I'm so careful I no longer recognize myself. You know that I was also scared of starting to write you again? I was afraid that I wouldn't be able to identify my intentions, to understand what I'm writing, to undo my tangles. My mind is so exhausted and messy, and my body trembles with the effort of taming this storm that's too big to contain. I didn't know how I'd be able to write you with that storm inside. But at some point I realized that the internal chaos was so great that ironically, it left me with only one intention, one great desire, thanks to which I do manage to get out of bed every morning. The desire to return to myself, to pick up the pieces. To regain control.

To: Sheera and Michael <softspoons@gmail.com>
From: Sheera and Michael <softspoons@gmail.com>
March 9, 2016 at 9:34 p.m.
Subject: Don't keep the faith

Avi called today. When I answered he immediately said – I can't believe you still haven't called. What's up, when are you coming back?

Next week, I stuttered, I'm not totally okay yet, I need a few more days.

That's not the Sheera I know, he said. The Sheera I know would continue to run the world from her bed, and would've been back here ages ago. What are you hiding from me?

I froze. Was it that easy to see through me?

Nothing, I said, don't you know how lethal mono can be?

You don't have to tell me if you don't want to, but all kinds of stuff is happening, and you're not here, and I can't look out for your interests alone. I can barely look out for my own.

What do you mean, I asked, what's the stuff that's happening?

In the past couple of days Erik and Moni had a few meetings about "The Write Stuff", he lowered his voice as if afraid someone would overhear, and for some reason nobody else was invited. They asked me not to say anything to the advertisers for now, and I know that Gaya is also worried that something doesn't smell right. I asked Moni and he avoided me, and I couldn't get anything out of Erik either.

What do you think they're up to? I asked.

How would I know? He bristled. You're the only one with the Mossad ability to get Moni to sing. And we have the premiere of "The Human League" to deal with. Get back here already!

Oh please, "The League" is going to flop with or without me, I said.

Just don't jinx it like you did that drama series I couldn't sell, he said, and keep in mind that your replacement's a bomb and Moni's starting to get angry.

The conversation was a wake-up call. I realized I'd taken it too far. I'm not talking to anyone, I display no interest, no wonder Erik is leaping at the chance to take over and Avi is suspicious. I still had absolutely no desire, but I forced myself to get the laptop and respond to the flush of emails from the past few weeks, to make up for what I'd lost. It was a little depressing.

At some point I began deleting everything that seemed less relevant or had expired, and focused only on the emails related to "The Write Stuff". I read them all thoroughly, but there was no real information. Only technical details, meeting updates, scheduling conflicts, nothing really interesting. Avi was right. Someone was keeping me out of the loop. Guess who.

This kind of thing used to blow my fuses, get me to furiously put everyone in their place. But the space where that anger used to be was now occupied by something frail and delicate, maybe a feeling of helplessness. An internal announcement that I didn't really have the strength to come back and fight Erik as if nothing had happened. Something in me had known from the start that this program was too brittle, as if it weren't really meant to be. We both know that if you hadn't invaded Moni's thoughts to convince him, he never would've given me the program, and maybe since you disappeared Moni's returned to his real self. This show was a little like you – too good to be true. In my life, things that good don't just naturally fall into your lap. I have to work very hard for my achievements, and even when I finally achieve something, it's never so incredibly good.

I got up to make coffee. When the water boiled and I was about to stir in the sugar, I paused as I looked at the spoon, and smiled. The spoon and I, we go way back. That moment from a few months ago flashed in my memory, when I stood here and couldn't make it bend. Suddenly it seemed so long ago. I stirred my coffee and tossed the spoon into the sink, and remembered that you said that if I wanted to learn how to use my power, I had to shed my old beliefs. But what exactly does that mean, "old beliefs"? What am I supposed to shed? What can I say I believe in?

I believe that Avi really does need me back, but also that Moni doesn't want me to develop a show, that he only gave me "The Write Stuff" because you used your own spoon to stir the thoughts in his head, while he only needs me as a PR slave. I also believe I'm not talented enough to run a successful show, and therefore mysterious breakthroughs in my career are something that's never going to happen. You were right, Michael, true faith doesn't need any proof, and these are the things I believe in. Look how easy it is for me to believe in them, they seem obvious. So is this my toxic placebo? Are these the beliefs I fuel with my power that later makes them come true?

These thoughts only made my internal tremor grow, as I recalled the beliefs that took over me on that frenzied night, after the bracelet fell off. Beliefs in what seemed entirely real, sending me hurtling at breakneck speed to the end of a dark road I'd never driven before. For a moment I choked on my fear of myself, of the things I was capable of doing. It happens every time I get flashbacks from that night. I slammed the laptop shut and began pacing the apartment. I wanted to drive those memories away, burn them, purge them out, kick them to hell, destroy them forever.

I picked up the phone and called Ruthie, my hands shaking. How are you, dear? She asked, and I said – Better, thinking how that word "dear" pretended to be warm but was actually alienating and cold. I told her I was coming back to work on Sunday, so she could count me in for any meetings she scheduled. Oh, that's great! She chirped, overemphasizing the "R", I'll go right in and tell Moni, he can't wait to have you back.

You may find it funny, but that call soothed me, I was glad to hear that Moni is waiting for me to come back. Supposedly I was afraid that nothing would get done without me, but apparently what really scared me was that they'd suddenly realize they were getting along just fine without me. Everyone thinks I'm so strong and domineering, but deep down I don't really believe they need me. That's why I'm constantly looking for proof, and even when I find it, it never really convinces me.

When Tom got back from school we had lunch. Then he asked if he could watch TV and I sat next to him on the sofa with my laptop. I continued reading my work emails, trying to get back in the running, to feel a hint of desire to go back. When I saw that Tom was completely focused on his show, I logged onto Facebook for a minute. Oh yeah, I forgot to tell you that I've developed this little obsession with checking your Facebook page every few hours. It never changes, stays exactly the same, as if frozen in time. Like the photo of you on the beach. Your hair tossing in the wind, your white shirt, the stubble, that smile. I almost jumped to the ceiling when Tom suddenly leaned on me and asked, Mommy, who's that man?

Oh, he's just a Facebook friend, I said, my cheeks burning.

I saw you looking at his picture once, he said nonchalantly.

As I quickly scrambled for a response even an eight and a half year old wouldn't find idiotic, he suddenly gave me Ziv's honey-eyed look and said – I thought that maybe he was my dad.

A tiny pebble hardened in my throat. Where did that come from? No, no, I coughed, of course not.

I looked at him, not knowing what to say. He hadn't stumped me with questions like "who's my dad" since kindergarten. I wanted to recite that I don't know who his father is, that it's impossible to know, but I was incapable of saying the words. As if that lie had reached its expiration date, and I couldn't keep cultivating it anymore. I wanted to be a responsible mother, to take the opportunity and maybe finally tell him something about you, but where should I begin? Is there anything left to tell? After all, you no longer want to be with me. So I ended up not saying anything.

Tom went back to his program, turned up the volume and leaned back on the sofa. His face seemed totally calm, giving away nothing, but I kept stealing glances, suddenly afraid of the thoughts running through his mind. He's growing up right in front of me, he's not a little boy anymore, doesn't take everything I say at face value. He's stopped fighting with me over these past few weeks, but who knows which beliefs have formed in his mind in this time, and whether he even believes me.

I went back to my emails, and saw that Avi sent me the PR layout my replacement had written for "The Human League".

Look what that Pita-brain did, he wrote, you couldn't write something so bad even with all the jinx in the world.

Do you really think I did a bad job with that drama series? I asked.

No way babe, you're a pro, he replied, but haven't you noticed that the only shows that succeed are the ones that you like? Everyone at the station jokes about how you jinx the shows you don't like, I thought you knew that.

I paused for a moment. No one had ever said anything like that to me. Or maybe they had but I just hadn't made the connection, or waved it off as a joke. I really did like "Big Fear", or at least wanted very much for it to succeed, and I couldn't stand "The Human League" from the beginning. Could that have something to do with my power? My beliefs? Is it possible that the programs in which I believe, and write their promotions out of those beliefs, are the ones that eventually succeed?

I don't know what to think anymore.

Maybe everything I thought about you also stemmed from old mistaken beliefs I insisted on clinging to. I don't know why I was so stuck on believing it would never happen between us. But how am I supposed to believe now that it can? I'd really like to believe that you're all right, that you'll be back soon, that you're listening in on Tom's principal and secretly looking out for him, but that's so detached. You've completely disappeared. I can't feel you. It's been a month and you haven't written a word. How can you just get up one morning and change the things you believe in?

To: Sheera and Michael <softspoons@gmail.com>
From: Sheera and Michael <softspoons@gmail.com>
March 10, 2016 at 2:53 p.m.
Subject: Tea break in Jerusalem

I don't even know what started it all, because I was sitting with the coffee and the papers this morning after Tom and my mother left for school, and suddenly for no reason, I remembered the pink note and said to myself – wait a minute, why don't I try again now?

I got up and looked for that pink note, which I thought I'd left in the mess drawer in the kitchen. I rummaged around and found it by a stray butterscotch drop, a loose screw and a few stamps. Joseph Eden, it read, and underneath were nine numbers in shaky, almost illegible handwriting. I picked up the phone, dialed, and an older man's voice came through. Hello? This startled me a little, as if I wasn't really expecting him to pick up, like he hadn't when I called him the first time, two days after you left.

Uh... hello, I stalled for a moment, is this Joseph?

Who's asking? He asked me.

This is Sheera, I said, Sheera Leitner. We met once at Michael's apartment.

Yes, yes, I remember. Hello there. If you're looking for Michael, he's not here.

May I ask where he is?

The voice on the other end coughed lightly and said – he's gone up north and hasn't returned yet.

Up north? I asked.

Yes, he wanted to get some rest.

And I thought – why does he need rest, what happened to him, and why is he off the grid? There were a thousand questions I wanted to ask, but I didn't feel comfortable questioning him. A memory flashed through my mind and I tried to recall what you wrote me once, after driving your father home. What was it you'd said? That I needed to understand the sense of responsibility you had for him. That if anything ever happened to you, you'd want someone to drop by to see how he was.

Actually, Joseph, I wanted to ask whether you have some time to meet me, I heard myself saying.

There was silence on the other end of the line. Why do you want to see me? He asked wondrously, perhaps suspiciously.

I just… want to talk to you, and not over the phone, I said.

All right, he said. You can come tomorrow at noon. Or in fact today at noon if you like.

I ended the call and was suddenly filled with motivation. I had a mission. Though I didn't know what happened to you, I was going to meet your father, to see if everything was all right on your behalf, I owed you at least that. I tossed aside the newspapers and poured the remains of the coffee into the sink. Energy suddenly flowed through me, as if an invisible hand had appeared during that phone call and turned on some switch. According to the kitchen clock I had enough time to go before Tom came home. I glanced in the mirror. You can't go like that, I scolded my reflection, who wore brown sweatpants that had been with me since forever and a huge t-shirt that used to be white. I changed into jeans, slipped into my flip flops, ran a brush through my hair, made sure I had some money, and it was only as I got on the freeway when I realized that other than the few times I'd gone to the therapist, this was actually the first time I'd left the house in nearly a month.

There was some traffic on the way to Jerusalem. People are busy. Apparently the world continues to turn even when I'm not working. I flipped through the radio stations. Music filled the car and it managed to soothe me somehow. I tried to think of what I would say to your father when I got there. What did I want from him? I realized I had no clue. A song was playing, by a singer I didn't know. I'm still walking fast, *don't know where anymore, things that kill me in life, aren't deadly after all...*

I drove by Ben Shemen Forest, then the green stretches of land near Latrun, humming the unfamiliar song, no longer caring that I didn't know what to say to your father. All I knew was that I was doing the right thing.

At the entrance to Jerusalem I tensed. Left. Straight. In four hundred meters, continue straight. As I approached the yellow star on the blue map I started feeling that tremor, which had quieted down over the past few days. But I kept driving obediently until the metallic voice announced – you have reached your destination. Tschernichowsky Street. I started looking for a parking space.

The building was simple, just like the others, in a series of rugged stone blocks down the street. There were green trash cans by the side of the stone wall, a tabby cat dozing on one of them in a little triangle of sun. The entrance was modest. My steps echoed through the stairwell as I walked up. On the second floor I stopped in front of a door bearing a flat slab of wood with white lettering reading "Eden". I stood there, a little out of breath, but mostly asking myself what the hell I was about to say. I knocked. Inside I could hear those dragging steps I'd once heard outside your door. The door opened with a little creak, and there stood the slightly shorter, older Michael. I smiled at him. I held out my hand, and he squeezed it with his dry, cracked palm, and a sudden pain jolted through my elbow. Come in, he said, leading me inside. I smiled with a childlike embarrassment. I thought I could smell you in there.

Would you like something to drink? I'm making myself a cup of tea, the kettle will boil in a minute or two, he said. I smiled and said I'd have some too. The yellowing kitchen cabinets with their red stripes were a sad reminder of their former glory. The family pride that you spoke of had sagged with the years and grown old. I looked around, drinking in the details, as he took two glass teacups out of the cabinet. My parents used to have those exact same teacups, made of that paper-thin glass which always made me anxious that if I held them too loosely I'd lose my grip and drop them to their tragic death, but if I held too tight they would crack and break into my palm. The living room was a little dark, and I didn't feel comfortable asking why the curtains weren't drawn. An old pillow in a crochet slipcover that was beginning to fall apart sat alone on a green sofa, beside it a silent matching armchair.

I wondered if this was the sofa on which you sat watching the Camp David Peace Treaty signing, or if it had been replaced. A thin-legged wooden table stood on a faded Persian carpet covering the freckled tiles. I stared at the intricate patterns on the rug where you used to sit and practice with your mother. Your father suddenly asked – do you like it? And it took me a second to figure out what he meant. I said – Yes, it's beautiful, they don't make cabinets like that anymore.

I used to have a woodshop, he said, Eden Carpentry, have you heard of it?

I haven't, actually, I smiled apologetically, but looks like those cabinets are still in good shape.

He waved his hand dismissively. Anyone who buys this place after I die will probably want new cabinets, he said, without looking at me.

The kettle blew a jet of steam. Viciously boiling water was poured into the cups, and the rusty color of the tea leaves pierced it, bleeding into the clear water and slowly billowing upwards. Funny how neither of us was bothered by the fact that we were just standing there silently, looking intently at grains of sugar dissolving into the tea as if they were the center of the universe.

Your father picked up both cups and walked into the living room, and I suddenly noticed that what you said was true, he does walk in a syncope, asymmetrically. The second step is always quicker than the first. I sat on the edge of the sofa and your father sat on the armchair that seemed to have adjusted perfectly to his body over the years. He carefully put his right arm on the armrest, looked apologetically at me and said, my elbow is not what it used to be.

He took a cautious sip of his steaming tea. So why does a pretty young woman like you want to visit an old man like me? He asked. I straightened. I raised my cup to stall for time, and took a little sip, burning my tongue. I decided it would be best to start talking about you, so he wouldn't think this was some pity visit.

The truth is I'm just worried about Mikey, I mean Michael. I don't want to bother him but I think something's not right, so I wanted to know if there's anything I can do.

He looked at me and just nodded. I tried to find a flicker of expression on his face, but the shadows in the gloomy room prevented me from seeing clearly. My son is somewhat complicated, he finally said.

Has he ever disappeared like this? I asked.

He has, your father said.

Have you spoken to him? I mustered courage to ask, and he paused for a moment before mumbling - In a manner of speaking.

Is he all right? I asked.

Yes, he said simply. A silent sigh of relief spread through my body, tickling my fingertips. My sweet Mikey, do you have any idea how worried I was about you?

What about his migraines? I asked carefully.

There's nothing to worry about, smart alecks always get headaches, your father said, but he's doing better than he was a few weeks ago.

His words were like a needle through my heart. At first it stung and then the pain blossomed out like the tea in the boiling water, staining everything inside. So you're all right, but you're all right because you're not with me. With all of my power to take away your headaches at night, the bottom line was that I only caused you more pain.

Somewhat complicated, he said again. And I just nodded, trying to swallow my sorrow. I wondered what he even knew about your abilities. How much you and your mother hid from him. How much he even knows who you are.

Just out of curiosity, I said, trying to sound casual, what was he like as a boy?

Your father didn't smile, but through the shadows I thought I could see a flicker of light in his eyes, or maybe a longing. He slowly got up and said, you want to see? He started his slow syncope shuffling towards the hallway and said, here's the room he shared with Daniel. I got up to follow him. I saw a small bedroom, and on the right an even smaller room with a bookcase, a wood desk and an armchair identical to the one in the living room. There was an old soccer ball on one of the shelves. Squinting, I could see the word "Daniel" on it in faded black marker. This is where he grew up with his brother, Joseph explained, and when they left home I turned it into a study.

I looked around quietly, examining the tiny room, trying to imagine how it could fit two beds, amazed that there were such basic things I didn't know about you, like the fact that you have a brother. Look, here's a drawing Daniel made in kindergarten, he pointed at some colorful scribble in a faded wood frame. He drew that when he was five, can you believe it?

Talented, I said, is he an artist today? Your father looked at me with surprise and said, Didn't Michael tell you? He went off to Belgium to study medicine and decided to stay there.

I looked around the little room and tried to imagine what it used to look like long ago. Did they have a bunk bed? I asked with a smile.

Yes, and Michael always insisted on sleeping on the top bed, there was nothing anyone could do, he was willing to give up anything but that. He paused for a moment and then muttered something about having donated the bed to an orphanage years ago.

What kind of medicine does Daniel practice? I asked.

He's not a doctor, he has a big pharmacy near Brussels, in a very nice suburb. He took a framed photo down from a shelf. Three grandchildren, he said proudly, they all speak fluent French. And look at his wife, have you ever seen such a beauty?

I smiled and murmured my agreement, but before I could see the faces in the photo it was returned to the shelf.

He looked at me for a moment, as if examining me, and then continued in a rush of words – and Michael, he had all sorts of crazy business in his head, but he went into hi-tech and did rather well. He used to work hard, never come out of the office. But since he sold that company, he just wants to work alone.

I smiled. He was suddenly silent, and I didn't know what to say. We stood there quietly, and I looked around at the faded wooden shelves. It's not good for a man to be alone, your father mumbled, even at that cabin he goes to. I looked back into his eyes.

He's somewhat complicated, and doesn't like to talk, he said again, looking out through the window, maybe somebody should go up there and bring him back to Tel Aviv. He swept his eyes back at me, as if asking me something.

Where exactly is it? I asked.

Oh, I thought you knew, he said, with a trace of disappointment. Never mind, he recovered, don't worry, he'll come back on his own.

He turned and reached out to the shelf again, pulling down an old photo album with a worn-out fake leather binding. Here, you want to have a look? He asked, holding out the album.

We went back to the living room. He slowly collected the half-empty teacups and went to put them in the sink. I jumped at the chance to spend some time alone with your photos. I opened the first page directly into a giant close-up of your face, and those smiling eyes caught me off guard. Could it be that you were staring into the camera, smiling lovingly at me thirty years ago? As if you knew that one day I would sit on this sofa, and you'd surprise me with those clear-pool eyes of yours. I was captured inside that gentle gaze, and without any reason, it was suddenly clear to me that you weren't mad at me, that it wasn't what I thought. A gentle stream of love coursed through me. I could barely tear myself away from the photo and turn the page, but I wanted more and more of you. In one photo you were proudly holding up your first grade report card. In another you were laying on a stone wall with your eyes shut. I wanted to send out little arms to hold you, to slip into those photos. But as you grew in front of my eyes, I realized that in all of the photos it was only you, no friends. No brother. Lonely. On the last page I stopped at another close-up of your face, apparently from the same set, a glimmer of a smile on your lips, a young, unripe Mikey. But beyond the handsome features and the pools in your eyes, you had already had that expression as a boy – of someone who's pretending everything is fine and he's in control. Someone who doesn't want to know so much, and has no one to tell what he knows.

Do you know that girlfriend of his? Your father suddenly asked, shaking me out of my time travel. What girlfriend? I asked, flipping back, certain I'd missed a photo of Ella Cinderella. The girlfriend who just left him, your father said.

I could feel the color draining from my face and my heart slowing down, then picking up the pace, then slowing again. Uh, I... you could say I know her, I stammered.

Is that what you told your father? Is that what was easiest to say? That I left you?

Is she pretty? Your father looked at me closely.

Well, you know, it's a matter of taste, I tried to be diplomatic while not flattering myself.

It's a pity she left, he said, Michael needs someone, it's no good being alone all the time.

I glanced at the clock and noticed that the time I had given myself for the visit was about to run out. I had the impression that he suspected "the girlfriend" was me and was trying to squeeze some information, and that I should watch what I say. I wanted to look through your childhood some more, to picture you standing at your mother's side by the sink, imagine how you'd run around as a thin little boy, maybe jump on the couch. But it was getting late.

Your father took the photo album and began returning to the other room, engulfed in his task, as a small envelope slipped out of the album and fell silently on the carpet. I got up to pick it up and wanted to call out for him, but something made me look inside. It was a simple old-fashioned envelope that had greyed over the years. It seemed so thin. Could it be empty? I opened it carefully, and a light shiver rushed through my entire body as I saw what it contained. Two delicate tie-on hand-knotted bracelets made of colorful string.

Astonished, I looked up, and only then did I notice her, though she'd been there all along. That's why I'd felt something from the second I walked in, those sweet remains of your childhood. Beautiful and noble, high cheekbones, a smooth bare forehead, smiling with closed lips, her eyes caressing me from within the frame that stood right in the middle of the sideboard. The fact she was gone filled me with a gush of sorrow, but I was unsure whether it was my own sorrow or your father's or yours. How had I missed her? For some reason the sideboard had gone completely unnoticed the whole time I was there, and with it, the framed photo of your mother.

There was something in her look that was quiet but drenched in emotion. I imagined her looking at you that way, innocently explaining how to do things with love. Without thinking too much

I slipped the envelope into my purse. I hope you understand that I wasn't stealing it, Mikey, I can't explain why but I think it was forgotten there for me to find. I shut my eyes for a second, trying to concentrate all my intentions. When your father came back I stood facing him and gently placed my palm on his right elbow. I could feel all of my intent draining into that one movement, and he looked at me, finally giving the slightest hint of a smile. You know, in the car later, on my way back home, afire with so many thoughts, I realized that I didn't feel the need to ask him how his elbow felt afterwards, if it still hurt. Maybe I did learn to believe after all.

I also thought that my biggest problem with what happened is that I really love you. There's something so excruciating, hurtful and infuriating about a person who has abandoned you. You're supposed to feel anger, resentment, maybe even hatred. But when you took me to that edge, I discovered I don't want that. I'm simply not interested in those feelings towards you. Yes, you were evasive, we barely met, and you never whispered in my ear that I was the best thing that had ever happened to you. But even if I never see you again, I choose to love you. I refuse to erase you like I erased Ziv. I don't want to focus on everything I didn't like about us, but on that special feeling that welled up inside every time we saw each other, or talked, or wrote here. I want to preserve those nights alone in bed when I could feel you in some twilight zone, merging with me in a way I never knew was possible. I'm not going to taint that feeling with the mud of resentment. I suddenly realize it's a matter of choice. So even if your choice is to stop loving me, it's not going to affect my decision. If you don't want to love me, it's your problem, not mine.

When I stood there facing your dad with my hand on his elbow, I felt something delicate flowing from me into him, tickling my fingertips. Do you have to go? He asked, and I nodded. I have to pick up my son, I said. He escorted me to the door, and I suddenly felt really uncomfortable. As immersed as I had been the entire time in me and you, I hadn't shown enough interest in him. An elderly man living out the remnants of his life alone, and now even his son is not around, mostly because of me, and I hadn't even asked how he was. Be a little nicer before you leave, I scolded myself.

Do you live here alone? I asked.

Since my wife passed, twenty years, he said.

And does someone clean, or cook for you? I asked, and immediately regretted it, afraid it was too invasive. But your father didn't seem troubled, and simply said – every other week there's a girl who cleans, but I cook for myself. Between you and me, he leaned over to me as if sharing a secret, it's not so bad because my wife made everything too spicy anyway. And when my hand was already on the gold door handle, he suddenly mumbled, as if casually: he's complicated, but my son and I do have something in common.

Yes, I agreed, turning towards him, you both live alone. He looked at me with the expression of someone who's not sure if he's giving away state secrets, and said: yes, that too, but also because we're both widowers.

3:30 p.m.	It's you, isn't it?
	My sweet Mikey... I came back home, and turns out I shouldn't have rushed because my mother picked Tom up from school and took him straight to a friend's house. But instead of succumbing to the emptiness and wishing he'd return to chase away the silent vacuum, I sat down to write you. I was so enthralled with you, it was as if we'd spent all morning together. The buzz of my fear disappeared, the quiver had died down completely since I left your father's house. I was so happy you were all right. It wasn't just happiness. It was more like starting to breathe again after lying in a drawer at the morgue. A basic joy of life, sheer happiness

just for feeling the air flowing into your lungs. But I also felt sadness, or more like a shadow, a faded silhouette of sadness. I don't know whether it was the bracelets I found, or the visit to your childhood home that connected me to you again. All this time I was obsessed with the physical pain I caused you, but never once stopped to consider how deeply I'd scarred you inside. All I wanted to do was to come close to you and gently kiss you where it hurt. So when I realized that I still had some time to myself, I went to the bedroom, closed the shutters and the door, and just stood there, hugging myself. When I shut my eyes my hand became your hand, stroking my neck, hesitating a little, slowly taking off my shirt, fluttering over my waist, undoing my pants, sliding under my bra. My sweet Mikey, you're back. You don't have to tell me, you don't have to write anything, I felt it. I thought you'd abandoned me and I crashed so hard that I completely left myself, and maybe that's why you thought it was I who was leaving you.

Your presence thickened around me, strong and clear. The desire swelled in my body, crashing on the shore of my thighs and then pulling back to ripple against yours. One of your tears slipped out of my eye, and you used my hand to wipe it away. I undressed you slowly, careful not to touch where it hurts, focusing my entire being on that one place in my imagination, afraid to move or speak so as not to lose it, so you don't suddenly run off. That place where you're right in my soul, loving me so powerfully, so present, so strong. Just don't stop, my love, don't expel me from our garden of Eden. Please, just don't send me back into the real world.

I wasn't worried about you anymore, Mikey, I knew exactly where you were. Maybe up north but also here with me, at the foot of the Tree of Knowledge, closer than ever. And suddenly a foreign scene surged into my imagination – as if it weren't mine. You turned me around and sunk your teeth into the back of my neck with a sudden burst of passion that surprised me. It wasn't mine, that part, I know – there was the part I had directed, and there was your part, which was erupting out of your consciousness and invading mine. A moment later we were two people in one body, out of breath, lost in a parallel universe, displaced of our senses. Finally I understand what you meant when you said our fantasies intertwine. Our tears mixed in my eyes, Mikey, you came back, and today for the first time I felt that we really were one.

To: Sheera and Michael <softspoons@gmail.com>
From: Sheera and Michael <softspoons@gmail.com>
March 10, 2016 at 11:54 p.m.
Subject: I've stopped waiting for you to tell me. I wrote your story on my own

Tom fell asleep in my bed. I lay on my back with the TV flickering at a low volume, and stroked his hair distractedly as he cuddled against me like a cub. I'd taken in too many details throughout the day, and my body was in shock from the abundance of information that seeped in through the skin. In the past I would've tried to shake off this overload, afraid of drowning in it, but this time I tried not to move too much. I let it all linger, a mixed doughy mass that slowly cleared into distinct sensations. I noticed that my tremor had entirely disappeared, that I felt stronger. But I also felt a stabbing in my back and arms, my jaw ached, my temples throbbed. I wondered if I was just feeling where you hurt, and my head was flushed with questions. Why didn't you tell me? And how is all of this connected to your strange headaches? And if she were still alive – which of us would you prefer?

Eventually it became pointless to pretend I was trying to sleep. I gingerly separated my limbs from Tom's small body and got up to get a butterscotch drop from the drawer. I put it in my mouth, but this time I sat at my desk in the corner of the living room, opened the laptop, shut my eyes, and took a few deep breaths, trying to calm my thoughts. Remember how you once told me that I was so busy asking questions I couldn't see there was a lot about you I already knew?

It was strange, how this story just wrote itself of its own accord. I stepped outside of my body, and was able to see it all as if I was sitting in the audience. Without my pain, without the fear. I just looked straight at you, from above my jumble instead of through it. And suddenly... I understood. A story was formed out of all the sporadic details. Once I let go of the questions there was room for everything I'd seen during my visit with your dad, and it connected with the fragments of history, and the hints that you scattered here among the words. And yes. After your father told me what had happened to your wife, I found some old articles on Google as well.

I have no idea if you're back here, if you're even reading this. But if you are, you should know that although it took a while, I think I've finally found the answer to your question. Here it is.

Soulmate

They say you get to know yourself as a person through the people you love. So what has he learned about himself from the three women he's loved? Odd, because they had almost nothing in common. Different personalities, different temperaments, different styles. His mother was quiet, like him, and his wife wasn't much of a talker either. The third was different, maybe because ultimately the silent types need someone to force them to talk once in a while.

No one had taught him to be silent, it just happened, as he was too busy listening. Born into a continuous cacophony of voices, an infant that was tossed into a salad of thoughts, and he'd never known anything different. The headaches were there ever since he could remember – as a child he thought everyone had them, just like everyone felt that pressure every now and then, when they needed to go to the bathroom. But over time he realized that everyone has an assembly line in their head that never stops – as one thought emerges and gets conveyed along until it's packed up and sent far away, another thought appears. If you don't organize the merchandise, it piles up. So of course he has headaches, how wouldn't he?

He needs to handle his own thought factory, but also to be the blue-collar worker in everyone else's.

When he was little he had trouble distinguishing his thoughts from those of others. In kindergarten, for instance, his father had thought he was a screwed up little smart aleck who knew too much, just like his mother, and there was no way he could differentiate that from what he thought about himself. When he grew up a little, he started to separate the inner voices, like listening to a symphony and distinguishing the various instruments. After learning to recognize what was being thought by whom, he learned how to tune out unwanted thoughts. In high school it turned out to be helpful during exams, because he could tune in only to the smart kids' thoughts.

But let's get back to the issue, because the issue is love. And the way he listened to those he loved was always different. It was so much more interesting. When he was attracted to someone, he found himself following processes from a distance. It's like finding a really good television series and making sure you don't miss the next episode. Ella Cinderella was the first series he got addicted to. He wanted more and more of her thoughts, just one more, and then another. He couldn't stop. At one time he caught her thinking about how he understood her better than anyone else. That filled him with unexpected happiness. He kept that thought of hers in a velvet jewelry box inside his head, and would sometimes pull it out and linger on it, admiring it. But over time he realized that it wasn't very unique. We're all on a search for someone who will understand us, it's a pretty basic need. Like a sedative that eases the existential loneliness. He'd been given a gift that allowed him to understand the people around him quite easily, but as the years went by he began to fear it would never be reciprocated, and he would never find someone who truly understood him.

It's true that throughout his childhood, his mother understood him more than others did, but it didn't change his situation at home. He was always expected to know what everyone wanted and never to say "no" to anything, while his brother won all the praise. He knew his father thought that he should be cut down to size while his brother needed encouragement, and that his mother didn't like to argue. Still, he kept trying. He became used to pretending that he could handle anything, but this tactic became a double-edged sword. No matter how hard he tried to be the beloved son that everyone's proud of, he was always taken for granted. When everybody's sure that you can easily handle anything, resentment towards you flourishes while expectations only keep growing.

He'd pretended for so long that nothing was too hard for him, that he became convinced that difficulty was good, a source of motivation. But nothing prepared him for that sudden difficulty that came out of nowhere. The worst punch is the one you're not ready for, and it wasn't just the knockout, but the realization that he had no desire to get back up on his feet anymore. No desire for time to heal everything. The pain was unbearable, but even more unbearable was the thought that one day the pain would dissolve because he would forget. At first he would obsessively replay in his mind that moment that slashed through his life, he could remember every detail, every millisecond before the blow. After the shock wore off, when he realized that the woman he loved had ceased to exist, the anger became ever-increasing. How could she do that to him? They were just married, she wasn't supposed to leave. But his fury at her was just a phase, a cover for what came next and seemed there to stay – the swamp of hatred he felt for himself.

The headaches became more frequent. They were no longer just regular headaches, they grew stronger, spreading out to the neck, to the jaws, settling in the shoulder blades and radiating down his back. Every person has their own form of self-destruction, and his sent him straight for the strongest painkillers they make.

They always loved going to the open market together, it was right near the house, but one morning they had a stupid argument, and she needed some air. When she left the house alone, he was struck by anxiety and shortness of breath, and fell on the carpet after momentarily losing sensation in his legs. But instead of collecting himself and running to stop her, he allowed doubt to trickle in. He persuaded himself that he was just being hysterical; that his genetic instinct was to be controlling, like his father is. The anxiety grew, the pressure was hurting his chest, but he stalled for four whole minutes, and the explosion occurred one minute after she got there. When he finally left the house, running frantically to catch up with her, it was too late.

Doubt is the enemy of power, they wrestle each other in a war of survival. He paid such a high price for allowing doubt to win. All it takes is one tiny crack in confidence, and doubt takes over. He could feel the danger distinctly, but doubted it and failed to stop her. He'd asked himself – is it really possible, what I'm feeling? And his doubt had responded – no way, you're delusional.

Only a few years later, when the sadness had already hardened like sediment on the bottom of life, he awoke one morning realizing there was no choice. He knew he'd have to forgive himself or he'd drown. It sounds easy, but forgiving yourself is much harder than forgiving someone else. It's exhausting and needs to be renegotiated again and again, every day. Every morning you open your eyes with a corpse of guilt lying beside you, and you're raring to forgive. But somehow, by the end of the day, you discover that you're still filled with self-loathing. Time and again he had to forgive himself for failing to understand, for not believing in himself, for hesitating. For stopping to wonder if it even made sense. For being an idiot. For being too slow.

He used to insist on deciphering everything down to the smallest detail, but life is too strange – there are some things he's simply stopped trying to understand. How could the most tragic thing he'd ever experienced, lead nine years later to an encounter with the best thing that's ever happened to him? One day he walked into a bakery and suddenly caught her out of the corner of his eye, and what his mother had told him as a child flashed and reverberated inside him.

"People like us find each other somehow, because you can't be like us and get through life completely alone." It was like being hit in the back with a club – the realizations smashing into his body, one after the other. The knowledge that it would happen had kept him going during those nine years when he shut down. But he'd never known it would be a woman. He never knew he'd be attracted to her like this. He didn't know she would be his soulmate, alike yet so different, on so many levels.

That random encounter blew life into him. For an entire month he just listened, studied her. He wanted to do everything right, so he held back. Vanished from her life and came back only when he knew she was ready. But nothing worked out as he expected. How can you convince someone who has built her entire life on a lie, to just give you her hand and cross the lines into a different world. Turns out that the fateful encounter where you meet your soulmate is just the beginning. You still have to work hard afterwards for it to really happen, to bend the bars of the cage.

The three of them, they're so different. The way they understand things. With his wife it was a silent understanding, and within the clamor of his life, her melodic thoughts had given him a silence he'd never known before. After she left he started going to the market alone, staying there until dark. The glaring neon lights were merciless, and he was surrounded by thousands of sounds – studded high school students, calloused-hand laborers, a hunched woman in a kerchief, young ladies thinking in Russian. A mass of passersby, and none of them her. He'd walk for hours, the chaotic overload on his senses was the only thing that could banish the demons. Middle-Eastern music, street chatter, the competing shouts and banter of merchants. So many things caught his attention – melons shaped like alien skulls, pale corncobs emerging from green collars, malicious red peppers, piles of synthetic underwear in toxic hues. But the real magic of the market was that only there he would suddenly feel her, quiet like a shadow, slipping into his steps.

He would buy some cheese and remember how she used to taste it off the edge of a knife. He'd pass over the exotic spice stall with a slight sadness, though now he could season his food as hot as he liked. He missed her quiet thoughts, the notes that always played in her head just before her long fingers touched the piano keys, but they gradually faded in his memory. Time and time again he'd rewind the first moment he saw her. That serendipitous ride in the taxi-van to Jerusalem, the whisper of his spine as it straightened when she got in and sat beside him, and his heartbeats as he heard her imagining her hands softly playing that piece by Chopin, that used to play during his sessions on the carpet with his mother.

He began running on the beach in the evenings to exhaust himself. He yearned to escape into his own moments of temporary death, but couldn't fall asleep. Darkness always dragged him into mute conversations with her. Sometimes he couldn't bear the thoughts, he'd long for her touch so badly that the skin on his face would almost sear.

An absence of something produces longing in your body, but longing comes in many forms. Sheera hated that longing, hated the distance between them and the need to wait. He hated waiting for her but loved it as well, because he knew it was a longing for something that would be, and not for something that would never return. But maybe only those who have experienced longing for the dead can feel the pleasure in longing for a living love yet to be attained.

So what had he learned from the women he'd loved and were now gone from his life? Funny, because all of them had taught him about his power. He'd learned from his mother how to disengage himself from everything, but also how to connect. From his wife he'd learned of his second ability, to feel danger before disaster occurred. From Sheera he'd learned what he asked her in a heated moment of argument: if soulmates were supposed to understand each other better than anyone, why was she the only one he couldn't persuade? He was simply unaware of the fact that there was someone else in the world with a force that was equal to his. He had the ability to dissolve words within thoughts, but she could recreate them. When they were in sync - they could achieve anything together, but when their wills were opposed, her power would always neutralize his.

It took him a long time to figure out that there were things that no matter how badly he wanted, he just couldn't get them done on his own. You can't force someone to do something when they simply don't want to.

So now he's there and she's here, and at night it sometimes seems that he's whispering – Hey Sea Song, you just don't want to. Something is standing in your way – you don't want to cross the lines, you still don't want to know who you are, you don't want to believe or to see the signs. And you have to understand why, what is that one hidden thing that you want more than anything. I can't do it for you. You have to solve your own riddle if you ever want to be truly alive.

11:11 p.m.	Mikey, I've been going over some stuff for work, and suddenly my eyes filled with tears for no reason. Empty tears that just appeared and began trickling down my face. It took me a few seconds to realize I was feeling you, what you're feeling right now, after coming back here today and reading everything I wrote. These are not my tears, I'm sure of it. They began flowing way before the sadness came in. As if the tears are the lightning and the feeling is the thunder, and it works the other way around when you cry someone else's tears instead of your own.
	Strange, I haven't removed the bracelets from that old envelope in my purse. But ever since I took them I can feel you like I did before you left. Maybe even more.

To: Sheera and Michael <softspoons@gmail.com>
From: Sheera and Michael <softspoons@gmail.com>
March 13, 2016 at 9:47 p.m.
Subject: The television machine must stay in motion

I'm back at work, Mikey. I had a weird day. I'm not sure if it's good or bad that it's finally over. I felt like the lead in someone else's movie, God knows whose. I knew all the routines, gave Oscar-worthy imitations of expressions, remembered all my lines.

I didn't write you at all over the weekend. I wanted to spend as much time as I could with Tom before going back to work. We cooked together, rode our bikes through the neighborhood streets and drew a thousand paintings that were hung crookedly to dry on the laundry lines. You wouldn't believe it, but we even laughed. I've regained my laughing ability. I guess it was no accident that I went to see your father just before going back to my old life. I could feel you every minute of the weekend, smelled you in my morning coffee and tasted you in the kisses I gave Tom. I hoped you'd make some sort of contact, I don't really understand why you haven't written, I guess I'm still missing something.

When I took Tom to school this morning, he paused for a moment before entering the car, looked at me hesitantly, then took the backpack off his back and put it in the back seat. One of the walls in my heart collapsed as he sat beside me. He's afraid of me, I think I've crippled my son's courage to rebel. Are you gonna come late today? He asked indifferently when I dropped him off, trying to hide the worry brewing inside of him. I'll be back early, I promised, we'll do homework together. He forced a little smile, then got out wordlessly, loaded his backpack on his back and ran heavily into the schoolyard, maybe preparing himself for the fact that I was going back to the labyrinth of work where I would get lost again.

Parents are always lying to their kids, but I went a little too far with the lies I have told this child, in my efforts to protect him from life. I didn't tell him the truth about his father, thus depriving him of the truth about himself. Without noticing I'd sentenced him to a life of deception, just like mine. How could I change that now? I still have no idea how to untangle this complicated jumble of lies, which nobody knows about except you and me.

The guard at the parking lot welcomed me with a huge smile. Where've you been? He beamed, and I smiled apologetically and said I'd been a little sick. It was strange to park in my regular spot with the old oil stain, to smell the dank air of the parking level, press the cracked elevator button and enter to find my image in the mirror, simultaneously familiar and estranged.

Outside it was warm but I wrapped myself in a sweater. My office door was open and a small colorful clump of helium balloons clung merrily to the ceiling. One minute later, Moni himself appeared, accompanied by Ruthie who pasted a smacking kiss on my cheek and welcomed me back in impeccable Hebrew. Moni drew me to him with a warm, lengthy hug. He'd never hugged me like that. He was a little discomfited at first, then said welcome back and I'll see you at the meeting later, then finally answered his phone which was ringing like crazy in his pocket, and left. Just then, Erik came in with his everlasting boots. He's back to his old self, looks exactly as he used to. I suddenly felt so vulnerable that I actually considered asking Ruthie to stay and not to leave me alone with him. He hesitated for a minute before coming closer and giving me an awkward kiss. I smiled, and thought how strange it was that even when I'm weak he's afraid of me. Julia came in with her enormous smile, and placed a slice of cake on my desk. I was flattered by the attention, but felt so out of place.

After that welcome I turned on my computer, and fear sent a pang of regards from my stomach, driving a slight tremor through me. I knew I had to do this, but had no idea where to start.

Thousands of emails I'd missed over the past month began flowing menacingly onto the screen. I scanned them, having seen a large share of them at home last week. How I used to charge at them once, focusing on my goal, yearning to finish my tasks as quickly as possible, to move on. I'd reply, delete, measure my pace, just wanted to cross them off the list. Today I was so disinclined to read anything that I found myself logging onto Google and typing the words "Eden" and "Suicide bombing", waiting for the results as if I hadn't done this twenty eight times over the weekend.

2006. A suicide attack at the Carmel Market in Tel Aviv. Four dead, one of them Irit Eden, thirty years old. One of the articles mentioned her being a pianist. Then I looked for some more information about her. Her name appeared in an old chamber orchestra program, and in a review of a festival concert. I couldn't find a photo. Maybe it's for the best.

Her last name may be identical to yours, but there was no chance I would have discovered the whole thing without your father's kind assistance. There had been so many suicide attacks back then, just about the time I broke up with Ziv. How could anyone remember who had been killed, when or where. They became a horrifying bloody routine, a series of tragedies that unwillingly crystallized into a lump instead of receiving the minimal dignity of being distinct, with identities of their own. Your name was not even mentioned in the article, it was dry and factual. An event that had vanished into the nooks of history. Blended into the statistics.

So is that what you've been doing since, Mikey? Is this what you do, God knows how? Crushing yourself to the bone, ridden with guilt for your wife's death, so you save others from imminent disaster? I can't stop thinking about it. About the way you learned that you could sense something terrible was about to happen. To know that someone was about to commit murder, certain that that was their calling in life. I keep imagining you feeling it again and again, finding that locked person whose mind needed to be changed, and then starting to mix the words around in his thoughts. How do you do it? How do you convince someone that you can't solve one catastrophe with another? Which words do you dissolve? I tried, but I couldn't imagine it. I also tried to think about how it was related to your headaches, if they'd increased because of what you'd been doing since, or because of the grief that had accumulated inside you. I imagined you shutting your eyes, searching for that crack in the stiff pack of thoughts, that little speck of humanity. The crack through which you would be able to restore someone's sanity.

I was suddenly jealous of her, of Irit, whose existence I hadn't even been aware of a few days ago. That perfect woman who'd been killed nine years ago, your own private heroine. I didn't know what she looked like but I knew I could never affect your life as she did. I suppose you might feel the same regarding Ziv, but it's not true. Although he's Tom's father, there's no comparing him to you. The force of your influence on me is so much stronger than his was. I've tormented myself enough with these comparisons, until I finally concluded that this is the kind of destructive thinking that should be pushed out of my mind, comparisons that never amount to anything good.

In the morning roundup nobody mentioned my absence, and it appeared that a whole month had gone by, but everyone was talking more or less about the same things. As if I'd fast forwarded a large share of the movie, but the plot hadn't developed and I hadn't missed anything important. The changes in "The Human League", a mini-campaign for the final episode of the loathsome drama series, and how to boost ratings even higher on the next season of "Big Fear". I was relatively quiet. I looked at them like an observer, knowing that on the outside I looked exactly like they did. Dead serious, demonstrating with their hands, struggling to impress, competing to be the wittiest.

The important things I'd missed only surfaced later. Moni asked me to stay after everyone got up and left.

You're still a little pale, he said.

I'm fine, give me a few days and you won't even remember I was gone, I promised. I had a feeling we both knew I was lying but preferred to ignore it. He suddenly became serious, and it was obvious he was about to say something unpleasant.

Look, he said, we've decided to freeze "The Write Stuff" for the moment, we thought about it a lot while you were gone, and we realized that no matter how you spin it, bottom line is that it's just too trivial, a bunch of gimmicks that might bring in the ratings and turn a small profit, but maybe we should aim higher.

And what about Gaya and the partnership plans? I asked.

It's a little complicated with Gaya, he said, as far as I'm concerned the partnership is good for us regardless of the show, but she and Erik are having some differences. Then he glanced at his computer and mumbled – I have to finish up here but I promise to keep you posted.

It wasn't that surprising, Mikey. I found it hard to argue because it was exactly what I thought, I told you. Besides, it was obvious, wasn't it? I knew the whole time that that program and I were not really meant to be. I'm the woman who's destined to do PR so that all kinds of talents would make it big and people like Erik could take their cut. So I was disappointed, sure, but not like I used to be. I knew Moni was expecting me to resist, to ask – but why? To argue. I tried to fake an expression of devastation. What does "freeze" mean, I asked, that it'll be defrosted at some point?

I really don't know yet, Sheera, Moni said. But I know him so well, it was clear that during my absence, "The Write Stuff" had withered away and is now dead and buried.

We're two impostors, Mikey, you and I. You're a lifeguard who poses as a hi-tech entrepreneur, or an angel, or whatever. But since your wife was murdered you've been dedicating your life to the thoughts of people who are planning atrocities. Preventing pain, preventing suffering, and nobody even knows how bad it could've been without you. No one is grateful. Nobody thinks you're a hero, no one says you're a wonderful person. Nobody wants to interview you or even give you a like on Facebook. The world keeps turning and you're spinning on the same axis but exactly in the opposite direction. How can you even live like that? Only with yourself and your thoughts forever imprisoned inside your head, detached from everyone.

I'm not like you, but I'm also an impostor. I realized that when I walked down the hall from Moni's office to mine, straight-backed and proud, pretending, as usual. But this time my faking was doubled: I walked with false pride, pretending I was pretending not to care. I really didn't care, but I didn't want anyone to know. It was strange – I couldn't understand how something I'd wanted so much could lose all its appeal at once. Until now I had posed as an ambitious corporate girl, my goals were clear, but suddenly I have no idea what I want to be. I'm lost, Mikey, I'm no longer here, but I'm still not there. I've given you my hand so we can cross those lines, but now I'm stuck in the middle, hovering in that small space that opens when a seam between two universes is suddenly undone.

Avi only got in at noon, his face shining with sweat from the blinding sun outside. Too many meetings, he apologized as he came into my office, I see I've missed your welcome back party. When we hugged my body immediately grew stiff, and I wondered how I'd never fully realized the stress he was under. He said he'd ask the secretary to set up a meeting about the promotion of "The Human League". You've gotta help me, I have no idea how to resell this crap to the advertisers. I looked at him for a minute, sweet Avi, who can always be counted on, my only true friend at the station. Hey, I suddenly said, why would we even want to sell crap? How did we end up where this is what we do in life?

He studied me suspiciously. He didn't like the question, he had work to do, goals to attain, ad time to sell. Sweetheart, take another day or two but we need you here, he said, please don't tell me you've decided to form deep theories on the meaning of life, okay?

How long have you known about "The Write Stuff"? I asked.

A couple of days. Moni suddenly lost interest, and Erik and Gaya had this fight. I don't know what it was about, but emotions went wild. Now that you're back, maybe you can milk the details from Moni and fix it somehow.

I looked at him without saying a word, a little stunned at my indifference to the news, the kind that used to make me boil with rage in a second. That moment when I sat at home and deleted "The Write Stuff" proposal in disgust suddenly flashed before me. Maybe it's for the best. You told me there was a reason I got that show, and maybe there was a reason I lost it. Could you have meant that it would teach me something completely different? Maybe you wanted it to spark something inside of me, something I had put out years ago. Before becoming an expert on PR and ratings and intrigue, I wrote all the time, and I loved it so.

I hope you're not mad at me for not telling you, I thought it was better if you got well and came back and we just started working again, Avi said.

No, don't worry, I'm not mad, I shook myself out of my reverie.

You need to pull yourself together, he said before leaving, I'm worried about you, something in your eyes is blank, aren't you better already?

I don't know how I can go on from here. I don't want to give up Avi or Moni, I've got to be one of the gang. For years I've known how to work with them, to say the things that will activate them. But what is there behind it all besides common interests? I want them to keep liking me even if I suddenly change. But do they even like who I really am, or just the fictitious character I've been cultivating? I think I know the answer, but still, something inside of me doesn't want to put them to the test, doesn't want to know the truth. Something wants to go back to who I used to be, to live on their fake love and in exchange – go on pretending.

In the afternoon I went to see Gidi from the Promo department. Sis, you're back! He rejoiced, we've missed you around here. We argued passionately about whether to call the season finale of the drama series "a once in a lifetime moving experience" or "a must-see, brilliant and unforgettable", and I suddenly sensed how easily I could wrap myself back into the arms of habit, fall into that safety net. If I continued walking for a few more miles, over time I would forget that anything ever happened. I could once again bypass the fear of the change I had to make. The fear of surrendering to the unknown, burning the ships, leaving my old life behind. And then it occurred to me that maybe that was the reason you wanted me to invest in Fire Island. Maybe you wanted me to have enough money put aside so I wouldn't be afraid to call it quits. So I would have one less excuse not to work up the courage to leave.

On my way home Rona called. Well, how did the first day go?

I'm back in the saddle, I said, and she immediately said – Great, next week I'm finally interviewing Mr. Rafi-Hard-to-Get-Hadar, and that's going to be the glorious grand finale for our marvelous survey.

At the word "our" I felt a slight stroke of panic. I tried to remember if I'd mistakenly inserted some unintentional motives or powers or God knows what to those posts I'd written with Rona, if I'd hurt someone without meaning to do so by helping to edit her stories. It all suddenly seemed light years away. I couldn't even remember what I'd been thinking when we wrote them.

What's going on with Eyal? I asked cautiously.

He's going abroad for a couple of days, the ball and chain, I'll have some air, we can go out, I'll get a babysitter, it's been forever since we did that.

Perfect, I said, and we made plans for the weekend, and suddenly I knew that it happened, I was out of the chasm. My life was calling me back from all directions, and it seemed I'd gotten what I wanted most. I'd managed to re-glue my parts. I was back together.

I got home just in time for dinner with Tom. He didn't get up when I came in, but didn't resist when I walked over and gave him a long hug. Not that I haven't appreciated his presence in my life until now, but now I appreciate it much more. I cherish it. I dwell on the moments, the sensations. When I put him to bed, surrendering to our connection, I didn't understand how I could've even thought I could leave him. You said that the ramifications for people like us are more extreme, but still, I can't comprehend what I did. Apparently there are some things you can't explain rationally, they just happen without any explanation, no matter how much you try to analyze them later.

I think it's time to tell you, although you probably know already.

To: Sheera and Michael <softspoons@gmail.com>
From: Sheera and Michael <softspoons@gmail.com>
March 14, 2016 at 10:58 p.m.
Subject: The night I got on the fast train to hell

Here's something else I figured out on my own, Mikey, like your mother said you're supposed to. I finally understand the snowball you talked about. Apparently not only can our fantasies intertwine, our fears can too. I was so intoxicated by the feelings that engulfed me when you finally surrendered to me on our evening together, that I didn't realize how much my fear of you had also increased. I didn't know how the ping pong of influence worked. I didn't know the depth to which I could feel your emotions or you could feel mine. And then when I hurt you and you said you were leaving, your fear mixed with mine, and we threw this mad mixture at each other until it swelled into a petrifying horror. After you disappeared the horror grabbed me from behind with an ether-soaked rag, took over the steering wheel and tossed me aside.

I don't remember everything about that night, and maybe it's for the best. I just know that I've never broken down like that. That these past few weeks have been an everlasting attempt to survive the flashbacks, the vivid memories. What about you, Mikey? Have you told anyone, or are you also totally alone with all of this?

That night, after we had that fight, everything began toppling down like dominos. A black tile falls and hits you in the head, and you have no way of knowing it's only the first in a long series of tiles. You were like an overripe fruit, and your contents just burst all over me when I wounded you. Right after you disappeared, I stood in the middle of the house, feeling my entire body collapse into itself, in a dry and quiet landslide. It was scary, and I didn't understand what the feeling meant. What have I done? Have I hurt you again, like I had with Erik? And if so – who could tell me how to fix it? I can't get close to you, and I don't understand what happened, and when I touch you without complete awareness all I do is damage, so what the hell should I do now? The sensations raced through my organs like mercury, and I panicked at the notion that the collapse I was feeling in my body was actually your death.

I felt haunted. I'm used to being so goal-oriented, to ask and fully understand and then check and double-check until I get things done – but I just didn't know what to do. If I was hurting you unknowingly, I might only hurt you more by finding you. I was trapped in a nightmare of a parallel universe with rules I couldn't comprehend. I didn't sleep a wink, but when morning came I pretended everything was fine. I had no choice. I had the season finale of "Big Fear" to deal with, so I took Tom to school and went to work.

The terror only increased when the bracelet suddenly broke and fell off my hand. I'm used to faking it at work, but this time it was too hard to cover what I felt. People kept asking me what was wrong, and I said I didn't feel so well. That's why later it seemed logical to run with that line and invent the mononucleosis – or whatever the disease I'd been infected with since kissing your soul.

The fear gnawed at me relentlessly. I was worried about you, but for the first time in my life, I was worried about me as well. I was always confident I could get by, handle things even with a shattered heart. But with all these powers I had no idea how to use, I didn't know how I'd be able to survive. How would I manage on my own, without any guidance? You put a machine gun in my hands, it was firing away randomly on its own, and I had no control. Who would be next in the line of fire? And how the hell do I get rid of this thing? How do you stop intending? How do you shut off those channels? How do you stop this madness?

I didn't recognize myself. I tried conducting myself as usual, but something very basic had gone awry inside, that hard core that had always maintained me was cracked. I couldn't concentrate, I couldn't eat or sleep, I was ridden with anxiety and there was nobody I could tell. This was before you deleted everything, but you weren't answering your phone or the email, so all I could do was read and reread our last argument in a desperate attempt to find a sign, to figure out what had happened. You told me to think about what I was creating here, so what have I created? If I put Erik in the hospital, and love mixes with hate, and the bracelets only intensify the feelings, then what happened to you? From your words I could feel your regret about getting mixed up with me to begin with. It hurt all over every time I read what you wrote, that you can't live like this. But I didn't understand what you wanted. What all that rage was about. I meant well. How had I managed to destroy everything?

I wanted to get in the car and just drive to your house, but you warned me not to. I was arrested by the rules of a virtual world I hated, with monstrous fears and thoughts that were racing wildly. The intense fear put me in a different mode. At work there were constantly people around me, I could see their mouths moving, but couldn't make out what they were saying. I tried to avoid sending messages, thinking eight times before sending each email. How would I know if I was doing something harmful? My anxiety level was so high that my body was deep in emergency mode, an animal instinct for survival that was stronger than me. On the inside I chewed away at myself viciously, and on the outside I was no longer able to maintain my cool. It wasn't just my broken heart. I trusted you, I'd agreed to cross the lines with you, and you'd suddenly abandoned me midway. I was stranded. I'd become so dependent on you, how had I let that happen? I'd never been so dependent on anyone.

At some point I told Julia and Ruthie I wasn't feeling well, that I had to leave. My hands shook as I gathered my things. I took the elevator down, got into the car, praying that I'd soon wake up, that this was just a bad dream. All I wished for was to disappear.

But once I got home, it was even worse. I couldn't sleep, and when I could no longer pace the apartment in an aimless trance, I sent Tom to my parents' and accessed our email again. You said all the answers were here, screaming at me, so I read our last argument again and again, unaware that I was swallowing more and more of the poison we'd vomited over each other in our moments of despair. I didn't understand the destructive power we inserted into our words. The way we mutually affect each other, Mikey, it's so beautiful at some moments, but in those dark moments it was lethal. I didn't notice how I was deteriorating each time I read it. I really thought it was the only way to finally make some sense of everything.

I remembered you told me that an ability was a duty, not a privilege. You can't escape, you have to use it. But how can I do it if you don't guide me? And if I keep it all inside will I get sick and die, like your mother? And if I don't... who will I hurt? Moni? My parents? I remember the moment when my heart stopped. Tom? No, not Tom. That's impossible. I can't have any bad intention towards my son, not hidden, visible or imaginary.

But up until a few days ago I was sure that I couldn't have any bad intentions regarding you, either.

The blood stabbed through my veins. I affect everyone around me, with my presence, my touch, my feelings and my visible and hidden intentions that ooze out uncontrollably through my pores. I searched back at all sorts of things you wrote over time. "How did a poetic soul such as yours get stuck with such a pragmatic personality?" Something was so fundamentally wrong with me, like a baby being allergic to its mother's milk. Maybe you'd meant that something was preventing my personality from coping with my soul.

When Tom came back that evening I mumbled something about not feeling well. He looked a little angry, barely ate or spoke to me, and the anxiety kept consuming my insides like corrosion. I had lost any certainty that I could manage our lives. I tiptoed to him quietly as he fell asleep watching the final episode of "Big Fear". His eyelids were darker than usual, his breathing low, and I wanted to put a hand on his forehead, but I was afraid to touch him. I glanced at the contestants on the screen, specifically at that crass and violent one who I knew would soon win one million shekels and buckets of fame, and suddenly I could no longer stand them, their stupid, frivolous shouting invaded my boundaries, trespassed my skin.

I stood there facing the TV, alarmed, scared out of my wits. Not only do I allow him to watch this stuff, he worships it more than other kids do. He thinks it's good and right and worthy, because this is what mommy does. And just then, my previous blindness immediately flipped: from believing I had no control over anything around me, suddenly, in my terrified train of association, everything in the world was entirely my responsibility.

Suddenly it hit me, Mikey – my power is destructive. That's the answer you wanted me to find. I put Erik in the hospital, I crushed the love of my life, and without noticing I'm destroying my son. In a momentum of self-persuasion, I frantically searched for more evidence to prove my new theory. The journals I'd filled as a girl when I was mad at my father flashed in my memory. I wrote how crazy he was, but I wasn't documenting reality, it was the other way around - that's what happened later only because I was writing with such passionate anger. But I didn't stop there, because if this was true, what had I written about Tom? Have I caused damage there too? Jesus, what have I done to my boy?

I couldn't contain all these perceptions about myself, a wave of nausea hurled through me. I ran to the bathroom, just making it in time to retch into the toilet. I looked in the mirror as I washed the cold sweat off my face. I'm a bad person. I just never realized it before. It makes sense, even the most evil people in the world don't realize they're wrong. Those head choppers and suicidal fanatics that blow up in buses, they justify their behavior, they're sure it's the right thing to do.

The thoughts rushed wildly, like bumper cars in my brain. You said that love meant putting yourself aside, doing something for someone you love without receiving anything in return. It all came together with a recognition that shook me to the core. If I'm making you sick, so in what I've amounted to in my life, I'm just an intrusive force. The best thing I can do for others is to die, that's the missing piece in this huge chaotic puzzle. My heart beat so fast it made me dizzy. I tried refuting my theory, which seemed insane, but there were no loopholes. Everything around it fell into place in perfect order. My personality is preventing my soul from flourishing, which is why I have to return it to creation, that's all. If I die, my destructive power will cease to exist. If I die, I'll be putting the benefit of the people I love before my own. The love of my life will finally be freed of the pain I cause him without being able to control it. And most importantly, if I die, Tom won't have a mother, but since I'm damaging him, he'll have a better life. That's it, I've found the answers. I've solved the puzzle, haven't I?

I completely believed it, Michael, at that moment it just seemed to make perfect sense. The thoughts lined up immaculately in my head, they locked in place.

But what would Tom do? Fatherless and now motherless - how would he manage? No, no, I stood there in the middle of the house, vigorously shaking my head. But wait, what's better? To be an orphan raised by his grandparents, or to rot with his mother and eventually die of pain?

My sweet little Tom... I went back to the living room and looked at him. My beautiful boy. We are one, we're connected by blood. How would I be able to end it knowing I'd left him alone?

Tom's eyes suddenly opened, red and confused. My sweet baby, how are you feeling, I asked, tears welling in my eyes. Fine, his voice cracked as he whispered. He got up slowly, coughed, and began shuffling slowly towards his room. When he passed by me I stroked his arm but he yanked it away sharply. I was stunned. Stop it, Mom, he said aggressively, I hate when you treat me like you think you own me.

He left me planted to the floor. What happened to that boy? I followed him slowly to his room and asked, are you sure you're all right? Maybe you're a little sick, too.

I'm fine, leave me alone already! He yelled hoarsely, I don't want to be with you right now, okay? I want to be alone. I'm calling Grandma and Grandpa. Can I go back there and sleep over?

I was silent. The fear paralyzed me. I walked hazily to the bathroom, rifled through the drawer and pulled out a thermometer, of the old-fashioned kind my father insists is far more accurate than the digital plastic ones, and forced him to take his temperature. He fought me, resisted, then eventually gave in and stuck it in his mouth, but in a moment of sudden rage he bit down forcefully at the thermometer, which just shattered in his mouth. I screamed – Tom, what do you think you're doing? And forced him to spit out the shards and wash his mouth a thousand times. I was terrified. This child has gone crazy, why is he so mad?

He stood there demanding to go sleep at my parents' house, not letting me touch him and unwilling to listen. It only reinforced what I thought – I'd lost him anyway. There, that's what Mikey had meant when he said "learn how to read the signs already". Tom can feel it on his own – in order to survive he'd have to be without me from now on. I was just no good for him, like a baby allergic to its mother's milk. He wouldn't be alone, he'd be with my mom. And with my father, and they're so connected recently. They'll be just like normal parents, only older. In a way his family will be more balanced, I persuaded myself.

My father came to pick him up rather quickly. When they left, Tom barely said goodbye. He wouldn't even let me help him pack some clothes or organize his bag.

I was alone. I started pacing the living room, back and forth, a lion in a cage. Your words echoed through my head – "You don't know how to love". But I don't really want to die. I want to live. I have Tom. I have to be his mother – no one else can take my place. Besides, why die? That's crazy, all in all my life is pretty good. And as I thought this, again I split into two – the scolder and scolded, and the scolder was furious. Listen to yourself! Thinking only about yourself, as usual, totally self-absorbed. I listened to her, frightened, knowing she was right. I really am in love with myself, with my bullshit, my career, with the lies I'd become used to. If I want to prove my love, I'd have to prove that I was willing to make a sacrifice. It's so twisted, but the only way I could really learn how to love is by ceasing to be. I smother, I intrude, I cause pain, that's just the way I am. But my love is true, and I won't let you down. Despite everything, I'm capable of loving, and I'll prove it to you.

How can I kill myself? I tried to shut my eyes and imagine it. Let's say I get a hold of a gun. Would I be able to put it against my temple and squeeze the trigger? Not a chance. With all the blood somebody else will have to clean, and God knows who that will be, probably my mother. I can't do that, definitely not to someone who loves me.

I soon concluded that the only thing I'd have the guts to do would be to swallow sleeping pills. The cowardly suicide, designed for the gutless. A quick calculation led me to realize that tomorrow was the cleaning lady's day, and she would find me in the morning. But what about Tom? Who would raise him? An orphan... how could I? No, I can't think about that. That's my way of chickening out of everything. It's for his own good. I'm hurting him without meaning to. I hurt everyone and everything I touch. I have to rise above myself. To just plain split, no emotions, no feelings. That's my specialty, after all, I'm an expert on emotional shutdown. No doubt that's something I'm capable of doing, that really must be my true, sick calling.

I looked at the clock. It was nine. Tom had probably already fallen asleep at my parents' house. What kind of a letter should I leave him? Would I even write one? Should I tell the truth? Should I tell him who his father is? Because if I die, the secret would die with me.

Maybe it's best if he doesn't know the truth about what his mother had done. Let him fantasize, it will help him get through it. My parents are still young, they can raise him at least until he's twenty. He'll have a chance at life. A normal family, a man and woman with old-fashioned values, the traditional Israeli ones. They'll have no tolerance for all the crap on which I let him grow up.

I was exhausted. Everything was surreal, like viewing the world from behind a screen. I paced back and forth, couldn't stop, couldn't halt. My thoughts dashed around madly like on a crazed conveyor belt that continues to accelerate. Once every few rounds I'd stop at the laptop. Refresh. Take a look. Maybe you replied. Maybe there's a sign of life. Maybe you posted something on Facebook. And suddenly I saw something I really had missed. You probably wrote it before our big argument.

"The truth may hurt, but less than the ramifications of the lie".

I read it and turned to stone. Yes, that also fit neatly into my psychotic puzzle. The truth did hurt terribly, but if I didn't accept it, the ramifications would hurt even more. Something would happen to Tom. It was obvious - that's what you were trying to say. You could hear my thoughts, and if you thought I'd reached the wrong conclusions you would send something or call. You would stop me. It suddenly dawned upon me that your silence was actually your way of giving me your approval. That my conclusion was right. It was really strange, because when I realized that you too thought it was the right thing to do, something inside of me became whole. I calmed a little. That's it. Now all I need to do is carry it out, and that's relatively simple. I am, after all, a doer – give me a mission, and I'll find a way to get it done.

Okay. So I need to write my parents a checklist. Organize the money I've saved. The special requests. The best thing would be for them to move in here, so that Tom will stay in the same neighborhood, at the same school with the same friends. They should sell their house, and with the addition of my savings, the three of them will be able to manage pretty well.

Now all I needed to do was to write Tom a letter he'd read when he was eighteen, a letter that would explain it all.

And a detailed letter to my parents, with all the instructions and how to's.

And to somehow get a hold of enough sleeping pills.

A walk in the park, really. That's a list of three things, no big deal.

I still get a chill when I think how from that moment onward I was as focused as a heat-seeking missile. I was sure I'd found the answer. Detached from any emotion, I had no more qualms, and all I could think about was how I'd carry out the deed in the cleanest and most effective way. How I'd get out of here as fast as I could, without time for second thoughts, and leave behind as small a mess as possible.

I wrote a goodbye letter to Tom. I said he was a wonderful boy, that he'd be fine, explained that he was actually better off without me. I'm so ashamed of that letter, Mikey, it was phony, cowardly, filled with clichés. I folded it into an envelope and moved on to my next task – the letter to my parents. Efficient, detailed, logical and withdrawn – containing phone numbers, accounts, contracts, technical explanations. And then I did something else, something kind of horrible. I called Tom's doctor, such a nice man who had grown slightly infatuated with us and sort of adopted us over the years. I'm sorry to call at this hour, I said, but a good friend of mine is getting on a plane to the US tonight and she can't sleep without a pill. I said he had nothing to worry about, she'd taken the pill before and wasn't allergic, and he didn't even pause before saying – for you? Anything. Stop by and I'll give you a prescription, just remind her not to drink any alcohol with it.

I did everything quickly, like a robot. I couldn't think of anything except checking the next item off my list. Less than an hour later, after stopping at the doctor's and the all-night pharmacy, after taking a shower and choosing the right dress, I put the two letters on the night table. They sat there next to a bottle of wine, one third of which I had already drunk, and a small pile of pills I had taken out of the packet. I shut my eyes and prepared for the final deed, but then, in a moment's decision, I grabbed a blank page and wrote one last letter. It contained only a few short lines that had been locked in a vault for years. *I never told you*, I wrote, *but I had a baby boy, nine months after we broke up. His name is Tom. We have a child together. He doesn't know you're his father, so do as you see fit. The ball's in your court.*

I couldn't take that secret with me to the grave. If Ziv wanted to be Tom's father, he'd know how to find him. If not – Tom would never know, and I would spare him the intolerable pain of knowing his father didn't want him. But at least he'd have a chance not to be an orphan.

I wrote on the envelope – for Ziv Peretz – and placed it at the bottom of the pile. The pills were becoming moist in my sweaty palm. I knew I shouldn't stop, so I poured some more wine and swallowed them, two by two, without even blinking. I wondered how long it would take until I felt sleepy. I lay back on the bed shivering, but after a minute the fear subsided. You're doing the right thing, I whispered to myself. I somehow felt lighter, maybe because of the letter to Ziv. I think I even smiled. A few more minutes and it would all be over.

But then I startled with a sudden realization - I hadn't taken my Directors' Insurance papers out of my desk. I sat up and then quickly stood, despite the slight dizziness. I knew I had to be fast, that soon the effect of the pills would completely kick in. I rifled frantically around the drawer, the one I never open except to shove another paper into, thinking that one day I'll have time to organize it. I found the insurance quarterly report, but when I hastily pulled my hand out of the drawer, an old notebook got pulled out along with it. That old notebook I wrote poems in with Rona as a teenager. I knew I had no time, but something urged me to read the poem I once wrote my mother, when the two of us were at home alone and my father was away at his "health sanatorium".

Some people's light has gone out.
It just happens sometimes
Like when the fuse box suddenly jumps.
They find a speck of bad in everything they see
Their bitter words keep crafting evil hypotheses.
People can go out like a light, and they don't even know it.
They blindly fume in the dark and they cannot control it.
They paint the whole world in a shade of pitch black
But all they need is for someone to push the switch in their fuse box for their light to come back.

I can't explain how or what exactly happened to me at that moment, but that naïve little poem written by the girl I had been, was the crack that split open in my elaborate scheme. That human crack in consciousness you told me about, and it saved me. I suddenly realized I was wrong, I'd been wrong about everything. Without thinking I grabbed the phone. I called the one person I knew would understand, and just said – Dad, come quick, call an ambulance, I took some pills. He didn't hesitate for a second. He just said, I'm coming Sheera, I'll be there in a few minutes. I whispered thanks, and could feel the fatigue starting to envelop me, so seductive, warm and pleasant. Just close your eyes for a minute, Sheera, it said sweetly, everything's all right, just rest a little. But my father's voice overrode it as he spoke firmly on the other end of the line.

No matter what happens, Sheera, don't let yourself fall asleep. But I'm tired, Dad, I whispered, almost from within a dream. Scream, Sheera, he commanded. Who would have dreamed that my crazy dad would become my lifeboat. I'm on my way, he said, but you, start screaming at the top of your lungs, and don't stop, no matter what, even if it seems like your voice is not responding and you can't hear anything coming out of your throat.

To: Sheera and Michael <softspoons@gmail.com>
From: Sheera and Michael <softspoons@gmail.com>
March 16, 2016 at 9:45 p.m.
Subject: Mrs. Ping

After I finished writing you the whole truth and nothing but the truth about that moonstruck night, a whole hour went by, then two hours passed, and then the fear attacked me. Is it possible that you won't respond again, even to this? All of a sudden it seemed perfectly reasonable. I checked for emails every few minutes. At some point I logged onto Facebook. I gasped when something suddenly moved on the screen, and then I saw the clip you shared on your page at that exact moment, just as I was staring at it. Which one of us had been here first and drew in the other? I clicked on the clip and listened to the song quietly, almost in a trance.

Dressed in black she appeared out of the darkness/ The queen of my dreams came to me / As crazed a woman as can be / we lost our air in a tango twirl / we barely managed to stop it / with her I'm always running against the wind / and I never know if she's real or I'm under a spell / she's a trip to heaven and then she's a fast train to hell.

I grabbed the phone. I tried calling you. After some discordant beeps I was thrown to the alienated sound of the voicemail. I hung up and tried again. But apparently, you're just as stubborn as I am when you decide to be unavailable.

In the past, if I wrote you something like this and you didn't respond, it would've crushed me. I don't know if you've ever spilled your guts out and then just had them left lying there, without any response. But I stopped myself. I don't want to be hurt by you anymore. I have no intention of devotedly feeding those old beliefs, I'm not stepping into that destructive circle with you again. I've seen where it leads, so somehow I've managed to convince myself there's probably a good reason you're still not getting back to me, and maybe someday I'll understand what it is.

Meanwhile I've become Mrs. Ping. I serve all day, there are hundreds of balls resting on the court around me. The ball flies up, I raise my racket, and when I hit hard it slices the air like an axe. Sometimes I totally miss and the ball lands out of bounds, and sometimes my racket hits it in that perfect sweet spot that makes a pure, springy sound.

I'm waiting for Mr. Pong. But he's hiding somewhere in the shade of the trees, just watching me serve. The days go by and I hit the ball again and again, but Mr. Pong remains unseen. Does he like my game? What's he thinking about? What does he do all day? Sometimes I stop and wonder if it's normal to play tennis like this, just with yourself.

Meanwhile my game has improved, my legs are a lot stronger. At night it gets cold and all you can hear is the chirp of the crickets and that damp sound of the racket hitting the ball. Sometimes the moon looks like a silver coin, and sometimes the color of the sky is so beautiful I suddenly feel like crying. I can't leave. Not really. All I want to do is to be here with this racket, and with this very specific Mr. Pong. But how long can I go on like this? I never knew how much loneliness could accumulate on one court, where one woman is waiting for a ball that never returns.

To: Sheera and Michael <softspoons@gmail.com>
From: Sheera and Michael <softspoons@gmail.com>
March 17, 2016 at 9:55 p.m.
Subject: What I'm creating here

You know how people think it's really good to go back to your old self after you've been through something traumatic? They say it as if it's a compliment – "Hey, I see you're back to your old self." I used to think that way too, but right now there's nothing that scares me more than being seduced back into the world I've created over the years, that keeps calling me back to be my old self again.

Rona called when I was on the way to work. What's up, got any hot merchandise for me? She asked before sharing her dilemmas about the interview with Rafi Hadar, which had finally been scheduled for the next week after endless delays. I don't want it to be too bland, I need to ask questions with juice potential, she complained, and I said – Okay, let's think about the message you're trying to relay.

Message?? Get real, Sheer, it's a celebrity interview so the women of Israel will have something to drool over during the weekend, she said, and that's it, I need an idea for a serious feature, because with all due respect, I'm done with this challenged-hairdresser genre.

But everything has some message, I insisted, seriously, think for a second. Lots of people are going to read this. What do you want to leave them with?

She paused for a moment. I can't see your face so I don't know if you're shitting me or if you're serious, she said hesitantly.

I'm dead serious, I said, we lured people into confessing their problems, but maybe we were kind of half-assed about it, you know? We didn't really search for the truth.

What could be more true than confessions? She was puzzled.

I knew it would be a grave mistake to say something about people who rush to put their theory together before they have all the facts, so I just said – well, the question is what we were looking for... besides ratings. What were we really searching for when we wrote those posts inviting people to talk?

Okay, and what do you think we were looking for? She was becoming impatient.

I'm suddenly thinking that all we wanted to find is what we already knew in advance. We just wanted to fixate on our old beliefs, justify our fear of love.

There was silence on the other end of the line, and then Rona burst into laughter. Oh, you're my heroic poet! She gushed, you really had me going there for a minute! No, wait, not a poet, you're a philosopher, you think therefore you are! At this point she totally got a kick out of herself – that's it, from now on I'm calling you Descartes, the feminine version, and we both laughed, but I knew I sounded ridiculous and that I hadn't made myself clear.

Turns out it's not so easy to decide not to go back to your old self. When I came into the office I turned on the computer, put my cell phone on the desk and my bag on the little side cabinet, sat down, and suddenly I noticed those tiny automatic motions of habit, the motions that give you some sense of confidence, luring you back to into their arms so softly, you can't even hear them. A few minutes before the morning meeting Avi came into my office and shut the door behind him. What's up? I asked.

I'd like to know what you plan on doing now, he frowned.

What do you mean? I tensed.

I mean everybody's shocked, nobody understands why you're not fighting to bring back "The Write Stuff". Have you even tried talking to Moni? The whole partnership with Gaya is about to collapse because of Erik, this is our chance to bury him, and you're playing uninvolved, like you joined the UN or something. Even Erik came sniffing around me to see what you're up to.

I smiled. Why is it so hard to believe I reconsidered, and I'm not so sure it's what I want anymore?

Are you kidding me? He said, annoyed, what's up with the secrecy? I thought we were a team, that we tell each other everything.

I swear I'm not keeping anything from you, I found myself apologizing.

Look, he said impatiently, sitting down and leaning towards me, you're not someone who takes things lying down. You're a tiger. When you want something you never let up, and everyone here knows it. So if you don't want to share your plans with me, that's okay, but at least say it to my face and don't make me feel like an idiot.

I don't know what it was exactly, but something he said was off, sounded like a flat note. But I just said softly – Look sweetie, truth is I'm just not at my best yet, and I promise to let you know once I have a battle plan in line, okay? You know I won't make a move without you.

Somehow this appeased him. He snapped something about wishing he had time for a cigarette, and we both headed to Moni's office for the morning meeting. I tried to figure out what bugged me about what he said. Me? A tiger? It seems that people were expecting me to react in a very particular way, and if I didn't, they were sure I was scheming something. I guess that when you cultivate a false image, at some point it takes over and you find yourself increasingly adapting to the expectations that go along with it.

Avi and I walked towards Moni's office, each with our own truth – he was certain I'd gotten the show because I'm a tiger, while I thought I only got it thanks to you. But why had your powers been effective on Moni and mine hadn't? Why hadn't I ever been able to persuade him to give me what I really wanted?

Halfway down the hall I suddenly saw it, the answer was right there in my steps – every time I walked to Moni's office this way I was preparing myself for his refusal, and also preparing the way I'd console myself. It's okay, I'd whisper to myself, worst case he'll say no. Every time I stepped into that office, instead of focusing on the possibility of success, I was focused on the potential failure. You said I had to understand my true desires, to be honest with myself, so here, now I get it – my real intention was to prove that I wasn't good enough and to fail. That's how I planned it, and that's how it worked every time. I did it to myself.

Michael, could that be the reason I've lived all these years without knowing? That's how I was when I started out trying to find my power – I supposedly took a shot at it, but what did I really want on that crazy night when I tried to bend the spoon? My true intention was to prove that it was bullshit, that there was something wrong with you.

Nobody knows that underneath my battle-armor, I don't really believe in myself. Look at me, Mikey, I'm still afraid to go all the way, even when I have enough money. I've already realized I don't really want to stay here, but how can I just walk away from everything I've built? And where am I supposed to go from here?

In the afternoon, just before going home, Avi and I dropped into the Promo department to see the clips for the next episode of "The Human League". As we crowded into Gidi's little cubicle I suddenly saw a familiar face. I couldn't place it at first, but then Gidi said – Guys, this is Simon, he directs music clips, and he's going to be working with us. I smiled at him awkwardly. After all, I hadn't seen him in nine years, and the last time we'd bumped into each other was in the middle of the street on that night when I broke up with Ziv.

Simon smiled back. We stood there for a few seconds until he made the first move, leaned over and kissed me on the cheek.

How are you? He asked politely. Great, and you? I responded as expected. And then he turned to Gidi and said jokingly – I hope you're steering clear of this one, she's a known heartbreaker. Gidi and Avi immediately jumped at the chance to ask whose hearts I'd broken and Simon was glad to oblige by telling them how I was the legendary ex of one of his closest friends, who'd left the country after I dumped him. Have you heard his album? Simon turned to ask me. No, I mumbled, I didn't even know he had one.

Yeah, he recorded this album with some small band in New York, Simon said, "Sometimes Love Isn't Enough". Crazy that you haven't heard, I was sure it was about you.

From that moment on I could no longer concentrate. Simon said "don't be a stranger", shoved a business card into my hand and left, and I was weighed down with an avalanche of memories. When I got back to my office I shut the door, leaned against it, and started mumbling. Me? I'd broken Ziv's heart? Dumped him? I was his legendary ex? What the hell was he talking about? I suddenly wondered how I would've reacted if this had happened a few months ago. Would I have just pushed the whole thing aside and forgotten about it? Or would I have found some crooked explanation for what he said so that it wouldn't shatter my beliefs, God forbid?

Everything was suddenly clear, it was all connected. The beliefs that determine the true intentions, the sub-text of life that you can't always see. That's how I had planned it all – Moni's refusals, the breakup with Ziv, and apparently what happened with you as well. I live my life with this basic intention of failing at everything I care most about, just so I can do it first, have the upper hand. Just so that I won't be surprised by the stinging failure, just so that I won't be dumped by someone I love, because the worst punch is the one you're not ready for. I do it in order to spare myself the injury, but I'm injuring myself all the time.

When I got home to Tom, flushed with that embarrassing insight, I was ridden with guilt. I have to pay attention, make sure I'm not teaching my son how to counterfeit his life with false interpretations. Were the best men in my life really unattainable? Or did I decide they were unattainable in order to avoid the possibility of a failed relationship with them? Is that what I'd done with you, Michael?

Tom showered without any argument, then came to the living room. Can I watch TV? He asked, and I smiled and said yes. He's still a good boy, too good, scared of my reactions. He's developed this look that sort of asks my permission before doing any little thing. He breaks my heart with this look of fear and defeat. I obviously didn't tell him about what happened that night, in case you were wondering. He's too young. And then again, my parents never actually told me, I discovered those yellow pills on my own. God, I've woven so many lies into the life of that little boy.

Tom was watching TV and when I sat beside him with the laptop I saw an incoming email from Rona, with a link to an article about the Neanderthal who had won "Big Fear". Apparently he was offered a weekly column in her magazine. She added only one sentence – See what I have to compete with?

Sadness emanated from her words, seeping right into me. I could suddenly see her distress, see how she didn't believe in herself, just like me. I decided it was time. Rona was a close enough friend, and she'd understand if I only shared parts of the story with her. I took the notebook I'd scribbled in back when she came to visit me, and while Tom's nose was glued to the screen, I wrote her a long email. I didn't volunteer too many details, but I mentioned you too, and finally hit send.

After putting Tom to sleep I dimmed the lights and came here to write you. This day has left me confused. What am I doing, Mikey? I still don't entirely understand.

At the time you asked me what I'm creating here, in this strange mailbox journal. What am I writing about all the time? Sometimes

I think I'm writing about love. Or maybe I'm writing about the never-ending quest for my power, for the belief that it exists. What am I constructing here? It's a little depressing, but I still don't have a good answer.

Rona just texted me.

Well, well, you Descartes bitch, why didn't you tell me? Who's the hottie and why the hell wasn't I formally informed? Talk to me.

I sent her a smiling emoji, and wrote that I was busy with Tom and I'll call tomorrow. I was kind of disappointed. I thought she'd have something more meaningful to say about what I wrote, though I should've known she'd stick to the part with the gossip. Aren't I supposed to have power in my words? So why is that all she wrote after that long letter I wrote to her?

But I don't want to get dragged into those thoughts either. My lack of faith is my downfall, my Achilles' heel, also when it came to you. One of the few things I did confess to the therapist about was how I never really believe that someone can love me. And even if I do believe it for a moment, I fail to see how much.

You too, baby. Maybe you're still keeping your distance because you don't really believe that I love you. But I do love you despite everything, due to everything and regardless of everything. So what do you say we both create new theories and start looking for evidence in order to prove them right?

To: Sheera and Michael <softspoons@gmail.com>
From: Sheera and Michael <softspoons@gmail.com>
March 19, 2016 at 10:50 p.m.
Subject: This is what I wrote Rona. I thought it might interest you

Your article reminded me that "lonely pairs" is what I used to call those mismatched socks that inadvertently ended up with each other after losing their original partners in the laundry, but I guess it can happen to people as well. People who maintain a life together, but no longer feel. They meet in the kitchen, in the living room, in the bathroom, in bed, but lose interest, lose hold, never really touch anymore. That's what I've tried to avoid all these years, but eventually I ended up with another kind of lonely pair. Two people who never lose hold, touch each other constantly and feel down to the bone, but never really meet anymore.

You can lose love in so many ways. Nobody ever tells you how much fear is enfolded in this emotion, you have to find out on your own. But the story of how your relationship died isn't really relevant, because the reason love is lost is always some covert fear. I lost my love because I was afraid to be weak. I bent over backwards just so I could feel powerful, but I forgot one thing – real power doesn't need to be proven. You can feel it. You believe in it. You simply know it's there. And the thing is, once you know it exists, you don't feel the need to battle anymore.

I had a stroke of luck. Or perhaps it was fate. I met the love of my life, "the one". The guy from the fairytales. But when he actually got here, I got spooked. Scared of the change, scared I'd get hurt, I finally found the emergency exit and came right back to my old familiar place. I could've insisted on challenging the fear, maybe dared to trust him a little more, but I preferred to be "powerful" and blame him for everything. Ultimately he cracked. In a twisted way, I guess you can say I won.

Have you ever thought about how scary it is to just feel things? And once you get hurt, your instinct is to shut down and shut out even more. The results of this instinct are all over your survey. So how the hell do you muster the courage to still be there, feelings and all? Maybe by realizing that courage is complicated. You shut down in order to protect yourself, especially after you've been hurt, but if you want to heal the pain, you need to be able to differentiate. To know which of the muscles you've tightened really protects you, and which needs to be released despite the fear, because it's depriving you of something you really need.

I don't really know what to do now. In some parallel universe we're still together, because there's no real exit once "the one" enters your life. But in this universe, I fell apart. I discovered that even when fate attacks you in commando gear, you still have a choice. So once again I chose the position of power over true power, and I hurt him. In return - he chose to give up and leave. Turns out people don't always make the best choices when they refuse to admit they're simply afraid to love. Afraid to feel.

Maybe I'm one of those people who are somehow always fucked up, always the oddball, no matter what they do. Look at me, forty years old and I still understand nothing. Why did fate arrange for us to meet if we're not together? What's the point in living life alone after meeting your "one" and losing him? At least within that fog of frustration I have these lucid moments, when I can dwell on the connection between us, freeze all the irritating questions and just push them aside. It's such an addictive sensation, but I have to focus and differentiate it, separate it from all the rest in order to refine that unique feeling of connection. That's all I have left of our love, and I'm willing to do a lot just to feel it again for a few seconds every now and again.

Do you think that's normal..?

I don't know, maybe nothing about love is normal. Maybe the formula is that there is no formula, and the survey conclusion is that there are no conclusions, and "the one" is not necessarily the one who completes us, or the one we're most comfortable with, or the one we should marry. The more I think about it, it seems that fate only arranges the initial encounter, that moment of inevitable clash, but nothing else is inevitable with "the one". His only significance is that he's the biggest challenge to our nature, because he's able to evoke the greatest level of emotion. That's it – there's nothing to understand apart from the intensity of emotion. The rest of the story with him depends on our habits and tendencies, on what we think we deserve, and on the only way we believe we can manage. We can learn how to manage differently, but it's exhausting. You need to keep in mind that whatever happens to you with "the one" is actually the strongest reflection of who you are. And what you need most is the emotional fortitude to cope with it.

The good sensations with "the one" are the best you'll ever experience, because sensations with him are more intense. But when things go bad, it can become intolerable. He maxes out your emotion. Your will-power, but also your vulnerability, and that's where his fateful, pre-written role ends.

We write the rest of the story ourselves.

To: Sheera and Michael <softspoons@gmail.com>
From: Sheera and Michael <softspoons@gmail.com>
March 20, 2016 at 9:10 a.m.
Subject: Mikey.

When I left for work this morning, there was a pink flower laying on the doormat. When we met on the boardwalk you gave me that exact kind of flower, so beautifully rare, crazy and frail. It was so long ago I'd almost forgotten. When I picked it up, just as a slight shiver passed through me, Tom asked who left it there. I smiled, not really knowing what to say. Finally I just said, someone you don't know.

On our way to school he said – When you came back from the hospital there was a flower just like that on the doormat.

Really?? I tried not to shriek with surprise, so why didn't you give it to me?

I didn't think it was for us, he said. I thought the neighbor dropped it on her way upstairs so I threw it in the waste basket down the hall.

To: Sheera and Michael <softspoons@gmail.com>
From: Sheera and Michael <softspoons@gmail.com>
March 20, 2016 at 10:56 p.m.
Subject: Houston... problems again.

I somehow managed to avoid Rona all day. I screened her calls, texted that I was overloaded with my return to work, and I didn't even reply when she tried to change the subject by asking if I'd seen what's happening on her Facebook page. I promised that we'd meet up on the weekend and talk about everything, including you and including her next feature. By then I'll try to figure out what to say.

I left work early because I promised Tom I'd take him to his favorite restaurant on the beach. We got there just before sunset and walked barefoot on the sand. Everything was perfect - we ordered the ultimate healthy cuisine, a burger and French fries. We laughed, talked about school, took turns imitating the principal, and attempted to plan our Passover vacation. He mentioned this camp some of his friends were signed up for, including that boy who used to tease him and now doesn't anymore, and then he suddenly blurted it out. Quietly, indifferently and even laconically he told me about a conversation he had had with that kid who used to call him "Mama's boy". He told Tom he had a cousin in America who was also a sperm donor child, but unlike me, his mom had promised that when he grew up he'd be able to get in touch with his dad.

I knew it would eventually happen, the moment when the more difficult questions would surface. But it's the kind of thing that no matter how ready you may think you are, will always catch you off guard. The greasy French fries stuck in my throat like an anchor and made me want to dash to the restroom and throw up. Tom continued to dip his fries leisurely into the ketchup and watch the surfers on the beach as if nothing important or unusual had been said, and I sat there praying he would keep his eyes on them and not on me, at least until I regained the ability to breathe.

About two minutes went by, then Tom looked back at me and smiled, pushing a strand of hair from his eyes and waiting for an answer. I smiled back, incapable of speaking. My tongue was glued to the roof of my mouth. I drank some water, trying to maintain hold of the glass with my trembling hand. I put it back on the table and then recited the answer I'd been rehearsing for nine years: look, sweetie, it's complicated. America has different laws, and in Israel sperm donors remain anonymous.

He looked at me silently, and I asked – do you know what anonymous means?

Yes, he said.

And that's it. He didn't ask anything else, and I wanted to keep talking, because I'd rehearsed the whole speech about Israeli laws vs. American laws, and had the perfect explanation about how in Israel kids don't have the option of knowing the identity of their father because the sperm donors do so on the condition that they can just continue with their lives. But it felt so cruel to say that, to hurt him so badly just to maintain the lie, so eventually I didn't say anything else, and just kept my mouth shut like the worst mom in the world.

The whole way home I felt awful. I'd waited too long, and the secrets I'd tried to protect Tom from were suddenly poking their way out of their graves. I tried to spare him the pain, but I hadn't spared him anything. I'd prevented a certain kind of problem, but new problems had been born to replace them, and were now imminent and threatening to eat him up from the inside like a black hole. So what's the better option? To spend your life in a futile search for your genetic father, or to have your genetic father reject you? I used to be sure I knew the answer, but today it's obvious that I don't.

I kept sneaking peeks at him, but he just sat there quietly in the dark, staring out the window at the passersby and the illuminated shop windows. What's going on inside his head? His expressions gave away nothing. Apparently everything has its price – the ability to hear other people's thoughts, as well as the inability, and the realization that sometimes there's just no way of knowing.

I have no idea how I'll fall asleep tonight. I suddenly realized that Tom is almost nine, and what I thought was right for him when he was a baby, no longer seems right. Neither of us can continue living with this lie, I can't understand how I once thought I'd be able to carry it forever. I have to figure it out somehow, it's not something I can keep postponing, and my time has run out.

To: Sheera and Michael <softspoons@gmail.com>
From: Sheera and Michael <softspoons@gmail.com>
March 21, 2016 at 12:43 p.m.
Subject: A moment of truth

Michael, you're not going to believe this, but I'm sitting in my car in the parking lot at work again, laptop on my lap, writing you. I'm in emotional turmoil again, still shocked by the chain of incidents, and again you're not around and there's nobody I can tell. But this time it's so different. I just couldn't wait until tonight after Tom falls asleep to write it all.

I have no idea where to begin. Maybe from the start, from the way I got up this morning, thinking only about one thing – Tom. He was quieter than usual, and I was so mindful of his every little movement, alert in case another trick question popped up, but he didn't mention last night's conversation on the way to school. After he got out of the car and into the schoolyard like the walking backpack he is, I called Rona. So I guess you've seen Facebook, she said right away. No, I haven't had time, I said impatiently. It's been there since yesterday, she enthused, you're totally spaced out ever since you became a philosopher.

It was hard to relate to our regular chatter and her glowing mood. I promised to take a look later and asked whether she knew of a good child psychologist. Yeah, sure, what's up? She immediately sobered. It's a long story, I'll tell you this weekend when we meet, I said. And inside I thought – here's another item on that growing list of things I'd have to find a way of explaining.

I knew I would have to schedule a session with a specialist today or tomorrow at the latest. I had to find the best way of telling Tom the truth, the way that had the least chance of messing up his life and turning his mother into a pathological liar that could never be trusted again.

I only had a few minutes before the morning meeting, and I was totally unfocused. I started scanning my emails, looking over the media clippings. Everything seemed so bland. Luckily there was nothing that required my immediate attention.

Any progress? I texted Rona, and she wrote, yes, found someone, sending you the contact details in a sec.

As I waited anxiously I distractedly logged on to Facebook, to her page, and I suddenly saw it. I could almost hear the brakes screeching as the whole world came to a halt.

Without asking, without even notifying me, she'd posted the letter I sent her. I was so astonished I read the whole thing twice to make sure I wasn't hallucinating. My fury made the letters a blur, I was flooded with horror. It took me a few minutes to notice she'd posted it as an anonymous reader's comment on her series of features. My heart was pounding so loudly it hurt. She's insane. What has she done, that stupid girl?

The office phone rang and shattered my thoughts. It was Ruthie. I'll be right there, I said, but obviously I didn't get up. I had to call Rona.

Are you nuts? I asked when she picked up, stretching my self-restraint to its max.

Hey, don't bite my head off, I just want to make sure he's recommended by everyone before I send you the number, she said, offended.

No, I said through clenched teeth, not the shrink, I mean my email, the very personal email I wrote you!

Oh, you finally saw it? But it's anonymous, what do you care? She played innocent and only angered me more.

So what if it's anonymous? I yelled, and when I realized I was yelling I immediately lowered my voice so nobody would hear. Post it on Facebook? Without asking me? Did you stop to think that maybe I didn't want anyone other than you to know all this?

Sorry, I didn't know you would get so upset, she said defensively. You barely said anything, it was all implied, who could possibly know it was you? Besides, did you see how many likes and shares?

I couldn't believe that's what she had to say. Did anyone ask you who it was from? I asked icily.

No, of course not, she was defensive again, what's the big deal? There are no revealing signs. I wanted you to lose your virginity already. Isn't it a great opportunity? Just so you know, the Predator read it and loved it, and wants to publish it in the Letters to the Editor.

Virginity? I was dizzy with reined fury. Rona, listen, I said, with all the restraint I could muster, don't you dare let your editor publish anything anywhere, and you, delete it! Right now! And I ended the call.

My phone buzzed, it was Ruthie texting that they were all waiting for me to start the meeting. Horror scenarios began flashing through my head. What if the letter had reached Moni or Erik, who had immediately figured that I was the anonymous friend and it hadn't been mononucleosis but more like a manic nuclear meltdown, and now that information will somehow find its way to Tom? I was so scared that the familiar tremor returned.

I'll be right there, I wrote Ruthie, but before leaving I read the letter again, just to make sure there was nothing there that could give me away.

I started walking towards Moni's office like a spy whose cover was about to be blown. I was flooded with panic. Rona's name flashed incessantly on my screen, but I didn't pick up. Eventually she texted me the contact details for Dr. Haim Rosenberg, a child psychologist from Ramat Gan, adding that he was the best in the field. I wanted to answer but I was immediately frightened by the rage I felt towards her, by the effect my words and intentions might have. So I cursed her quietly and held back from writing. I tried to soothe myself but my restlessness only increased. I couldn't see why all of my secrets were suddenly emerging, closing in on me.

When I entered Moni's office I was sure everyone was staring at me. There was a strange vibe in the air – was it just me or were they exchanging secret smiles? My paranoia ran wild.

Sheera, is everything okay? Moni asked. Yeah, sure, I said, in a desperate attempt at faking indifference. Were they onto me? Did they put two and two together?

I was quiet for the entire meeting, sitting on pins and needles, but when everyone finally began to leave, Moni asked me to stay. He walked Erik to the door, and as if to infuriate me, they stood there for a few minutes, whispering. Something about their body language was out of the ordinary, but I couldn't put my finger on what it was. When Moni came back in I was on the verge of a breakdown. I tried to convey business as usual, but my voice cracked when I asked – what did you want to talk about?

I promised to keep you posted, he said, and though nothing is official yet, we talked to Gaya last night and looks like we're putting the partnership back on the table.

That's great, I exhaled, relieved that I wasn't the issue, crisis averted?

Yes, Moni said, Erik set things straight. He gave me a long and penetrating look, and I started stressing out again until he said – but that doesn't mean we're bringing "The Write Stuff" back. Only then did I realize he'd just been waiting for me to ask. Too bad, because the host we wanted is a hot ticket now, Moni uttered, did you read that he came out of the closet? Maybe we should take him for another show.

I had no idea what he was talking about and didn't feel comfortable asking, so I just made a mental note to Google it later and said – great idea, and Moni gave me another look that seemed a bit worried. Are you sure everything's okay, Sheera?

Sure, I gave him a big phony smile, peeking at the time so he could see I was pressed, and stood up to get the hell out of there.

I literally ran to my office. Before I could even sit down, Avi called. So, did Moni tell you about Erik and Gaya? He asked. That they're bringing the partnership back? I asked impatiently, and he said – no, you're on slow-mo, they're a couple now, can you believe it? I paused for a moment despite my desire to end the conversation. Who's a couple, Erik and Gaya?

Yes, Erik told me himself, Avi vented, he's not even hiding it. They had a fight so the partnership went bust, but then they had make-up sex and we're back in business. You realize how the whole station went crazy just because of his personal issues?

Normally I'd spend an hour analyzing the scandal, punctuating my commentary with vomiting sounds as to express my opinion of Gaya's bad taste, but I really wasn't up to it. Avi was pretty shocked when I said I had to go because I had an urgent phone call to make, but as I dialed the psychologist's number, Rafi Hadar poked his head into my office. Got a minute? He asked.

I didn't have one free second, but Rafi Hadar is not someone you can say no to. I forced a smile and blurted - Sure.

How's life? I asked, trying my best to project mundanity.

Sweet, he said, sitting across from me with a mysterious smile. Again I was sure they were all talking about me in the hallways, that everyone except me had seen the letter yesterday and that he was also here to milk me for the juicy details.

Everything all right? He asked, you seem a little stressed.

Yeah, just a busy day, I smiled apologetically.

Well, I'll make it quick, he said, first the bad news – I have to call off the interview.

I was so preoccupied I almost asked him what interview, but then I remembered. Yes, Rona's interview that had been postponed a hundred times already and was supposed to finally happen tomorrow.

Why? I asked, what's wrong?

I guess there was a reason I kept going back and forth on this like some pussy, he smiled, we've decided to give it another chance. So I'm not leaving for the time being.

He sat there with his huge smile, waiting for me to applaud, expecting me to go wild with enthusiasm.

Wow, that's amazing, I tried to pretend I cared.

So you'll let your reporter friend know? I hope she takes it like a good sport, he said.

Sport? If jumping off the roof is a sport, then yeah, I said, and for a moment I thanked some unknown deity for making this happen today of all days, since no matter what I told Rona today, she'd have no justification to kill me.

Good thing you decided to stay, I said as he got up to leave, it's probably best for the kids.

That too, he said, giving me a meaningful look as if he were doing a close-up dramatic scene on camera. It's not easy to survive the crises, but I've come to realize that there's no real exit sign once "the one" enters your life.
What? I asked, pretty sure I hadn't heard him right.

Forget it, he said, just pondering. Sorry about the mess, but at least we got a happy ending, right?

He winked and moved towards the door, but then suddenly stopped, came back to give me a quick hug, and even thanked me.

I continued to sit there like a mummy, a million thoughts racing through my mind, trying to understand what had just happened. Was he quoting from my email to Rona or was I losing the little sanity I had only recently regained?

I woke the computer with a shake of the mouse, and with trembling fingers Googled the name of that actor who wouldn't host "The Write Stuff" and who had decided, today of all days, to come out. When I saw his quote on the first article that came up, I froze: "Maybe nothing about love is normal".

And all at once, my paranoid thoughts froze in my head. As if someone had yelled "Cut!" and in a split second the riot was over, and all that was left was a soft, quiet hush, like after a snow flurry. I remembered what had happened with Erik, what you said on the boardwalk, that even if someone read what I didn't want them to read, the effect was different from what I imagined. That I had to learn to interpret things differently from the way I was used to. I could feel you beside me so strongly at that moment, Mikey, whispering to me within the chaos of my anxiety, as if you were right next to me.

It's you, Sheera, do you really not get it? I heard your beautiful voice from inside, as if you were in my head.

That's the way you wanted things to happen, read back, it's what you wrote yourself. When will you finally get it? Nobody besides you needs to know, don't get carried away by all those fears. Focus on what really matters – your words. Your true feelings. You touch people's lives when you dare to feel pain and touch your own soul. Look what you did with one real letter. When your intentions are pure, it filters through the cracks of everyone who reads you.

And as I sit here in the car writing to you, somehow trying to make sense of this hazy day, Rona texts me – Sheera, don't kill me but I haven't deleted it yet... once you've calmed down we'll do what you say, k?

I didn't reply. Should I tell her to delete it..? I'm so overwhelmed, Mikey. I don't know anymore.

To: Sheera and Michael <softspoons@gmail.com>
From: Sheera and Michael <softspoons@gmail.com>
March 22, 2016 at 1:34 a.m.
Subject: Can't sleep again

After tossing and turning for two hours I remembered that old story I wrote about sanity that goes out for some air. I shivered. I suddenly realized why I'd given it to my mother instead of submitting it to the competition, probably because I knew she was the only one who would stop me. Now I could finally be glad I'd burned it on the rooftop. Without realizing it, I'd burnt my intention and the fears I'd poured into the words, and had demolished the story instead of giving it life.

It's all echoing through my head, without any rhyme or reason. It's crazy, Mikey, I still can't digest it. I've written so many things in my life, it'll take years to put the whole puzzle together, to figure out how they hushed behind my back, creating my reality.

When I gave up on the idea of sleeping and got up out of bed, I remembered that small, forgotten notepad in my nightstand. Only when I took it out and reread that old dream with the motorbike in the desert, did I realize how clueless I'd been. The whole time I thought you were the one who had planned our first meeting, but now I think it was me. When I gave in to that vague urge to write it down, I was actually giving power to my desire that it would happen.

I went to the kitchen with the notepad in hand, hesitated for a moment before pouring myself a glass of red wine. I had to wind down. I paced around the house for a while, and then took the laptop and sat at my desk.

I began rereading things I'd written you here after you deleted all of our old correspondence. Maybe the answers were still here, and I just had to find them. I paused on what Avi had said, that I could jinx things, and that somehow only the shows I liked succeeded. I kept reading back, and saw what I wrote about the proposal for "The Write Stuff", and then I scrolled forward to see what Moni had said about cancelling the show. He'd used my words, the same exact words, Mikey, I swear. I know it was just a stupid rehashed old paper, but as long as I believed in it, others had too. And when I wrote you that it had lost its appeal, suddenly Moni felt the same as I did.

I was so frustrated. Why had you deleted everything? I can't sleep anyway and I could've read everything now, see what else I'd written that had materialized over time. But then it hit me. Wait, is that why you'd erased everything? All that was written here, that you were afraid would actually occur? You couldn't have deleted everything just because of our fight, right?

It was useless, there was no chance I'd remember all my rambling. But it slowly began coming back to me. I wrote that we had a destructive relationship, didn't I? I'd been so certain it was true, Mikey, but now I realize I'd written it with so much passion... I hadn't noticed how caught up I was in the web of my own Big Fear. How I'd infused all of my power into those fears and eventually made them come true. I can't believe you didn't tell me. Why did you insist that I figure this out on my own?

Actually, now that I think about it, there were things you did tell me. But you only hinted. You told me to consider my words carefully, to rethink definitions, to go back and change things, but I didn't. Is that why you said I should start over without you? You wanted me to start clean, to start creating a new reality. But how did you think I would figure that out, Mikey? No normal person could ever begin to comprehend such a thing.

God, what a moron I was. That's the reason you wanted me to open this email account in the first place. You wanted me to understand that simple fact I steadfastly refused to see: the things I write fucking happen. That's how I defined it, that was my intent, I made up the password myself. I've created everything. I sat here rambling on every night, and it was just like Rona's series of features, I delved only into the pieces of evidence I wanted to find, and all I did was reinforce my old beliefs.

I started opening drawers, looking for other old things I'd written, and suddenly... I saw them. The three letters. I'd completely forgotten about them after shoving them into a drawer that night, when I screamed my lungs out as I paced the house in a desperate attempt to stay awake.

I took them out hesitantly. What should I do? The whole time I'd thought I was the student in your bizarre guided course, but only tonight I understand that I wasn't only the student but also the teacher, and the janitor, and the only one who ever opened the complaint box. I guess that's what you meant when you said that I shouldn't forget that I was the one writing this manual.

So what do I do with these explosive letters? I clutched them in my hand, knowing that as long as they exist, Tom is affected by them, trying to be extra good, afraid to lose me. As long as they exist, my father is becoming more alienated and estranged. So without overthinking, I checked to make sure Tom was asleep, took a matchbox from the kitchen, grabbed the house keys, the cell phone, and shutting the door softly behind me - went up to the roof. There I stood, in the middle of the dark night, breathing the cold city air. Without opening the sealed envelopes, I lit a match. The first to go up in flames was the one containing my letter to Tom. The letter to my parents was next.

I watched the scorched paper as its scraps scattered in the air, but then I paused with the sudden memory of the cover story I wrote for myself when I was pregnant with Tom. How I'd used my focused intention to weave the perfect lie, which I successfully made everyone believe. I took the cell phone and the remaining letter and went home. I rummaged through my bag to look for the business card Simon had given me, hesitated for a moment, and then texted: r u awake?

He replied a minute later – Just got back from a gig.

I smiled. Could you do me a favor and find something out for me? I asked.

Sure, he replied.

Mikey, I thought very carefully about the intentions I had that night. I was searching for the truth, not trying to embellish it. What had I really wanted to happen when I wrote Ziv that short letter? It contained only a few lines written during the frenzy of an emotional overflow. I ran my finger along the envelope, feeling the incredible turmoil that had been carved into the paper on that fervent night. Yes, I know what I wished would happen. I wrote two long letters, elaborate in detail but cold and stuffed with panic, and only this short letter contained an intention that was entirely pure.

I copied Ziv's New York address on the envelope exactly as Simon had texted it to me, and added a stamp I'd found in the mess drawer. I went downstairs, in the dark, in pajamas and slippers, marching defiantly down the street like a true lunatic. Luckily nobody saw me. But I did it, Mikey. Without waiting, or doubting, or thinking why he wouldn't want to, fully aware that the intention I'd put into the words that night, was that the letter would work. That's it, there's no going back. I slipped the letter from that night deep into the recesses of the neighborhood mailbox.

To: Sheera and Michael <softspoons@gmail.com>
From: Sheera and Michael <softspoons@gmail.com>
March 23, 2016 at 11:56 p.m.
Subject: The riddle

I have an important announcement: I went out tonight. For the first time since you left me, or since I left you (I suggest we don't make too big a deal out of that debate because I've decided we're both wrong). But the important thing is that I went out. Rona and I went to some hip bar on Lilenblum Street to set things straight between us. So I spiffed myself up, my mother came over to watch Tom, and I didn't even have to lie when he asked where I was going.

We got there early so the place wasn't crowded. Macy Gray sang in the background about trying to say goodbye and choking, her velvety sandpaper voice scraping my skin a little. The whole way over I pondered how to ask Rona not to press me for more details about you, how to say I needed more time, that it's complicated. I thought we were headed for some serious girl talk, so it was quite a surprise, when a few minutes after we'd ordered our drinks, a friend of hers from a competing newspaper came in – a serious journalist who doesn't do crappy television but appears on the news every now and then. Hey gorgeous, want to join us? She stood and asked him with a sweet smile, and he put a hand on her waist and kissed her on both cheeks and then, without batting an eyelid, pulled up a chair and sat down. Sheera, this is Ronen, she said, and then we all naturally flowed into a conversation about the future of journalism in Israel. There was something naughty about the way they looked at each other, and for a second I wondered if something was going on. Only during my second round of whisky I suddenly realized that the so-called random encounter had been prearranged, but not in the way that I thought – she was trying to fix me up with him.

We had a lot to drink. Three rounds of whisky straight up is a lot to take in for someone who was completely off alcohol over the past few months. At some point he looked at me with bedroom eyes and said he was impressed with my capacity.

I observed us from the outside for a moment. On my right was Rona, who as opposed to me, had naturally become a journalist. On my left was this celebrity writer, who was about to get his book published, and seemed like a cat that was sitting there next to us, constantly licking itself. I've been trying to figure out how I should work with words from now on, and that's why it was weird to feel so out of place, so removed from the conversation about writing with the two of them.

I live to write, he said, clinking his glass against mine, the need to do it is stronger than me.

What's the book about? I asked, and he smiled and said – our own homegrown apocalypse.

What do you mean? I asked.

It's a compilation of articles written over the past few years, arranged in the order of the text of our Declaration of Independence, and showing how the articles actually contradict every clause.

I raised an eyebrow. It's a reflection on Israeli society, which has removed itself from all of its founding values and has no legitimacy anymore, he explained gravely, and then leaned back in his chair and ordered another drink.

You don't think that's going just a bit overboard? I asked cautiously, and he rattled the ice cubes in his empty glass before saying that these days, you have to be radical if you want to have any impact, if you don't shock the masses they don't respond. I smiled understandingly. He really didn't need to explain, after all, I was the expert on radicalizing messages. We'd all stopped telling the truth a long time ago, but when everything is a "must-see" and "unforgettably brilliant" and "like never before", ultimately nothing is a must-see or unforgettably brilliant or like never before. Maybe manuscripts don't burn these days, but the words have been so overused that their meanings have worn out, and that's why real masterpieces don't exist anymore.

You think Moni would be interested in a documentary about the book? Rona asked, and I mumbled – he might be, slowly realizing there were a few more goals to this so-called random encounter.

After the second drink I wondered what I was trying to drown in all that whisky, because I could see them peeking out, those sprouts of jealousy that had been burning in me for my entire life. I looked at that Ronen character and knew he was right, Mikey. That's the way to write if you want to succeed, but how will I ever make it if I have to triple-think everything before writing one measly word? Why do they get to go wild with their overdramatizing? And why aren't they scared? Look at me – even after you made sure I would have enough money for two years, I still find it hard to believe I can write for a living.

When we got the check, Ronen went to the restroom and Rona leant towards me and asked, well, what do you think? Cute, I said.

Cute? She asked, he's heartbreakingly hot! I smiled out of my warm fuzzy buzz and said, I thought he was your Wasabi on the side. Get real, she waved me off, I'm just a big talker. Besides, I don't want to jinx it but since Eyal came back from Europe he's got this Humphrey Bogart thing going on, and it's been a mini-honeymoon for the past few days.

Honeymoon? I was surprised, and she said, yeah, the stars are lining up or whatever, so until he pisses me off again it's the beginning of a beautiful friendship, just don't say I didn't bring you any hot merchandise today.

So there. I hadn't understood why my letter hadn't affected Rona, but turns out it just took a little time. Maybe I'm not as different from Ronen, the celebrity journalist, as I'd like to think. I may not have 70 thousand followers on Twitter, but I too am addicted to immediate feedback that confirms whether what I just did was good or bad.

You should still network with him, Rona said, help him promote his book, what do you care? You know what one mentioned tweet of his can do for you if you ever decide to publish something yourself?

She's right too, of course, that's the way it works. But I'm confused. I don't really know what to aspire to anymore. I don't want to hold a mirror up to society or smash it in society's face. As long as my ambitions matched those of the people surrounding me it was simple, but now what? I'm no VP Communications or Content Manager, I'm certainly not a journalist, so what am I?

When Ronen returned we left the bar, and Rona quickly said goodbye and left us alone on the sidewalk. You want a ride home? He asked. I said I'd rather walk and get some air. He asked whether he could call me sometime to talk about his book, and I said yes. I saw him hesitate for a moment, unsure what I thought of him. Before we said goodbye he put a hand on my waist and gave me a kiss on the cheek, and his discomfiture really got under my skin. As I began walking, I grew lighter with each step, and his discomfort gradually faded. I suddenly saw him in a different light and could really relate. Relate to that mask he put on for the world, to the endless need for more affirmation, without realizing that he wasn't obtaining any real internal power, but only a position of power – power that comes from an external source. Who could relate to the immense pressure to succeed in this fucked-up industry more than I could? An industry that demands you to do whatever it takes, just to get the right feedback from your peers.

When I entered the house, for a moment I thought I was hallucinating. My mother sat on the sofa in front of the silently flickering TV, but she wasn't alone. My father was sitting beside her. He straightened as I walked in, looking at his watch and saying – you're home early. Yes, I smiled. A memory of the letter I burned on the roof flashed through my head and I didn't know if I should say something about his sudden return, so I just came closer and gave him a light kiss on the cheek. What's up? I asked, and he said, no news. Just like old times.

I exchanged a quick look with my mother, and was suddenly filled with a swell of love for her. I'd always thought she was weak, never realizing the extent of resilience she'd needed just to be with him all these years. After they left, I went into Tom's dark bedroom, sat on the edge of the bed listening to his rhythmic breathing, staring at the shapes created by the shadows on the closet, stroking his hair. I tried to calculate when my letter would reach Ziv, imagining his face as he opened the envelope, speculating how much time I had left before I got a response. When I went back to the living room, just as I was sitting down to write you, I got a text from Ronen. Just wanted to say one last goodnight, he wrote. I felt like replying – who the hell do you think you are? If you want to get on my good side start with a dream, slowly progress into random encounters, disappear, keep your distance, and then make your way to butterscotch drops. For a second I wondered why he had really texted. Maybe I'd been so enigmatic he wanted to make sure I'd given him the right number.

But the point of the story, Mikey, is not the failed attempt to fix me up with Ronen the celebrity journalist, but that it was through him that I finally found the answer. Sitting across from him this evening I wondered whether he really believed his apocalyptic story could have a positive influence. I remembered how pissed off I was when you told me – do you want to feel what it's like to really affect people? Then separate your desires, and begin only when you're certain that you're focused, that you're doing it only for yourself because it makes you feel good, and you don't expect to receive anything in return.

I think that Ronen isn't lying, he really does want to affect things and make a change, to fix things in society, but he fails because there are other things he wants more. He wants so badly to get something in return from his book that it just keeps standing in his way. The same thing had happened to me. It's not only ratings or followers or recognition, he wants the sense of belonging. The knowledge that he's part of a very particular group of people he values, but that requires him to embrace a certain manner of thought and code of conduct, if he wants to continue to belong.

For my entire life I've envied normal people, Mikey, I wanted to be just like them. It's the one thing I wanted most – to belong. That's what made me deny who I was and then prevented me from understanding everything you tried to explain. That's why I preferred to ignore my powers, my sensitivities, my strangeness, everything that made me different. If I'd acknowledged my power, I would've had no choice but to admit that I wasn't really normal, which was the last thing I wanted to do. That's why I didn't want to cross the lines with you and leave my old world. I've always lived as someone who wasn't normal but who insisted on proving she was. It's pretty stupid to live for a goal that was doomed to fail from the start. No wonder that even before we met I always felt isolated despite my efforts to belong. And now I still feel isolated, so I guess it doesn't really matter anymore.

That's my Dr. Seuss riddle, Mikey. I think I've solved it. Between you and me, I still want to be like Ronen. To say I write because it's stronger than me. It just sounds so dramatic, so good. But it's not the truth. For me it's the other way around. The need to write is strong, but the cage of my personality is much stronger. If I don't insist on bending the bars, it'll defeat any urge, deafen any emotion, kill anything. Even me.

And I have something else to tell you, Mikey, it's not only my riddle I've solved. I've solved yours as well. There's something I haven't told you, I hope you won't be mad. A few days ago I worked up the nerve to call Yanky again, on his cell. I didn't care anymore, I had to ask him how you were. This time I didn't pose as someone else, I decided to just be me. When he answered I said, Hi, this is Sheera, I don't know if Michael has mentioned me.

Sheera? He paused for a moment, trying to remember. Oh, he might have said something, he said in a faltering voice, you know what he's like. I didn't know if he was trying to be polite or you really had mentioned me. But wait, he suddenly said, are you by any chance Sea Song?

I blushed. Sort of, I said, and for a moment I even thought you'd told him everything.

Okay, I heard him smiling, gratified, fifty four missed calls.

Excuse me?

No, it's just that I had Michael's phone for the past few weeks, and I saw there were fifty four missed calls from Sea Song. I didn't know who it could be. Now I get it.

My cheeks burned. I didn't know he left his phone with you, I stammered.

Yeah, he said, he forgot to leave it at home when he wanted to disengage.

I really wanted to milk him for more details, but I was afraid to sound nosy so I just tried to play along as if I understood. Forgot to leave his phone at home when you went up north with him?

Yes, he said, it's part of his disengaging protocol after a serious seizure. His phone has been charging at my office for like a month. But that's it, yesterday he came back to Tel Aviv and took it back. You can try calling again.

I was silent. He thought I knew, so he just said it – a serious seizure.

My heart went wild but I tried not to reveal that I had no idea what he was talking about. So I improvised. I asked whether you've been taking the Tramadex or something else this time. He said not to worry, that a doctor had seen you and given you something new and you were pretty much okay. Just a little depressed.

Then I Googled the new medicine and read its leaflet, and I connected all the dots. I read the signs. I tried calling again and you didn't answer, and the truth is I waited for a few days so maybe you'd finally come out and tell me what you have, but that's probably not going to happen. So maybe you should know that I already know.

To: Sheera and Michael <softspoons@gmail.com>
From: Sheera and Michael <softspoons@gmail.com>
March 24, 2016 at 10:04 p.m.
Subject: Hi. It's me.

Welcome back to my head. I swore I'd never listen to your thoughts again, but like a true junkie, tonight I said – fuck it, just for a few minutes. So I heard you when you put Tom to bed, and then when you got up to the laptop and entered the password and came in here. It sounded like hesitant steps towards a door when you're not really sure anyone's home. Maybe he finally wrote something? And if so – how awkward is it going to be after all this time? What will I say? And how would he react?

Hi, Sea Song, it's me.

Cool it, OK? Your heart is beating almost as fast as mine. I know you're here and you can see these lines as I write them. That's why I started to write now, so I'd be in the middle when you came in here, and I wouldn't be able to delete it all and run away this time.

I've been home for a few days. Just got back from my first run on the beach. Run on the beach, yeah right, more like a limp on the beach after this six week break, but you have to start somewhere.

I had this song on repeat the whole time, do you know it? *Every night I would come to you, to look for remains of myself, and you would always save me...*

You don't know it. I should've known. Just don't tell me you're a snob who doesn't like Middle Eastern Music.

OK, I guess I owe you an explanation for the last six weeks. Yanky has a B&B cabin by the Hula Valley that's pretty much empty most of the year. I used to fantasize about taking you up there. Like an imbecile I ended up going there on a romantic weekend with myself. It was right after the mess between us. I'm a loser, I know. Nothing like that was supposed to happen. It would be an understatement to tell you I'm sorry now, right? But I don't know what else to say. I fell off the edge. Stuff like that sometimes happens to imbeciles like me. I swallow and keep it all in until I explode. But I was sure you understood that I just needed to get away for a while. You're so tough, I never imagined you'd take it that way. Haven't you ever walked out on anyone? I still don't get how it wasn't obvious to you I'd be back.

I went up north for a while. I asked Yanky for the key so he offered to take me, I probably didn't sound so hot and he didn't want me to drive alone. He stayed there the first night. Tried to convince me to see a doctor, but I said that all I needed was some time away to disengage for a while. Eventually he agreed, took my phone with him and told the cleaning woman to check on me.

That's the whole story, understand? That's the way it was supposed to end.

I settled into the quiet of the cabin. Did nothing, barely got out of bed. After a few days everything was calmer. I even managed to go for a little walk in the woods. When the cleaning woman came I asked her to call Yanky and tell him to come get me and bring my phone, I wanted to go back to civilization. When I waited for him I couldn't stop myself any longer and connected to you. To your thoughts. God. Even now I can't stand to think about it. I didn't know anything, Sheera. It was like a piano dropping straight on my head from the sixth floor. I connected one day too late. The day after you got on that train.

It didn't affect me very well. I meant to recuperate and try to start over with you, saner. I still can't believe I almost lost you. When Yanky arrived and saw me he freaked. Why did you say you were fine if you're flat on the floor? I told him it was another seizure and I'll be OK in a minute, but it didn't seem to calm him. Said he'd never seen me like that. He called a doctor without asking me. Dragged me to the couch, and I lay there like a wuss and tried to figure out what to do. I considered asking Yanky to do something, but I didn't know if it would help. But as the minutes passed those thoughts about "what do I do" were replaced by an understanding. By reality. I realized what it meant, that I'd pushed you over a cliff. At your hardest moments I was powerless to help you. I even made it worse. I can't be the man you need.

The doctor arrived, examined me, prescribed some new wonder drug that's supposed to help with fibromyalgia pain. Told me to rest for a few days and avoid external stimuli. Oh gee, thanks for the input. As if I could do anything but. I couldn't tell him normal people's medicine doesn't always help me. I asked Yanky for the phone for a minute, just to come in here and erase everything. So you could start over without me, clean slate. It took me an hour, I was kind of out of it. Then I went to some shopping site, sent you a flower. That's it, right after that I disengaged again. Talk about Zombie Mode. But when I reach the edge like that, I don't really have a choice.

How could you think that I heard your crazy thoughts about having to die and didn't stop you? How could that even cross your mind? That's what killed me the most. You had zero faith in my love for you. It's probably my fault. But I was disengaged from you that night, Sheera, I didn't know squat. That's what I despise myself most for.

The new pills worked pretty well. It took two weeks, and I could start working a little. I didn't dare connect to you, I was sure you never wanted to see me again. That I'd let you down like no one ever had before. I listened to your mother so I knew you were getting better, knew you were being taken care of. Knew I could only ruin things. So I moved some stuff around so things would be easier for Tom. Other than that I was pretty useless. Total silence. Isolation. Doing nothing. La dolce vita, right?

Yanky came up every week. Texted my father that I'm OK. He knew the drill, we've been through this before, only not for such a long period of time. At some point he brought my laptop over. I didn't have the nerve to turn it on. But that day you went to see my father, I felt something. I hesitated, then couldn't stop myself. True junkie, I told you. I managed to avoid your thoughts, but I missed reading you. At first I was stunned that you still wanted me, but I also knew you didn't realize I was sick. Still, your words healed me. The more I read the less it hurt. You brought me back to life. You've learned to combine your two powers, Sheera. You rock.

Sorry I didn't write back, I couldn't. I should've told you about the illness from the start, I know, but along with all the other things I had to tell you when we met I was sure you'd freak and tell me to go to hell. Later, when you began to discover your power, I had this fantasy that maybe I wouldn't have to tell you, that it would just disappear. But things got pretty complicated. And then I couldn't find the right moment. Or the right words. And I was scared shitless of how you'd respond. Sometimes Yanky's big mouth is a good thing.

That's it, Sea Song. Now you really know everything. Or almost everything. And now I'm going to stop listening to your thoughts, and that's final. There are things I can't take hearing even if I already know them. I don't think you realize all the ramifications, the consequences. It's a bummer to be with a sick person, but it's always more complicated when it's you and me, with the way we affect each other. For us things are always more extreme. Really, Sheera. You won't be able to take it. When I'm OK it looks doable, but you've never seen me when it's not. It's not for you. And I love you the way you are, I don't want you to change. You're a drama queen that mesmerizes me, but when you get into one of your scenes, everything starts hurting. And it's no picnic as it is, believe me.

I know the fantasies you had about me. You thought I was some sort of an almighty magician. You love power, and I'm not what you think I am. You're passionate, hot blooded, you need someone who can stand and face you when you're at the height of your storm. I swear I tried, I gave it my all, but I'm not that man.

I want you to be happy. But you don't really need me. And things will work out with Tom and Ziv. You ultimately got what you wanted, have you noticed? I'm no longer your guide, you're your own guide. You've been flourishing without me. Look how much you've figured out on your own since I've stopped standing in your way.

That's it. Do me a favor and don't blow off everything I said, OK? Trust me, I've thought it through, from all angles and in every direction, I've had plenty of time. Look what happened to you when you were with me. My only way of protecting you is not being close to you. I don't just love you, Sea Song, if anything happens to you I won't be able to take it. I have no more capacity to forgive myself. Even without talking to you or hearing your thoughts, your existence dominates me.

To: Sheera and Michael <softspoons@gmail.com>
From: Sheera and Michael <softspoons@gmail.com>
March 27, 2016 at 11:34 p.m.
Subject: A sneak peek into the next episode

I suppose you understand that it's been hard to sleep these past few nights. Turns out the more I get to know myself, the more I realize there are things I'll never understand. Like us, for instance. Allegedly so simple. A connection between someone suffering from chronic pain disease and someone who can make pain disappear. Pretty corny, when you think about it like that. Almost boring. Yet so fucking complicated.

After you came out of your hiding place and finally wrote me, I paced the house, storming with crazy thoughts. Is he really that fucked up? The guy who used to talk to me about the meaning of love in Tibetan, teach me about separating emotions, bending bars, how could he now say it was impossible? You used to be the one who believed, maybe the tables have turned.

This morning I woke up tired, and Tom was a little nervous too. For a moment I thought maybe he felt that his father had called me last night. I don't think he heard the conversation because it was late and he was asleep. But who knows, maybe I'm raising a little Harry Potter myself. When I saw the American number flashing on my cell I immediately knew it was Ziv. I answered after one ring, and something in his "Hey Sheera" made me freeze, I could barely pronounce a cracked little "Hi". At first we were mostly silent. Then I told him I was sorry and apologized about eighteen times, and he didn't really answer, he just breathed. Then he asked me to send him a picture, and I scrolled through my phone until I found the sweetest photo of Tom rolling with laughter on a good hair day, and sent it to him as we spoke. From there on something softened and we ended up talking for about an hour. He even sent me a link to a new song he'd just released. Then we agreed that he'd make arrangements and come to Israel in about three weeks, by which time I would somehow have a talk with Tom. And with my parents too, and with Rona. In other words, I'm thinking of stuffing a few things into a small backpack and running off to Nepal.

This morning on the way to school I played Ziv's song in the car without saying anything, "Sometimes Love Isn't Enough". Something about its rhythm caught on to both of us. After I dropped Tom off I listened to it again, and thought how twisted life's path can be sometimes, if an Israeli guy makes music in Hebrew in New York, and his son listens to it on the way to school in Tel Aviv without knowing it was his dad.

As I stood in traffic at the entrance to Ramat Hachayal, Ruthie called. How spontaneous are you feeling today? She asked merrily. I rolled my eyes and said, depends. Moni has a meeting at a café in Tel Aviv, he forgot to tell you, I know it's last minute but he really wants you to join him, she said. I asked who it was with, and she said there was this app for promoting reality shows that Moni wanted my input on. Actually, I wasn't in the mood for that kind of stuff, I've already told Moni I was quitting and we were supposed to work out how and when. But over the years he's become sort of a father to me and I still feel the need to please him. So I made a U-turn in the middle of traffic and started heading south into the city, while consoling myself - how boring could it be?

I couldn't find a parking spot and it was getting late, and when I entered the café I was still kind of dazed. I hadn't had enough sleep at night and the morning coffee hadn't done the job. So I just didn't notice, Mikey, I can't believe it but once again I didn't see. I went up to Moni who sat at a corner table with a few other men, and he introduced me to Boris, the creator of the app, and I found myself gravely shaking the hand of some pimply twenty year old.

But when Boris started introducing me to the others, the air suddenly escaped my lungs. I've brought my angel with me, he said. And only then did I see you, Mikey. With your boyish smile and the silver streaks in your hair. You look great, although that doesn't necessarily mean anything, since even when you're in complete agony you manage to hide it most of the time.

Ten thousand emotions swelled in me simultaneously, and my heart went wild as I was drowning in them. Somehow I managed to hold out a trembling hand and utter a "nice to meet you".

I hope nobody noticed that I didn't sit down in the chair across from you – I collapsed into it. Mikey, my love. You really took me by surprise. I wasn't sure if you came to see if I'm all right, or if you were worried because I haven't written in two days, or if you finally cracked and listened to my thoughts and understood what I think about your totally idiotic theory.

When you saw I cooled down a little, you winked at me. I had to keep myself from laughing when you wrinkled your brow and asked me with a pensive look – Hey, haven't we met before? I wanted to tell you it was the oldest pickup line in the book, but was afraid the words would come out wrong. I guess it's pretty hard to be witty and sharp when you can't breathe normally.

I don't know how to break this to you, but that stupid meeting this morning (sorry, no disrespect for your startup or anything) brought back that feeling, the one worth living for, the one I only get when I'm with you. I had no idea how messed up I was until suddenly, in one moment, all my inner organs arranged themselves in perfect order.

When you said it was late and you had to go, a stinging lump of salt hardened in my throat. I realized that I don't really know what's going to happen now. If there's anything I've learned over the past few months, it's that with you I can never really know. Maybe you were just there to say hi. I snuck one last look as you were almost out the door, and at that exact moment you snuck one back at me. I felt something crushing inside. That spot where our eyes locked hung in the air and will remain hanging there forever. The locked eyes of two people who should be together all the time, but for some reason haven't managed to do so. Or maybe the locked eyes of two souls that were still locked in two separate cages.

I stayed there with Moni and Boris a little while longer, barely able to follow the conversation. When I got up to leave the café a smiling yellow sun welcomed me, along with an angry black cloud. Some happiness still floated inside, but I was already starting to drown in longing. I walked down the street with that emotional milkshake and tried to find the car for about ten minutes before realizing it had been towed. I cursed. Was it just me or was this day taking a bad turn? I looked down the street to see if there was a taxi anywhere, and only then did I see your motorbike, which had been there the whole time, with you on it, just looking at me, and eventually taking your helmet off.

An awkward little laugh escaped my lips. I walked over to you, trying to maintain my balance. Wait a minute, did you know my car would be towed? I smiled, and you said – when we were still in the meeting I saw the traffic cop walking by, and I couldn't resist sending him to your car, I really wanted a chance to rescue you.

And this was your only idea how to accomplish that? I bristled, and you got off your motorbike and said, come on, show a little compassion, sometimes I need to feel that you need me and don't know what you'd do without me.

You wrapped your arms around my waste and drew me to you in a huge wave of sensations. And when you gave me a long kiss, with that taste that makes me dizzy, I immediately forgot we'd ever had any issue to work out.

You pulled out another helmet and gave it to me. Who's driving, you or me? You asked, and I said that today you seemed well enough to drive. I sat behind you, wrapping my thighs around yours, and when I clung to your back and wrapped your waist with my arms, for a moment it felt like we'd been poured into the same mold. Where to? You asked, and I mumbled that as long as it wasn't to your place or mine, I didn't really care.

The memories of today are so vivid, they still dance around me in a slow waltz of a fancy ballroom. They've been with me since sunset, when you dropped me off at that romantic municipal parking lot to pick up my towed car. I'm especially shaken up by the memory of that smoldering, intoxicating passion when we started taking our clothes off, a feeling no words can ever describe.

As we were about to leave Yanky's cabin I asked what made you change your mind.

I haven't changed my mind, you said, I just moved it a little, by four or five degrees.

What does that mean? I asked.

It means I still can't figure out how we can be together, but that won't stop me from living this particular day the best I can, and believing that I'll figure it out somewhere down the road, you said.

When we got back to the city and the remains of sunlight caressed our backs, I thought of how much you've changed, Mikey, it's not only me who's changed. We're no longer those two people from the bakery who were scared out of their wits by that random encounter. We've left them behind. So after we've been saved, maybe instead of waiting for "all or nothing", it's best to take what you can and just live.

My sweet and beautiful Mikey.

We both know that's not what really happened to me today. We both know that none of this ever happened, I made it all up. I wrote my heart's desire. I've made up every word, but I had a good reason. I did everything I could to make it credible, because I really believe this could happen. If my power is in words, then I can create the reality of the future, right? I type reality on my keyboard, with all the intention that flows out of my fingertips.

I wrote down my purest intention though I know I can't affect you if you don't want me to. It's just like you couldn't persuade me when I didn't want to, because our powers are equal. We both need to want to set our souls free. To bend the bars. Each of us from within the cage he's been locked in.

My fantasy is to give up the fantasy for real life, Mikey. To give up everything I thought you were at the start for who you really are. I love power, but I love you when you're powerless too, and I don't care that you're weak sometimes. Sometimes I'm weak too. We're quite the odd couple, but if we really want to, we can learn to get along somehow. I'm sorry I hurt you, and that you hurt me too. But I'm willing to be hurt by you again, I swear I am.

I don't know if you've ever thought of it this way, but our story began as two parallel stories, nine years ago. Our hearts were broken at exactly the same point in time, so that we would have enough time to heal before meeting one random afternoon with a sudden lightning bolt that woke two people that were living but dead. I've given it a lot of thought, Mikey, like you asked, and I've concluded that I really shouldn't let you get in the way, because I fully understand. Remember when you told me that using your power is not optional? Well, a love like ours is not optional either. We have to act on it. You're not really protecting me when you want to spare me your pain, you're just causing me a different kind of pain. Your problems are my problems too, and the only choice we have is to face them alone or together, which is the only thing that can heal us. And yes, I can't believe you actually need me to explain this to you.

So just before I let go and embark on a two-year adventure to see how I can make a living as a writer, I have one last question for you: what's stronger, the cage of your character or your love for me? You're the one who's going to have to decide.

I got up to make myself one last coffee for the day, and stirred it with a spoon. The spoon looked at me dismissively and said, get serious, Sheera, you're such a hopeless romantic. Oh shut up, you're hopeless yourself, I said, and tossed it straight into the sink.

Acknowledgements

During my four years of work on this book, I was fortunate enough to be aided by many. Some kindly offered their knowledge; some spent long hours conversing and thinking with me; some casually said some words that sparked ideas in my mind; some read the manuscript, gave me their insights and became my partners; and some helped by their mere presence in my life. I truly hope I hadn't forgotten anyone, and if I did – I apologize. At my age, it's the sort of thing that can happen sometimes. This list is organized randomly and not by importance. I would like to deeply thank everyone mentioned in it.

Prof. Eyal Schiff, Prof. Dan Caspi, Prof. Nadir Arber, Dr. Jacob Ablin, Dr. Hanan Netter, Anat Hezroni, Ligad Rotlevy, Ronnie Rotlevy, Mika Rotlevy, Ronit Weiss Berkowitz, Eyal Waxman, Shilo De Ber, Tamara Chotoveli, Sean Keddem, Liat Bein, Gila Harmatz, Rachel Dasberg, Orna Rudi, Anati Landau, Ilanit Hayut, Yael Gaoni, Anat Bein, Mabel Efrat, Tzipa Levi, Eynat Meyron, Danny Cohen, Simha Sigan, Ronen Sigan, Noa Sigan, Efrat Tsori, Maya Karvat, Tali Goren, Tirza Gortler, Idit Lev-Zerahia, Merav Cohen, Sharon Unger, Zach Unger, Roi Deutch, Sigi Eshel, Shira Rotlevi, Rafi Ben Shachar, Zvika Limon, Ghila Limon, Ori Lazer, Danny Tocatly, Yaron Merhav, Nirit Yaron, Eyal Goldman, Zamir Dahbash, Dan Eblegon, Yoram Ascheim, Ofer Golan, Mor Arditi, Sharon Keddem, Yael Kehat, Shyan Ben Sira, Heli Shoshani, Goel Pinto, Shirly Mazliach, Yoav Pridor, Edna Maor, Ronel Mor, Eran Yuval, Zipi Rolnik, Meir Brand, Paul Solomon, Ricky Drori, Shira

Margalit, Moshe Alima, Yonatan Segal, Imi Iron, Yona Weisenthal, Karni Ziv, Shirly Rachel Rochman.

I owe a special thanks to my incredible literary editor, Michal Heruti, for her patience, delicate hand, and professionalism. I am lucky to have her as a companion for the second (and hopefully not the last) time. A huge special thanks to the one and only Dovi Eichenvald, the head of Yedioth Books, who leads the Israeli publishing world with strength and sensitivity. A very big thanks to the professional and devoted team at Yedioth Books, and especially to Eyal Dadosh, Navit Barel, Ika Zaluf, Yael Madar, Irit Arav, Gili Michaeli Schiller, Renana Sofer, Zachi Foks and Hila Shafir.

And yes – a much needed thank you to the charming staff at Turquoise Restaurant on the beach in Tel Aviv, who put up with my presence and my laptop for so many hours so many times, some ending with a check for a mere coffee and sparling water. Thank you for hosting my writing.

Printed in Great Britain
by Amazon